I0604772

weeping
| angels |

weeping angels

RILEY CHANCE

By the same author
Surveillance
The Democracy Game

Published by Copy Press Books, Nelson, New Zealand 2024
Copy Press Books, 141 Pascoe Street, Nelson, New Zealand

ISBN 978-1-067010-05-8 (International Edition – Print-On-Demand)

© Copyright Riley Chance 2024

The right of Riley Chance to be identified as the author of this work in terms of section 96 of the Copyright Act 1994 is hereby asserted.

All rights reserved.

Except for the purpose of fair reviewing, no part of this publication may be reproduced or transmitted in any form or by any means, electronic or mechanical, including photocopying, recording or any information storage and retrieval system, without prior written permission from the publisher.

COPYPRESS

Designed by CopyPress, Nelson, New Zealand.

{REAL**NZBOOKS**}

Distributed in New Zealand by Real NZ Books, Nelson, New Zealand.

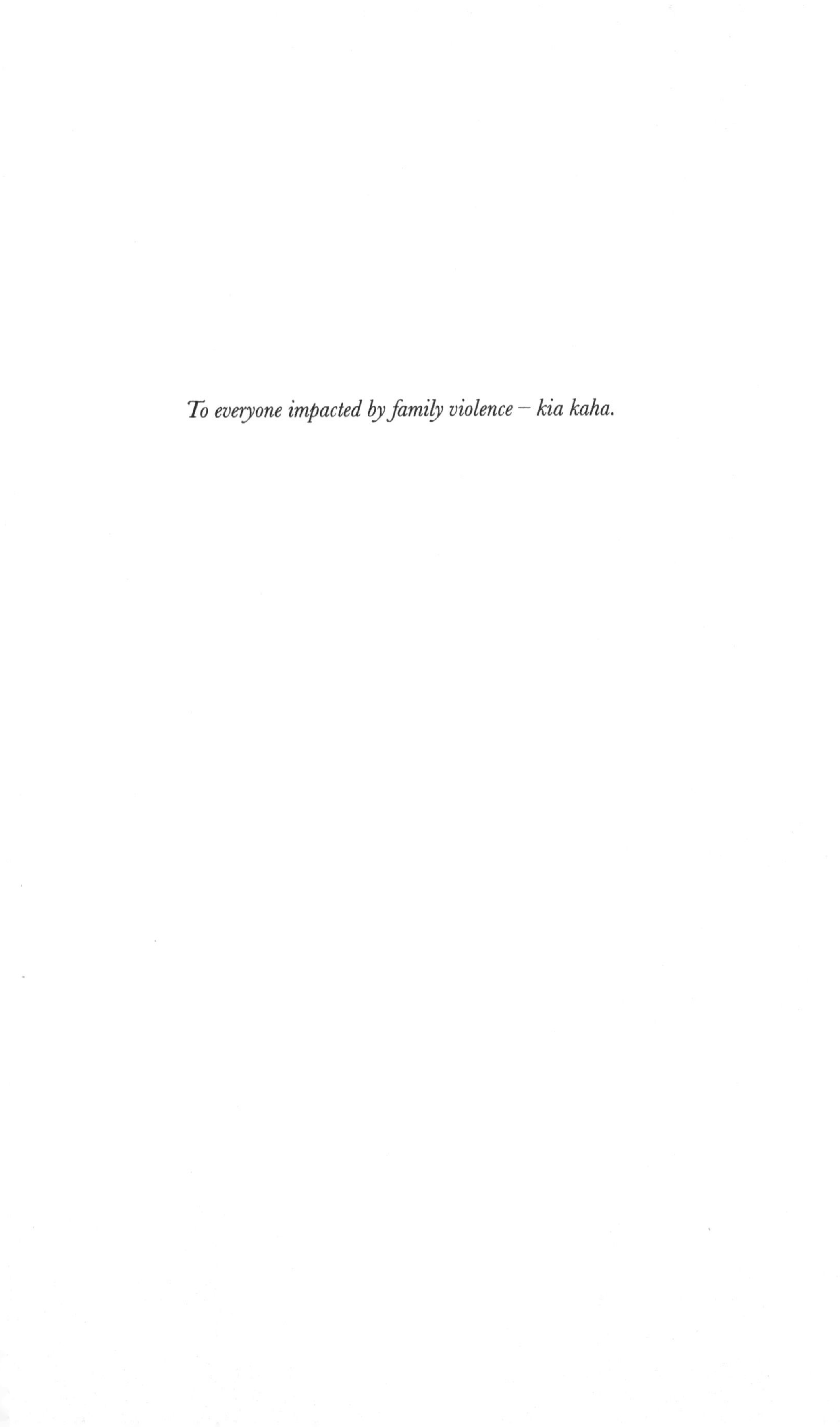

To everyone impacted by family violence – kia kaha.

CHAPTER 1

Stooping unsteadily, he picked up his keys.

'Are you sure you're okay to drive, Keith?'

Turning slowly as he stood, he saw Melissa Palmer, the wife of the community leader, watching him from her back door. His keys in one hand, the other jammed into the pocket of his overly-blue pants, Keith Leslie forced out a short laugh. 'I'm good. Besides, my car knows the way home.'

Arms crossed, she ran her eyes over him. Her community-prescribed full-length blue dress flapped around her ankles, though the breeze had no impact on her stiff, white head-scarf. Behind her the sound of raucous male laughter spilled from the door.

'If you're sure,' she said slowly. 'Take your time. We'll see you on Sunday.'

'Sure thing, Mel.'

It was a warm evening, the wind strong and gusty. With a final wave, he walked consciously towards his Audi A4 sedan, letting out a long, alcoholic breath. It wasn't a practical vehicle, but as the community's accountant he spent time outside the community looking after Reverentia's many and varied business interests.

Behind the steering wheel, he let his arm hang from the driver's window. In the rearview mirror he saw that Melissa had gone inside, rejoining the remaining elders at their regular end-of-the-week drinks. The Palmers' impressive house sat on the lower tier of the community's extensive property, closest to the church that towered God-like over the nearby buildings and multi-storey accommodation complexes. His position in the community allowed him a house on the upper level of the farm where he lived with his young wife, his second wife. His first wife had abandoned him and the community when their first child hadn't survived. Those events had bitten deep but he kept himself to himself. It was what Reverentia men did.

Looking up, he searched the stars.

Nothing.

Alcohol quietened his mind. It numbed, but it enraged too. It wasn't his new wife's fault, but she was … convenient. He had loved her, his first wife. And she would have loved him, in time – he was sure of that. Was it really, as everyone kept saying, part of God's plan? A test of him as a god-fearing man? It couldn't be. It had to be something else, but what?

Gazing up towards his house, he started the car. When he arrived home his wife would be cooking dinner, steak perhaps, as she knew that's what he liked. While she cooked, he would head to the shed with a bottle of Jack Daniel's to keep the edge off.

Then, if she stayed quiet, if she left him in peace, the evening might play out smoothly.

'You still here Keith?' The deep, throaty voice of Reverentia's leader Nathaniel Palmer bounced over the gusts of wind. 'Mel said she'd seen you off.' Dressed identically in blue pants, a light-blue shirt and dark tie, he was a once-strong man run to fat. Walking awkwardly, he came over, leant on the car and looked in the driver's window. 'You okay, Keith?'

'I'm great thanks, Nate. I was looking at the stars. Thinking about God – I guess.'

The large man reached into the car, a powerful smell of gin on his breath, clapping him on the shoulder. 'He has his purpose for us, Keith. Never forget that. He will bless your marriage soon, I'm sure.'

The engine purred.

'It's in God's plan,' said Palmer, pushing himself off the car. 'And in God's time. We'll meet up next week and go through the accounts, there's lots to, ahh … plan. We leave in a few weeks.'

'True,' said Keith putting on his seatbelt. Turning on the car's headlights, he let the Audi ease forwards.

Holding his arm up in farewell, Palmer called out, 'Drive carefully, you're one of God's chosen.'

As he drove onto the gravel road he inhaled deeply, breathing out slowly. Anger simmered as the powerful car crawled along the gravel road that led to the upper part of the farm. Leaning over, he tried to grab the near-empty bottle of spirits rolling around in the passenger footwell.

Unable to reach it, he undid his seatbelt and, with a final lunge, grabbed the bottle. Carefully taking off the top, he drank deeply as the car rocked over the uneven surface.

Before the road commenced its steep climb, he pulled over, turning off the car's headlights but leaving the engine running. He often stopped here, hidden behind the church, before he made the final push for home. Closing his eyes, he sat still, listening, sensing.

Nothing.

More evidence that God had abandoned him.

Yawning, he clicked his neck. It had been a long week of work, planning and drinking. Tonight, like most Fridays, was playing on repeat. After drinking again from the bottle, he recapped it, dropping it onto the passenger seat. Flicking the headlights back on, he pressed down on the accelerator. The tyres bit into the gravel as the Audi started its ascent.

CHAPTER 2

'Just take us through what happened,' said the female police officer.

Joy Leslie, teeth clenched, dabbed at her eyes with a freshly laundered white handkerchief.

She sat at her plain wooden kitchen table with three other people – two uniformed police officers, a woman and a man, who had introduced themselves though Joy had already forgotten their names. They had come in respectfully, taking their caps off, looking around curiously at the modest furnishings and bare timber walls adorned with a lone cross.

The final person at the table was the wife of the community leader, Melissa Palmer, sitting next to Joy, a supportive hand on her arm. The two women looked an unlikely mother-daughter combination, dressed identically in long blue dresses and white scarves. Noticeably shorter, Melissa was twice Joy's age and easily twice her weight. Ostensibly she was there as a support person, but Joy suspected her motives.

Over the years, Melissa had assumed the role of a Rottweiler to Reverentia's women, a role she threw herself into with gusto. Under the guise of 'doing God's work' she kept the women working impossibly hard, helped by the fact that it was difficult to trust others not to pass on information to improve their standing.

'It was a normal Friday.' Joy spoke barely above a whisper, her hands wound tightly around the handkerchief. 'He, my husband that is, worked in his office until about four, though he came out for lunch. I'd made him a steak and kidney pie.' She looked towards the older woman who smiled without warmth. Joy looked back at the table, dabbing at her eyes.

'What time did he leave for …' The police officer checked her notes.

'My house?' interrupted Melissa. Turning to speak to the male officer, she said, 'He arrived punctually at five. Keith was always on time. He was a good man. A reliable man.'

'That's right,' said Joy. 'It takes around ten minutes. He must have left around quarter to five.'

If the female officer was annoyed by the older woman's snub, she didn't let it show. 'And what time did he leave your house, Mrs Palmer?'

Forced to look at the female officer, bristling she said, 'Just after eight.'

The male officer followed up. 'Three hours. How much alcohol had he consumed?'

'I have no idea,' she said. 'My husband might know. It's not my place to keep a check on how much the men drink.'

Joy looked blankly at her. *The honest answer was heaps. It was always heaps.*

In the hours since members of the community had discovered the fatally crashed Audi upside down on the gravel road, Joy had experienced a range of emotions, but primarily shock. Shock that it had happened. Shock that she was … what? Free?

'You must have some idea how much Keith Leslie had drunk?' the male officer asked matter-of-factly. 'Your husband told us you spoke to him before he left. Did he seem intoxicated?'

'No.'

'How about your husband,' he asked. 'Was he intoxicated?'

Joy dropped her gaze. Melissa's face would be a picture, her double chin prominent when she raised her shoulders.

'How dare you,' she said. 'My husband is a pillar of this community. He only ever drinks in moderation so he can be one of the boys.'

Without looking up, Joy said, 'He drank a lot the last time we had the drinks here. You had to pick him up.'

'You didn't provide enough food,' said Palmer eyeing her coldly. 'It hasn't happened anywhere else.'

Joy stayed quiet. *Liar.*

'Did your husband usually come home drunk on a Friday, Joy?' The female officer's tone softer.

Joy nodded.

'And did he drive?'

'Always,' said Joy. 'I mean, it's too far to walk.'

Through gritted teeth, Melissa said, 'The men of Reverentia work incredibly hard all week, they deserve to relax. They keep our community running and safe. Without them we'd be destitute. All I can say is that when Keith Leslie left my house, he was capable of driving. I wouldn't have let him go otherwise.'

Joy dabbed at her eyes.

The male officer asked, 'Did he usually drink in the car on the way home?'

'I think so,' said Joy. 'I don't know.'

'Well, that explains it,' said the older woman. 'He must have been under terrible stress. Keith is ... was, Reverentia's accountant. My husband called him his right-hand man. It's been a struggle lately, financially.' Palmer paused before adding icily, 'He possibly wasn't looking forward to going home.'

Joy glanced at her.

'What do you mean?' asked the male officer.

An uneasy silence descended as Melissa Palmer hesitated, her face calculating.

'It was common knowledge Keith and Joy were having difficulties conceiving,' she said. 'Keith was ... disappointed that God had not yet blessed his marriage.'

Joy didn't move. *His marriage. Not hers or theirs. His.*

The officer glanced at her colleague, who gave the slightest of eyebrow raises. 'That's all we need now, Joy,' she said. 'We'll leave you information about where you can get help if you need to reach out.'

Intruding on their conversation, Melissa said, 'Our community has its arms wrapped around Joy. She doesn't need *outside* help.'

'We'll leave it anyway.' The police officer's tone was, for the first time, strained. 'Joy may like to know about other options.'

A short, tense silence ensued before everyone stood.

'I'll come by tomorrow,' said Melissa, hugging Joy with the least amount of body contact possible. 'Nobody is expecting you at work, not until after the funeral. Take care. You're in all our prayers.'

Joy followed them to the front door, watching the ungainly woman hurry to her husband's ute, knowing the next time she would see her would be at the funeral. Not expected at work – that was a bonus she hadn't anticipated. She wouldn't have to get up at 5am tomorrow, what would that feel like?

'Thanks, Joy,' said the female officer. 'I know this is an awful time, but it will get better.'

The male officer solemnly nodded his agreement.

'Thanks,' said Joy. 'It's been a nightmare.'

'The Serious Crash Unit investigators will be here tomorrow to make a detailed scene inspection.'

Joy drew in a quick gasp. 'Why?'

'It's standard for fatal accidents, nothing to worry about. After they've finished, they'll send a tow truck to recover the car. They'll take it to the police yard, but as it looks like a write-off, you'll need to contact your insurance company. That can all wait a few days.'

Joy nodded, dabbing at her eyes.

Putting on their caps, the two officers walked to their patrol car. Joy watched Melissa drive through the gate and onto the gravel road that wound down the steep hill.

I'm free.

The joyful thought didn't last. She clenched her fists tight, keeping her face blank as the police officers got into their patrol car. Melissa knew what went on, she had to. Was she too a victim? How likely was it that Joy's husband – *he* – was the single bad apple? Nobody talked about it. The men, the women, even the children, all maintained a stoic silence. The community were complicit in each misery she had endured.

The patrol car's lights snapped on.

The real Joy, who nobody knew existed, who they had failed to mould into a 'Reverentian', was free – but she had to get away. If she could escape, no longer would she need to suppress her thoughts, or feel guilty for thinking them. No more hiding books or ensuring she left no trace of her internet browsing on *his* computer.

If.

Joy watched until the patrol car had disappeared, staring at the seemingly endless expanse of land and stars. This real Joy had to be smart, she had to hide for a few more days.

With her foot she pushed aside the triangular-shaped rock she used to stop the front door from banging, and shut the door. *Had God blessed her at last?*

CHAPTER 3

The day after the funeral

With a final look around the bedroom, Joy zipped closed the black backpack that contained all she was taking from this life. Clothes, a small framed picture of her and her siblings when she was ten, a soft pencil case containing rolled up banknotes and several miscellaneous items, each with a story. The money, over $8,000 in $50 notes, was cash her husband had kept hidden in the shed to take on business trips.

As she had expected, apart from her friends, the only elder to visit her before the funeral had been Reverentia's leader – Nathanial Palmer. Dressed as usual in blue trousers, his belt straining against his stomach, a light blue shirt and dark-blue tie, he had spoken to her at the kitchen table. She had never been so close to him; his breath smelt of the onion soup they regularly served for lunch. His face was deeply lined, and through the thick lenses of his black-rimmed glasses, his eyes were red-rimmed and watery.

He had arrived with two men from the community who she didn't know well. Dressed identically, but younger and fitter, they had packed up her husband's computer and files, taking them away in two cardboard boxes. They had worked quickly, not looking at her as they removed her link to the outside world. After they had finished, they had waited outside while Palmer had assured her that the whole community was there for her. He had spoken gently, parentally, saying, 'The speculation about the accident will die away in time.' And, 'When the time's right, we will find you a suitable husband.' She had looked down nodding, playing the part of the grieving wife – the grieving ex-wife.

Palmer had left seemingly convinced she was desperate to put this sad episode behind her, to become a leading light among the women of Reverentia. Because he believed himself one of God's representatives on earth, it wasn't hard to pull the wool over his eyes – he saw what he wanted to see.

On his way out he had assured her that they would take care of the financial and insurance issues, she didn't need to get involved in what he called 'men's business'. He had added that she would need to sign some documents but that it could wait until after the funeral – yesterday.

Turning off the lights, Joy locked the front door for what she hoped was the final time. She checked the time on her watch – his old watch before he came home from an overseas trip wearing an expensive watch, a gift from a client. It was nearly 4am. The sun was an hour from rising but there was enough pre-dawn light to safely walk down the gravel road.

Dressed in the community-mandated blue dress and white headscarf – she had no other choice – with her long hair tied in a pony tail, she stopped at the front gate for a last look at what was and wasn't her home. Turning away, she breathed in the cool morning air as she set off. From the top of the gravel road, she could see the long trek she had in front of her. Down to the farm's lower level, quietly past the accommodation complexes where she had spent her childhood, then down the long driveway that led to the gates of the community. Then, in the outside world, she planned to walk the long, narrow road that led to the Waikato Expressway and Hamilton.

Reaching the bottom of the gravel road, she emerged behind the enormous church, its spire straining towards the fading stars. Walking stealthily, she hustled past the accommodation complexes. There were lights on behind a few curtains, people having started their brutally long day. Alarms for most of Reverentia's community started blaring around 4:30am, pressing the compliant, unpaid workforce into action – cooking, farming, cleaning, preparing food, washing and folding laundry and caring for children. They were berated for any sign of slackness, and the work was long, hard and relentless.

Enticing aromas from the bakery were wafting over the community as Joy plodded forwards. At any time, she expected to hear her name called out, like a question. *'Joy?'* If anyone did see her, the news would circulate faster than the wind. Her chance of making it to the expressway would become zero. Worse, they would then keep her on a short leash – this was her one shot.

Her thoughts swirled as she concentrated on each step, not looking back. It was an anticlimax when she finally stood outside the main gate. Turning, she looked at the community bathed in the weak morning light, the church's spire glimmering like a beacon. The scene was picture-postcard serene. Shaking her head, she adjusted her backpack and headed towards the expressway.

The day was dawning bright, clear and warm. Although her backpack was heavy, each step outside the community felt effortless. Only one car passed her as she walked. She had stopped, holding her breath, but they had sped past taking no interest in her. Just after 6.30am, sweating after clambering through flax and over a wire barrier, she stood on the edge of the Waikato Expressway.

Dropping her backpack, she smoothed her dress, straightened her head scarf and stood self-consciously with her thumb out. Her internet research had warned her that while hitchhiking was a cheap way to travel, it wasn't without risk. Hitchhikers had fallen victim to abuse and assault. Even murder, though rare, wasn't unknown. Adding to her nervousness, she recalled community elders constantly preaching that the men outside their community were beasts, waiting for their opportunity to strike.

The road wasn't busy, cars speeding past at roughly thirty-second intervals. It was light enough for the drivers to see her but none had slowed; if anything they had increased their speed. Those drivers that did make eye contact looked surprised, shocked even. Time crawled as cars hurtled past, each one making Joy feel more exposed. Looking back the way she had come, she expected to see the lights of Palmer's ute bearing down on her.

Her despair was growing when a yellow and red courier van slowed, the bearded driver staring at her as he drove past. Its red brake lights shone brightly as it pulled over a short distance up the road. Joy stared wide eyed, expecting the van to drive away. Instead, orange lights started flashing. Throwing her backpack over a shoulder, she ran as fast as she could.

She inhaled deeply as she reached the lowered passenger window. Before she could speak, the male driver, who was eyeing her sternly, said, 'Jeez girl, you're not allowed to hitch on the expressway.' Dressed in a red and yellow shirt, the same colours as the van, the driver was a powerfully built Polynesian man. Bald with a trimmed, greying beard, he radiated concern.

Panting, she said, 'I … It's legal to hitchhike in New Zealand, isn't it?'

'Yeah, but not on the expressway, girl. Quick, get in before a cop sees us.'

Joy froze. She had seen Māori and Polynesian men before, when they came to help with shearing or to pick up stock, but she had never spoken to one.

The driver threw his head back, his laugh a high-pitched chuckle. 'Jeez, girl, I'm not going to eat you. I've two daughters though they're a bit younger than you. Come on, throw your bag in the back. Are you heading for Hamilton?'

Mouth open, eyes wide, Joy nodded.

For years Joy had known the world outside Reverentia was nothing like how the community elders painted it. When her husband was away, the ability to access the internet, always using the incognito function, had allowed her to travel New Zealand and the world beyond. Prior to that she had been a frog at the bottom of a well; the Reverentia community *was* the world. Unlike the frog, who was at the bottom of the well through circumstance, she was there because the community had created a carefully crafted fiction.

Cars flew by as she opened the rear sliding door, placing the entirety of her possessions in the van before cautiously climbing into the passenger seat. As soon as she shut her door, he accelerated hard, throwing her back in the seat.

'Put your seatbelt on, girl. I'm Tana. What's your name?'

'Joy,' she said breathlessly, buckling her seatbelt, as they flew towards Hamilton.

'It's good to meet you, Joy. I don't get to talk to many people during the day. Where are you headed?'

'Hamilton.'

'I know that, where in Hamilton?'

'I'm meeting a lawyer. The office is on Victoria Street.'

'Really?' His eyes flicked over her. 'What's your story?'

'My story?'

'Let's start with your age. What are you, twenty-one? A bit older?'

Joy shook her head. 'I'm seventeen.'

'Whoa,' Tana stared at her briefly. 'No offence girl, but dressed like that you don't look seventeen. I should know, my daughters are your age.'

Joy glared down at her ankle-length blue dress. It was ugly but it was all she owned. It was what all the women and girls wore. The elders had explained that it was to prevent expressions of vanity and to make the cost of making and maintaining clothes economical. She had kept on the compulsory head covering, a sign to the angels that she had placed herself in submission to the authority of her husband. It was stupid to wear it, but when she took it off briefly walking to the expressway she had felt strange, vulnerable.

'You're from one of those funny places, aren't you?' he said. 'You know, a religious hoo-ha.'

She nodded, her face reddening as tears threatened. She hadn't cried since she was seven or eight, not real tears.

In a quieter voice, he asked, 'Are you leaving? You know, escaping?'

Again, she nodded, realising how obvious it must look.

'Are those all the clothes you have? Anything' – he flicked his head towards her backpack – 'in there?'

'No, this is it,' she said without looking at him.

They drove on in silence, slower now as the traffic grew denser.

Tana spoke into some sort of radio. 'Bob, I've a family crisis, I'll be a bit late back.'

Over the radio's crackle, Bob swore. Tana chuckled with delight.

He looked over at her, serious. 'I'm taking you to my house.'

Eyes widening, she said, 'What? Why?'

'Don't panic, girl. You need different clothes, that's all. My daughters are your size. Well, they were your size but they're into their sport and they've shot up a bit lately. They always want money for new clothes. I tell them to stop growing.' He giggled at his own joke and Joy relaxed slightly. 'They have heaps they don't need that you could fit, you can take your pick. They won't have gone to school yet and they won't mind helping you out.'

Joy opened her mouth but no words came out.

The driver's face turned solemn. 'You can't walk around like that, girl. It's like you're wearing a sign around your neck. I'd take that scarf off too, if I was you. Nobody wears scarfs like that except ...'

You lot. He didn't need to finish the sentence. The few times she had visited town she heard people use that term. *You lot. That lot.* Worse.

Pulling off the scarf, Joy glared at it, her eyes moistening. She had left behind a dozen similar but subtly different scarfs. They were the one item of clothing that could set you apart, the smallest hint of personality. Throwing it at her feet, she looked at Tana. The community had preached that the man she was sitting beside had a devil inside him – but it was hard to see.

Smiling at her, he said. 'That's it, girl. You look years younger. Wait until my girls get a hold of you.' He chuckled away to himself.

'Thanks for giving me a lift,' she said. 'You might have saved my life.'

'I couldn't leave you there, you looked pretty tragic. We can't take too long, that's all, girl. But we'll get you looking like a regular seventeen-year-old. Don't you worry.'

He weaved swiftly around the streets, stopping in the driveway of a house on Vivian Street. It was a brick house with a wooden picket fence half painted white. Tana, who must have noticed her staring at the fence, said, 'Don't look at me. Catherine, that's my wife, she's the one who needs to pull finger.'

Joy didn't get a chance to ask what that meant, Tana was already heading to the front door.

It was a whirlwind half hour. Tana's daughters, who were tall and stunning even in their unflattering school uniform, were delighted to help, using her like a dress-up doll. When she got back into the van, she was wearing tight white jeans, a light-coloured blouse, the first she had worn that hadn't covered her neck, and a red cardigan.

When she had taken off the hated blue dress, both Tana's daughters had raised their eyes in alarm at her underwear. One had said, 'Dad doesn't need to know, but you're not leaving in those thunder-pants.' Joy's cheeks had reddened when they gave her underwear that included a tiny item they called a thong – she hid it at the bottom of her backpack. When they had finished, they wished her luck and hugged her tightly, crushing her twice.

'You look great,' said Tana. 'I told you my daughters have an eye for clothes. How do you feel?'

Joy stared at her legs, her feet in light-brown strappy shoes. They looked and felt as if they belonged to someone else. It would take time to feel comfortable in what was a new body. She turned to Tana, who was grinning. 'I know I look great,' she said, 'but I feel weird.'

His head rocked back with laughter. 'You'll get used to it, girl. Life's too short to be stuck where you were. Get out and enjoy yourself.'

Joy smiled tentatively. She couldn't go back, that fact pleased and terrified her in equal measures. The only life she had known, her world, her family and friends, gone – as though they had never existed. The Reverentia elders would make sure no one ever communicated with her. Whatever happened from now, her life, short or long, would be different.

Tana dropped her in the middle of Hamilton outside a bank on Victoria Street. As she reached for the door, he asked, 'Have you got money?'

'A little,' she said. 'How much do you want?'

Tana chuckled. 'Don't be silly, girl. I just wanted to make sure you could buy something to eat.' His face turned parental. 'Take care of yourself, Joy. It's a different world from where you've come. Not everyone's a good guy, like me.'

'Thanks, Tana.' She wanted to say more but couldn't find the words.

With a huge smile, he said, 'Good luck, girl,' and he roared off to catch up on his deliveries. As she watched his van disappear, she shook her head at what had happened. Was Tana one of the guardian angels she had heard so much about? Well disguised, but evidence of God's divine plan? But the stories she had read online – Ben and Olivia Hope, Urban Höglin and Heidi Paakkonen, Mona Blades and many other names – they were surely evidence that there was no all-seeing God. Had she been lucky and they hadn't?

'Phwoah.'

Joy jumped at the voice that had shattered the quiet, putting a self-defensive hand across her chest. The scraggly, bearded young man in the passenger seat of a slow-moving ute was wearing a white singlet and black beanie. Hanging halfway out of the passenger window, holding a brown paper bag, he sang loudly, 'Come on baby light my fire', before giving her an enormous grin and disappearing into the ute.

The few people that were around took no notice of her or the scene that had taken place. In the reflective glass of the bank, she scrutinised herself – a stranger stared back, frowning. Seemingly taller, the stranger was slender and it occurred to Joy that she rarely saw the *shape* of her body, always hidden under the unflattering blue dress. Was she … pretty? Attractive? The stranger in the window gave her a shy smile before her frown returned. Did she want to draw that sort of attention? She stared hard. *Who are you?*

A feeling of vulnerability swept over her – she was on display. If the community was aware that she had left, they would be looking for her. She walked away quickly, eyes on the pavement.

Her appointment at the lawyers was at 10am, over an hour and a half away. She spent the time nursing a large mug of coffee in a busy café whose clientele were mainly men and women in high-viz jackets. The elders had permitted coffee, but they frowned on women drinking it – it would apparently make them too excitable. Before she had married, she and her friends had used to secretly meet and drink black coffee 'borrowed' from the community kitchen.

Joy spent the remaining time before her appointment in a state of delight – she found another café in a bookstore where she ate chocolate cake, read magazines and drank another coffee so strong it made her teeth buzz. She might be doubting God's existence, but she had found heaven!

CHAPTER 4

'Sit down, Mrs Leslie.'

'Please, call me Joy,' she said in a quiet voice.

Putting her backpack at her feet, she sat opposite Emma Blackburn, a lawyer in the Hamilton family law firm. In the waiting room, she had sat in a plush leather chair surrounded by walls of legal tomes that smelt dusty. When the receptionist had ushered her through the impressive book wall, Joy had expected to emerge in an old-world library, complete with a large eighteenth-century globe. What she found was a meanly decorated office that smelled of the same cleaning products the community used. Strangely, they had hung pictures that resembled art but featured random words like, *Endeavour, Triumph* and *Leadership*. They reminded her of images in the community, only without God.

Still feeling the effects from her last coffee, Joy opted for a glass of water in response to Blackburn's offer of tea or coffee.

Dressed in a coal-black suit with a light-green collared shirt buttoned up to her neck, the lawyer could have been attractive but her appearance was severe. Everyone looked different outside Reverentia and Joy found herself scrutinising women for looks she might try.

After organising Joy's water, Blackburn knitted her hands together. 'Now, Joy, what can I help you with? I must confess I was surprised you contacted our firm. Reverentia always uses its own lawyers.'

'Is this conversation private, Miss Blackburn?'

'Please, call me Emma. Do you mean privileged?'

'Privileged?'

'It means I can't disclose what you say. You can talk freely.'

'That's what I meant then,' said Joy. 'This conversation is privileged?'

Blackburn smiled as she nodded

'I'm leaving the church, Emma. I want nothing more to do with it or them. I want to settle everything so I can leave and never go back.'

Blackburn looked at her intensely. 'What's there to settle?'

'My husband was killed in an accident.'

Blackburn's eyebrows raised. 'Oh. I'm sorry –'

'It's okay,' she cut in. *Don't be.*

Taking a brown folder out of her backpack, she said, 'I have all his personal papers here. He was insured for $100,000, but I couldn't find a copy of his will. I'm not sure if he made one.'

Still staring, Blackburn said, 'Right. First, let's get you signed up as a client. That will allow me to look at your files and access information on-line.'

After the lawyer had explained the ins and outs of the contract, Joy completed the form, signing and dating it without asking any questions. For an address, she used Tana's.

'Do you post much?' asked Joy as she had filled out the form.

'The physical post? Hardly ever, it's all electronic.'

Smiling, Joy handed the form back to *her* lawyer. Joy had an email account at Proton Mail, and if they communicated by email, Tana would never need to be involved.

Taking the form, Blackburn pointed at Joy's folder. 'May I?'

Joy passed it over. 'If you need more information, I might have it on this.' She held up a small flash drive. 'Do you want it?'

'You keep it for now,' she said as the firm's receptionist brought in a glass of water.

'Perfect timing,' said Blackburn. 'Finn, take Joy through to the visitor's lounge. I'll have a quick look at your files so I can get an idea of what we're dealing with and what we'll need to do. I'll need to contact Reverentia's lawyers; will that be a problem?'

Putting the flash drive in her backpack, Joy frowned. 'What details of mine will they want?'

Blackburn shook her head. 'Nothing. It's about me getting all the relevant documents they may hold.'

'Fine,' said Joy shrugging.

They had decorated the visitor's lounge in a similar style, minimalistic. Sitting at the table, she took out the notepad that she used to hide in her underwear drawer to make a list of what she needed to do.

At the top of the list was a place to stay. The entire focus of her planning had been on escaping the community. But she'd doubted she would succeed, so this was all new territory. She was making it up as she went.

In terms of money, she had her husband's hidden cash which she doubted anyone in the community knew about. Although over $8,000, which sounded like a fortune, her internet research told her otherwise. But it should buy her enough time, if she stayed in cheap accommodation, though she didn't know how long her lawyer would need to finalise her affairs. She hoped the life insurance would pay quickly – he was dead – and that she could use the money to establish herself in a new city. Settling his will, if he had one, would take longer but she wasn't planning on waiting. Besides, apart from his life insurance what would he own? As far as she was aware, the community owned everything.

Clothes like the ones Tana's daughters had given her were second on her list. New clothes were a luxury, she would shop in second-hand stores. The third and final item of immediate concern was food.

Under the heading *Luxuries*, she wrote *cosmetics* and *alcohol*. Tana's daughters cluttered their rooms with a dazzling array of makeup, accessories and products she had never heard of let alone knew how to use. From her former home she had taken her toothbrush, toothpaste, two hairbrushes, a myriad of hair ties and a bar of soap – that was all she had ever used. As for alcohol, it was the one vice the community not only tolerated but encouraged. She had been sneaking drinks since her baptism and she looked forward to being able to drink in public – like a man.

Staring out the window at the grubby rear entrances of shops and restaurants, she remembered her baptism as though it was yesterday. She had been thirteen when she pledged her life to God, the elders dunking her in a freezing river on a glorious sunny day. It had been exhilarating – at the time, her parents watching with obvious pride. Or had they? It was hard to know what was real and what people did because they knew it was expected.

Like a dark cloud obscuring the sun, a coldness washed over her. Was it hatred? Anger? Or was it confusion? Resentment? Maybe it was all those and more. The day after she had married, the marriage her parents had helped arrange, her parents had become distant. Joy had eventually concluded that they must have considered they had done their duty, that she was on her own. They had her younger brothers and sisters to care for. So they had kicked her out of the nest, but not to fly. She became someone else's property in a different flightless nest. The feeling of abandonment had bitten deep but Joy had to suck it up. No one would care, especially her new husband.

From the moment the idea had struck her that a different life was possible, her parents hadn't featured in her plans. Their actions had made it clear that they had their own life. They must have known about Keith Leslie, what he was like – every adult in the community must have. They had left her with a violent alcoholic; she had left them to live their lives.

'Emma's ready for you.'

Joy jumped, startled by the receptionist's reappearance. She hurriedly closed her notebook, tucking it in her backpack.

Blackburn appeared serious as Joy again sat opposite.

'I'm afraid, Joy, there's not a lot of good news.'

She stared at the lawyer, her face pinching.

'I contacted the life insurance company. They informed me that Reverentia has lodged a claim on behalf of your husband.'

'My husband? How?'

'The policy was *owned* by your husband.'

'So?' The word snapped out.

Holding up a calming hand, Blackburn said, 'It means any payment goes to your husband's estate, not directly to any beneficiary.'

Shaking her head, Joy said, 'I don't understand.'

'It means your husband's will determines how his estate, including any insurance money, is distributed. It also means it will take longer. The High Court needs to grant probate to recognise your husband's will as valid.'

Blackburn paused but Joy could only stare.

'There's more bad news,' said Blackburn. 'I contacted Reverentia's legal people about the will. They seemed' – she pressed her lips together

– 'surprised to hear from me on your behalf. They were very guarded, but they told me they have a copy of your husband's will.'

'What does it say?'

'I don't know. I requested a copy, they said they'd send it in due course.'

'What does that mean?'

'It usually means they want to strategise about how to deal with a circumstance they weren't expecting.'

Joy again shook her head, her mouth open.

'This will take longer than I think you hoped, Joy. The conditions in your husband's will – they dictate what, if anything, you're entitled to. Then there's the police.'

Joy stiffened. 'The police?'

'Their lawyer mentioned the accident is the subject of a police investigation.'

'Why?'

Blackburn shrugged, a sigh escaping her. 'I don't know.'

Joy's frown was intense. *No, no, no.*

'I'll keep the pressure on them,' said Blackburn. 'When I have a copy of the will, I'll work out what next steps to take.' The lawyer bit her lip. 'I'm sorry to have to ask this, but this will all take time – and it might get expensive. Can you afford to retain our services?'

'To pay you?'

'Yes.'

'When the will gets settled, yes,' said Joy.

Blackburn grimaced. 'That's not how we operate.'

'Okay,' said Joy. 'I have money. Can I let you know if I can't pay anymore?'

'That's okay,' said the lawyer. 'We normally invoice monthly, but I'll make sure you're invoiced on a time and materials basis.'

Not understanding, Joy nodded.

With a smile, Blackburn said, 'This hour, we'll make that pro bono. I'll call it "initial research" to keep my boss off my back.'

'Pro bono?'

Blackburn almost laughed. 'Free.'

As Joy walked back through the impressive reception area, Finn called out in a chipper voice, 'See you again.'

She turned and gave him a warm smile, a smile that faded as soon as he couldn't see her face. Walking slowly down the stairs, for the second time that day she had to fight back tears.

CHAPTER 5

The backpackers, where Joy was sharing a communal room, was clean and cheap. When she first arrived, she had been the only occupant in a six-bed room but two German tourists, a couple, had arrived later that evening. In their mid-twenties, they spoke passable English and she was fascinated by their description of life in Germany. She was still getting her head around the fact that New Zealand was vastly different to her former home, let alone the world.

Since arriving her days had become ordered. After a life of regimentation, it made her feel in control. In the morning she visited the lawyer's office to check for news. Finn would normally smile and shake his head when she arrived at the top of the stairs. 'You need to get a phone,' he would say and she would smile and reply, 'When I can afford one.' Apart from the cost, the truth was she had little idea how smart phones worked. The men had phones in Reverentia, not the women.

After visiting the lawyer's office, she would go to her favourite café and bookstore, treating herself to cake and coffee for breakfast. Next, she headed to the public library where she browsed the non-fiction books at random, reading them in a comfortable chair. That or she surfed the internet on their free computers.

The last stop for the day, around 4pm, was the supermarket, the novelty of which hadn't yet worn off. She tried to spend her money frugally, but it was hard to resist the temptations on offer – pies, cakes, pre-made salads, and the huge range of desserts and chocolate. On her first visit, she found she wasn't old enough to buy alcohol. Flustered, she had said, 'I've been drinking for years.' The look that went along with the 'Sorry, love,' made her cheeks burn.

She ate in the backpackers' communal lounge, conversing with people from a wide range of nationalities about their day, home and plans. If they asked about her, she would deflect by saying, 'I'm between lives.' It was a line everyone accepted at face value – they didn't press.

After dinner she watched TV until she felt tired enough for bed. One night her German roommates asked if they could have a little "private time". She knew what they would be doing, and although she was aware that her own sexual experiences weren't likely to be typical, it surprised her that the woman seemed genuinely excited at the prospect. The constant messaging the community had delivered on sex, especially a woman's role, would take time to unlearn.

When she was alone, she counted her money, working out how much longer she could stay, keeping aside enough to pay for her lawyer, though she hadn't received a bill – yet. The money from the will, that was what she needed to come through, then she would ... *What will I do?*

She was into her second week at the backpackers when her new life received twin body blows.

The first had occurred when she visited her lawyer's office. Finn, expecting her visit, wasn't wearing his usual friendly expression. 'Emma would like a quick word.'

In Joy's mind, the will taking longer to settle meant a few weeks, maybe a month. Blackburn had told her it would be months – plural. As the will was being contested, it could take a year. With her hand on Joy's arm, Blackburn had said, 'There's no point coming in each day. When I have any news, I'll be in touch.'

Joy had carried on with the rest of her day as usual, what else could she do? The only good news Blackburn had was that until she needed to act there would be no bill to pay.

Sitting in the communal lounge, having determined that she needed a job, the second body blow landed when two people, clearly not backpackers, arrived. They weren't, as she had feared, from Reverentia. They were worse.

It was around 4.30pm and she was watching a game show on TV. The owner of the backpackers, a solidly built man who dressed like a once-successful businessman, came into the lounge. Scowling, he pointed her out to a man and a woman who had come in with him. The man, older, his hair and beard greying, was wearing a dark suit, blue shirt and striped tie. The woman, taller as well as younger, wore black pants and a tight paisley blouse which accentuated her athletic build. They radiated confidence and importance.

Joy returned her stare to the TV, but she felt that she was back in the community, an elder about to publicly shame her. Her one hope, that they were looking for someone else, didn't last long.

'Are you Joy Leslie?' asked the man as he approached, his voice low and accusing.

She stared at each of them in turn, nodding.

'I'm Detective Inspector Jeffries.' He angled his head towards the woman. 'This is Detective Sergeant Kerr.'

Detectives?

'Hi,' she finally managed. 'Am I in trouble?' Joy's sole interaction with the police had been on the night of the accident. Now, towering over her, were two detectives.

'Not at all,' he said, his voice unconvincingly light. 'We'd just like to ask you a few questions.' Pointing at a dining table away from the TV, he said, 'Do you mind if we sit there?'

'Sure.' As she stood, she asked, 'Is it about the death of my husband?'

'That's right,' said the female detective. 'It's about the accident that caused his death.'

'I've already spoken to the police,' she said as she sat down. 'And how did you know I was staying here?' She had tried to make the question sound as though she was mildly interested in their answer.

The detectives shared a glance, the male detective answering. 'Your lawyer let us know.'

'Oh,' said Joy. *Is my lawyer allowed to do that?*

'Let's start with how old are you,' said DI Jeffries.

'Seventeen.'

The detective wrote the number down, adding an exclamation mark. 'The Serious Crash Unit have reviewed the accident,' he said stroking his beard, 'we're just squaring away a few details. We'd like you to take us through the events on the night of the accident.'

Tensing, she said, 'It's all a blur.'

They sat still. Keen. Eyes unblinking. Forced smiles. Silent.

Taking her time, she walked them through what happened – him not coming home, her getting worried, calling to see where he was, finding out about the crash. She kept her story plain, sticking to the facts. Besides, they wouldn't be interested in what else was happening in her life, what would've happened, what always happened, if his car hadn't gone off the road.

When Joy had finished, DS Kerr asked, 'So, you were home all evening?'

'I was making dinner.'

'Was your husband abusive?' she asked. The detective's question caught Joy off balance. Her hand went instinctively to her jaw. *Yes, he was a mean, abusive bastard.* She lowered her hand casually, hoping the movement wasn't obvious, knowing that it had been. 'I'm ... I'm not sure.'

The detectives stared at her like the elders used to when they were unsatisfied with an answer she had given.

'I mean,' said Joy, 'I thought what was happening to me was normal.'

The female detective leaned closer. 'What did happen to you?'

Joy took a moment to process the question, to think carefully about what to say. She spoke slowly. 'He was kind, when he was sober. But when he'd been drinking ...' She let her sentence fade.

'Did he hit you?' she asked.

'He slapped me mostly. Not hard, but ... hard enough.'

'Why?'

You'd have to ask him that, wouldn't you? Anger tried to claw its way to the surface. She put her hands in her lap. Speaking evenly, she said, 'I always tried to please him, but he was hard to please.'

The female detective waited a moment before asking, 'Did he rape you?'

Her eyes widened. 'Rape?' She looked at each of them. 'No,' she lied.

DI Jeffries asked, 'Did you, um ... dislike your husband?'

'Did I dislike my husband? At times, of course. At times it was hard not to *dislike* him.' The words came out with a sharp edge, she breathed in deeply through her nose.

'Of course,' he said quickly. 'But your life will be different now. Now he's deceased.'

Warning bells rang. 'I don't know,' she said. 'It's all so recent. It'll be different, now I've left.'

'Why have you run away?' asked DS Kerr.

They were taking turns to ask questions, coming from different angles, trying to unsettle her. Licking her lips, squeezing her hands together under the table, she said calmly, 'I haven't *run away*. I decided to leave the community. There's nothing there for me now.' It was an answer open to interpretation.

The female detective pinched her bottom lip. 'And you're challenging your husband's will.'

It was a statement that sounded like a question.

'I haven't seen his will. My lawyer has requested a copy.'

'If you're successful' – DS Kerr licked her lips – 'do you stand to inherit money?'

'I don't know.' Joy knew what she was implying, but her escape wasn't about money. It was about saving her life. Living her life. Her own life, not the scripted one they had planned for her – part slave, part domesticated mother.

'What do you have planned?' It was the male detective's turn. 'With the money, that is.'

'Nothing,' she said. 'I haven't had time to think about anything like that.'

'Did your husband drink gin?' he asked.

Joy blinked. It was such an abrupt change in the line of questioning; she suspected that he was losing patience.

'He drank anything alcoholic.'

Pursing his lips, the detective said, 'According to his church friends, he never touched gin. Hated the stuff.'

All Joy's muscles below the table clenched. She was a proficient actor, able to play the part people expected. It was how she survived inside Reverentia, never letting people know what she was thinking or feeling. But this was different. These weren't doddery elders, they were detectives used to detecting lies – it's what they did. Lying to them was a risky strategy, but she didn't need to lie.

'I didn't monitor what he drank.' It was true statement. 'It's not the place of a wife to do that.' Another true statement. 'To my knowledge, he drank all sorts of alcohol.' A third true statement.

Again, the detectives exchanged the briefest of glances.

DI Jeffries put his hands together. 'A bottle of gin, half full, was found in your husband's car. According to eye witnesses, he didn't take any bottle with him when he left the … party.'

Joy kept her face neutral.

'In fact,' he continued, 'that bottle was left at your house by a Mr Pious Wright. He confirmed he had left it a few weeks earlier.'

The source of the detective's concerns had clearly originated in the community. A scene formed in Joy's mind. It had been their turn to host Friday drinks. Once everyone had gone home, once *he* had staggered off to bed, she had cleaned the house. Sprinkled among the empty bottles and cans that adorned most flat surfaces was the odd half-full bottle of spirits. She had put these in his liquor collection. Now the detective was informing her that one of those bottles had found its way into his crashed car. He had taken a bottle of spirits when he left, but not gin – she knew that for a fact.

Nodding almost imperceptibly, Joy remained silent. DI Jeffries hadn't asked her a question. He was hoping she would start talking, to fill in the silence. She wouldn't. She'd had ample experience of men questioning her, trying to make her confess to things she had and hadn't done. Silence was your friend.

Playing as a tag team, it was the female detective who asked, 'Do you know how that bottle got into his car?'

Shaking her head, she said, 'I told you, I didn't monitor my husband's drinking. Or his drinks collection.' Almost true.

'Did he take the bottle of gin with him on Friday?'

Joy paused before saying, 'No.'

DS Kerr made a note. She asked, 'Did your husband often come home dishevelled?'

'Dishevelled?'

'You know, dirty. Like he'd been rolling on the ground?'

'Dirty? No. He was an accountant, he didn't work on the farms.'

'No,' she said. 'I mean, did he get his clothes dirty when he'd been drinking, say on a Friday night.'

Joy looked at the table. 'Once or twice, not often. If he'd been drinking a lot.'

'Did you worry about his drinking and driving?'

'It's not a wife's place to question what her husband does.' *Hell, no.*

A young couple bounced into the room, giggling and holding hands. They sat in front of the TV, smiling at Joy as they had entered, but apart from that they took no interest in what was happening around the table.

'Right,' said Detective Jeffries exhaling. 'Your husband suffered a range of injuries in the crash, most of them consistent with him being unconscious at the time of the accident and not wearing a seatbelt.'

Joy stared unmoving. The detective hadn't finished.

'The majority of his injuries weren't life threatening,' he said. 'The car has a good safety rating and the airbags deployed, but the autopsy revealed that your husband suffered a' – he took his time flicking through his notes – 'ah, yes, a vertebral artery dissection leading to a subarachnoid haemorrhage.'

Shaking her head, Joy said, 'I don't know what any of that means.'

'It *can* happen in a car crash, but it's not common,' he said. 'Especially in what was a relatively low-speed impact. The trees slowed the car until it hit one head on, flipped and skidded down the hill.'

'I'm still not following.'

'Your husband was unlucky,' said the female detective. 'Statistically, it was a one in a million chance.'

Taking a handkerchief from her pocket, Joy started to sob. It was a valuable ability she had developed from a young age. If it didn't save you from a beating, it lessened its intensity. Through her sobs she said, 'I don't know what you're telling me. He was unlucky, as though that makes it better.'

In unison, the detectives sat back.

'We're sorry,' said DS Kerr. 'We didn't mean to upset you. We're …
we're just doing our job. Following leads to make sure nothing's missed.'

Joy dried her eyes.

'How long are you planning on staying here?' asked the male detective.

Sniffing, she shook herself, sitting upright. 'Not long, I hope. A few
more weeks while my lawyer sorts out my affairs.'

Glancing at each other, the detectives stood.

'I don't think we will,' said DS Kerr, 'but we may need to ask you
further questions.'

Joy stayed seated. 'Sure.'

They turned and left, talking inaudibly.

Joy watched them leave then closed her eyes. *Damn.*

She needed to make sense of what the detectives had said, asked and
implied. The state of his clothes and his injuries were understandable in
a car crash, but it was the gin bottle that made no sense. He might have
taken it to give back to old 'wandering hands' Wright, but he hadn't put
the gin bottle in his car, not that night – she was sure of that. Either he
had put the bottle in earlier, which she doubted, or someone had put
it there after the accident. And while she didn't know exactly who, she
knew roughly who – the same sort of men who took away his computer
and files, following instructions.

They could have taken the bottle from her house on the evening
of the accident, when everyone was milling around before the police
arrived. Then, before the Serious Crash Unit arrived the next day, they
had planted it in the car. But why? They didn't know she was planning
to escape. They can't have.

Drumming her fingers on the table, she felt tired. The detectives
would return, she was in no doubt of that. Now that she had left
Reverentia, now she was challenging the will, God only knew what
they might dream up. The members of the community would rally
around whatever story the elders concocted. It would be the word of
the community against hers.

Would they 'find' more evidence, which couldn't exist? Would the
police charge her with a crime? She didn't know, but waiting around to

find out didn't make sense. Forming a fist, she banged it lightly on the table – she had to change plans yet again. Getting a job while she waited was out of the question. Her dream of the insurance money allowing her to set herself up in another city, maybe attend university if she was smart enough, was dead.

Other members had left Reverentia. Apart from erasing them from the collective memory, the elders had let them go. Why did they want her so badly? Why not let her go too? Whatever the reasons, she needed to disappear in the next few hours.

In the bunkroom she packed her belongings into her backpack. It was heavier; she had more clothes now having bought several items second-hand, and there were even a few cosmetics she was experimenting with. When she had finished packing, she sat on the bed.

Could she really escape … again? This time it wasn't from the community; it was the police who would be looking for her. Would disappearing make her guilty? But what was the alternative? Stay and wait for the detectives or community to arrive – to make her look guilty? No, that wasn't an option. Neither was going back. The only option she could see was to keep going forwards.

Back downstairs, she retrieved her remaining food from the communal fridge, adding it to her backpack – she would eat while she walked. On the backpackers' computer she plugged her destination into Google maps, an application she had become familiar with when surfing the web on 'his' computer. Her destination was just under an hour away by foot. If this didn't pan out, she wasn't sure what she would do.

After a final check, she was ready to leave. Noiselessly opening the window in the lounge, raising her eyebrows conspiratorially to the young couple watching TV, she dropped her backpack onto the lawn outside, keeping an apple. She strolled casually through the lounge, past the manager's office and towards the front door.

The manager poked his head out and, after giving her his usual once-over, asked, 'What's going on?'

Smiling widely, she said, 'Nothing.'

As she reached for the door, he asked, 'You're not in any trouble?'

She shook her head. 'No.' He wasn't concerned about her – he was concerned about his business.

'The police are bad enough,' he said glowering, 'but when a couple of detectives want to speak to a guest, that usually means trouble.'

Her smile still in place, she said, 'It's fine, honestly. They won't be back.' *Well, they might, but I won't be here.*

Turning away to end the conversation, she left the building. Out of the manager's sight she retrieved her backpack. She had been right to be cautious.

Taking a bite out of her apple, she started walking.

CHAPTER 6

'It's all right, girl, there's no need to cry,' said Tana.

Arriving at Tana's house at 6.30pm, Joy had spent the time walking rehearsing her story. How she was running low on money, her legal issues were complex and she needed a place to stay until she had sorted herself out. After drawing in a deep breath, she knocked on the front door. She had heard Tana shouting at his daughters in his warm, parental manner.

'Turn that bloody awful music down. There's someone at the door.'

The door swept open and a smiling Tana stood framed in the doorway. His face instantly morphed to concern. Her prepared story evaporated in a flood of tears. Real tears, not strategic tears. Once they came, she couldn't stop them.

'Gimme your bag, girl. Come in, come in.'

Tana's daughters shrieked with delight when they recognised Joy, stopping when they saw she was crying.

'Put the kettle on, girls. She needs a cuppa.'

Tana guided her into the kitchen, still crying, a handkerchief over her eyes.

In an accent she recognised, a soft female voice asked, 'And who's this, love?'

'This is that girl Joy. I told you about her, the one running away from one of those … places.'

'What's the matter?'

Steering Joy into a chair, he whispered, 'I don't know.'

Joy felt a gentle hand on her shoulder. 'It's okay, child.'

It took a couple of minutes, and many ragged breaths, before Joy regained control. The kitchen was hot and, after her walk, she had to mop sweat from her brow as well as dry her eyes. She sipped the sweet tea Tana's wife had put in front of her, mainly out of politeness. Joy did a momentary double-take when she first glimpsed his wife, who wasn't Tongan. At least, she assumed she wasn't Tongan, she was as fair as Joy.

'Take your time girl,' said Tana. 'There's no hurry.'

Her voice was croaky, like she had a cold. 'I … I haven't anywhere to go.'

'It's all right girl, you can stay with us,' he said. Turning to his wife, he added, 'I mean, that's all right, isn't it?'

Smiling, his wife said, 'Of course. She can stay as long as she needs.'

Tana spoke softly. 'Can I ask what happened?'

Joy bit her top lip. *What can I tell them?*

Patting her husband's hand, his wife delayed her decision. 'Easy on the girl. There's plenty of time to find out. I think she needs a shower, to freshen up a bit and we'll get her settled in one of the bedrooms.'

'She can sleep in my room,' the two girls yelled in unison as they burst into the room. They must have been listening at the door.

This family had known her for less than an hour, yet for the first time in years Joy felt genuinely wanted. The tears came again but this time also laughter. Later that evening, with the girls watching TV and his wife reading, Tana had said, 'Come and sit outside with me, Joy. It's a nice evening.'

They sat on the front porch in two well-worn wicker chairs. People wandered past bouncing balls, listening to music, walking dogs or holding hands. Eventually Tana interrupted their silence. 'You better tell me what's going on. As much as you can. As much as you want to. We can do lots to help.'

Through all that she had endured, Joy had never confided in anyone – the risk was too great. She couldn't even be sure how her parents might have reacted. It was known for parents to denounce their own children, and not being able to trust them had stung. While spouting love, the community actively drove a wedge between parents and children. Joy assumed they did it because it was easier to control isolated individuals than tight-knit family units. To be fair, she didn't know what Tana would do either, but he seemed honest and decent. If she didn't trust him now, would she ever trust anyone?

Exhaling, she said, 'This is going to sound … strange. The community I lived in, Reverentia, it's not like Hamilton with shops and libraries and food and coffee. I knew more about the world than my brothers, sisters and friends because I was always sneaking on to my parents' computer, then the one in our house.'

'Googling?'

Joy nodded. 'It was amazing, but it wasn't real. It only existed for a short time on a screen, then I was back in the community with the endless work and strict rules. That's what I mean about strange, you have to put yourself in my shoes, otherwise it sounds crazy.'

An intense look on his face, Tana nodded.

Taking him back in time, she started her story when she was fifteen. The education she had received preparing her for the life of a Reverentia worker, wife and mother. If you deviated from that, you came in for public shaming or physical discipline. The insanely long days of work – all in the service of the community and God. Finally she told Tana about her marriage, when she was nearly sixteen.

'*Nearly* sixteen? That's not right,' he said. 'I thought even wacko communities had to obey the law.' He held up his hands. 'Sorry, Joy. I didn't mean *wacko*.'

'Don't be sorry,' she said, 'I think they're *wacko* too. And the community keeps itself to itself, how would anyone know what went on? When outsiders visited, we put on our best clothes and acted happy – we didn't need to be told.'

Tana grunted angrily. 'I guess it isn't hard to fool the world.'

'It isn't,' she said. 'And don't get me wrong, it wasn't all bad. We did find time for fun. But as I grew older the fun evaporated.'

'So, you were married. I take it you didn't choose your husband?'

Joy shook her head. 'That's not how it works. And that's when my life went from tough to shit.'

Tana shifted in his chair.

In almost a whisper, she said, 'He was not a nice man. His first wife died a few weeks after their first child was stillborn. The elders said it was an accident, some in the community said she had killed herself. I don't know. I guess the elders thought he'd get over it quicker if he married again, started a family. I tried to be a good wife, that's what they'd trained me to be, what else could I do?'

Tana's face was stern. 'Did he knock you around?'

Pursing her lips, Joy paused as a young man walked past bouncing a basketball. 'He was an alcoholic. He was violent. He slapped me mostly, sometimes he'd punch, not often. Nights could be worse. A constant tension hung in the air – it was like waiting for a bomb to explode.' Smiling sadly at Tana, she said, 'The violence was actually easier to deal with.'

Tana had a face like thunder. He snorted. 'Sorry, it's just hard to listen to what happened to you. You're a child for Pete's sake. Married, a runaway and now nowhere to go. And what, you're seventeen?'

She nodded.

Tana pushed himself out of his chair, came over and hugged her. She blinked away her tears, safe in his huge, warm embrace.

Sitting back in his chair, he said, 'Life will different for you now. Much better.'

'I hope so,' she said. 'It feels better even though I'm not sure what I'm going to do.'

'So, you decided to escape your shitty marriage,' he said. 'Good for you.'

In her story, Joy had reached the fatal accident. Licking her lips, she said, 'He, my husband, had an accident. He was driving home, we lived on the top of a hill, he was drunk and drove off the edge. He died.'

A long silence descended.

'Jeez,' said Tana. 'I don't know what to feel about that. If he was as bad as you're saying, maybe it was for the best.' Looking at her earnestly, he asked, 'Were you sad?'

'Hell, no. I'm sure he would have killed me, eventually.'

Tana shook his head.

'I couldn't show it, though,' she said. 'I had to play the grieving wife. The day after his funeral, I left the next morning before the community was awake.'

'Is that when I picked you up?'

Grinning, she said, 'Yep, you're the luckiest break I've had. An hour later, with you and your daughter's help, I looked normal.' Reaching over, she squeezed his arm. 'You'll never know how much that helped.'

Tana smiled shyly. 'Where've you been staying?'

'I was in a backpackers. It was nice, apart from the pervy manager. I was hoping my lawyer would settle things fast, especially the insurance, but the community's lawyers got involved.'

'I bet they're saying he left everything to the community.'

'That's what I reckon.'

'How long will it take?'

She sighed. 'I don't know. My lawyer said ages. And then today …' She looked at him then at her feet. 'The police came to the backpackers, two detectives.' She waited for him to speak, to ask questions, but he remained silent. 'They asked about the accident. The community are making things up, they put a bottle of gin from our house at the scene.' Tears came but in single lines, not torrents. 'They're trying to make it look like I was involved.'

'Easy girl,' said Tana. 'Take me through what happened, slowly. Start from the night of the accident.'

Using her sleeve to dab her eyes and sniffing loudly, Joy repeated her story from finding out about the accident to the detectives questioning her at the backpackers. Tana listened intently, not interrupting. When she'd finished, he sat surveying the street painted a weak orange by the streetlights.

Eventually he said, 'Detectives. You're in a bit of a pickle, girl.' He looked at her seriously. 'What do you want to do, Joy? I mean, I know you're only seventeen, but it's your life. Only you should make decisions about that.'

'I'm not sure, Tana.'

'Can't say I blame you.'

They sat again in silence. A car drove slowly past, only one headlight working.

Tana broke the silence. 'Do you want to know what I think?'

'Please,' she said. Her plan had fallen apart, she had no idea what her next step should be.

'You need time,' he said. 'Maybe lots of time. You need to consider what you want to do, what you can do and, maybe, what you should do.'

She stared at him.

'How does this sound for a plan? Take a week to chill out, no one knows you're here. Then, if you decide you don't want to go back, or talk to the police, we can enrol you in high school for the rest of the year. I'll have to make sure Catherine's okay with it, but she will be. You'll be in year thirteen, the same as my eldest.'

'But the community … the police will find me,' she said.

'For as long as you need to be, you can be part of my family. We'll enrol you as Joy Brown, that's my last name. No one will ask questions. No one ever does. I'll say you've been living in Australia.'

Joy's eyes lit up, but the light didn't last long. 'Look at me, Tana, I look nothing like you or your family.'

'True, you make a pretty pale Tongan. But, as you saw, Catherine's not Tongan, she's an Aussie. We can create a believable story.' Shrugging his shoulders, he said, 'You're Catherine's sister's child sent out from Australia. Schools see it all the time – adoptions and extended families raising children.'

'Does her sister have children my age?'

Tana laughed his high-pitch chuckle. 'She doesn't have a sister, girl. See what I mean. Besides, once you're in school, no one will care. You'll get questions from the kids, but girls are only interested in where you fit in. And the boys, well …' He stroked his beard.

Looking down, she shook her head.

'You're not to blame, girl. It'll take time for that to sink in but this might give you that time. You strike me as pretty smart to have educated yourself when no one was looking. Take the week to think about it.'

'It does sound good,' she said. 'It sounds like a possible future. And I'll be able to pay you back, when my lawyer settles with the community.'

'Don't worry about that,' he said. 'What will be, will be.'

Frowning, Joy asked, 'What do we do if they find out who I really am?'

'We'll paddle that canoe if it happens. Until then, welcome to the fāmili.'

CHAPTER 7

Four years later

Emerging silently from one of the legal firm's offices, a tall, well-dressed woman closed the door quietly behind her. After blowing her nose, she walked towards where Lauren Brown, the receptionist at the Auckland family law firm, sat. The woman's clothes, a matching dark blue skirt and jacket with a white shirt, gave her a professional but casual look. If Lauren had to guess, as she liked to, she would pick university lecturer.

As the woman reached her desk, Lauren smiled when they made eye contact, asking, 'How did that go?'

Forcing a brief smile, she said, 'Fine. Now I know what it'll take, what it'll cost and that there's no guarantee. I need time to think.'

Lauren reached under her desk and took a business card out of her bag. She knew what 'thinking' the woman was going to do – could she afford to pay? A victim of family violence where the price of justice was more than she could afford. Not sad, wrong.

Leaning closer, Lauren said, 'Give me a call,' and handed her a card for her fledging business. 'Let's have a coffee. I can help make it less expensive and a bit more guaranteed.' That was over-selling it, but the line usually got her foot in the door.

'Weeping Angels,' said the woman.

Even though no one was nearby, Lauren whispered, 'Give me a call. The coffee's on me.'

Putting the business card in her bag, she forced another smile before hurrying away. Tapping her lip, Lauren watched her go. *She'll call. Next time it happens, she'll call.*

Lauren had worked as the firm's receptionist for two years since she had moved from Hamilton. She had changed her name from Joy to Lauren, keeping Tana's surname, to minimise the chance that her past life could find her. It was after seeing too many women in the predicament she had just witnessed that she had started Weeping Angels – an unregistered company she ran in her spare time. Her receptionist job paid the bills, just, but she was finding the role a mix of discouraging and unstimulating.

Lauren saw many women in obvious distress come in needing help. But after learning the process, the time, the chances of success and the cost, many never came back. Where did these women go? What did they do? From her time at the firm, she knew that if it was bad enough to need a lawyer, it was dire.

From the cases that made it to court, and from talking to the firm's lawyers, she knew that the abusive behaviour, illegal as it was, was unlikely to change unless the women obtained a protection order. And that wasn't a guarantee. Her boss, a part-owner of the practice, was fond of saying, 'Family violence is an iceberg, two percent of the abuse is visible and dealt with through the courts, the rest lurks beneath the surface.' It was an ugly side of New Zealand society nobody wanted to acknowledge.

Sensing an opportunity, Lauren had started the company, joined a karate dojo so she could learn how to handle herself and began handing out business cards to women she considered unlikely to come back. Over coffee, while they unburdened themselves, she tried to convince them of the results she could help them achieve. By acting as their private investigator, she could gather the evidence they needed and write the affidavit in legal speak so their lawyers had little to do and hours to charge. Lauren's plan was that by providing solid, irrefutable evidence, the abusers would agree to sign a protection order, saving the significant costs associated with a court appearance.

It was a no-brainer, at least to Lauren.

Most women loved, and badly needed, the opportunity to talk – to confide in someone outside their circle of friends and family. Many confessed that they thought they were going mad. The world around them was oblivious or, worse, disbelieving of what they were enduring. Friends were unable to square away their stories with the reasonable, tolerant façade their partners or exes maintained.

The sticking point was always money. Naturally they wanted the abuse to stop, they wanted to fight back. But the majority couldn't afford the relatively modest fees she was charging to help them secure a protection order, let alone the sums needed if the fight went through the courts. In many situations, the abuser controlled their access to money, wielding the financial power like a battle-axe.

After nine tearful chats over coffee and no clients secured, Lauren knew she needed to change tack. She had worked hard writing a business plan, and had started rewriting it, when help came from an unlikely corner.

Carter Donaldson, a fellow karate attendee, had joined the dojo around the same time as Lauren and they had developed a friendship. Older than her by a decade, and too handsome to be single, he was the first man she had met since escaping Reverentia who she had felt a genuine attraction to. Chatting to him one evening after class, she had discovered that he was a business consultant.

'If I buy you lunch,' she had said, 'can I bounce an idea I have that's brilliant, but it's not going so well?'

'Brilliant, but not going so well,' he had said. 'Sounds intriguing, count me in.'

She arrived at the café early to give herself time to order her thoughts. She had dressed for a normal day at the legal firm, though she had changed outfits three times before she was happy with how she looked. And although she liked her hair short, she had stared into the mirror wondering if it made her look boyish.

Arriving right on time, after ordering lunch and enjoying a little small talk about last night's karate, Carter asked her to explain her idea. He listened attentively as she talked, maintaining eye contact even when he took off his expensive-looking suit jacket, hanging it on the back of his chair. Finally she presented him with her weighty plan – *Weeping Angels Strategy and Marketing Plan*.

Adjusting his cuff links and smoothing his blue and green diagonally striped tie, he scrutinised the plan's cover, looking at it in the same manner a dermatologist might dispassionately inspect a discoloured, angry lesion.

'Weeping Angels,' he said slowly. 'I like the name.' He indicated the plan on the table between them. 'Who advised you to write *that?*'

'No one.' Lauren crossed her arms. 'Unless you count the internet as a person.'

'Right.' He turned the document face down. 'I need to tell you about the birds and bees of the business world. I don't normally tell people this because they'd stop paying my invoices. But, with you, Lauren, I get the distinct vibe I'm unlikely to make any money.'

Lauren's nostrils flared, and she wanted to argue the point, but currently he was right. That made his comment even more infuriating. Putting her hands in her lap, she stayed quiet.

'I don't mind,' he said smiling. 'I like helping friends and that means you get the non-bullshit version of me which, if I do say so myself, is far superior. You see, consultants like me' – he showily smoothed his tie again – 'and every business internet site you'll visit are trying to sell you their expensive recipe – none of which work.'

'Don't work?'

'Well, they sometimes work, but that's more down to luck. If you hit enough golf balls you'll get a hole-in-one, but that makes you lucky not a good golfer. You see, recipes only work in static worlds when you have the right ingredients and the right tools – the bowls, the stove, that sort of stuff. A kitchen is perfect for recipes, you have all the items you need to make a chocolate cake. Right?'

'I guess,' said Lauren, arms still folded.

'The business world isn't like that. Every situation is chaotically unique. So, following a recipe is like buying random ingredients, combining them in a random manner in a random room using random equipment and being surprised when you get anything but a chocolate cake.'

Lauren huffed. 'What are you telling me? That what you do is all *bullshit*?'

'Pretty much,' said Carter laughing. 'The big consultancy firms, expensive bullshit. When no one is around, they call themselves con*slut*ants rather than consultants. I used to work for a big firm. I applied their trademarked version of the recipe and hoped it worked to justify the eyewatering invoices they submitted.' He flicked the pages of Lauren's plan like a deck of cards. 'How many pages?'

With a single nose twitch, Lauren turned over the back page. 'Fifty-two.'

'The typical consultant's formula says we'd charge fifty-two thousand for that – a thousand a page.'

'Why are you telling me this? It's putting me off you, big time.'

Carter seemed delighted with her comment. 'I'm different. I refuse to follow a recipe. But first, tell me, why haven't you registered Weeping Angels as a company?' She went to speak, but he added, 'I stalked you online, at least I tried to. Lauren Brown, if that's your name, doesn't own or direct any companies. It's all publicly available …'

'Is it?' she said, staring at him. 'I'm doing this on the quiet, okay?'

He held up his hands in surrender.

Frowning, she asked, 'If you don't follow a recipe, what do you do?'

Leaning forward, speaking seductively, he held up two fingers like a peace sign. 'Tell me in two sentences, what are you trying to achieve?'

Lauren used ten convoluted sentences to *not* tell Carter what she was trying to achieve. He sat looking serious, nodding encouragingly. Finally, having confused herself, she sat back. 'Fuck, you must be single. You're so annoying with that – "your call is important to me" – shit-eating look.'

He almost tipped off his chair as he laughed. When he had finished, he flashed his eyebrows at her. 'I am, as it happens.'

'Am what?'

'Single.'

She gave him a hard look. 'I hope you get paired with Allen at karate. I'll enjoy seeing you gasping for air.'

He made a face. 'Nasty. Allen's too old school for me. All that "if you're not bleeding, you're not trying" bullshit.'

Their lunches arrived. Lauren used the interruption to take in a long calming breath. *He's doing me a favour.*

As they ate, Carter said, 'I think you get my point. Until you can articulate what you're trying to achieve with *blinding* clarity, making plans – developing recipes – can't work. It's like building a house when you don't know what you want or where, but you start drawing up plans.

Worse, you pour concrete and let builders bang pieces of wood together.'

Lauren sighed. 'That makes sense. Do you have any good news for me?'

Picking up his glass of water, he said, 'Let's take a step back. What's the problem you're trying to solve?'

Putting her cutlery down, she leafed through her plan and tore a page out that featured a graph. 'That,' she said, slapping the page onto the table.

Pulling it next to his plate with a single finger, he read aloud. 'New Zealand has one of the worst records in the OECD for family violence.'

'In some categories, we're number one by a considerable margin,' she said. 'And, if you read on,' – she pushed the rest of the document towards him with her finger – 'the police estimate that only one in three episodes of family harm is reported.'

'That's a problem,' he said. 'A big problem by the sound of it. But it's a problem for the police and Ministry of Justice, isn't it?'

Scoffing, she said, 'That's a typical male view. It's a bigger problem for the victims, wouldn't you say?'

'Ouch,' he said nodding.

'Reports of family violence are going up, but fewer men are going to court.' She flicked through her document, showing Carter a copied news article – *More victims are reporting family violence, but abusers aren't facing court. No-one knows why.*

Shaking his head, he said, 'No-one knows why? That's lame. It means no-one's done the work to find out why.'

'Exactly,' she said. '*I* know the major reason – money.'

'Money?'

'Abused women come into the legal practice where I work who desperately need help that they can't afford.'

Carter positively beamed. 'That's great.'

She scowled. 'What?'

Shaking his head vigorously, he said, 'Not what's happening, that's shit. What you said is great. Write it down, that's a crystal-clear problem statement.'

Huffing out a breath, she found a pen in her bag. Turning over the page she had torn out, she asked calmly, 'What did I say?'

'Abused women desperately need help that they can't afford.' When she had captured the sentence, he asked, 'Isn't that what legal aid is for?'

Lauren trilled her lips while she shook her head. 'You have to be on the bones of your arse to qualify for legal aid. Then you have to find a lawyer who'll take the work. There's also a chance you have to pay the money back.'

'Jesus, that's … broken.'

'Technically speaking,' she said, 'it's fucked.'

'Why don't they fix it, then? That's what I pay my taxes for, even though the government doesn't need my tax.'

'That, I don't know,' she said, not following his comment. 'What I do know is, when it comes to family violence, we don't have a justice system. We have a system that benefits the abusers, especially if they're rich abusers.'

'Wow, you have a noble cause too. That's a great base to build a business on. So, what does Weeping Angels do to help?'

'I want to help these women gather the evidence they need, so they can secure a protection order and get these men off their backs. But …' She shrugged.

He seemed to follow her logic easily. 'But they can't afford to pay. What happens to the women who have enough money?'

'The wealthy can afford expensive lawyers, PIs, security systems – the lot. Couples scrap like sumo wrestlers over the house, children and dog.'

'That sounds right,' he said. 'If you're rich, you can afford whatever you need, including justice, it seems. That leaves the people in the middle – not on the bones of their arse or rich-as – what do they do?'

'If they can, they borrow money off family or friends, but the first step is to get them to document the abuse. It's often not physical violence and they have to demonstrate to the court that they're the victim of a clear pattern of abuse. The abuse happens behind closed doors or becomes tainted as she-said he-said evidence.'

'And that's what you're going to do?' He raised his eyebrows. 'Be like a PI?'

Lauren nodded. 'They need help gathering the evidence. The men are sneaky: stalking, prowling, letting themselves in when the women aren't home or banging on the door whenever they feel like it. Without evidence, they can deny everything and gaslight the women into doubting themselves. Doubting how bad it is.'

'Gaslighting,' he said nodding.

'Have you heard of the term?'

'Sure. It's how narcissists operate in business too. Lie and alter the facts so people have difficulty working out what's real and what's not. It's tough to fool *this* consultant though.' He gave her what he no doubt considered was his winning grin.

Puffing out her cheeks as if she was about to vomit, she couldn't stop herself from smiling on the inside. He was growing on her – fast.

'You're planning to stalk the stalkers,' he said.

'Yep. And get the women to use their phones to record what happens outside their house. You know, use their phone camera to record then review the footage later. That way they can carry on with their lives *and* gather evidence.'

'Clever.'

'Then there's the deluge of calls and texts that they can save, screenshot and record. Their exes contact them because they're confident in their male superiority, they never consider they'll have to face any consequences. If I can help them present a slam-dunk body of evidence, they should get a protection order without having to go to court.'

'What about the men who do want to go to court?'

'If their lawyer can't talk them down, it'll be more expensive and that'll put some off. The men believe they'll charm the judge, brush aside the evidence and be back abusing their exes before the day's over.'

'Fuck, I had no idea about this,' said Carter. 'Count me in. I'll help you out, pro bono.'

'Free?'

'Sure. Only the consultants that work for the big companies don't have consciences. It withers and dies the moment they can afford to put on an over-priced brand-name suit and designer sunglasses.'

Lauren grinned. 'What do I … what do *we*, do now?'

Carter ate the last of his lunch, paused and drummed his fingers on the table. As much as Lauren wanted to hurry him along, she was due back in the office, she didn't want to interrupt his train of thought.

Eventually he said. 'Off the top of my head, you're talking about three different groups. Those who can afford lawyers who don't need your help. Then those with no money, I can't see how you can help those women, at least not right now. But the legal aid safety net, pathetic as it sounds, should catch some.'

When he didn't carry on, Lauren couldn't help herself. 'That leaves those with money, but not enough.'

'And you're saying the majority of those never come back.'

'Or never come in at all.'

Carter stayed quiet for a long moment. 'You have a fulltime job, were you planning to do your investigating after hours?'

'Yeah. People are busy during the day: working, school, whatever. The abuse, the stalking, typically occurs in the evening.'

After another pause, he said, 'You don't need paying immediately, your job gives you money to live on. So why don't you let them pay you later?'

Lauren squinted at him.

'I can see what you're thinking,' he said. 'Hear me out. If I put myself in these women's shoes, and an organisation helped make my life amazingly better, when I could I'd pay them back. Some won't, they'll never be able to, but you can write those off – reduce your tax a little.'

Lauren let the idea bounce around inside her head. He was right, she didn't need the money immediately and she would be helping women whose lives were a misery. When they were back on their feet, happy, balanced, they would be more than grateful. On a limited scale, she would be giving women failed by the justice system exactly what they needed – a no-strings-attached helping hand.

Speaking slowly, she said, 'That sounds like it could work. Would the same logic work for legal fees?'

Carter's face soured. 'Lawyers expect payment pronto, if not sooner. If they get stiffed, they'll likely set the debt collectors on their clients. I consulted to a legal firm once, their talk was all *he tāngata, he tāngata, he tāngata,* but their actions were strictly *Money, Money, Money.*' Carter had sung the words flatly.

Lauren laughed. 'I've noticed that where I work too. They can't be all like that though? I mean, how many houses do they need?'

'At least four,' he said. 'Don't forget the flash EV, overseas holiday, private schooling for Montgomery and Brittany —'

Lauren joined in. 'Brittany's pony and the thoroughbreds trotting around the manor preparing for a tilt at the Melbourne Cup.'

'Carp to catch in the moat.'

They both laughed.

Lauren shook herself gently. Partly because she needed to get back to work, partly because she wanted to write down what Carter had said, but mainly because of the strange feeling in her stomach. 'I need to get going. You've been so helpful, Carter. Thank you.'

'No sweat.' He pushed her plan back towards her. 'File that. There'll be useful stuff, but see if you can condense your thinking into one page. That's clarity.' He made to stand, but eased himself back down. 'Can I ask a personal question?'

'Sure,' she said, feeling anything but sure.

Resting his chin in his hand, he asked, 'Why the focus on domestic violence?'

'It's called family violence,' she said, meeting his gaze. 'And I guess you can't ask a personal question.' *We're so not going there.*

A smile slowly emerging, he said, 'Fair enough.' Standing, he asked, 'See you at karate?'

'Wouldn't miss it,' she said, pleased he hadn't pressed the subject. 'As payment, I'll pair up with Allen.'

She could hear him laughing as he weaved his way through the tables. It must have been his regular café because a female server nipped out from behind the counter and gave him a warm hug before he disappeared in the lunchtime human traffic.

That was easily the best twenty-odd dollars she had spent. She would need to tread carefully around Carter – she didn't want to give him the wrong idea, whatever the wrong idea was. Besides, despite what he said, he must have a partner, maybe a couple of women on the go. Good-looking single men like him, she suspected, would flirt as a matter of course. She smiled, the warning about men from outside Reverentia being devils came back to her – she chuckled the notion away.

'You want another coffee, love?'

Snapping her out of her introspection, the woman server who had hugged Carter was clearing the table.

'Sorry, no. I have to get going.' Lauren put the torn plan back into her bag.

'That's better,' said the server. 'You had quite a look on.'

Smiling, Lauren said, 'Did I? I was lost in thought. Do you know Carter well?'

'Yeah, we went to school together.' She stopped clearing the table, looking into the distance. After letting out a sigh, she said, 'When I was in year twelve, I had a huge crush on him.'

'Did you?'

She flashed her eyebrows. 'He wasn't like the other boys. They were only interested in getting their hand down your pants.'

'Did you, um … go out with him?'

The server laughed. 'Twice. It crushed me at the time. I thought he didn't fancy *me* but it turned out he didn't fancy *girls*.' She shrugged. 'What can you do?'

Lauren sat with her mouth open as the server disappeared into the kitchen.

CHAPTER 8

The woman sitting opposite Lauren accepted a tissue. Even though no one in the busy café was taking any notice of them, she looked around the room self-consciously before drying her eyes. In a similar vein to breast-feeding or men kissing, crying in public was not how society preferred to operate. Like family violence itself, tears were for the privacy of your own home.

Having accepted Lauren's offer of coffee, the woman, Carole, was unburdening herself about the harm she was suffering. Her ex-husband, who she described as a high-flying businessman in a soul-less insurance company, had followed her one afternoon and caught her cheating. This was, in many men's minds, the ultimate betrayal, even though he'd had three affairs, to Carole's knowledge. When she had arrived home, he'd confronted her, pushed her around but stopped short of hitting her, before storming out of the house.

'How long ago was that?' asked Lauren.

Carole glanced at the ceiling. 'Maybe three years.'

Taking the odd note, trying not to interrupt, Lauren hid her surprise.

'I didn't hear from him for three days, but when the man I was seeing came over, my ex must have seen his car. He created a huge scene, threatened to "give him a hiding". The children were crying, it was just awful.' She sniffed. 'David, the man I was seeing, stopped returning my calls a week later.' Laughing sadly, she added, 'Not that I blame him. With my ex shadowing me, I've been on my own since then.'

'From what I've seen, it's common,' said Lauren. 'Men want their victims isolated. It's easier to control someone when there isn't another adult to witness their actions.'

Carole slumped. 'It's worked. I've had the odd date, when he's looking after the children.' Her eyes briefly lit up. 'I went on a dating app for a while, but I couldn't risk bringing anyone home. And he always seemed to know where I was. He'd call and leave messages or send a text.'

'Why didn't you turn your phone off?'

She shook her head sadly. 'In case something happened to the children. He would leave messages like, Sara, that's my daughter, wants to talk to you.'

Lauren grunted. There must be a book available – *How to stalk your ex and get away with it!* The playbook of these men was so similar you would swear they'd had training. Checking the time on her phone, she said, 'I'm sorry Carole, but I need to get back to work.'

Carole's face pinched.

'What I suggest you do,' said Lauren, 'is write your story down electronically in bullet points. Everything you can remember. Add dates and times. It can all go into an affidavit which we'll submit to the court.' Carole appeared to be listening but Lauren wasn't sure her message was getting through. 'What's happening now? That's what the judge will focus on.'

'Everyone told me it will blow over,' said Carole. 'But it hasn't and it's getting worse. He drives past my house mornings and evenings to make sure there's no one there. I catch him doing it all the time. Honestly, he's a useless stalker.'

'If you see him, what does he do?'

Carole faked a big smile. 'Grins like an imbecile and waves.'

'He's not a useless stalker then, he wants you to see him.'

Carole frowned.

'He could drive past earlier or later, you'd never know,' said Lauren. 'He wants you to know he's there, that he's always there. If you bring home a date, or have a friend over for coffee, he wants you to see him. He wants you to believe that he knows what you're doing every minute of the day.'

'God, that makes sense. It's like I'm under surveillance.'

'That's the psychological tactic men like your ex like to employ. If you believe you're constantly under surveillance, you self-police. You don't bring dates home or have friends over for coffee. You become your own jailer.'

Carole's mouth hung open.

Lauren nodded. 'It's common enough.'

'How do they … I mean, he's not a master criminal. In fact, he's as thick as two short planks.'

'It's an interesting question,' said Lauren, one she had spent time turning over herself. 'I'd bet there's research to explain it, locked away in the bowels of universities. And the reason we're talking today is that the way the justice system operates favours them, not us. Not you.'

'Isn't the purpose of the law to protect people like me?' said Carole.

'It is, in theory, but it's how the law *operates* that loads the dice. These men sit back and say "prove it". That's fair, they should be innocent until proven guilty. But if you get burgled or have your car stolen or you're attacked while walking home, it's the police's job to investigate and catch the criminals. With family violence, the police may intervene, even have a chat with the abuser, but they don't have the resources to document what the court demands – a clear pattern of abuse over time.'

Lauren checked herself as she could see Carole was getting worked up. Discussing why there were gaping holes in the justice system was like chasing your tail. 'Sorry,' she said. 'That tangent's due to me. Let's focus on what your ex is doing. He drives by constantly, what else?'

Carole knitted her fingers together. 'He seems to know where I'm going and when. He tailgates me to the supermarket. Turns up in cafés when I'm having coffee.'

Lauren made a note. 'That's not good, but if we record him doing it, that's solid evidence.'

Carole looked away.

Lauren waited. *Here it comes.*

'I'm not sure I can afford to go through with this,' said Carole.

Lauren was expecting that sentence, or a variation of it – she was ready. 'I know, but you only live once, Carole. You shouldn't have to live looking over your shoulder. Nervous. Worrying. Hoping it'll get better. Knowing it won't. What I can do is help you build a solid case that your ex is guilty of family violence. Get you a protection order.'

'I doubt that will make him stop,' said Carole.

'It will,' said Lauren. 'Believe me. There are real consequences to breaching a protection order – the police can lock them up for twenty-four hours, for a start. Remember, your ex's goal is to keep his abuse under the radar so his colleagues and mates don't know he's a bastard. That's a harder pretext to maintain if the police chuck him inside then drag him into a public courtroom to explain his actions. Journalists can't attend Family Court sessions, but breaching a protection order, that's a criminal offence.'

Carole smiled as Lauren spoke, but her smile didn't last. She made to speak, but Lauren held up a hand. *Here goes.*

'Hear me out. I can help you gather the evidence and prepare it so our firm's lawyers don't have much to do – that'll keep the costs low. The goal is to get your ex to agree to a protection order without you having to go to court, that will save you even more. Obviously I can't *guarantee* results, but this is your best chance to free yourself – and your children.'

'If the legal bill is at the lower end of the scale, I could manage that. What about your costs?'

'I'm prepared to wait until you can afford to pay.'

Carole looked confused.

'I run a business,' said Lauren, 'but it's also personal. I've been in your shoes.'

Shaking her head, Carole said, 'You don't look old enough to have been in my shoes.'

'Imagine how hard that was,' said Lauren. She let her words hang. 'I think you, and everyone who's in your position, will thrive when you can live without dread.'

'What say I can't pay, even later?'

Lauren shrugged. 'I'll write it off, no hard feelings. If you can't pay, you can't pay. My business advisor's hunch is that when you can, you will. It's as simple as that and I'll never hound you for the money. There'll be no letters or nagging reminders and especially no debt collectors. I'll send an email out once a month about how Weeping Angels is going, that's it.'

'And if I see you in the street, Lauren?'

'I'll give you a hug.'

'That'd make me feel guiltier,' she said.

'Sorry about that,' said Lauren laughing. 'My advisor thinks some women will be so much better off, when they can, that they'll contribute additional money. We'll apply that money to everyone's debt.'

Carole's confused look returned.

'If you won Lotto, would you settle your bill?' asked Lauren.

'Of course.'

'And, with all that money, would you consider helping the women who couldn't pay? Help us carry on?'

'Of course.' Carole's eyes lit up. 'Oh, imagine being in a position to help others going through this.'

'You've got it,' said Lauren. 'Do you want to proceed?'

'Where do I sign?'

On her way back to work Lauren texted Carter – *First client secured. I'm bringing champagne for a post-karate celebration!*

CHAPTER 9

Lauren sat in her 2010 grey Holden Cruze, classical music playing softly, sipping coffee and generally blending into the suburban scene. It was a pleasant, warm evening allowing her to dress in shorts, a t-shirt and sunglasses. The entry level camera – a Canon EOS 3000D – that lay on her lap had the ability to take high-definition images as well as record video. To anyone who glanced her way, she was waiting to pick up someone, maybe a date. What she was doing was staking out Carole's house, collecting the required evidence to detail a pattern of abuse.

Carole's ex, who she ironically called 'Guy Smiley', drove past her house morning and night. He wasn't difficult to spot as he drove a white van decorated with his employer's distinctive logo. Subtle as an elephant, as expected – he wanted her to see him skulking around her house.

To capture these incidences, Lauren made Carole employ a low-tech surveillance method. Setting her smart phone up like a security camera, she positioned it where it recorded the comings and goings on the street outside her house. Choosing times likely for a drive- or walk-by, she left it recording until the battery died or night fell, carrying on with life and reviewing the footage later. As well as gathering valuable evidence, Carter thought making their clients feel part of the investigator team would work from several angles.

For each encounter Carole captured, she uploaded the video to a shared drive, noting the time he featured in a separate document. She also uploaded screenshots of each text he sent as well as phone calls to document their time and frequency. Lauren added Carole's entries to a spreadsheet that Carter had created where she recorded the evidence she obtained. The evidence trail needed to be watertight so, as Carter liked to say, 'the fuckers can't wriggle off the hook'.

If an unknown car was in Carole's driveway, a favourite tactic of her ex was to park across the entrance and interrupt by calling. This made evidence gathering a matter of scheduling, not serendipity. Carole asked a male work colleague, who was happy to get involved, to visit around five. That was why Lauren was sitting in her 2010 grey Holden Cruze, classical music playing softly, sipping her coffee and generally blending into the suburban scene – she was waiting for 'Guy Smiley'.

A creature of habit, he drove the same route past her house on his way to work, reversing the route on his way home. He should arrive within the next five minutes and, with Carole's colleague's car parked in her driveway, he would attempt to inject his presence into their evening.

The first time she lay in wait, Lauren was worried that he would see her. Positioning her car so he would arrive from behind, and parking in front of another car to further obscure his vision, she was confident she was well hidden. After researching how private investigators rolled, she sat in the driver's seat, taking her sunglasses off when he appeared, looking normal. Hardened investigators had warned that sitting in the backseat, wearing hats and sunglasses, had the opposite effect – oddness drew attention.

As it turned out, it was the single-minded focus of Carole's stalker that almost guaranteed her anonymity. When he neared Carole's house, he slowed to a crawl, staring intently, giving himself maximum exposure time. He wouldn't have seen Lauren if she was sitting naked on the car's bonnet.

He was running behind schedule when Lauren saw his white van approaching in her side mirror. White vans were common enough but she had become used to this man's features framed behind the wheel, they were as distinctive as they were unpleasant. The van predictably slowed, the driver wriggling in his seat. Lauren slowly raised her camera, which she had set to video snapshot mode, capturing the scene perfectly as the van idled past her position.

She placed the camera back on her lap as the van pulled over to the side of the road. When there was a break in the traffic, he performed a tight U-turn and headed back towards Carole's house. Lauren, now fully on display, picked up her mobile and acted as though she was having a semi-animated conversation. If he did glance at her, he took no notice as she stared straight ahead looking concerned.

This part of the operation put her most at risk of detection. As expected, he parked across Carole's driveway, staring at his phone. Lauren exchanged her phone for the camera, set it to video capture, and pressed record. She zoomed in slowly until he was easily identifiable. After recording his antics, she put the camera on the passenger seat and recommenced her fake phone call. Four minutes later, with a final rude gesture towards the house, he drove away.

Lauren imagined that on any given day similar scenes occurred all over Aotearoa – with only the victims bearing witness.

Though the world of private investigation was new to Lauren, her work in the legal firm meant she knew the ins and outs of the Family Court. Documenting a month's worth of constant appearances spiked with episodes like the one she had just captured was enough to demonstrate a clear pattern of abuse to any judge.

As the white van shrank in her side mirror, she called Carter.

He answered immediately, which was rare for him. Her calls usually went to his voicemail though she seldom left a message. It had become their way of saying 'Call when you can'.

'All good?' he asked.

'All good. How's tricks for you?'

He groaned.

'Anything in particular?'

'Just this university gig,' he said.

'I thought you said it was easy money?'

'It is,' he said. 'But I'm helping them run a sham restructure so it doesn't look like a sham restructure. I fear this work is damaging my moral compass.'

'Do consultants have those?' she asked.

'Ha ha. Anyway, how's New Zealand's latest amateur investigator getting on?'

She filled him in on her evening's work.

'Sounds like you're nailing him good and proper.' After a short pause, he said, 'I've come across a snag.'

'Really? What?'

'I researched the laws regulating investigators,' he said. 'We need to get you registered and approved.'

'Why? This is working out great, running under the radar.'

'I thought so too,' he said. 'But if the defence challenges how the evidence was gathered, the fact you're not licenced could get it ruled as inadmissible.'

'Fuck, really? Can't we say I'm doing it in my spare time?'

'We could, but it's dodgy. And it would only work once.'

'Good point.'

'We can manage this,' said Carter. 'I've started the process to get a new company registered, then you and I can go through the PI registration process together.'

'What *new* company?'

'I know you don't want to register the company in your name. Rather than convince you otherwise, the way to get around it is for me to register Weeping Angels under my name.' In response to the silence, he said, 'Unless you *do* want to do have it under your name.'

'No,' she said. 'No, I like your idea. It's just that … well, I need time. And why are *we* going through the PI registration process?'

'If we do it the way I just suggested, I have to,' he said. 'It's a legal requirement for the sole director of a company providing investigator services. Plus, you never know, I might try it out one day. Buddy-up with you.'

She smiled briefly at the thought. 'If I have to register as an investigator, that'll create a record, won't it?'

'It will, but I thought about that too. Apart from your name, we can use the company's address and contact details. If you're uncovered as an investigator, and they check you out, all they'll find is the company you work for.'

She processed what Carter was proposing. 'I'll need to make sure I'm okay with this, but it sounds good. What about what I'm doing now?'

'They could challenge it in court, but remember that you're aiming to get them to roll over before court. Once their lawyer sees the evidence, they should realise they've no chance of winning.'

'That's right. Some men will plough ahead regardless, but from what I've seen most prefer to sign voluntarily rather than have a judge rule against them.'

'Is it because of the money?' asked Carter.

'Partly, but it's more so they can maintain their fantasy. You know, they can say, "I would have won in court but I rolled because she's mad".'

Carter grunted. 'That's the narcissist gene in full command. So, while we dot the I's and cross the T's on becoming registered, we keep going.' After a brief silence, he added, 'We can chat at my place after karate if you like. That's if you don't have a better offer.'

'I don't.'

'You can stay the night if you like. You know you're safe with me.'

Lauren, smiling widely, said, 'That means I could have a couple of wines, not have to worry about driving home. Do you have a spare bedroom?'

'Two,' he said, 'but … you're safe with me.'

CHAPTER 10

Nine months later

Carter's body made a bone-jarring thud as he landed on the flat of his back on the wooden floor of the make-shift dojo. Lauren winced. Allen, the cause of Carter's heavy collision with the floor, stood over him, his *gi* open to the waist. He looked like a super villain crossed with a Bee Gee. The hard man of the dojo, Allen was much older than Carter but toughened after decades of karate training. Taking Carter's hand, he yanked him onto his feet as though he was a child. They faced each other, Allen adjusting his *gi* and staring hard, Carter holding in his frustration and anger. They bowed and sat back in line.

'That's how it's done,' said the *sensei*, giving Allen an appreciative nod. 'Now pair up and practise. Alternate between attack and defence. We'll finish with line work.'

Lauren flashed her eyebrows at Carter as an invitation. They took turns dumping each other onto the floor, albeit in a less forceful manner than Allen's ragdoll demonstration with Carter. After an intense session of the promised line work, set moves that had them moving up and down the dojo sweating profusely, the session finished.

For Lauren, karate had become the perfect release. For ninety minutes she had to focus solely on what she needed to do to survive the training session. The cares of the world, money problems, a struggling business, her past, all disappeared – karate muted the volume on her life. Each evening after training she had a *Fight Club* feeling of being reborn. Among all humans on Earth, she alone was ready to put the world to rights.

Going to Carter's house for dinner after training had become a regular feature of her life. They trained twice a week; after Monday's class she cooked and on Thursdays he cooked. The rest of the class must have thought they were an item and it was easiest to let people leap to conclusions than explain the reality of their situation.

'I think Allen has it in for you,' said Lauren as she sat at Carter's breakfast bar with a glass of red wine.

In the kitchen, cooking a stir fry, Carter said, 'He has a *thing* for me, more like it. It's his way of hiding the fact he's gay.'

'He hides it bloody well,' said Lauren. 'Besides, you think everyone's gay.'

Carter's home, a townhouse in the well-to-do suburb of Ellerslie, was immaculate. There was a right place for everything and everything was always in its right place. She enjoyed putting her feet on the table and putting items back in different places. 'I know what you're doing,' he would say, adding, 'It doesn't bother me,' as he replaced each item. When it was her turn to cook, she enjoyed watching him fight his desire to tidy the kitchen in her wake.

Carter didn't look or act stereotypically gay, at least in Lauren's limited experience. In truth, she knew little about homosexuality, in Reverentia it hadn't existed. Well, as she knew now, it must have existed but it was never acknowledged, certainly never discussed.

As he was slicing carrots, unexpectedly Carter asked, 'Are you bi?'

Judging by Carter's look, her face must have displayed shock. Even though she had been away from the community for years, their puritanical views on sex and relationships lingered. *Bi?* In truth, she hadn't thought about it… much. She was happily single, answerable only to herself. She imagined herself heterosexual. She found men's bodies intriguing, but it was what women wore that intrigued her.

'Sorry, I didn't mean to be blunt,' he said.

Taking a larger than normal drink of wine, she said, 'Why's it important?'

Carter shrugged. 'It's not important. I'm just curious, that's all. You don't give off a full-blown cis-hetero aura.'

'Don't I?' Lauren laughed, relaxing into the conversation. 'I understood it's women who have a *gaydar.*'

'God no,' he said. 'Women think every man they want to shag is gay. It's their way of justifying flirting.' He held up hands in mock shock. 'I was sure he was gay, right until he popped it in.'

Lauren laughed.

He stopped stirring. 'Are you avoiding the question?'

'Pretty much,' she said. 'Honest answer – I don't know.'

Carter stared at her. 'What do you mean you don't know?'

Labouring each word, she said, 'I don't know. I've never tried … um …'

'Muff-diving? Really?'

Wincing, she said, 'No.'

Judgelike, Carter said, 'You don't have to have tried it to *know*. You don't have to fall off a cliff to *know* it hurts.'

Lauren shook her head. 'You're schizo. I think I prefer the strait-laced, hetero-pretending consultant. Besides, have you tried it? You could be closet hetero.'

'I've tried it.'

'Didn't do it for you?'

'No, though no one could've faulted my enthusiasm.'

Lauren closed her eyes and shook away the image.

Carter sighed. 'I wanted to like it, at the time. I wanted to feel *normal*.' A cloud briefly passed over him before he was back. 'I realised it wasn't for me. My mind kept wandering off to … well, never mind.'

He dished up, they clinked their glasses of red wine and attacked dinner – both were starving. Karate didn't finish until 8pm, which meant that after their twice-weekly sessions they didn't eat until nine, often later.

Too hungry to talk until each had made a dent in their dinner, Carter was first to speak. 'How's the life of an unpaid investigator going?'

Weeping Angels had been running for nearly a year. It was giving Lauren a huge kick to help women secure protection orders, but the company was financially hanging on by its fingernails. Eating a piece of broccoli, she rocked her head back and forth. 'Great, apart from the money, of course.'

'How many are paying now?'

'A few are paying weekly, small amounts.'

'Your patience will be rewarded,' he said. 'I love your business model.'

'You should,' she said, 'it was your idea.'

'There is that,' he said. 'But you've helped, what is it now, twelve women?'

'Fifteen.'

'Fifteen women's lives are now indescribably better.'

'I know,' she said. 'We've only had the one case go to court'

'I was amazed McMahon didn't demand to go court too,' he said.

'I know,' said Lauren. 'His lawyer must have made him sign. He didn't stop harassing his ex, even after the court had served him.'

'The police can throw him the cells for that, can't they?'

'I don't think they can, not until the protection order is in place. I need to check that.'

'And all the rest rolled,' said Carter. 'As we expected.'

'As you expected. I was more hoping.'

'Now, you just need money,' he said.

'I'm happy to wait … if I can. They've all written glowing recommendations, and have been spreading their good news, which has created a different problem.'

He nodded, saying, 'Ahh. Word-of-mouth recommendations are the strongest endorsement you can get. They'll be telling their friends how wonderful you are.'

'I'm getting inquiries,' she said. 'More work than *I* can cope with. But I can't —'

He cut in. 'I know, I see the problem. You can't scale.'

'Sorry?'

'There's only you. You can only cope with what, two, three clients at a time?' She nodded. 'To put more people on the payroll, you need cash because they need to pay their bills.' He jabbed vegetables onto his fork. 'You've a chicken and egg problem.'

'When you talk business, you talk in cliches. Have you noticed?'

'Sorry,' he said. 'Management speak is full of those and worse. You need cash —'

'Oh, I get it,' she said cutting him off this time. 'I can't expect others to work for free but, at this rate, it'll take years before I'll have enough money to pay myself, let alone expand the business. A chicken and an egg.'

Carter stabbed together another large forkful, chewing deliberately. Lauren kept eating, still hungry.

After a prolonged period of silence he said, 'The only answer is a cash injection.'

'That's what I figured, but …' She finished her sentence with a shrug.

'You need cash now, as in yesterday,' he said. 'But even if I put together a drop-dead-gorgeous business plan, no one' – his eyes widened – 'and I mean *no one*, is going to invest in a business focused on family violence. They'll run a mile.'

'I figured that,' she said putting her fork down. After a slow sip of wine, she continued, 'There's a situation in my past, a legal situation. It's a door I had to turn my back on, but I'm becoming reconciled to the fact that I might need to kick it open.' After the lawyers had settled her husband's will, Lauren had been left with a small legal bill, zero inheritance and the on-going concern that the police were keen for a second chat. That's where she let sleeping dogs lie until, tidying her home office, she had rediscovered the flash drive of files she took with her when she escaped from Reverentia.

'Will the door lead to cash?' asked Carter.

Lauren frowned. 'If I win.'

'What's behind the door?'

Monsters.

Picking at a rough bit of skin on her thumb, Lauren said, 'Let's leave it for now. I'll make a couple of enquiries. If it looks promising, I'll let you know.' Holding up a finger, keen to change the subject, she said, 'Besides, I've been thinking …'

Lauren grinned but stayed quiet. Carter said slowly, 'Go on.'

'I agree,' she said. 'Family violence *is* the opposite of sexy' – she paused for a long beat before delivering her punchline – 'to *men*.' She flashed an eyebrow raise across the breakfast bar.

Pointing at her with his fork, Carter's eyes widened. 'You *have* been thinking, haven't you. That's genius. Why didn't I think of that? *Women*. It's not sexy but they would *totally* get the problem and grasp the beauty of the model.'

Lauren picked up her fork. 'But how do we find women investors?'

'Hold your horses,' he said. 'To appeal to women, it would look better if you, a woman, was running the company.'

'I figured that too,' she said. 'I was leaving it as long as I could, that's all.'

'Can I ask why?'

She pushed around the last of her food before pushing away her plate. 'My past needs to stay in the past.'

Carter nodded but stayed quiet, so she added, 'I'm pretty sure my name won't set off any alarms, but if it does ...'

'Lauren Brown isn't your real name, is it? Before our first lunch, I did some research and I couldn't find you on the internet. That's ... rare.'

Giving a slight shrug, she said, 'I invented it when I came to Auckland.'

'Invented it? How did you do that? Get ID cards? A driver's licence?'

'It's not that hard. Once you have a bank account, the rest of the dominos tumble. I opened an account in my previous name, adding a middle name – Lauren. I told the bank I never used my first name, and *voila*, I have a bank account and credit card in the name Lauren Brown.'

Carter stared at her. 'How bad is your past?'

'More unpleasant than bad.'

Carter steepled his hands together, pressing the tips of his fingers to his lips. 'Do you trust me?'

'Of course. It's not –'

'No' – he shook his head – 'I don't mean you should tell me your past. Do you trust me not to run off to Barbados with your money.'

'What money?' she asked.

'I mean later, when the business is successful?'

'Of course, I trust you. I'm not following you, though.'

'If we can successfully find an investor, it'll take a little time, the company will have the money it needs – at least access to money. We can keep the company under my name on the company's register and make you CEO. We'll organise it so all the communications come directly to you, I won't see them because it's really your company. But, and it's a big but, I'll be able to do what I want because the company is in my name – get me?'

Lauren nodded. 'Legally it's your company, but because I trust you it's my company. *And* I keep below the radar.'

'What would you do if I did go mad, run off to the Bahamas with the captain of the All Blacks?'

'You wish. And I thought it was Barbados?'

They grinned at each other.

'Seriously, what do you think?' he said.

'It sounds perfect. What if my company in your name goes broke?'

Shrugging, he said. 'With me as an advisor, I'll only have myself to blame.' She went to argue but he put a finger to his lips. 'The rules around limited liability protect me and, besides, it's the sharpest business model I've seen. The main danger is if the government fixes the justice system.'

Lauren scoffed. 'Not much chance of that.'

'Zero,' said Carter, 'with the bloody right-wingers in power.'

She refilled their glasses. 'Isn't this all academic? I mean, where's the cash injection going to materialise from?'

Tapping his nose, he said, 'You leave that to me.'

CHAPTER 11

A year later

Lauren's phone vibrated in her pocket. Judge Carr hadn't arrived in court so she read Carter's text. *All good? I missed you at karate.*

Lauren smiled. She hardly ever missed karate, but there were times when she needed to get away, to hide at Tana's. It happened if a client's situation was too close to her own experience. This time it was a young woman who had fallen pregnant and was pressured into marriage – a recipe for dysfunction and disaster. Escaping to Tana's, hanging out with his family, helped her regain perspective – she only needed the weekend, sometimes Monday too. Talking to Tana about her previous life – the work, the psychological pressure, the punishments, the controlling men, the constant threat of God's wrath – helped.

She texted back. *All good. Just needed a change of scenery.*

He replied immediately. *There's someone you need to meet. Can you make 4pm at our usual haunt?*

Lauren checked her calendar. It was nearly 10am, the hearing about to start shouldn't last more than two or three hours. They normally didn't, but every now and then they dragged on, occasionally into a second day. She replied, *Should be okay. Do I need to prepare?*

Carter had helped her produce a two-page strategy outlining what Weeping Angels needed in terms of finance to fulfil its mission to deliver justice for family violence victims. He had used it to successfully raise money through a Kickstarter campaign – an internet funding platform for creative projects. Then he had organised meetings with several government agencies, who seemed enthusiastic. But they never met anyone who had the authority to spend more than $7.50.

The judge swept into the room, everyone stood. Judge Carr was a veteran of the Family Court who had a nose for the truth. A diminutive figure, as soon as she stared at you with her sharp, grey eyes you couldn't miss her gravitas. Lauren had heard stories of men swaggering into her courtroom, taking one look at her and expecting to dominate proceedings. They invariably left with their tails between their legs, run over by a judicial force of nature.

As the judge settled herself and arranged her files, Lauren glanced at Carter's answer. *No. Just be prepared to jump for joy.* He might not look or act in the least way gay, but he loved having news, being the centre of attention. It was why he was so easy to socialise with at functions. She could keep a low profile because he networked like a pro, introducing her when he sensed an opportunity.

Before the judge took control of the courtroom, Lauren leaned forwards and gave Polly's shoulder a squeeze. A Weeping Angels' client, Polly was applying to the Family Court for a protection order. Her story was common. Her ex stalked her constantly, monitoring and controlling her life. According to the evidence that they had collected, he also arrived uninvited when she was out with friends, playing the totally-cool-with-it ex. He would then text her later with a range of unpleasant observations about her physical appearance and that of her friends, especially any men who he liked to refer to as 'homos'.

Turning around, Polly gave Lauren a nervous smile.

Her ex-husband, sitting next to his lawyer across the room, stared hard at Lauren. She matched his stare until he looked away, hands behind his head, smirking. As he was challenging the protection order application, this was a defended hearing.

As the business had expanded, Lauren had taken on the role of general manager, a role the company seldom needed because Carter had trained her to become an excellent delegator. That allowed her to spend her time as an investigator and as a support person for clients like Polly. It was a role Lauren relished. She had a front-row seat enabling her to watch the result of the Weeping Angels operation.

Each judge was different. Each case was unique, but they ran along similar lines. The judge pre-read each side's position so would have formed an opinion. In this case, on behalf of Polly they had outlined the evidence they had collected in detail. Their goal wasn't to spring a trap in court – the defence saw the evidence well before a date was set for the hearing – it was to avoid court, to avoid the expense. Via his lawyer, the respondent, Polly's ex, had countered that the evidence was incorrect and misrepresented his actions. It was a strange claim given what they had documented.

After formally accepting the affidavits, and listening to both opening statements, it was the judge's role to work out where the truth lay. After sitting quietly, listening for over an hour, Judge Carr intervened.

Addressing Polly's lawyer, she said, 'Miss Beaumont. How reliable is this evidence? That seems the key to understanding what has and hasn't happened. Let's take a date that's in dispute. On the twenty-fourth of November, your client claims Mr Hawkins took photos of her house and car.' The judge picked up a different document. 'Mr Hawkins claims he was at home and has produced a witness statement to that effect. How do you explain that?'

The lawyer acting for Polly was one of the young breed Lauren liked to engage. In a black suit, light purple shirt and with her blonde hair tied in a tight bun, Beaumont looked both scholarly and menacing. Lauren knew the lawyer didn't need the dark-rimmed glasses but wore them to make her look older for credibility in front of judges. Remaining sitting, as was the protocol in the Family Court, she said, 'Mr Hawkins and his witness are, at best, mistaken. If I may use the screen ...' Beaumont worked the technology until an image of a suburban street appeared on multiple screens in the room.

'This video was recorded outside my client's house. The date and time stamp match the time entered in her affidavit.' Keeping her face neutral, Beaumont looked across at the respondent's lawyer, whose mouth was ajar. 'We're happy to submit copies of the files if the respondent doubts their authenticity.'

The recording started playing, Beaumont narrating over the action. 'This is Mr Hawkins arriving in his Porsche, the plate number' – she paused the image and zoomed in on the car's licence plate – 'matches, as noted in the affidavit. Mr Hawkins then walks to my client's house and uses his phone to take photos or possibly record a video.' Turning to Hawkins, she said, 'Those images are likely still on his phone.'

Hawkins' lawyer put a calming hand on his client's arm.

Turning back to the judge, Beaumont said, 'He then returns to his car and rings my client, the phone record is documented in my client's affidavit.' The lawyer paused the image showing a closeup of an angry Hawkins talking on his mobile.

The judge turned her head slowly, fixing her gaze on the respondent's lawyer.

'May I have two minutes with my client?' he asked.

'Very well.'

The lawyer left the room followed by a visibly seething Hawkins. The room plunged into a solemn silence.

Looking over her glasses at Lauren, the judge said, 'Miss Brown, could I have a minute, please.' Having registered the surprise on Beaumont's face, she said, 'Don't worry, Miss Beaumont, there's no cause for alarm.'

When Lauren reached the judge's table, the judge leaned towards her. Lauren bent down, noticing the judge was wearing a subtle perfume – she hadn't expected that. 'This is the second time you've been in my court in support of an applicant. Both times the cases have been prepared immaculately. They're slam dunks, as Mr Hawkins' lawyer is now hopefully explaining to his client. What's going on?'

'Nothing, your honour,' said Lauren, matching the judge's conspiratorial volume. 'It's satisfying to help deliver justice.'

'How was the evidence collected?'

Lauren answered semi-honestly. 'I don't know, I wasn't there. My role is to support –'

'I know about your role,' interrupted the judge. 'Don't get me wrong, I'm pleased to have such well-prepared cases in front of me' – she leaned even closer – 'and top-notch young lawyers too. But we judges talk, compare notes. The level of evidence gathering appears professional. The lawyers we've been seeing come from firms that are normally out of the reach of most applicants.'

'I believe the lawyers discount their rates significantly, for the experience.' Lauren spoke in hushed tones. 'I also don't think justice should be a purchasable commodity.'

The judge held up a warning hand. 'I'm not saying it's right. I'm just saying it's not usual.'

Interrupting their conversation, the respondent's lawyer came back into the courtroom followed by a red-faced Hawkins.

'Let's hope it becomes more usual, even normal, your honour.' Lauren stood, bowed her head and returned to her chair at the rear of the courtroom.

Looking at the respondent's lawyer, the judge asked, 'What do you have for me?'

The lawyer forced a smiled. 'Thank you, your honour. On reflection, my client feels he didn't scrutinise the original affidavit with sufficient care.'

The judge's eyes narrowed.

The lawyer quickly continued. 'He has decided that, given the circumstances, he will agree to a protection order being put in place.'

Polly grabbed her lawyer's arm before turning around and beaming at Lauren.

'Very well,' said the judge. 'Mr Hawkins, do you understand what you're signing?'

Hawkins, struggling to contain himself, nodded.

'Do you have anything else to want to say?' asked the judge.

After his lawyer had whispered into his ear, Hawkins shook his head, but said, 'The people who recorded me have ruined my life.'

Judge Carr rolled her eyes. 'Mr Hawkins, *you're* ruining your life. The people who recorded you were documenting it.' Addressing his lawyer, she said, 'Normally I let the costs fall where they may, but unless you can convince me that there's a good reason I shouldn't, I will be awarding costs to the applicant.'

'May I have time to consider our response, your honour?'

'Seven days.' The judge stood as she spoke causing everyone else to hurriedly stand. With a curt nod, and a final inquisitorial stare Lauren's way, she swept from the courtroom.

Hawkins tried to push past his lawyer to speak to his ex-wife. Before he could open his mouth, his lawyer firmly intervened, hissing, 'The protection order is now in place.'

Polly's lawyer, standing as she packed away her papers, looked down at Hawkins. 'You told the judge you understood what you were signing. The "no contact" condition means just that. Judge Carr won't take kindly to you breaching the order in her courtroom. So, unless you fancy cooling off in the cells, I'd leave.'

A fuming Hawkins followed his lawyer from the room.

From what Lauren had observed, there were two types of men who committed family violence. The first, when confronted with what they were doing and the consequences of their actions, took it as a wake-up call. They agreed to sign protection orders, attend non-violence programmes and were on their way to becoming better people. Hawkins was typical of the second type – they saw themselves as the victims, not the perpetrators. They obeyed protection orders solely out of fear of the consequences. They would never change. They were waiting for the day that they could convince their ex or the court to rescind the order – so they could get even.

'Is it too early to celebrate?' asked Polly.

'It is for me,' said her lawyer. 'I'm back in court this afternoon.'

'It's not for me,' said Lauren. 'Come on Polly, let's celebrate the first day of your new life.'

CHAPTER 12

Lauren took a grinning Carter through what had happened in the courtroom. They were sitting in the back of the bar that had become their unofficial local. Although not renowned for its food, its snack range was impressive and, as it was close to Carter's house, they could walk if they'd had one too many. Enjoying what Carter called a pre-celebratory drink, Lauren's second for the day, she had tried to get more information about the upcoming meeting but he had insisted that she needed to meet this mystery woman, adding cryptically that 'it's not guaranteed'.

'And his lawyer had to hold him back?' he asked.

'Almost,' said Lauren. 'I thought he was going to punch his own lawyer at one point. It was priceless theatre.'

'Is your success rate still one hundred percent?'

Carter, who acted as an advisor for Lauren, kept out of the day-to-day operations. Lauren shook her head. 'One stopped short of pushing for a protection order.'

'Did they accept an undertaking?'

Nodding, Lauren said, 'He promised to be a good boy and make sure his actions wouldn't breach a protection order.'

'Yeah, right,' he said. 'Are you going to keep tracking him? Catch him in the act?'

'No point,' said Lauren. 'The undertaking isn't enforceable. Plus, he knows how we gathered the evidence now, he'll be careful until he's confident we're not watching. And you never know, he might change, respect the undertaking. It is possible.'

Carter shook his head like a disappointed parent.

'You can't blame her, Carter. Most women are desperate to believe the people they once loved, the fathers of their children, aren't hopeless causes – who wouldn't? They just want a civilised relationship. And some men can, but it's less likely if they've gone down the family violence path. You know that better than anybody.'

Carter's face dropped.

'Sorry,' she said. 'I shouldn't have mentioned it.' It had taken Carter a year into their friendship, which had included sleeping together but not sleeping together, before he trusted her enough to let her in on that part of his life. His story came flooding out late one evening after karate and too much, or perhaps just enough, alcohol. In his case, Carter's ex sounded manipulative, fixated and wealthy – a terrible combination.

With a sad smile, he said, 'I'm pleased I told you. I wasn't going to tell anyone. You're right, nobody likes to admit the person they thought they loved is fatally flawed and that the best outcome is never seeing them again. I couldn't have taken him to court, though.' Sipping his wine, he asked, 'Does the Family Court have many applications from same-sex couples?'

'I doubt it but that could be because of the ratio of same-sex couples.'

'Not that the justice system's attitude to homosexuals is Victorian?'

'It's not that bad,' she said. 'But it's hard for *anyone* to go down the Family Court path, let alone people more likely to be victimised by the process. I know that your predicament, as you called it, ended when he moved to Australia. Did a protection order ever cross your mind?'

'God no. He was threatening to tell my clients that I was a fag, that would've pushed him over the edge. Besides, it's why your business is so successful. I couldn't afford the legal fees, not back then. That's the problem with the gig economy, it sounds empowering and life-balancing but it's just another way to use humans as docile resources. Keep them precarious, keen to keep their heads below the parapet, hoping that they'll survive and "make it", whatever that means.'

Lauren squeezed his arm.

'Sorry, this is a celebration,' he said. 'Now's not the time to wallow in self-pity and rail against the machine. How are the financials looking by the way? How long will it take to reach *Aqaba*?'

Created by Carter, *Aqaba* was a financial landmark named after Lawrence of Arabia's seemingly impossible World War One target. The actual number, expressed in months and days, was a complex calculation spanning multiple tabs of a spreadsheet. In simple terms, *Aqaba* was a projection of when the income from the women repaying the company exceeded their projected operational costs – it meant she had a viable, self-sustaining business.

'We're getting further away as we grow,' she said. 'My, actually our, accountant is nervous.'

'Accountants are always nervous,' he said. 'Is the gap growing fast?'

Lauren made a so-so gesture. 'The last time I looked it was a toss-up whether I'd reach *Aqaba* or fifty first. The Kickstarter money will run out in eight months, sooner if I don't stop hiring or make the women start paying, which I can't do.'

A disgruntled noise came from Carter. 'Never take business advice from an accountant.' Looking over at the entrance to the bar, he stood and flashed her an eyebrow raise. 'Here she is.'

Walking over to the door, his masculine business-consultant persona on full display, he greeted an elegant older woman. They hugged in an intimate not professional manner. *That's curious.* After ordering her a drink, they made their way towards Lauren's table.

The woman looked as though she had been torn from the front page of *Woman's Weekly*. Her unnaturally bouncy, shoulder-length blonde hair, overly white teeth, sparkling earrings and liberal use of makeup made her look like a pin-up for conservative wealth. In an attractive black and white diagonally panelled dress, it was only when she drew nearer that Lauren realised she must be in her sixties.

Lauren stood, her arm outstretched, hoping her smile didn't look fake.

Carter introduced them. 'Lauren Brown, this is Julianna Leftbridge.'

With a firm handshake, she said, 'Lauren, it's lovely to meet you. Carter has told me a lot about you and your business.'

Hesitantly, Lauren said, 'I hope it's all good.'

'You'll have to forgive me,' said Leftbridge as they sat. 'I don't normally go around looking like this but I've come from an NGO board photo shoot. Why they insist I look like a senile Trumpette is beyond me.'

Lauren laughed, warming to her, as Julianna took off her earrings.

'Now, Lauren, Carter has been nagging me to meet you, so here I am. He's told me a little about your business, and I had an investment advisor check you and your business out. Interestingly, she didn't find out much more than Carter had already told me. I found that intriguing, so here I am.'

Carter sat watching, looking like the Cheshire Cat.

'That's good to know,' said Lauren. 'I've deliberately kept Weeping Angels under the radar.'

'Why?'

'Safety mainly,' she said glancing at Carter. 'We employ women investigators who we protect by keeping their names out of the public domain.'

Staring hard as though she trying to read Lauren's mind, Leftbridge asked, 'In two sentences, what do you do?'

'The justice system is failing victims of family violence. It favours men with money and we exist to plug the gap until the system is fixed.'

Leftbridge laughed. 'You've answered that question before.'

'I haven't,' said Lauren, 'but Carter said I'd need an "elevator pitch" one day.'

Smiling, Leftbridge sipped her wine. Carter remained beaming.

'Take me through it,' said Leftbridge. 'High-level.'

After licking her lips, Lauren asked, 'Have you ever been a victim of family violence, Julianna?'

'No,' she said smiling.

'No? A partner or ex-partner hasn't pushed you around? Slapped you? Threatened you?' Lauren waited but before Julianna could reply, she added, 'Have you been raped in your own home?'

Her smile gone, Leftbridge closed her eyes, wincing briefly as she shook her head.

Lauren continued matter-of-factly. 'What about stalked? Gaslit until you doubted your sanity? A trolly bashed into you at a supermarket? Access to your bank accounts removed? Multiple, spurious legal challenges launched at you? Texted and rung at all hours? Your children used to blackmail you? Have you been called names? A whore? How about a —'

'That's quite enough, Lauren,' said Leftbridge holding up a hand. 'Your point is well made.'

Women, no matter their situation in life, understood. And who knew what Julianna's life was like behind closed doors? Wealth was no guarantee of safety. To a greater or lesser degree, family violence touched many women as the justice system watched on as a bored spectator.

Carter rubbed his hands together nervously.

She continued. 'Imagine if money wasn't a barrier for these women, these victims of family violence. They could afford the help they need to gather evidence. They could afford legal representation. Unable to confide in friends, because they were embarrassed or, more usually, their friends didn't want to get involved. Imagine if they were supported through the process, not left to navigate it alone, isolated.'

Lauren smiled broadly. 'That's where we enter the frame. We have trained investigators to gather evidence. We're small, but the demand is huge. We build watertight cases with the best chance of success in court, if it gets that far. So far, most abusers, or at least their lawyers, see the writing on the wall and agree to a protection order without the need to go to court. For cases that get to court, we contract young, keen lawyers to take the cases. Not disinterested, uninterested, well-meaning legal-aid lawyers.'

Carter, bursting to help, added, 'I was just asking before you arrived, Julianna, they've nearly a hundred percent success rate without having to go to court.'

'Hmmm,' said Leftbridge. 'I think I understand your business model, Lauren. It's admirable, but it's charity, isn't it? Providing services for those that can't afford to pay.'

Lauren and Carter shook their heads in unison. Lauren nodded at Carter. 'You explain, it was your idea.'

In full business consultant mode, Carter took the floor. 'You're right, Julianna, they can't afford the services *today* – that's the key. The model we put together recognises that, but, as you can imagine, women freed from abuse are more than delighted. They want to pay off their debt when, or if, they can. Since starting, around a quarter of the women Lauren has helped have started paying back what they owe.'

Leftbridge's forehead creased in concentration.

'It's slow,' admitted Carter. 'We add interest at the CPI rate to keep their debt fiscally neutral, but, and this is an important point, there's no pressure to pay. Is there Lauren?'

'None,' she said. 'The model works on the assumption that as these women get back on their feet, they'll eventually be able to pay most, if not all, of what they owe. We've made allowance to write off a portion of debts, but ...' She raised her eyebrows at Carter.

'We're anticipating ... make that *hoping*,' he said, 'that every now and again someone's life will turn around to such an extent that not only will they pay off their debt but they'll donate extra. We apportion that money across everyone else's debt.'

Leftbridge's frown intensified. 'Has anyone done that?'

'One has,' said Lauren. 'Abbey, freed from what she called "mental torture", went for and got a promotion. She paid an additional $2,000, part of a backpay deal that came with the promotion.'

Slowly nodding, Leftbridge said, 'And instead of banking that as pure profit, you apply it pro-rata to everyone's debt.'

'That's it,' said Lauren. 'We send an email to everyone advising them.'

Taking the baton back, Carter said, 'It's a way of reminding everyone of their debt, but in a positive way.'

'We also did it to thank Abbey,' said Lauren. 'She got a huge kick out of knowing she was helping other women who had gone through what she'd been through.'

Leftbridge grinned. 'I like it, but ...' Her face reverted to its serious expression.

'*Aqaba*,' said Carter.

Leftbridge looked at him. 'Pardon?'

'It's Carter's name for the time when the business stops burning cash,' said Lauren.

'Across the desert, of course. Our Carter is clever,' said Leftbridge. 'He under values himself. I'll bet he's charging you next to nothing for his services.'

Lauren smiled at him. *Our Carter.* 'Not next to nothing, actually nothing.'

Holding up a finger, he said, 'When the business is successful –'

Leftbridge cut him off. 'You'll both be older than I am and will need the money for Zimmer frames.'

Everyone laughed.

'I'll get another round of drinks,' said Carter.

When he was out of earshot, Lauren asked, 'How do you know Carter? Has he worked for you before?'

Leftbridge pursed her bright-red lips. 'He hasn't told you then. I'll leave that to him. Let's just say I feel maternally towards Carter. But, until now, he's never asked me for a favour.'

Lauren's eyes narrowed. 'What favour is he asking for?'

She reached across and patted Lauren's hand. 'Just that I listen and make a sound business decision.'

The bar was quiet and Carter soon returned. As the two women sat back, Carter looked from one to the other. 'What's up?'

'Nothing at all,' said Leftbridge. 'Now, tell me about how you're currently funding the financial desert you're trying to cross.'

Carter explained how the Kickstarter campaign had raised what he called 'initial capital', and how he had used that to convince his bank to lend an additional $50,000 at a mortgage-like interest rate. Lauren detailed their cash burn and how they would run out of cash in eight months.

When they had finished, Leftbridge said, '*Aqaba* sounds a long way away.'

'We're crawling closer,' said Lauren, holding her hands in a what-else-can-we-do gesture.

Carter grimaced.

Leftbridge stood. 'I'm going to powder my nose, as they say.'

'Well?' asked Lauren when she had gone.

Carter shrugged. 'I don't know. I thought I did, obviously, but now … She's astute when it comes to business but she has a strong philanthropic side. She's one of the few wealthy people I know who genuinely understand that she's been lucky in life. That she's no better than anyone else. The way you started. "Have you been raped in your own home?" That was brilliant. That punch landed.'

'It usually does,' said Lauren. Running her tongue over her teeth, she said, 'I asked her how she knew you.'

His eyes narrowed.

Shaking her head, she said, 'She didn't tell me.' *She didn't have to tell me.*

Carter smiled. 'I didn't expect she would.'

'If nothing else,' said Lauren, 'these last few years, working with you, have been the most enjoyable of my life.'

'Oh, gosh,' he said. 'You'll make me cry in front of Julianna. It's the most satisfying business I've been involved with too. Seeing the impact you're having on women the system would've let fall through the massive crevices, it's humbling. But' – he exhaled noisily – 'you need cash to get to the future.'

Lauren was about to ask how they should play it, when she saw Leftbridge was on her way back.

As she sat, Leftbridge said, 'I've made a decision, which comes with two conditions.'

She stared at Carter, all business. 'How much time are you spending currently? *Honestly.*'

'On average …' He rocked his head. 'Eight to ten hours a week.'

Leftbridge turned to Lauren. 'I want you to retain Carter's services, fifteen hours a week at $200 an hour – that's what he should be charging at a minimum. Heaven's above, idiot accountants charge $300 an hour for advice they're not qualified to give.'

Lauren opened her mouth but Leftbridge's raised hand silenced her.

'Let me finish. He's bound to be working more than fifteen hours a week, he always was a terrible liar.' She smiled at him. 'Just good friends.'

Carter looked down briefly.

Leftbridge said, 'Anyway, that's the first condition. Are you drawing a salary, Lauren?'

'Yes, I need money to pay my bills. I've had to resign from my job at the legal firm.'

'How much do you draw?'

Shrugging, she said, 'This year, just over $40,000. If we can afford that much.'

'You can hardly live on that and perform all the duties expected of a CEO,' said Leftbridge. 'The second condition is you pay yourself $125,000. It's an okay salary, for now.'

'The business can't – '

Leftbridge waved her into silence. 'If you agree, I'll invest whatever is needed to get you to this *Aqaba*.'

Her eyes bulging, Lauren again went to speak, but Leftbridge hadn't finished.

'And I expect you to scale up, not down. I imagine the demand is huge, obscene really. You should plan to double the size of your operation within twelve months and double it again in the following year – that's at a minimum.' She looked at Carter. 'Is that possible?'

'Anything's possible,' he said. 'It's just that we'll need ...' Lauren waited as Carter desperately calculated the amount Leftbridge was possibly offering. He spoke slowly. 'That's in the ballpark of maybe ... a million.'

Leftbridge shrugged. 'It's an investment.'

Carter asked, 'How much equity would you want for that?'

Leftbridge fell back in her chair laughing. 'Carter, you dear boy. You didn't spend enough time with me, did you. I'm not a so-called "Angel Investor"' – she shook her head grunting disgustedly – 'who pretend they're philanthropic but want to get their greedy hands on as many companies as they can. I will simply tell my trust board that I expect Weeping Angels, when they are fully on their feet, will start repaying the CPI-adjusted loan at a future date.'

Carter grinned broadly. 'Now where did you get that idea like that from, Julianna?' He held his glass high. 'To Weeping Angels.'

Lauren, not quite speechless, said, 'To us.'

They clinked glasses.

CHAPTER 13

'How did last night go, Trudi?' asked Lauren.

Trudi, red-faced with a towel over her shoulders having come from the gym, yawned loudly before saying. 'Sweet as, boss.'

Smiling, Lauren said, 'You didn't need to come in, you know. Friday meetings are optional. What time did you get to bed?'

'It wasn't late,' she said. 'It's just hard to fall asleep. You know, all that adrenalin flowing after the thrill of the chase.'

Lauren did indeed know what it was like, having been the company's first investigator, and she still filled in when investigators were sick or on leave. Trudi was part of their rapidly expanding team. A student by day, her role as an investigator was to document incidents of family violence against their clients. The team in the Auckland office had expanded to twelve. Unfortunately, but predictably, business was booming.

Lauren loved her varied roles as general manager and backup investigator as well as in the expanding client-support team. The company employed women able to work flexible hours, including evenings and nights. All employees had to be actively training in a combat-focussed martial art or self-defence discipline. On top of that, they employed local self-defence instructors to regularly train employees.

'The thrill of the chase,' said Lauren. 'What happened last night?'

Unable to suppress her smile, Trudi said, 'This one usually drives past a couple of times each evening. He waits until it's dark so I doubt we're getting good images of him on Rhonda's phone. She went out last night, took the kids to have dinner with her parents. I wasn't going to bother, but I was curious to see what he'd do if she wasn't home. Just after eight, he drove past as usual. When he saw her car wasn't there, he did a U-turn, parked about fifty metres away from her house and went back on foot.'

'And …' Lauren's voice had a parental tone.

'I couldn't resist. I had Zeek with me, so after I recorded him entering her property, we jumped out so I could have a look. You know, I'm just taking my German Shepherd for a walk. As we went past the driveway, he was coming out the gate by the side of her house.'

'Go on.'

Grinning, Trudi said, 'He came out of the dark and surprised Zeek, who went ballistic. The bloke absolutely shat himself. After I calmed Zeek, he apologised – said he'd forgotten his keys. I used my phone to record him heading back to his car.'

Lauren patted Trudi's shoulder. 'Trudi, you need to be careful. Recording him entering her property is solid enough evidence. How much have we got on him?'

Trudi woke the computer in front of her. 'Let's see. Rhonda's logged his morning drive-by for nearly a month and I've recorded him outside her house six times, plus last night.'

'That's a clear pattern of abuse. Fire it through to legal, see if they think we have enough.'

Trudi grinned. 'Cool.'

'Redeemable?' asked Lauren.

Wrinkling her nose, Trudi said, 'I doubt it. He's a dedicated fuckwit who looks like he enjoys stalking. You never know, though.'

As part of the protection order application, they often requested additional education and support. The ideal outcome was to have the order safely rescinded in the future. That was the best outcome, especially when children were involved. As Lauren told everyone, Weeping Angels wasn't anti-men – it was anti-family violence.

'I'll grab the next on the wait list,' said Trudi.

The wait list they maintained was growing. This was partly due to their reputation but mostly due to what the government dispassionately termed 'unmet need'. The justice system was broken, it was failing women and it had been for decades. Unless you were independently wealthy, you were in with the lions. If you could endure the abuse, scrape together enough money, you might survive. The system doomed the rest to remain as prey. Despite the impressive increase of women in Parliament, including multiple Prime Ministers, the way justice was dispensed remained a firm supporter of the male right to do whatever they wanted.

After making sure the operation was running as it should – and it was – Lauren headed for the airport. Auckland Airport's domestic terminal was hectic, as usual. Even though air travel in New Zealand was meant to be 'back to normal', the cancellations, eye-watering prices and low numbers of available flights told a different story. Lauren had learnt the hard way – now was not a good time to fly.

As it was, she wasn't flying, she was waiting for a journalist arriving from Palmerston North. Although it was only eleven o'clock, the airport seemed to be at rush hour. Hassled travellers, tired parents with tired children and business men and women yelling into their phones filed past Lauren in an endless stream. Smiling, she recognised Grace Marks as she walked casually through the arrival gates, took a sidestep to get out of the pedestrian flow, pushed her sunglasses onto the top of her head and looked around.

While Lauren recognised Grace, whose image was often in the media, Grace had no idea what she looked like. A journalist with RNZ, Grace had written two insightful pieces on family violence. It had been that, her reputation as an investigative journalist, the fact she was a woman and Carter's nagging that had convinced Lauren to contact her to see if she was interested in covering Weeping Angels. Now the operation's financial needs were no longer dire, and they were achieving their growth targets, Lauren wanted to turn her focus back to the company's overall mission – fixing the justice system. For that to happen, she needed to take the company out of the shadows.

With her blonde hair in a neat shoulder-length ponytail, Grace had dressed casually in jeans, a black hoodie and black ankle boots. Solid, but feminine, she was much shorter than Lauren had expected. Her stories, and the recent feature article on her, had made her seem larger than life, but had she not stepped into the open, Lauren would have struggled to see her. But, as she was at least double Lauren's age, Grace looked fantastic.

Lauren, dressed in unassuming business clothes – a grey pants suit and white shirt – stepped away from the pillar, waved out and headed towards Grace. Smiling in recognition, Grace headed towards her.

Offering her hand, Lauren said, 'It's great to meet you, Grace.'

'Call me Ace, everyone does. It's great to meet you too, Lauren. After I researched you, I wasn't sure you existed.'

'I'm pleased to hear it,' she said. 'I'm a private person. Do you have bags to collect?'

Grace shook her head. 'I travel light.'

As they walked to her car, Lauren asked, 'What do you want to do first? Head to your hotel to see if you can check in and freshen up?'

Grace smirked. 'This is as fresh as I get.'

Lauren laughed. 'Great, let's head to the office. I can show you around and you can ask questions, I figure that's the best way to start.'

They chatted amiably on the drive, covering a range of topics. Lauren swung her anonymous grey Holden into an equally anonymous carpark outside a building that had seen far better days. It was part of a row of buildings occupied by businesses that looked like they were struggling to make ends meet. The only other car in the carpark was Trudi's well-worn student car. The name on the building, painted deliberately in faded black lettering, was *Tomorrows Solutions Yesterday Ltd.*

Out of the car, Grace looked at the carpark and building. 'I must say your digs are … understated.'

Lauren smiled. 'It's deliberate.' In response to Grace's questioning look, she said, 'That's what we're aiming for – the abandoned look.'

'And the grammar?' asked Grace.

'My business advisor's sense of humour,' said Lauren as she walked towards the building's only door. 'You'll appreciate this, Ace.' Lauren pointed to a grey electrical box on the wall with a triangular yellow warning sticker.

Stepping closer, Grace bent to inspect the box. 'A miniature security camera, expensive too. Why?'

'I want to ensure this place is secure. Apart from one pest, no one knows this is our operations centre apart from our staff, who know to keep it secret.'

'Pest?'

'He's a serial pain in the arse,' said Lauren. 'He files claim after claim against his ex-wife. We found out he knows about this place because we pipe the feed from the camera through an algorithm which looks for patterns of unusual activity. He was a repeat drive-by.'

'Is it expensive technology?' asked Grace.

Lauren shook her head. 'I like to believe only we can access the feed, but I've read your stories investigating New Zealand's surveillance scene.'

'I might have only delayed the inevitable,' said Grace. 'Let's hope the much-touted government safeguards work.'

Lauren tapped her security card on the grey box. A loud *clunk* indicated serious bolts were retracting and she pushed open the door. Inside, a short corridor led to a second security door which opened after she again tapped her security card. Finally, they stepped into Weeping Angels' operations centre.

'I expected a phone booth,' said Grace. 'Did you model your security on *Get Smart*?'

'Get what?'

'Google it,' said Grace, grinning.

After Lauren had showed her around the office, highlighting the technical aspects of their operation, which Grace took a particular interest in, they adjourned to her office.

'Where is everybody?' asked Grace, taking a seat on a bright red couch.

Sitting at right angles on a similar-coloured single-seater, Lauren said, 'Most of our team work parttime in the evenings and, as you can imagine, they spend most of their time offsite. We have regular Monday and Friday meetings which most try to make but many join remotely. Coffee?'

'Too late in the day for me,' said Grace, getting out a notepad. 'I assume the operations centre is at the heart of how you function, can you take me through it?'

'Before I —'

Grace cut in. 'Every story I write, you'll get to read and approve, okay?'

'Good enough for me,' said Lauren. 'I don't know how you're going to approach this, but we model ourselves on terrorist cells.'

Grace looked surprised.

Shrugging, Lauren said, 'It sounds bad, I know, but they're an effective model to copy if you want to keep your operation hidden. In each geographic area in which we operate, first we recruit a lead investigator. We recently hired someone in Hastings. They operate from home initially, usually in the evenings, and we work with them to set up the office and recruit three to five investigators. We need a minimum number for coverage and backup.'

Lauren paused while Grace wrote furiously.

'Salaried?' asked Grace.

'Absolutely. Lead investigators are normally point sixes; investigators are point fours. Strong salaries though. Our aim is zero turnover, though people will leave to follow their careers.'

'Only women?'

'No, but yes. At least for now,' said Lauren.

'Why?'

'Women get what we're about instantly, and what we've learnt is that women investigators blend easily into suburbia. We will employ men, we're not anti-men, but we'll make sure they fit. We don't need anyone who thinks life is about "hardening up".'

'Don't be a soft cock,' said Grace. 'Men haven't stopped fascinating over their willies since they discovered they had one.'

Lauren grinned. 'Anyway, once the cell reaches a critical mass, and we're satisfied they'll be safe in the field, they're assigned a handler who operates out of here. We put the word out through local networks that we're in town and the cases tumble in.'

'How do you assess whether they'll be safe?'

'We require all staff to be actively training in a martial art or self-defence. We provide regular training sessions in-house too. I hope they never have to use those skills, but for the rest of their lives they have that training as a last line of defence.'

'What do you do?'

'Karate.'

Grace smiled. 'I did karate for years – loved it. Do your investigators operate alone?'

'Eventually,' she said, 'They're in pairs until their lead is satisfied they can fly solo. It's a big step.'

'Have you had many incidents?'

'Not many. Our investigators document every time they're in the field, to keep the evidence chain tight, but we also record all investigator-related incidents.'

'Readers love stories about PIs. And female PIs would grab a lot of attention.'

Lauren smiled thinking of Trudi and Zeek. 'I can arrange to give you our more colourful incidents.'

Grace's eyes lit up.

'Most of the time,' said Lauren, 'confrontations are easily diffused. If they're seen and confronted, we train them to employ deflection tactics. "I'm waiting for my boyfriend". Or they can go on the attack, "Get away from me you creep, I'm calling the cops".'

'But some aren't put off?'

'Some have got nasty. Then it's get the hell out of there. As I said, the self-defence training is a last line of defence.'

'Anyone hurt?'

Lauren paused briefly. 'Nothing serious. The men mainly demand their camera or phone – most of them know assault is a criminal offence. We document it, the lead investigator reviews the case as a matter of protocol and, when we lodge the protection order application, if the incident was serious enough, we lodge a police complaint.'

'Good,' said Grace. 'Those men must think the law doesn't apply to them.'

'We make sure they know it does.'

'Is that the reason for the security?' asked Grace.

Lauren nodded. 'We work hard to keep under the radar. When the court serves the papers on the respondent, their lawyer should advise them to keep away from their victim, our client. Most do, even narcissists recognise the need to *look* innocent. The odd hot-head wants to find out who's responsible for interfering in what they see as their private business.'

Grace wrote for a long moment. When she had finished, she looked up, eyes narrowed. 'It's a slick operation. I love it. But ...'

'How does it work financially?'

'Yeah,' said Grace. 'I mean, with my research and the stories I wrote around Elle's journey, money was a huge barrier. I don't need to tell you that bugger-all women qualify for legal aid, and few lawyers are interested in the work. The cost of going to court, the time, the stress and the prospect of losing and their life becoming harder. Any one of those factors is discouraging, let alone all of them.'

'That's why I started Weeping Angels. The justice system, as you've just pointed out, supports the abusers, not the victims. In financial terms, we provide benevolent bridging finance – that's what my business advisor, Carter, calls it. Simply, we've replicated what the women would do if money wasn't a barrier.'

Grace remained silent.

'We do the work,' said Lauren, 'help them build a case with our investigators and pay their legal fees. Because we do a solid job, we usually avoid having to go to court, which brings down the cost hugely. We record our client's debt as "unpaid but earned" and, when they're able, once they're on their feet, they start paying off the debt until it's gone.'

'"Unpaid but earned."' Grace bit her top lip. 'Isn't that a fancy title for future bad debts?'

Lauren had researched Grace's background. Before her recent move into journalism, she knew Grace had been a business consultant, so she was ready for these questions. 'That's one way you could look at it. We've developed a system that looks at it as delayed revenue.'

Grace squinted.

'Most women are beyond grateful,' explained Lauren. 'You'd be surprised how many start repaying immediately. We also champion our help-a-sister-out fund. We expect some clients to do so well after the abuse ends that they're able to contribute more than they owe. Any money over and above their debt, we divide equally and apply it to all existing debts.'

'Right,' said Grace slowly. 'Victims helping victims has a great feel-good factor – I get that. But unless New Zealand banks have developed a moral compass, which they haven't, they're not going to lend you $10 to help anyone's sister. How are you covering the debt?'

Lauren laughed. 'Carter has a similar view of banks. You're right, we *were* sailing towards a financial chasm, but we've been fortunate enough to attract a patron.'

'Who?'

'I'll need to get her okay –'

'Her?'

Lauren laughed 'I meant *their* okay first.'

Grace tapped her pen on her notepad. 'Either way I can make it work. A named patron or a mysterious *unnamed* one. Where did you get the idea from?'

'For the bridging finance? Carter, my business advisor.'

'I'd like to talk to her, possible?'

'Sure,' said Lauren. 'And Carter's a he.'

'Oh,' said Grace.

'He's not technically an employee,' said Lauren. 'And he's happy to talk about the business side of our operation. When I next see him, I'll get him to call you. He developed our stretch goal too – to ensure everyone impacted by family violence has access to quality legal representation.'

'That's good,' said Grace as a short laugh escaped her. 'Wouldn't that mean you're doing what the government is meant to do?'

'Exactly. If we can get them to change the law, add funding or improve the legal aid system, we can step back and target our money into related areas like education and support services. But realistically, what's the chance of any government intervening meaningfully?'

'I hear you,' said Grace. 'Not enough votes in family violence.'

'Most of our clients,' continued Lauren, 'blossom when the abuse stops, but some are badly damaged and the court system doesn't help. We can only do so much, and recidivist abusers find ways to keep abusing their victims while staying within the law. It would be great if psycho-social help was available but that doesn't exist, not in any practical way.'

'What you're doing, it's fantastic.'

A warm feeling swept over Lauren.

'If my friend Elle had access to your services,' said Grace, 'it wouldn't have just made it simpler and less expensive, you would've saved her scores of horrible hours battling her ex. You can't put a price on that.'

Lauren smiled. 'How's she doing?'

'Getting the protection order was life changing. She's dating again, which she thought impossible. I can fashion great stories from this, but no matter how carefully I write them your organisation is going to attract attention. That will be great for business but you will be stepping out into the light.'

Biting her top lip, Lauren nodded.

'You'll be in demand,' said Grace. 'Personally. Are you ready for that?'

'No,' she said. 'But I know I have to be, if we want to tackle the system.'

'What about hiring a PR firm to help?' asked Grace. 'They're worth the cost if you can afford them.'

'That's a great idea,' said Lauren. 'If I'm going to come out of the closet, so to speak, I may as well have as many people in my corner as possible.'

CHAPTER 14

Grace's phone vibrated rhythmically on the table as she lay on the couch, her feet on her daughter's lap. Her son lay sprawled on the adjacent two-seater. While her furniture was past its best, it worked and Grace didn't see the point of upgrading when her teenage children were still prone to slopping their breakfast, lunch or dinner. It also meant she didn't care when Roxy, her partner Sean's often wet retriever, curled up on the couch.

Grace's phone was trying, but failing, to interrupt the movie they were watching, *The Castle*. They had seen it before, and it was a classic.

Without moving, Grace asked her son, 'Who was it?'

Tapping the screen, he said, 'Caller ID blocked.'

'Fuck them, then,' said Grace.

In a low growl, he said, 'Mum.'

Apart from her job as a RNZ journalist, Grace was kept busy as a single parent to two near-adult children – her son Kane was at university and her daughter Sophie was nearing the end of college. Recent journalistic successes had secured Grace a fulltime role in the politics and society fields but RNZ, like every state-owned entity, was constantly tightening their belt because the Government mistakenly viewed the country as a company. With the sword of redundancy hanging by a thread over her head, she needed to keep the stories flowing. Despite her efforts, she remained what she had been trying to escape her whole adult life – a rat on a wheel.

'Still fuck them,' said Grace in response to her phone's dying-fly buzz that indicated the caller had left a message.

Her son shook his head, tutting.

When the movie finished, the children bounded off to their rooms via the kitchen, her son to recommence online gaming, her daughter to upload a few thousand selfies. Alone, Grace dragged herself into a sitting position, snatching her phone in the process to listen to the voice message.

'Kia ora. Constable Manderson of the Auckland Police. I want to discuss a missing person's report, if you could call me on …'

Grace wrote the number on the back of an ACT Party leaflet that must have come in with the junk mail. The words *IGNORANT AF* had been neatly written across the forehead of the grinning, white, male, business-suited candidate. No doubt her rebel daughter's work.

It had gone 8pm. Manderson was likely making these calls in the evening as the chances of people answering was higher, though who answered when the caller blocked their ID? Grace drummed her fingers on the table. The tired parent who had worked all day and cooked dinner wanted to leave it until the morning. The journalist wanted to know who was missing. And what was her connection to the person or disappearance?

The journalist won.

The officer answered the call immediately with a crisp, 'Manderson.'

Grace smirked. 'Manderson. Marks.'

'Marks?'

'Manderson?'

Grace enjoyed toying with the police. Through her various run-ins she had long ago lost the nervousness that most people experienced when dealing with them.

She heard him breathe out. 'Grace Marks, the journalist.'

'You left a message to call.'

'I'll open the file. Hang on Miss —'

Grace cut in. 'Just call me Ace. That'll save me having to give you a lecture on the stupidity of female honorifics.'

'Honour whats?'

Grace smiled. 'You called about a missing person. Who's missing?'

The sound of a two-finger typist conscientiously punching a keyboard came down the line. 'Lauren Brown. Does that name —'

'Lauren's missing?' she said, cutting him off. 'Since when?'

After more deliberate keyboard punching, he said, 'She was last seen at her place of work last Friday. She left in her car … with you.'

Grace's eyes rolled. The police had a knack of making a statement sound like an accusation – what did you do with her?

'Hang on,' said Grace. 'That sound's right but I'll check my diary.'

In her office, Grace woke her computer from the sleep she had intended to give it until morning, putting the call on speaker phone. Her diary confirmed what Manderson had said. 'I was with her on the twelfth. She picked me up from the airport around midday. We went to her office to discuss business and, after that, we spent the evening together.'

There was a long pause before the officer said, 'Very good. That's why I'm calling.'

Grace's eyes nearly managed a three-sixty. 'I said evening, not night. We had dinner.'

After another pause, he said, 'Very good.'

Grace simultaneously clenched her fists, shut her eyes, gritted her teeth and shook her head. Why do males view two women having dinner as the equivalent of foreplay? Inhaling deeply through her nose, she mentally dropped the bone she wanted to chew – now was not the time to educate what sounded like a young police officer. 'That was five days ago,' she said. 'Why are you only calling now?'

Manderson let out a loud sigh.

Grace knew he was about to tell her what she already knew, what he had to tell everyone who was anxious over a missing person.

'Most people who go missing turn up within a couple of days,' he said. 'An impulsive trip with a friend, or they need time out of their lives. According to her friends and workmates, she was reclusive, had been known to disappear for a couple of days, but was always contactable. When she didn't answer calls or reply to texts, their concerns escalated.'

'And no one's heard from her for the last five days?'

'No.'

'Is that all you have?'

'A patrol car found her car parked outside St James Anglican Church on Church Road – they recognised the plate number and had it towed to the police yards. We believe it was parked close to where she lives.'

'You believe?'

'We've been unable to determine her address. As I said, according to her colleagues who reported her missing she was careful with her privacy.'

'Was her laptop or phone in the car?' asked Grace.

'No. If we'd found those it would have been … concerning.'

'Fair enough,' she said. 'I take it you want to know what happened on Friday?'

'That would help. Also, what was her mental state? Did she seem depressed or worried?'

'Quite the opposite,' said Grace. 'The reason she invited me to Auckland was because she wanted to go public with Weeping Angels' success.'

'Is that her company's name.'

'That's right,' said Grace. 'I don't think it's registered in her name?'

'Why?'

'I didn't ask her that.' She started explaining what Lauren's company did, but Manderson cut her off.

'That's all very interesting but this is a missing persons case, not a criminal investigation. I just want to know what happened on the Friday night you spent with her.'

Gritting her teeth again, Grace knew this was a battle she couldn't win. In front of Manderson would be the online equivalent of a stack of missing persons files. Update the file, hopefully stamp 'RESOLVED' on it, and move on.

'We left her offices about 5pm,' she said. 'She dropped me at my hotel and picked me up again at 6.30 — we went to a Vietnamese restaurant for dinner. We discussed business and she dropped me back at my hotel around 8.30.'

'Did you notice any mood swings during dinner?'

'No. As I said, she was nervous about the future, but excited. Nothing about her said I'm about to do a runner. She said she was going to see a friend on her way home. She called him Tana.'

'Tana? T-A-N-A?'

'I presume so.'

'No last name?' asked the officer.

'She just called him Tana.'

Blowing out a breath, he said, 'There are thousands of people called Tana. Where did you stay?'

'The Quest Highbrook. It was near her offices.'

'And you weren't planning to see her the following day?'

'No. I met a journalist friend for lunch. He took me to the airport and I caught the 3.25 back to Palmerston North.'

Grace listened as Manderson pecked at his keyboard.

'Thanks for calling back … Ace.'

'Hold on, Manderson. What now?'

'What now what?'

It was hard to tell on the phone whether he was being dense deliberately or whether it was part of police training. She said slowly, 'What are you, the police, doing to find Lauren?'

'Unless someone comes forward with more information, or there's evidence of a crime, there's not much we can do. As I said, most people eventually turn up.'

'Can't you track her car?' asked Grace. 'I know you have all sorts of surveillance tools you don't like to let the public know about.'

He laughed. 'You've read one too many conspiracy theories. It's not like the movies, you know.'

He was wrong, but he was right and she wasn't talking to the right person. Agent Jenna Parata, Grace's SIS contact, and her spooky mates had access to that technology, but not the ordinary police. Not Manderson.

'Thanks for your assistance.' He terminated the call.

Grace put her phone down and chewed on her thumbnail.

CHAPTER 15

Grace had been standing, sitting and even tried jumping up and down outside Weeping Angels' operations centre. She had waved her arms, banged on the door and yelled before resorting to sitting in the middle of the carpark. Even though there were three cars parked outside their offices, she had no idea if anyone was inside. This was, however, the only lead she had and she was going to stay until someone came out.

After her conversation with Manderson the previous evening, she slept on the problem of what to do. More accurately, she tossed and turned, trying the patience of her partner Sean. He had two younger children he shared the care of and he stayed with Grace when he wasn't looking after them. Last night he likely wished he had stayed at home.

The police's position was clear – without new information they wouldn't act. Grace had considered reaching out to her SIS contact, a lead agent in the domestic terrorism unit. Playing possible conversations in her head, they all ended with Agent Parata saying, 'There's no way, Ace. It's a missing person.'

Marla Simmons, a former US agent for hire now living secretly in the South Island, was another option, but involving her would take time and put Marla's anonymity at risk. The two women's paths had crossed several times, most recently when the alt-right had designs on subverting New Zealand's democracy. Prior to that, Marla's former colleagues had tried to throw her under the bus when an assignment cratered. Now she was wanted by the police, the SIS and covert American agencies, who viewed her as a problematic loose end.

After turning possible options over and over she decided to head back to Auckland to see what she could find out. It may be that Lauren had taken off for a few mental health days, that's what the police expected, but that explanation didn't sit right. The last time Grace glanced at the dim red digital clock in her bedroom it had read two-seventeen.

She crept out of bed at 4.45am, moving silently to let Sean sleep. Unfortunately Roxy, his ever-alert retriever, took this as a signal that it was time for breakfast. Sliding nosily off the bed, she shook herself with such vigour that the room moved. Sean muttered a few choice words as he rolled away. In the lounge, closing doors silently behind her, Grace shook her head at a smiling Roxy. 'You've got me into trouble, young lady.'

After letting Roxy out for a call of nature and feeding her, she booked a ticket on the soon to be departing 7.20am flight to Auckland. She used the RNZ credit card she had memorised – it was a work trip. She would have to justify this later to both the regional finance controller and her political editor, both parental in their attention to expenses.

She woke Sean to let him know what she was doing – he was surprisingly supportive. Her children took the news with sleepy grunts; she told them she would call to let them know what was happening. After hurriedly throwing clothes into a carry-on bag, she taxied to the airport. When she arrived in Auckland, she hired a car, again on RNZ's tab, and headed to the Weeping Angel's operation centre – where she was now sitting cross-legged, scowling at the building.

An idea occurred to her. Finding a nearby office products store, and buying a much-needed coffee, with her recent purchases she wrote in bold, black capitals on the large piece of cardboard – I'M LOOKING FOR LAUREN!

She held the sign above her head – the security door opened almost immediately. A wary woman came out, surveyed the carpark then walked towards Grace. The young, fit woman, dressed as though she had just come from the gym, regarded her with a deeply suspicious look from a safe distance. 'Who are you?' she asked.

Putting her sign down, Grace stood. 'Didn't you see me before?'

'We saw you.'

'Why didn't you come out? Do I look like a threat?' said Grace.

Easily a head taller than Grace, the woman's eyes flicked over Grace. 'No, but we never come out, it's procedure. We never acknowledge this place exists. Your sign, though, that was clever.'

Grace smiled. 'I'm Grace Marks. I'm –'

'The journalist,' she interrupted, her facing losing its look of suspicion. 'I heard you were here last week, before –'

Grace finished her sentence. 'The Friday before Lauren went missing, I was. The police rang me last night, I had no idea Lauren was missing until then.'

'That makes sense. We've been trying to get the police to treat this as … well, serious.' She frowned. 'They keep saying she'll turn up.'

'Shall we go inside?' suggested Grace.

'Sure. I'm Trudi. One of the investigators here.'

Grace followed Trudi through the Maxwell Smart-tribute security doors, through the offices and into a small, well-appointed kitchen. The few people she saw stared at her keenly, as though she had arrived to explain the mystery. Trudi sat opposite Grace, edgy, concern engraved on her face.

'Take me through what happened,' said Grace, taking out her notepad. 'The last time I saw Lauren, she had just dropped me at my hotel and she said she was going to visit someone called Tana.'

Trudi nodded. 'Lauren occasionally mentioned Tana.'

'In what context?'

Trudi took a moment. 'From what she said, which was never much, he sounded like an old friend, a trusted friend.'

'So, not a concern she was visiting him?'

Trudi shook her head. 'I'd say the opposite.'

'What happened after Friday?' asked Grace.

Holding her hands in a you-tell-me gesture, she said. 'She wasn't at work on Monday for our regular meeting. That wasn't like her, she loves those meetings, but she'd missed them before.'

'It wasn't unusual for her go missing?'

'Not missing,' said Trudi. 'She'd always answer emails and texts at any time of the day or night.' Trudi suddenly frowned and shook her head. 'Sorry, why are you here? What can you do, you're a journalist?'

'That's a fair question,' said Grace. 'The police are waiting for her to reappear. Like you, I'm concerned so I'm giving them a hand. I'm an investigative journalist. Digging up stuff is what I do. If I can find new information, it might spur them into action. Sometimes someone needs to do something.'

'True.' Trudi grinned briefly. 'After we hadn't heard from her by Tuesday, we decided to ring the police. After they found her car, and it hadn't been messed with, they asked if I had concerns for her safety. I wasn't sure. Maybe I should've said yes, then they would've taken it more seriously.'

'When Lauren dropped me off, she was in good spirits,' said Grace. 'She was the opposite of depressed.'

'I know,' said Trudi. 'She was getting ready to battle the justice system. We were excited too.'

'What's your best guess as to what's happened?' asked Grace.

'It's not my best guess, but all I have left is that McMahon's involved. I don't know how, but he's the only one we've had serious trouble with.'

'McMahon?'

Trudi sighed. 'He's a serial abuser who knows we operate out of here. Our cameras have caught him driving past more than once, it's not a coincidence.'

After Trudi supplied his first name, Grace wrote a large question mark next to his name. 'I take it he's unhappy that he can't keep on abusing his ex.'

'McMahon's a vindicative arsehole who's rich enough to use the justice system as a weapon to hound his ex.'

Grace tapped her lip. 'There are a few them around.'

'There sure are,' she said. 'McMahon drags his ex through the court every chance he gets.'

'How many times has he …' Grace waved her hands in the air.

'Filed applications?' Trudi groaned. 'I don't know, maybe thirty.'

'Thirty?' Grace's mouth stayed open.

'From what I hear, it's not uncommon,' said Trudi. 'Talk to Women's Refuge, they'll have stories. I think one man has filed over a hundred. The courts seem powerless to stop them.'

'A hundred, what the absolute … Do they hold a cricket bat aloft in the pub to celebrate?' Grace scribbled some notes, this was a story that needed telling. When she had finished writing, she huffed out a breath.

Trudi, smiling sadly, said, 'Welcome to our world.'

'When I wrote about Elle's experience of family violence, and the courts, I had to almost shame my editor into running the pieces.'

'People don't want to know,' said Trudi. 'I mean, I didn't know until I joined. I guess everyone prefers to pretend it doesn't exist, which makes it easy for abusers and a nightmare for victims.'

Grace shook her head. 'Back to McMahon. He's driving his ex-wife mad, that's shit, but I get it. What's his beef with you?'

'We keep paying for her lawyer. Without us, she'd have given up by now. Judges don't always award costs, though they should.'

Grace spoke slowly. 'And you think he's worked out who Lauren is and ...' She finished the sentence by holding her hands palms up.

'Yeah, that's where the logic falls down,' said Trudi.

'Did you tell the police about him?'

She nodded. 'They told me they contacted him, that he's not involved.'

'Do you have his details?'

Trudi paused for an instant before saying, 'Sure, he's not our client. We don't owe him a duty of care. Hang on.' Jumping up, she returned with a square of paper containing his details.

'I'm not sure what I can do, but you never know,' said Grace. 'Did he ever threaten Lauren?'

'I doubt he knows who Lauren is.'

'Do you know if Lauren's had other threats?'

Trudi shook her head. 'Hardly anyone knows Lauren runs the company, so if men do their nuts they aim their anger at the lawyers we use, sometimes us investigators, if they catch us on the job. He probably got lucky, followed someone he recognised. That's why we keep the building secure.'

'Given the type of men involved,' said Grace, 'I can imagine how they lose their shit, but if we're talking, what ... abduction, that's an extreme step.' She shook her head. 'It doesn't sound right, does it? He would have had to know who Lauren is and start following her. She'd be alert for anything like that. I mean, even the police don't know where she lives. Do you know?'

Again, Trudi shook her head. 'We tried to find out, to see if she was okay, and to tell the police, but every address we found is care of here.' In response to Grace's obvious look of incredulity, she added, 'Why should we know? It's not the sort of question you ask your boss.'

Grace tapped her lip for a moment before saying, 'I suppose not. She obviously never hosted staff functions. Can the business survive without her?'

'For a while, it'll be no problem.'

'It sounds like she thought this might happen,' said Grace. Trudi's face tightened; the possibility had clearly crossed her mind too. 'Is there any point talking to your colleagues?'

Her face scrunching, Trudi said, 'I doubt it. As you can imagine, apart from work it's all we've talked about.'

'Is there anyone else? What about this man Tana? Does anybody know more about him?'

Trudi shook her head. 'We've been around that block, several times.'

'What about people she's mentioned? Family? Business contacts?'

'There's Carter. She calls him her business advisor. We're hoping he turns up. Like Tana, she talked about him like he was a friend.'

'Lauren mentioned him.' Grace wrote his name in capitals. Her pen poised, she half laughed. 'That's it though, isn't it?'

'We've tried Googling him,' said Trudi. 'Combinations of "business", "advisor" and "Carter", nothing worked.'

'Really?'

Trudi nodded. 'Smaller firms don't list their staff, or even have websites. Larger firms have too many staff to list. We thought we had him, there's a business in Auckland called Carter Consultants – no connection.'

Grace grunted.

'I know,' said Trudi. 'We run teams of investigators, and we've been digging hard. We've come up with blanks on Lauren, Tana and Carter. It's as though Lauren exists in this business but nowhere else. We're good at tracking people, but Lauren's a ghost.' After a pause she asked, 'Are you still going to look for her?'

'Sure. There's not much to go on but I'll give it a crack. I'm here now.'

'You'll need her picture.' Trudi left the kitchen returning a few minutes later with two copies of a head and shoulders shot of Lauren. It was a group photo that she'd cropped Lauren's image from, the photo taken at a distance so the image wasn't crisp.

'I assume this is the best you could dig up?'

'For security, we have a policy of no staff photos. This was from an early team-building event with family members that someone snapped. It was posted on social media not long ago, until Lauren saw it, that is.'

'Really,' said Grace as she studied the image of a serious Lauren staring into the distance. 'She was smart, and knew when to be on guard. These days you can drop an image into Google, who knows what you might find. It's how we, journalists that is, try to identify people standing in the background of photos.'

'Then there's Clearview AI,' said Trudi. 'God knows how many images that dark star has scraped from the internet.'

'Indeed,' said Grace, impressed that Trudi was aware of Clearview AI and its billions of images. 'Their collection methods are dodgy. I'm not sure if all the privacy lawsuits against them have been resolved yet.'

Back in the carpark, after giving Trudi an assurance that she would keep in touch if she made progress, Grace sat in her rental car, drumming her fingers on the steering wheel.

'What would Marla do?'

CHAPTER 16

Having missed breakfast to catch her early morning flight, Grace demolished a large Mongolian stir-fry for lunch. In between mouthfuls she rang Sean then her children, explaining that she might need to stay in Auckland overnight, or even for a few days. Sean was concerned, her children delighted to have the house to themselves. 'Yes, you can borrow my car but leave more than a whiff of petrol in it,' she had said to her son.

After she had finished lunch, she checked her emails. There was the usual spam that beat her tireless efforts to block it. Among the legitimate emails, most related to the various stories she was working on. Her editor wanted to know when she was filing the story on the changes in the tertiary education sector. The new education minister, who viewed education as a public good and not through a profit-making lens, was in the process of implementing a raft of changes. For universities, that meant the disestablishment of the Stonehenge-esque university councils and the law-unto-themselves Vice Chancellors Committee as the sector refocused on collaboration, not competition. From her interviews with university staff, the overall feeling was unbridled delight.

Having attended to everything that needed attending to, she booked a budget room for the night, RNZ's credit card again to the fore. Why RNZ expected you to get your expenses approved in advance was beyond Grace – the stories journalists chased were never neat and tidy. Grace stuck to the adage that it's easier to ask for forgiveness than permission – and it took a few days for charges to appear in the accounts.

An idea had struck her over lunch. Rather than trying to think like Marla, it would be easiest to contact her and get her thoughts on how she'd tackle the problem. There was no guarantee Marla would get her message and that was the deciding factor – what's the worst that could happen? Launching a Tor browser for invisibility, she sent her a message from one of her many anonymous Proton Mail addresses.

Hey, I hope you're enjoying the quiet life (wherever you are). I'm in Auckland in

Even if the message did make it to Marla, she might not see it for days. She was about to close her Tor browser session when a message pinged into her inbox. Her eyes widened – it was from Marla.

Hey Ace. What's up? It must be you because nobody else on the planet knows this email address. Sorry though, this is an automated reply. I don't sit around waiting for your messages but, if I'm still alive, I'll get in touch. M

Marla was alive. If the New Zealand authorities, or any of the spy agencies, had caught her, Grace's SIS contact would have heard and let her know. What she expected Marla could advise from her bolthole in the South Island, that was a different question.

It had gone two when Grace checked in to her hotel. She hadn't showered before leaving, employing copious amounts of deodorant instead. It is an unwritten rule of society that women needed to smell like floral tributes, whereas men ranged from *Brut* to *Evening-in-Gallipoli*.

Her room was a replica of every hotel room she'd had. Stretching, she could almost touch opposite walls and the view from the window, secured so you could only open it a crack, was of a brick wall. The only possible reaction anyone could have on opening the door was the one Grace had – this is adequate.

After showering, she set up her laptop on the tiny desk to work on a plan. Even if Marla contacted her, she was on her own for now. On the hotel stationery, she drew a mind map. In the middle she wrote *Lauren???* circled in red pen. She leaned back in her chair, staring at the minimalistic diagram.

Ten minutes later she flopped onto the bed. Her diagram, apart from the addition of a single swear word and exclamation mark, was unchanged. Lauren's colleagues, her only link to Lauren, had used their combined skills and knowledge and had come up blank. Unless she could uncover a lead, where would she even start? Looking around, Grace felt the room's adequate walls were closing in on her.

The one piece of information she had was where the police had discovered Lauren's car, parked outside a church on the aptly named Church Road. Manderson said they assumed it was near where she lived, which sounded plausible. Park on the street where it was free, walk home a short distance making sure nobody followed you. It did make Lauren sound paranoid, but given what had happened it looked as if she had justification.

The hotel where Grace was staying was a twenty-minute drive from Church Road. Needing to get out of the room, to do something, she drove there, parking where the police had found Lauren's car. On the footpath, she scanned the environment. St James Anglican Church and its parklike cemetery grounds dominated one side of the street. The other side contained an eclectic mix of suburban housing – from "picture-perfect home" to "unpolished gem".

Pushing her sunglasses onto the top of her head, she said to herself, 'The person we're looking for, Watson, is over six foot, left-handed and walks with a limp.' Her laughed turned into a sigh – what was she expecting to see?

Deciding to make her trip worthwhile, she strolled to the church. Pushing open the heavy wooden door, she stepped back in time. Stone walls, the smell of furniture polish, wooden pews, plush but well-trudged carpet, with an ornate altar at the end of the long rectangular room. In the silence, the scene was more nineteenth century than twenty-first.

'Can I help you?'

'Jesus,' said Grace, involuntarily stepping away from the voice. A man had appeared out of nowhere and was standing smiling by her side.

'Not quite, sorry to disappoint you. I'm the senior priest here at St James.'

Heavily bearded and wearing jeans, a collared shirt, cheese-cutter cap and glasses, he looked nothing like Grace's vision of a senior priest. He did, however, look a little like Jesus.

Recovering her poise, she said, 'Sorry. Kia ora, I'm Grace Marks.'

'Kia ora, Grace. Have you come in for a particular reason?'

Pressing her lips together, she said, 'This might sound odd, but I was wondering if you'd noticed a car parked on the street outside your church. It was −'

'A grey Holden?'

A journalistic tingle of excitement snaked through Grace. 'That's the one.'

'Yes, I saw it quite often. Few people visit in the morning, so it was noticeable. Is there a problem?'

'Um … No. It's my friend's car.'

The senior priest employed a well-practised smile. 'Oh, yes.' His tone suggested he was thinking − *I know you're lying, but I hear a lot of lies.*

'Confession time,' said Grace. 'Well, sort of. I'm a journalist and the car belongs to a woman I was helping write a story − a woman who's gone missing.'

'Oh.'

Grace wasn't sure if he was surprised by what she said or that she wasn't lying.

'Did you ever see the driver of the car?'

'Yes, but infrequently. We'd say hello if we passed each other.'

'You didn't −'

He cut in again. 'No, I never talked to her beyond saying hello.'

'Did you see which way she went after she parked?'

His face creased. 'Not after she parked, but I saw her walking *to* her car some mornings. She arrived from that way.' He pointed out the window. 'Like she was walking to the shops. She would do a U-turn when she left, if the traffic wasn't busy.'

A few more questions revealed that was all he knew and a satisfied Grace went back to her car. Lauren lived somewhere in front of her. Her doing a U-turn in the morning fitted as that was the way to the Weeping Angels' operation centre. After studying the area using Google maps, she drove the neighbourhood in a haphazard grid pattern. When cars weren't behind her, she drove slowly, looking at the houses.

After driving around in ever decreasing circles, she pulled over. 'Marla sure-as-hell wouldn't be doing *this*.' The street she had stopped on stretched away in front of her, unemptied wheelie bins outside many houses. Before she headed back to the hotel, she drove back down Church Road, where the scene was unchanged though more wheelie bins had appeared.

'Maybe,' she said. 'It can't hurt.'

As she drove back to the hotel, she decided she needed to have a serious planning session – with a glass of wine.

CHAPTER 17

Grace woke early with a dry mouth, the result of one too many wines in the house bar as she'd forestalled her return to the claustrophobic room. She hadn't slept well, having woken several times during the night, the alcohol combining with her mind restlessly chewing over events. Deciding to attack the day early, after showering, devouring a large hot breakfast at the hotel's breakfast buffet, checking emails – disappointingly there had been no email from Marla – and dropping her card-key into the hotel's drop box, she headed back to Church Road. Unless she discovered new information, staying in Auckland was pointless.

Dressed as though she was going jogging – sunglasses, cap, hoodie, three-quarter leggings and shorts – it was 7:15am when she once again parked outside St James Anglican Church. Her plan was to observe the comings and goings near the church, near where Lauren parked. She hoped to identify utility vehicles, like council rubbish trucks emptying wheelie bins, and see if the crew remembered seeing Lauren – what street she may have come from. It was a longshot.

At 7.25am a large green rubbish truck headed towards her position, emptying bins on the other side of the street. She nipped deftly across the road and stood near a wheelie bin in the truck's path. Grace had no idea how this would play out.

The lefthand drive truck stopped directly in front of her, the driver metres away. Glaring down at Grace from the cab was a young, tough-looking woman in a high-viz vest, her cap on backwards. Clearly unused to interruptions in her schedule, she looked at Grace as though she'd rather tip her into the truck than talk.

Taking off her sunglasses, Grace had to shout over the noise of the engine. 'I'd like to ask you a quick question.'

Turning back to her controls, in an out-of-place Australian accent, the driver said, 'Ring the 0800 number, lady. I don't organise *beens*.'

The truck's mechanical arm shot out, grabbing the bin as Grace semi-yelled, 'I don't need a … bin.' The truck consumed the bin's contents like a thirsty drinker draining the last drop from their glass. 'I'm looking for information. Do you do this run every day?'

The driver's eyes narrowed. 'Why?'

'It's all right, I'm not with the police. I'm a journalist.' Stepping closer, she held out her phone showing the driver a picture of a similar car to Lauren's. 'A car like this usually parked by the church. Can you remember seeing it? You might have seen a woman getting in, going to work? I'm hoping you might have seen which street she usually came from.'

The driver's face contorted as though Grace had asked her to solve a quadratic equation. 'I dunno lady, there are cars all over the place. That doesn't ring any bells.'

Grace looked around, seeing the scene through the driver's eyes. Blowing out a tired breath, she said, 'Thanks, it was a longshot.'

As the truck lurched to the next bin, Grace put her sunglasses back on. It was a longshot all right, what now? A woman walking her dog stopped on the footpath next to her. Grace smiled briefly, concentrating on the small black and white dog who was wagging its tail desperately. As Grace crouched to pat the dog, the woman took off her cap and, in a slight American accent, asked, 'What did you get?'

Standing, Grace said, 'Sorry?'

The well-tanned woman, her face hidden behind sunglasses and sporting a jet-black crewcut, said, 'From the driver. I mean, why would anyone interrupt a random garbage collector unless you hoped she had information?'

Grace stared, her mouth open as she recognised that former US Marine and agent for hire Marla Simmons had once more dropped into her life, out of thin air. The same height but leaner than Grace, a grinning Marla looked like a suburban dogwalker in her jean shorts and a loose, long-sleeved T-shirt. Not even her crewcut would get her a second look.

'What the fuck,' said Grace. 'How?'

Putting her cap back on, Marla smiled broadly. 'It's great to see you too, Ace.'

Dozens of emotions ran through Grace; the main ones were relief and confusion. They hugged warmly. The last time Grace had seen her was a year ago, outside a pub in Paraparaumu. To her knowledge, Marla should be hiding in the South Island.

Marla picked up her dog. 'Indy, this is Ace. You didn't get to meet her last time.'

Indy tilted her head and stared at Grace. Scratching the dog's head, Grace said, 'You're okay, Indy. I'm the one who has no idea what's going on.'

'I know you'll have a few questions,' said Marla, 'I have too, but let's get off the street, go somewhere quieter. I doubt New Zealand's facial-recognition surveillance net is complete … yet, but I like to lessen my exposure.' Indicating Grace's car across the street, Marla asked, 'Is that a rental?'

Grace nodded.

'We'll use that, it's bland and anonymous. Who's paying?'

'RNZ.'

'Even better. I'll just get my bag.'

Handing over Indy's lead, Marla headed back the way she had come, turning down a side street. A few minutes later, she threw her bag into the back next to Indy and got in the front.

'I see you've gone back to your army look,' said Grace. 'You had a crewcut the first time we met – when I all but dropped dead of fright.'

Smiling and taking her cap off, Marla rubbed her head. 'Given there's no chance I'm dating anytime soon, this takes no looking after.'

Attractive, in different circumstances Marla would be sought after. Grace was about to say as much, when Indy interrupted. Standing with her paws on the centre console, as if she was on Pride Rock, she let out a long, lupine note.

Marla and Grace shared a look.

'I don't think Thelma and Louise had a dog,' said Grace.

Indy howled again as Grace started the car.

CHAPTER 18

Sitting in the back of the nearly empty café – most customers bought savouries, sandwiches and energy drinks to go – Grace brought Marla up to speed. She covered Lauren's background and the events that led to her disappearance as Marla tucked into breakfast. Grace, still full from her hangover-nullifying hotel buffet, had coffee. Marla ate and listened, not asking any questions until Grace had finished the briefing.

Pushing aside her empty plate, Marla asked, 'You're confident her colleagues can't add more?'

Grace nodded. 'I'm pretty sure. I only spoke with one but it sounded like they had worked together, had sprung into action and had come up empty handed. I didn't get a sense Trudi was holding back or had any suspicions she was keeping to herself – she seemed keen to tell me everything she knew.'

'Good enough,' said Marla. 'Think back. You spent a lot of time with Lauren, possibly on the day she disappeared. What did she mention that we can use?'

Grace went to speak, but Marla stood. 'I need another coffee.'

Grace smiled. Marla might want another coffee, but she really wanted her to take her time, to think hard.

'Anything?' asked Marla, having waited at the counter for the young server to make her coffee.

Grace grinned. 'Lauren and I mainly talked about their operation and stories that would add pressure on the Government to review the justice system. She talked about her advisor, the Carter I mentioned, but I didn't know at the time that I needed to dig out information on him.'

'What have you remembered?' said Marla, one eyebrow raised.

'When we went for dinner, it was awkward to start with. You know, no matter whether it's boy-girl, girl-girl or boy-boy, a business dinner always feels like a weird date. We chatted a bit and I remembered that she had told me she does karate, we discussed that.'

Marla asked, 'Did it feel like a date?'

'No, but the atmosphere in restaurant – low lights, romantic music.'

'I guess,' said Marla. 'If she's attending karate classes, we might have a lead.'

'She said she's actively training, but not the name of the club.'

'On the assumption she would've chosen a club nearby,' said Marla, 'there can't be many candidates.' Clearing a space for her laptop, she went to work. 'What we'll do is start where her car was parked and identify karate clubs nearby.'

'Sounds like a plan,' said Grace. 'Will they divulge private information about their members?'

Marla shook her head. 'No. That, and given how cautious she sounds, there's a strong possibility she'd have registered under a different name.'

As Marla worked her laptop, a dim light went on for Grace. 'We can check which nights they have adult training. Lauren said she trained Mondays and Thursdays.'

'That might work,' said Marla. 'I can check their website first, if they have one.' After numerous clicks and taps, she said, 'The closest club doesn't have a website.' She read out their contact number, Grace dialled.

A chirpy, Kiwi-male voice said, 'You've got the karate club, how can I help.'

'Hi. I'm new to Auckland and wanted to know what nights you ran adult training classes?'

'Have you trained before?'

'Not for a while. I was a blue belt,' said Grace.

'Do you know the style of your dojo?'

'Wadō-ryū.'

'Our style is based on Shotokan, they're similar but different. It'll take you a while to change techniques, but you'll get there. We train Tuesdays and Fridays; how does that work?'

'Not bad. Fridays might be an issue.'

'If it works, turn up and have a thrash. The first session is free.'

Grace terminated the call. In answer to Marla's raised eyebrows, she said, 'Tuesdays and Fridays.'

Grace repeated a variation of the conversation twice more until Marla found what they hoped was the jackpot on a club's website – if the Monday-Thursday combination wasn't common.

'Jyoshinmon shōrin-ryū.' Grace pronounced the words carefully. 'That's a mouthful. If Lauren trained there, they might have her address or someone might know her.'

'Let's hope it's not a dead end,' said Marla. 'It's skinny, but the next closest club, assuming Lauren lives close to where the police found her car, is much further away. We can also check whether her colleagues train there.'

'Why?' asked Grace.

'I'm sure they would have mentioned that they trained with her when they were racking their brains.'

'Glad to have you aboard,' said Grace. Marla seldom spoke about her life – past or present – but during the time they had spent together, Grace had learned that Marla had once been a highly regarded agent in a shadowy part of the US spy administration. She knew how to find people.

'Can you ring whoever you talked to at her work?' asked Marla. 'See if anyone is a member at that club or did karate with Lauren.'

Grace pulled out her notepad, finding Trudi's number. She answered immediately, saying she didn't think so but would send out a group message. Grace relayed this information to Marla before saying, 'And I completely forgot, how the … did you know where I was? And how did you get here so fast? I thought you were living in the South Island.'

Marla glanced at her watch. Packing up her laptop, she said, 'Come on, we've outstayed our welcome.'

Grace went to protest, but Marla was already making for the door. Shaking her head, and giving Marla's back the evils, she followed her out of the café.

In the car, Grace said, 'We're not going anywhere until you tell me how you knew I'd be waiting for the bin lady.'

Marla put on a serious look as Indy leapt into her lap. She took a napkin from her pocket – Indy devouring the bacon she had saved. After fussing with the dirty napkin while Grace glared, Marla finally said, 'Okay, okay. Drive us back to the church, I'll tell you on the way.'

Grace continued to glare but started the car and headed back to Church Road. In truth, she was delighted Marla was with her, but she was also damn curious.

Once they were under way, Marla said, 'You left a message through our … what did you call it? The bat phone?'

'Not my finest linguistic work,' said Grace.

'I got an alert straight away. I set it up that way in case time was a factor. Now, and don't take this the wrong way, Ace, ninety-nine percent of me considered your message kosher.'

'I'm surprised it was that high,' said Grace.

'I was being polite. I searched through your stories and I didn't see an obvious link to a disappearance. You told me you were in Auckland, I tried to narrow your location from your message, but you used a Tor browser – well done. So, I asked your partner, Sean.'

'What? He didn't tell me you contacted him?'

'He doesn't know.'

Grace shook her head.

'I spoofed your email address,' said Marla.

'What?'

'I created an email address close to yours.' Answering Grace's brief stare, she said, 'It's not hard. Dozens of websites let you do it.'

'And he replied?'

'Sure. He thought he was replying to you.'

'Why didn't I get the email?'

'Because the reply address was different, one that I could access. He didn't look closely. Busy people don't.'

'That's so wrong. What did you ask him?'

Closing her eyes for an instant, she said, 'Just dashing out, can you find the nearest street to the hotel that has free parking?'

Grace rolled her eyes.

'I figured you would have rung him from the hotel, let him know where you were staying. Anyway, I arrived before six this morning. Indy and I wandered through the carpark making a note of the rental cars.'

'Clever dog,' said Grace.

Marla laughed. 'Rentals usually have advertising on the licence plate surrounds. There were a few, so I waited. Then I saw you leave, alone and with no tail. I followed you.'

'It all sounds so simple. But how did you get here so fast?'

'That was the lucky bit. You're right, I am living in Te Waipounamu but, because I'm part artist, part lady-of-leisure, part bored-af, I was on, what do you call it, a tiki tour?'

Grace smiled.

'I was in Taupō —'

'*Tow paw*, listen to you,' cut in Grace. 'Are you taking lessons?'

'Sort of. When I walk Indy, I've been listening to *Māori Made Easy*.'

'That's awesome,' said Grace. 'If only everyone had your attitude. A few simple steps, an open mind — and ka pai.'

Grace's phone pinged. Glancing at her phone, she said, 'It's from Trudi.' At the next set of traffic lights, Grace read the message. 'No one does karate with Lauren or attends that dojo.'

'That's great,' said Marla. 'As a lead, it just got stronger. Let's head there after tonight's training, see what we can find out.'

For the second time that morning, Grace parked outside St James Anglican Church. She turned to Marla, who had been joined in the front by Indy. 'What now?'

After looking around, Marla said, 'We're going to need a bit of luck, that's what now.'

Grace waited while Marla put Indy on a lead and rummaged through her bag, stuffing green plastic poo bags into her pocket.

'What's the plan?' asked Grace.

'First,' said Marla, 'which way do you think Lauren walked home?'

Grace beamed, pointing at the houses bordering the far end of the cemetery. 'The senior priest in the church said she came from that way in the morning.'

'That limits our search zone.' Marla looked the other way. 'It makes sense, too. That way leads to shops.'

'I drove around a bit,' said Grace. 'Once you get past the cemetery, it's vanilla suburbia.'

As they walked towards the houses, Indy trotting in the lead, Grace asked, 'What are you hoping to find? A letterbox with her name on it?'

Marla took off her sunglasses. 'I wish. No, I'm trying to get a feel for how far she'd walk to feel safe. My gut feel says she lives on a side street. That makes a visible disconnect between her home and car – no chance of a tail parking near her car and seeing which is her house.'

'We just passed a side street,' said Grace.

'I know, it was too soon, too obvious. This next one, this feels better.'

Stopping at the corner, Marla looked slowly in all directions.

'You think she lives on this street?' Grace asked, her voice echoing her doubt.

Shrugging, Marla said, 'It's about the right distance but it's an educated guess, at best.'

'Are we going to take a look?'

Marla shook her head. 'I'm good, but I'm not psychic.'

Grace frowned. 'I drove down this street yesterday. I don't see how we're getting closer unless we let Indy see if she can sniff out her place.'

'Sorry,' said Marla stretching in the warm sun. 'It was an early start. I should've let you know what I was thinking. My hunch is that this street is *around* the limit where Lauren would have walked. Maybe a little further. Now, we're going to walk back and look for security cameras facing the street.'

Grace, feeling a little chastened, said, 'Ahh. That's great … and fucking ironic. We can use the same surveillance systems that almost got us both killed.'

'True,' said Marla. 'With any luck, we'll only need to find one.'

Crossing the road, they walked slowly, studying each house carefully as Indy tugged on her lead.

'There,' said Marla, indicating a house where a device that resembled a Dalek's eye from *Doctor Who* sat malevolently under the house's eave.

'It looks new,' said Grace. 'Bound to be high-def. A recent install because of the urban panic the Americans instilled throughout society. How do you plan to access its feed?'

'I'm going to take over a satellite, use it to interrogate the system, uncover the MAC address of the device, tunnel in –'

'Very funny,' cut in Grace. 'I thought you were serious for a second.'

Marla smirked. 'You've come on in leaps and bounds since we first met. Then you didn't know the difference between a dongle and a nibble.'

'I still don't,' said Grace. 'A nibble, that's IT geeks for you. Let's use a word that sounds like nipple. Tee-hee.'

Marla shook her head. 'No. A nibble is four bits: half a byte.'

Grace grinned. 'That's actually clever, though most IT jargon is created by aged adolescent nerds who think knob gags are funny.'

'Pretty much,' said Marla. 'Blame Gates, he was the world's biggest nerd.'

'And knob,' added Grace. 'So how?'

'Sometimes old-fashioned methods are best,' said Marla. 'Do you have your official media ID on you?'

'Always.'

'Cool. We're going to knock on the door, explain what we're doing and ask if they'll let us look through their files.'

'That should work.'

The house's driveway was empty and there were no windows open.

After knocking three times, the last time loud and a little desperate to Grace's ear, they wandered back to the street.

'Let's keep looking,' said Marla as she photographed the house's letterbox with her phone. 'We can come back if we need to.'

Two houses further down they saw the same model of HD surveillance camera installed under the eaves of a two-storey house.

'It would've been the same company,' said Grace. 'An agent going door-to-door.'

'At that height,' said Marla, 'it'll capture a lot of the street.'

Staring at the camera, Grace said, 'I know they shouldn't be, but do you think the feeds from all these cameras are being captured and analysed by US or Five Eyes algorithms?'

Marla pressed her lips together. 'Right now, I'm not sure. In the future, it's guaranteed. There'll be a false flag, the government will proclaim that they need to protect the population from subversives and people will abandon their privacy rights *en masse*. As you know, if you have nothing to hide ...'

'You have nothing to fear.' Grace finished the mantra used internationally to placate citizens. 'It's guaranteed, isn't it? What'll you do when they install cameras where you live?'

'There'll always be large pockets they can't cover,' she said. 'You know, like the mobile phone network – ninety-seven percent of the population get coverage but that equates to only fifty percent geographically.'

'They're trying to extend that as we speak,' said Grace.

'I know, I've been keeping an eye on developments. I'll find dead zones in which to live or maybe the US will have reigned in their rogue agencies and I'll be free to travel again.' Marla finished her sentence with a hopeful eyebrow raise.

'That's a slogan for the "yeah-right" marketers,' said Grace.

Marla's face changed to puzzled.

'Never mind,' said Grace. 'As much as I'd like to think society is developing towards a utopian future, as long as the rich are in charge we're fucked.'

'Let's keep the Nietzschean philosophy for –'

'When we have wine?' cut in Grace.

'Pretty much. While we've been chatting, the blinds in the house moved – someone's home.'

This time the door opened almost before Grace had knocked. Blocking the entire doorframe, his face serious and suspicious, was a middle-aged Polynesian man. He wasn't fat, though he wasn't thin either. Solid was the word that sprang to Grace's mind. He reminded her of her partner's retired rugby-playing friends who hadn't dialled back their calorie intake.

'What'ch you want?' He eyed them hard, his face softening when Indy stepped forwards and looked up at him quizzically.

Although they hadn't discussed their roles, it was natural for Grace to do the talking. Holding out her ID, she said 'Kia ora, I'm Grace Marks. I'm a journalist with RNZ. This is –'

'Kia ora,' interrupted Marla. 'I'm Norma. I help on the technical side of news stories.'

The man gave them a grudging nod. 'What'ch you want with me?'

'Shift yourself, Dad.' The voice came from behind the man, though it was impossible to make out who was speaking. 'It's Ace Marks. She's brilliant.'

The man took three awkward steps backwards, supporting himself with a walking stick, his left foot encased in a black moonboot. Barging around the bulk of his father, a young man came beaming into view.

Snatching Grace's ID, he read it with obvious delight. Handing it back, he said, 'Ace Marks, at my house. We've studied your stories in class.'

Grace smiled uncertainly. Although used to the odd person recognising her name, this was next level. The young man, dressed in designer ripped jeans and a T-shirt, seemed to recognise her confusion.

'Sorry. I'm Josh. I'm studying comms and journalism at uni. This *curmudgeon* is my Dad, Kevin, but everyone calls him KT. Come in.'

Josh half helped half shoved his dad back inside. Soon they were sitting around the kitchen table having declined hot drinks.

'What happened to your foot?' asked Grace.

'I twisted it jumping out of my truck's cab.'

Josh grinned. 'He was in a rush to get a pie.'

'Oi.' His dad's parental voice came out as a low growl.

Grace and Marla smiled.

'How's the study going?' asked Marla.

Josh made a so-so face. 'I'm doing well, and I love the subject, but most of the third-year classes are online. It makes it as boring AF. If I'd known, I would've gone to Auckland Uni. I went to uni to meet other students –'

'To chase skirt.' His dad cut in, looking pleased to get his own back, before his eyes widened. 'Sorry ladies, no offence meant.'

'You're safe, KT,' said Grace laughing. 'Unlike much of the world, I still have a strong non-PC sense of humour.'

Saving Grace from having to focus the conversation, Josh asked, 'So what are you here for?'

'We're working on a story about a missing person,' said Grace.

Josh put his elbows on the table, frowning. His dad sat back, arms crossed, serious.

Holding up a placating hand, Grace said, 'We know you're not involved, it's just that her car was found parked over the road, opposite the church.'

'You have a security camera covering the street,' said Marla. 'We hoped you might have caught her on film so we can get a clue as to what might have happened.'

Josh, his excitement having returned, looked as his dad. 'Is it still working?'

KT shrugged his enormous shoulders. 'It should be. We stopped paying for the monitoring when our free credit ran out. We used to look at what happened in the neighbourhood when we first got it installed, but not much happened – it was a waste of money. Why don't you go to the police?'

While Grace explained the police's low level of interest in missing persons, Josh left the room, returning with a laptop. After he exchanged comments, barbs and laughter with his dad over the password, Josh gained access. 'Yeah, the files are here. It looks like the system keeps them for thirty days.'

Grace glanced at Marla, who appeared eager to take control of the laptop.

'Lauren, that's the missing woman,' said Grace, 'dropped me off at 8.30 and was visiting a friend. She would've parked later, after 10pm last Friday.'

Josh clicked and tapped then pushed the laptop into the middle of the table. Grace and Marla moved their chairs together and leaned closer. The image was dark and grainy but there was sufficient streetlight to make out what was happening. The camera's field captured Church Road in both directions, further than they had walked.

'Can you speed up the action, Josh?' asked Marla.

'Sure.'

Josh played the recording at times three. Cars roared along the street as though it was a seldom-used motorway. The time in the bottom corner counted the night away. Twelve o'clock. One o'clock. Lauren had to have parked there, though it could have been any time before the police found her car.

Two o'clock rolled by.

At 2.17 a car whizzed into the frame and parked opposite the church.

'There,' everyone called out.

Josh paused the action. 'Is that it?'

'That's it,' said Grace staring at the screen.

Josh let the action resume at normal speed. For over a minute the image remained static, they could see Lauren sitting in her car, the flashes of light indicating she was likely on her phone. Then the driver's door opened ...

'What the fuck,' said Grace softly.

Josh paused the recording.

A person had got out of the car and walked to the footpath. Although the image was far from crisp, the person had short hair and was wearing a dark-coloured jacket and loose-fitting pants.

They all stared, KT struggling awkwardly around to look, at the image of what was clearly a man walking away from Lauren's car. The only sound was KT's tutting.

They collectively sat back.

'Marla?' said Grace.

Her face expressionless, Marla said, 'Unless Lauren has quite the backstory, it doesn't look good. It narrows the timeframe, though. Lauren disappeared between after she dropped you at 8.30pm and around two in the morning. Let the action run Josh, let's see what happens.'

The man walked briskly along Church Road, past Scott Avenue and down Tainui Terrace – the street Marla had identified as the one that Lauren might take. They continued to watch but the man didn't reappear.

'Speed it up again Josh,' said Marla.

They stared at the corner of Tainui Terrace and Church Road as the minutes passed by in seconds. Nothing of consequence happened. As the image lightened towards dawn, cars drove by more frequently and people started appearing in the street. The recording stopped at midday.

'Can you put that file on a flash drive, Josh?' asked Marla.

'Sure.'

Grace dug around in her bag, handing over one of the many she carried.

'Copy the files from the week before as well as up to today, please Josh,' said Grace. 'The police may want to have a look at them. I certainly do.'

After Josh had copied the files, Marla asked him to play one from the previous Friday. The action was similar, except Lauren's car arrived at 7.30 in the evening. This time a recognisable Lauren got out, walking in the same direction. And like the man who had driven her car a week later, she disappeared down Tainui Terrace.

'What do you think?' asked Grace.

Marla went to speak, but it was Josh who answered. 'Either it's a coincidence or he knew where your friend lived. That's where he was heading.'

Marla smiled at Josh. 'That's my gut feel too. We know Lauren was security conscious. Even though he had to have had her car keys, my money's on her having a working security system. That might've stymied him.'

'But who is he? And where did he go, though?' asked Grace. 'After, I mean.'

'Picked up nearby,' said Marla. 'A secluded spot, well away from her car and house. As for who he is …'

'She dropped you off at 8.30,' said Josh, 'but the man doesn't arrive here until 2.17. That's a big gap.'

'She said she was going to visiting a friend, Tana,' said Grace.

'It's a common name,' said KT. 'Do you know anything more about him?'

Grace shook her head slowly.

'What are you going to do?' asked Josh.

'Right now,' said Marla, 'Grace and I are going for a stroll down Tainui Terrace.'

CHAPTER 20

'She could live in any of them,' said Grace.

'That's assuming she lives on Tainui Terrace,' said Marla.

They had just walked slowly along the short street, returning to the middle where they stood surveying the houses. Indy, having given two dogs a piece of her mind from the safety of the other side of a fence, sat looking pleased with herself.

Marla clucked her tongue. 'I know I keep saying it, but this feels right. If she'd lived further away, I think she would've parked closer. She was carrying a laptop and groceries the previous Friday.'

'Throw in bad weather,' said Grace.

Checking her watch, Marla said, 'It's nearly three, what time does karate training finish?'

'Their website said eight. I didn't see any security cameras on these houses, did you?'

'Not a security camera,' said Marla, 'but I saw a video doorbell.'

'Really?'

Marla pointed at the house across the street

Grace's eyes widened as she looked. 'I see it. I've been reading about them. Yet another insidious way mass surveillance is creeping into society. I didn't think they were popular here.'

'I don't think they are, yet,' said Marla. 'But what's the easiest way to keep a watchful eye on every street?'

'Stick a video camera on everyone's front door,' said Grace. 'Fuck, we are so doomed. *And* we're paying for the privilege of imprisoning ourselves.'

Marla said, 'Everyone carries their global position in their back pocket. Soon security cameras will record people everywhere they go. But, if you have nothing to hide —'

Grace cut in, this time saying, 'The arseholes will invent probable cause, bend you over the table and —'

'Yes,' said Marla quickly, 'they likely will. You're involved in the campaign for an independent authority to monitor the privacy of information, how's that going?'

Grace groaned. 'Slowly. People still have this 1950s faith that it "couldn't happen in New Zealand". Fifty people murdered in a terrorist attack – not in New Zealand. The police trial facial recognition technology, take photos of Māori youths for a dodgy database – not in New Zealand. It's happening in New Zealand – wake the fuck up, people.'

Marla grinned. 'They'll make a statue of you one day and underneath they'll write, *We should've listened!*'

Grace laughed. 'Famous after I'm dead, probably rich too. Fucking typical.'

'Anyway,' said Marla. 'Let's see if anyone's home.'

They followed the unblemished concrete path, around the manicured lawn, past sculpted topiary and blooming roses, to the red-brick house's front door, where the owner had trained wisteria. A real estate agent would have described it as 'neat as a pin'.

Indicating the doorbell, Marla said, 'See, the video camera is aimed at the street.'

Leaning close, Grace pulled a face into the camera. Just as she was about to push the button, a scolding woman's voice assaulted her.

'I saw you pull that face.'

'Shit,' said Grace taking an involuntary step back.

Marla choked back laughter.

The voice, shrill and metallic through the speaker, was clearly that of an older woman, the prim tone suggesting a former teacher. 'What do you want?'

Recovering her poise, she said, 'Hi. I'm Grace Marks. I'm a –'

The voice promptly cut her off. 'Graham Sparks? You don't look like a Graham to me.'

Grace could hear Marla, who had ducked behind her, trying to keep it together.

'No.' Speaking slowly, Grace said, 'Grace Marks. I'm a –'

'Where did that other woman go?'

Grace heard Marla blow out a steadying breath as she emerged.

'I'm right here. I'm Norma Smith. Who are we speaking with, please?'

'My name is Glenda Wiffen.'

'It's lovely to meet you Glenda,' said Marla. 'We're –'

'Speak up. This stupid thing isn't loud enough.'

Marla bent towards the doorbell. 'We're journalists. We're searching for a missing person and your camera might have recorded her walking past.'

'Camera? What camera? I don't have a camera.'

'The one you're using to look at us now,' said Marla.

'Oh. Why didn't you say?'

They heard prolonged shuffling and the unbolting of locks, then the door opened. The woman, a broad smile on her face, with her glasses hanging around her neck on a chain, was indeed elderly, white and dressed in numerous layers and shades of blue. Her face lit up when she saw Indy. 'I didn't see your little dog. What's her name? Please, come in.'

Mirroring its outside, the house's interior was immaculate, as though Glenda was in the middle of running an open home. As they went into the lounge, Grace saw an open laptop on the dining table, presumably where Glenda sat when screening visitors. They refused multiple offers of tea and treats for Indy. Glenda's hearing wasn't the best but she persisted, and eventually they were sitting in her lounge, each with a cup of tea. She had maintained a solid one-way narrative about her health as she made the hot drinks. At one point she was clearly explaining the problem with her hip to Indy.

'I don't get many visitors these days,' she said. 'My son installed the video doorbell thingy so I wouldn't have to open the door to strangers.'

'That's wise,' said Marla.

'Now, how can I help you, dears?' Looking over her glasses, she added, 'Are you lesbians, by the way?'

The question came from so far left of field that Grace had to gulp down her mouthful of hot tea. Coughing she said, 'No, no – we're colleagues.'

'Oh.' Glenda's eyebrows shot up. 'You look like lesbians.'

Grace, mouth open, was lost for words. She could see that Marla was having to concentrate hard to keep a straight face.

Glenda, unaware of the impact her questions were having, kept on talking. 'Not that there's anything wrong with that. I've often thought I should've been a lesbian. I would've looked good with short hair, but we didn't have them in my day. Men are tolerable but terribly untidy with that' – she waved a hand in the air – 'thing dangling about and them weeing on the floor. I mean, why can't they sit down? What's wrong with them?'

'I … I don't know,' said Grace, composing herself. Glenda went to speak, but Grace knew she needed to take control of the conversation or risk being there for hours. 'We're looking for a missing person who might live on this street. Does your doorbell camera record when it detects motion.'

'That's right,' she said. 'My son set it up to send me a message when someone's at the door. I'll show you.'

They exercised their patience as Glenda first found her phone, unlocked it and opened the app. 'See.' She held the phone towards them. It showed a close-up image of Grace's contorted face. The message read *There's someone at the Front Door*.

Glenda beamed at Grace. 'I bet you won't do *that* again.'

They all laughed.

'Does it detect cars?' asked Grace. 'I mean, wouldn't it be sending you alerts all the time?'

'It did. I had to get my son to fix it. Now it only alerts me when it detects people – no cars or cats.'

'Clever,' said Grace.

Frowning, Marla took over. 'Can we have a look at the images on your laptop? We're hoping you recorded the person we're looking for. It might help us find her.'

'Sure,' said Glenda. 'My son wrote down how I can look at the images but I've never bothered.' She picked up a small pad from the coffee table, handing it to Marla.

Marla waited patiently as Glenda unlocked her laptop, which she managed after a couple of attempts. Marla's fingers danced over the keyboard like a concert pianist until the screen displayed a long list of files.

'This one,' said Marla. '2.22am Saturday morning.'

She double clicked the file and a box opened showing a night view of Tainui Terrace. The video ran for just over thirty seconds.

'I didn't see anyone,' said Grace.

'I didn't either, but the camera did, it wouldn't have recorded otherwise.' Marla replayed the video. 'There.' Manually moving the video back, she froze it and pointed to the edge of the image. It was dark, and the driveway of the house across the street had trees with overhanging branches, but Grace could make out the outline of a person. As Marla inched the action forwards, the man jumped over the low gate and was swallowed by the darkness.

'That's him,' said Grace. 'So, that's Lauren's house?'

'It has to be,' said Marla. 'No other explanation makes sense.'

'Did you find something?' asked Glenda, who had been patting Indy.

'We did,' said Grace. 'Could I get another tea please?'

Glenda beamed. 'Of course.' She bustled off to the kitchen, Indy in hot pursuit.

'Pass me your flash drive,' said Marla. 'I'll copy the files then ask, I'm sure she'll say yes.' Taking the drive from Grace, Marla started copying the files. 'He stayed for four minutes. The next recording happened at 2.26.'

The second recording showed the same man emerging from the driveway, walking away confidently along the street in the opposite direction to which he had come. He took an object out of his pocket which illuminated the outline of his face – his mobile phone. He was talking on his phone as he disappeared out of shot.

'There must be recordings of Lauren arriving home,' said Marla. She opened several files but none featured Lauren or Lauren's house.

Marla looked at Grace, who shrugged.

Glenda came back in with Grace's tea.

'Do you mind if I copy these files?' asked Marla.

'Not at all. I hope they help you find your missing friend.'

Grace glanced at Marla, who gave her a confirming eyebrow raise.

'We need to get going soon, Glenda,' said Grace taking the steaming cup from her. 'Before we do, how well do you know your neighbours?'

'Very well. Most of them, like me, have lived here for years. Why?'

'We're interested in the person who lives in a house across the street. I'll show you which one.'

Outside, Grace pointed to the house that the man who had driven Lauren's car had visited for four minutes. 'Do you know much about the person who lives there?'

'That was Patrick's house. He bought it around the time we bought ours. Lovely man, he was a butcher. His wife died early, cancer. They didn't have children. Strange.'

'How long ago did he move?' asked Marla.

'No, he passed away. Gosh, it was a while ago, at least five years. Let me see. My son's marriage, his first one that is, was in trouble so he was staying with me. His first wife, she was a piece of work, let me tell you, only wanted him for –'

Grace interrupted as gently as she could. 'Who lives there now?'

Glenda stood up straight, pulled back from her memories. 'Oh, hmmm. I'm not sure I know. It's kept tidy, and I see lights on from time to time, but … I'm not sure I can remember seeing anyone, not recently anyway.'

'Who didn't you see recently?' asked Marla.

'Well, when they first moved in, a Pasifika family arrived in a courier van. I say Pasifika, two of the women looked European. I thought it must be a *blended* family as two of the two girls were tall, tanned and athletic. The other girl, well, she was white and skinny – pretty, but she looked the odd one out. The man was built like a brick outhouse, he couldn't have … Well, you know.'

Grace and Marla smiled.

Getting Lauren's photo out, Grace asked, 'Was she one of the women?'

After studying the photo intently with ample muttering, she said, 'She could have been. Anyway, they must have bought Patrick's place, but I only ever saw them the once or twice early on. Not that I minded who was moving in.' Glenda made a disparaging noise. 'Some numpties have a problem with skin colour. Imagine, in this day and age.'

'You're spot on there, Glenda,' said Grace. 'How often do you see the gate open?'

Her faced creased, she said slowly, 'I can't remember ever seeing it left open. Gardening and lawn mowing people come regularly, that's why it looks so tidy.'

Grace glanced at Marla, receiving a second confirmatory eyebrow raise.

'Thanks Glenda, you've been super helpful,' said Grace, gulping down her tea.

'That's quite all right,' she said, giving Indy a final pat.

'Do you want to have a look at the house?' asked Grace when they were back on the street.

'Maybe later. It's not going anywhere and I reckon the system that put off whoever visited will mean we'll struggle to get in without a security firm turning up. I think I know why there are no videos of Lauren leaving or coming home.'

'Go on,' said Grace.

Pointing, Marla said, 'See that gate?' On the far left of the fence was a small pedestrian gate partially hidden by tree branches. 'It must be out of the security camera's field of view. The man who visited, he couldn't have seen it because he jumped the gate across the driveway.'

'He was only just in the shot,' said Grace nodding.

'That makes it work,' said Marla. 'Right, we've plenty of time before karate training finishes to organise dinner. What do you fancy?'

'Anything,' said Grace. 'All that tea, I need a wee.'

CHAPTER 21

'How do you want to handle this?' asked Grace.

Over dinner, Grace having used the restaurant's bathroom as soon as possible after placing her order, they decided to visit the karate dojo at the end of training when the *sensei*, the martial arts instructor, would be available to talk. With over an hour to wait, they headed back to what they were sure was Lauren's house to see if they could learn anything.

'Park in her driveway like we're visiting,' said Marla. 'I'll open the gate. People take little notice of everyday events. We'll look like a couple of real estate agents.'

'Lesbian ones,' said Grace looking around. 'If everyone in the neighbourhood thinks like Glenda.'

'It's the hair,' said Marla. 'I'm used to it. It keeps dickheads away, too.'

Leaving Indy in the car and the gate open, they strolled up the driveway as though they owned the place. The front section was immaculate, the lawn mown in pleasing bands with neatly trimmed trees. This house too appeared ready for an open home, it even looked freshly painted.

'Let's go around the back,' said Marla. 'Did you see the twin security cameras?'

Grace nodded. 'Hidden from the street.'

'The first time you notice them is when you're being recorded,' said Marla. 'Lauren wasn't interested in who was on the street, just people on her property.'

'That's security, not surveillance,' said Grace.

The back section was as immaculate as the front with a mix of fruiting citrus trees looking trimmed and orderly. A small table with a single chair sat on the back porch.

'Doesn't look like she entertained much,' said Grace, reaching for the back door handle.

'Don't, Ace,' said Marla.

Grace held up her hands. 'I was going to check if it was unlocked.'

'I know. But if it was, and you opened it, alarms would deafen us.'

Looking around, Grace said, 'I don't see an alarm panel, are you sure the house is wired?'

Marla pointed at the edge of a window. 'See that small, white plastic strip? It's a sensor. If you open the window, you'll get deafened. The alarm panel must be by the front door.'

Walking carefully along the porch, Marla peered through a window into the kitchen.

'What does it look like inside?' asked Grace.

'Spotless, like outside. What was her car like?' she asked, rejoining Grace at the back door.

'Clean and tidy, but not excessively. The centre console was overflowing with masks, containers of chewing gum, pens, that sort of stuff.' Grace kicked a green recycling bin with her toe – bottles clinked.

Pulling her sleeve over her hand, Marla lifted the lid. 'How often do they pick up?'

Grace shrugged. 'I'm not sure. Back home it's fortnightly.'

'That's a lot of wine bottles,' said Marla letting the lid fall back. 'But we don't know when it was last emptied.'

'Are we sure this is where she lives?' asked Grace.

After a small pause, Marla said, 'Yep. When we review the combined security camera footage from other days, I'm confident we'll see a pattern of Lauren parking opposite the church, likely at odd and quiet times, and walking to this street. This house is big, too big for one person, so she'll live in a small footprint, the rest of the house will be empty.'

Outside the front door, Marla pointed at the security panel which had the single word *Armed* highlighted in blue. 'I reckon the man who drove her car saw that and left.'

'Can you beat it?' asked Grace.

'Not without more time and the right gear.'

'The police could,' said Grace. 'If they had probable cause.'

'Do they have probable cause?'

'Probably not,' said Grace. 'We could tell them our suspicions, but even we're not a hundred percent sure this is where she lives. I'll bet if it's a rental, it's not in her name.'

'And if you go to the police, they'll take one of two actions,' said Marla. 'Most likely they'll add your suspicions to their file, but do nothing. Least likely they'll investigate and whatever they find they can't, or won't, share with you.'

'Either way,' said Grace, 'we'll be none the wiser.'

'The only outcome that would benefit us is if they found a figurative smoking gun. But from what we're learning about Lauren, I doubt they'll find a candlestick in the conservatory.'

'Is there any harm in sharing our information with the police?'

Marla pondered for a long moment. 'I can't see a downside. I can't be involved but I doubt they'll say "Let's work together on this, Ace".'

'It's not their style, is it?' said Grace. After puffing out a long sigh, she added, 'I'll put together a digital dossier for them from what we've gathered. Contact Manderson, see if I can get him interested. How vital is it that we see inside her house?'

'That's the $64,000 question,' said Marla. 'My hunch is not vital, but ...' she shrugged. 'It would be handy to have a poke around, at least confirm it is Lauren's house and there's no candlestick to find.'

Grace checked the time on her phone. The evening was drawing in, the shadows lengthening. 'That leaves us with our karate lead. Shall we head there?'

With rush hour long past, it took twenty minutes to get to the Manurewa Recreation Centre, which the karate club used as its dojo. With fifteen minutes to wait, Grace parked near the building. With the windows wound down, the sounds of karate training – yells and *kiais* – disturbed an otherwise tranquil setting.

'What belt did you get up to?' asked Marla.

'Blue. I lost interest because I didn't have the time to practise and the katas were getting long and technical. I assume you were a black belt.'

Marla shook her head. 'Brown. The marines had their own system – MCMAP. It combined different disciplines with self-defence and hand-to-hand combat. It became a pissing contest as you went through the grades. I got sick of having to prove I could handle myself.'

They listened to the training as the time ticked away. A yawning Indy curled up on the back seat.

'How should we play this?' asked Marla.

'If this is Lauren's dojo, they'll know of her but most won't know much else. Just after the *sensei* ends the training session, while they're still lined up, I'll ask if anyone knows her.'

'I like that approach,' said Marla.

Just before eight, they made their way into the centre, leaving a now alert Indy staring out the front window. The karate training was in the main indoor stadium – a large multi-purpose gymnasium with a hardwood floor. They took a seat on a bench, joining the parents and partners waiting for the session to finish. The class was practising their line work and, with sweat dripping off most, they made an impressive sight as they moved up and down the makeshift dojo.

At the end of the session, they lined up in *seiza* – the traditional kneeling position, their legs tucked underneath them, their backs straight. The *sensei* offered a few encouraging words before they bowed in the traditional manner. Just as the *sensei* was about to dismiss them, Grace, having kicked off her shoes, bowed and stepped into the dojo.

Bowing to the *sensei*, Grace said, 'Please, I need a minute of the class's time.'

The class eased themselves back into *seiza* as the *sensei* bowed an acknowledgement – though it was more a disgruntled nod.

Facing the class, she said, 'I'm Grace Marks. I'm a journalist with Radio New Zealand.' A few smiled in recognition, the rest stared blankly. A male black belt sitting closest to the *sensei* looked daggers at her. Ignoring him, she said, 'I'm investigating a missing person who attended your training – her name's Lauren Brown.'

Most in the class, including the *sensei*, looked at a man sitting in the second row. A purple belt, he had short hair and looked mid-thirties. Their eyes briefly met, the man staring at Grace with a mix of concern and surprise. Grace returned her gaze to the whole class. 'If anyone knows Lauren, or anything about her, we'd' – she indicated Marla who was now standing – 'like to have a brief chat. That's all.'

Grace bowed to the class and then the *sensei*. As the class scattered, Grace went over to Marla, whispering, 'Did you see the reaction?'

'You couldn't miss it.'

Grace whispered, 'Shit, it never occurred to me that he could be here.'

'It'd crossed my mind,' said Marla. 'But I dismissed it. Too much of a longshot. And anyway, we don't know it's him.'

'He fits the build,' said Grace.

'Thousands fit the build of a normal-sized man on a dark street.'

After turning around casually, the man was taking his time to put on his shoes – he wasn't rushing away. The *sensei*, having farewelled most of the class, strode towards them.

Grace hissed. 'Keep your eye on him.'

'I'm all over him. If he makes for the door, I'll intercept him.'

'Kia ora, Grace.' The *sensei* stood in front of them, not tall but not short. With a short-cut bob and a pleasant smile, she could have passed for a librarian if it wasn't for her black belt. She looked at Marla, who introduced herself laconically, 'Norma.'

Her attention back on Grace, she asked, 'If Lauren's missing, why are *you* here and not the police?'

'That's a good question …' Grace raised an eyebrow.

'Chantel.'

'That's a good question, Chantel. The truth is people go missing all the time and the police don't have the resources to investigate. I was working with Lauren on a story and I'm concerned. Do you know her well?'

Chantel shook her head. 'Only as a student. She's friendly and committed and a top trainer. Hardly misses a session.'

'What about your records?' asked Marla.

'I'm pretty sure her address is care of her work.' Answering Grace's raised eyebrows, she added, 'I prepare invoices at the start of each term.'

'Nothing else?' asked Grace. 'She didn't let slip any details that might help us find her?'

Glancing over her shoulder at the man who was clearly waiting for them to finish talking, she said, 'I think Carter knows her. Talk to him, but I need to lock up.'

Thanks,' said Grace, glancing at Marla who watched the instructor walk away before nodding her readiness.

'Carter?' said Grace, as he approached them cautiously. Still in his sweaty *gi*, he had a small gym bag in one hand, his car keys in the other. Grace noticed the smell of deodorant – not common for male karate trainers, in her experience. 'Are you Lauren's business advisor?'

'That's right,' he said. 'We better talk outside.'

Carter held his arm out and Grace started towards the door, but Marla said, 'After you, Carter.'

Frowning, he followed Grace. Marla followed him. Outside it was almost night, the carpark illuminated by sparsely located weak orange streetlights. The evening was cooling though it was still warm. Carter stopped under a streetlight. Marla and Grace stood apart, one on either side of him.

'What's going on?' he said. 'You said Lauren's missing? Are the police involved?'

Grace, unsure where to start, said, 'Hold fire, Carter.'

Looking at each of them in turn, he said, 'If I didn't know who you were, Grace, I'd be nervous right now.'

Grace glanced at a calculating Marla, before saying, 'Lauren is missing. The police rang me two days ago. We've been trying to trace her movements because the police don't have the resources to follow up every missing person. A man roughly your build was seen driving her car, parking it where we think she usually parks in the early hours of Saturday morning.'

Carter's eyes widened. 'And you think it was me? I don't know where she parks her car.'

'We don't think it was you,' said Marla, her voice friendly. 'But it pays to be careful. I don't like surprises.'

'Are you a journalist too?'

'Not a journalist,' she said. 'My name's Norma, I help Ace track down aspects of her stories. Where were you last Friday?'

'What? I was working. What time?'

'Relax,' said Marla. The lights in the centre blinked off, the increased darkness adding drama to the scene. 'You have no idea what's happened to Lauren, do you?'

'I don't,' he said, frustration and anger mixed in his reply. Their shakedown, as gentle as it was, had darkened his mood. 'I know Lauren missed class on Monday, she hardly ever misses class, but I thought she'd be here tonight. I've rung her to see what's up, to see if she's all right, but my calls went to voicemail. She didn't answer my texts either. I was getting worried, but I've known her to take off before for a couple of days.'

'How long have you known her?' asked Marla.

'Let's see, maybe four years.'

'Did you visit her house often?' asked Grace.

Turning to Grace, he said. 'No.'

'Why?'

Exhaling heavily, he said, 'This might sound strange, but I have no idea where she lives. She's extremely guarded about her private life.'

Grace smiled. 'We're finding that out.'

'You okay, Carter?' called out the *sensei* as she walked to her car.

'All good.' He gave her a thumbs up.

Grace looked around the near-deserted carpark. They had loads of questions but they needed to find somewhere more conducive. 'It sounds like you know Lauren as well as anyone. I know this has been a strange introduction, but if we could go somewhere we can talk. I was working with Lauren on angles to try and force a change in the justice system.'

'I know,' he said. 'I was the one who nagged Lauren into contacting you. The stories you had written, you seemed a great fit.' He looked down for a beat, lips pursed, before he said, 'I live quite close by. If you want, we can talk at my house. As you can see' – he tugged on his *gi* – 'I'm hardly dressed to go out.'

'That sounds great,' said Marla. 'If it's no bother.'

'I live by myself,' he said. 'Have you eaten?'

'We have, but you'll be starving,' said Grace. 'I always was after training.'

'Full disclosure,' said Marla. 'I have a small dog.' She pointed to the car where Indy was watching them, her paws on the steering wheel. 'She'll be no bother.'

Carter smiled. 'Follow me, you can park in my driveway once I've put my car away.'

'I need to get my car, too,' said Marla. 'What's your address? We'll be there asap.'

Half an hour later Grace and Marla were sitting at a large breakfast bar, each with a glass of red wine. Carter, who had changed into sweatpants and a T-shirt, was busying himself with dinner, Indy following him hopefully around the kitchen. His house reminded Grace of Glenda's, immaculate with nothing out of place – a state Grace viewed as possible only if, like Carter, you lived alone. If her children stayed with him for two days, he'd give up like she had.

While he cooked, Grace told him what they knew. Carter listened, concerned, asking the odd clarifying question. The conversation stayed relatively light until Carter had nearly finished eating. He took them through his relationship with Lauren: meeting her at karate, liking what she was trying to achieve, his small word-of-mouth business consulting practice and, finally, how Lauren came over after karate, usually staying the night.

'You two are an item, then?' said Marla, her eyes becoming keen. 'Shouldn't you –'

He cut Marla off. 'No, we're not an item, we're just good friends. She usually slept in a guest room.'

'Usually?' said Grace.

Carter shrugged. 'Occasionally we shared a bed, but not in the way you're thinking.' He sighed. 'I'm gay. It takes two to tango.'

'And six to do *The Dashing White Sargent*,' said Grace. In answer to their open-mouthed looks, she said, 'Never mind. You're gay, I didn't pick that.'

His face turned serious. 'I'm a business consultant. My clients are mainly men. No matter how enlightened New Zealand pretends it is, if they knew I was gay I'd never hear from some of them again. Unless they're gay themselves, that is, and then the situation can be fraught – I'm sure you can imagine. Besides, gay men don't look and act like Hudson and Halls.'

Grace laughed. 'We New Zealanders love to stereotype.'

'People take short cuts, it's simpler,' said Marla. 'In all that time, all that pillow talk, you never learnt more about her?'

Carter sipped his wine. 'Lauren made it clear she wanted – make that needed – to keep part of her life to herself. I respected that. It never became a topic of conversation. I helped her establish and run her business, I'm good at that. She's awesome company, I love having her in my life. Intimate, but at arm's length. There were parts of my life that I was reluctant to share too. Our two halves made a sort of whole, if that makes sense.'

'You're single then?' said Grace.

'At the moment, yes. And happily.'

Marla changed tack. 'Did she mention a Tana?'

'The mysterious Tana. Yes, but not often. She had to be in a certain mood.'

'What sort of mood?' asked Grace.

'After a wine or two her guard sometimes lowered an inch or two.'

'After she dropped me at my hotel on Friday,' said Grace, 'she said she was going to visit Tana, but that's all she said. Did she ever say his last name? Anything that might help us work out who he is?'

Carter topped up everyone's glass. 'Lauren mentioned he had two daughters and that he either did, or does, drive a courier van.' Seeing their reaction, he said, 'Is that material?'

'The lady who lives across the street from where we think Lauren lives mentioned a courier van,' said Grace. 'It might narrow the field. What about Lauren's relationship with him?'

Shaking his head slowly, he said, 'She never *said* much, but the way she talked *about* him, she gave the impression she owed him a lot. Thinking about it, Lauren made him sound more like a parent than a friend.'

They both stared, willing him to dredge his mind for more information.

He made a sorry-but-that's-all-I've-got gesture. They sat back.

Grace looked at Marla. 'What do you reckon?'

'I reckon we need to find a courier driver called Tana. If she made it to his place, he's the last person to have seen her ...' Marla's voice trailed off.

Carter gasped. 'Were you going to say "alive"?'

'No,' said Marla calmly. 'There's no evidence to suggest that's happened.'

'It doesn't sound good, though, does it?' he said. 'Shouldn't we go to the police?'

'I'm taking what we've found to them in the morning,' said Grace, 'but it isn't much. To get them interested, they'd have to upgrade her from a missing person. And to do that, I think they'll need more evidence than what we've found.'

'In the meantime,' said Marla, 'we're going to keep looking.'

His lips pursed, he nodded. Glancing at his kitchen clock, he said, 'Where are you staying?'

'Shit,' said Grace. 'In all the running around, I haven't booked a hotel.' She turned to Marla. 'You?'

Marla, indicating Indy, who was asleep next to their bags, said, 'No. Most hotels don't allow dogs. I figured I'd find a motel once we're done for the day. Sneak her in, if I have to.'

'You can stay here if you want,' said Carter. 'I mean, I know who you are, Ace. I doubt you're setting me up to steal my furniture – it's no problem. Indy hardly looks like she's going to cause trouble.'

At the sound of her name, Indy looked at them and yawned.

'I have two guest rooms,' he said. 'If you need two, that is.'

'Are you sure?' said Grace. 'And we'll need two rooms, we're colleagues not, um ...'

'Dykes?' he said.

'No,' said Grace. 'It's the second time today. Do we look ... no, forget it.'

'Were you going to ask if you look like lesbians?' he said. 'Most straight men think "lesbians" whenever they see two women together. And they certainly think all women with hair like Norma's swing that way. I had no idea. I was just being an accommodating host. If I'm honest' – he leaned in conspiratorially – 'I don't get women. Lauren's one of the few who made sense.' Grinning, he said, 'I can't tell this joke anymore, it's too un-PC, but did you know all women are *bi*?'

Grace and Marla frowned in unison.

After a period of comedic anticipation, he said, 'You just need to work out whether it's *sexual* or *polar*.

Carter started cleaning the kitchen as they sniggered.

CHAPTER 22

Having ordered an Americano, Grace joined Marla at a table in the back of the small, neat but generic café. While she had used Marla's car – an anonymous silver Nissan Leaf – to visit the nearest police station, Marla had returned her rental car before the company opened so she could drop the keys in the return box and leave without anyone seeing Indy.

'How'd you get on?' asked Grace as she sat opposite Marla, handing over her keys. Having brought only a limited wardrobe, Grace was wearing yesterday's I-look-like-I-might-go-for-a-run clothes. Thankfully, she had fresh underwear, though not a plentiful supply. Marla, who would have packed extensively for her 'tiki tour', looked fresh in a similar outfit.

'No problem,' said Marla. 'I took Indy for a long walk too. How did you go with the police?'

'I tried,' she said.

'They weren't interested?'

Grace made a face as she shook her head. 'I explained to the officer on the front desk that there's no point in me just handing over the information, that I needed to talk to someone, ideally the officer I spoke to, Manderson. I left a flash drive with a note for Manderson telling him to call me. They said they'd try to get it to him but he's based elsewhere.' Grace repeated the face.

'You can't blame them,' said Marla. 'They'll be understaffed and overworked. I imagine missing persons is near the bottom of their priority list. We need hard evidence that Lauren's disappearance is criminal.'

'I know, I know,' said Grace, forcing a smile for the server who brought her coffee.

'Without the police's help, getting into Lauren's house is problematic,' said Marla. 'Our best bet is locating this Tana, the probable courier driver. I've been thinking about that since Indy woke me early for a call of nature. I reckon talking to KT is the place to start.'

'That was bouncing around in my head too,' said Grace. 'Apart from ringing around courier companies, who would be reluctant to handout personal information, I wasn't sure how to proceed. What's your idea?'

'I'm hoping KT might have some connections. He's a truck driver, it's not a dissimilar occupation.'

'Plus,' said Grace, 'he looks like an ex-Tongan rugby or league player.'

'How do you know he's Tongan?' asked Marla.

Her face serious, Grace said, 'If you look close enough, you can detect subtle differences … like the Tongan flag in the hall.'

Marla grinned. 'Missed that, I'm slipping. Should have we said hello in Tongan rather than Māori?'

Grace shrugged. 'Do you know the Tongan for hello?'

'No.'

'That answers that. Besides, most people are supportive when you step outside English. Only ignorant Pākeha do their nut if you say *Aotearoa*. Anyway, rugby and league players, those guys and girls are usually well connected. Let's head there, we've nothing else to go on.'

Marla stared into her cup, nodding.

'What's up?' asked Grace.

'Lauren's obsessively security conscious and keeps her past guarded tightly – why?'

'Initially,' said Grace, 'I thought she was taking precautions against being doxed. I mean, there's a lot of angry, entitled men out there who are having their wings clipped because of her company. That's a reason for a grudge. But kidnapping?'

'At this stage, kidnapping is our best-case scenario,' said Marla. 'It's also the most likely. This wasn't random, there's something deeper about her disappearance.'

'Not a well-planned murder?'

Marla shut her eyes for an instant. 'No, a well-planned abduction. If it was murder, why take the risk of driving her car or visiting her house? I mean, we've identified *someone* on camera twice, and we don't have the police's resources. If the police knew it was murder, they would be all over the area.'

Grace finished her coffee. 'Let's get going.'

Marla relied on Google Map's somewhat-annoying female voice to direct her back to Church Road. After she put Indy on her lead, she said, 'It feels like we are chasing our tails. We've been here what, three times?'

'I was feeling the opposite,' said Grace. 'That we're narrowing in on what happened. Before you turned up, I had literally nothing. Now we know who Carter is and where Lauren lives. We're making progress.'

Josh answered the door this time, clearly delighted to see them. Following him to the kitchen, without looking at Marla, Grace nodded approvingly at the Tongan flag pinned to the wall – Marla simultaneously laughed and scoffed. They joined KT at the kitchen table where he was reading the morning paper, which he refolded as they entered the room.

'Hello again, ladies.' His voice was warm but guarded.

'Mālō e lelei,' said Marla.

A broad smile broke out on KT's face. 'Mālō e lelei.'

As they sat, Grace whispered, 'I thought you said –'

Cutting in, Marla whispered back, 'I looked it up while you were in the toilet at the café – one all.'

Grace grinned.

'What can I do for you?' asked KT. 'I assume it's to do with your missing friend.'

'We've made progress,' said Grace, 'but we keep running into dead ends. We're pretty sure Lauren, our missing friend, lives in Tainui Terrace but there's an armed security system protecting the house.'

Marla added, 'We gave the information to the police, but they've little time for missing persons. They're not going to investigate and, if we broke in, we'd have only a few minutes before the security company arrived.'

KT nodded solemnly.

'That leaves this Tana,' said Grace. KT opened his mouth, but before he could tell them again that there were hundreds of Tanas, she said, 'We think he's a courier driver.'

KT closed his mouth.

'There can't be that many courier drivers called Tana,' said Marla. 'We had hoped you might have connections that you could ask.'

Staring at them intensely, he asked. 'What else to do you know about him?'

'He likely has two daughters,' said Marla. 'Tall, athletic and attractive according to the woman who lives across the road.'

Scratching at his stubble, KT said, 'I can make some phone calls. I can't promise anything, but you never know.'

'I could go around the courier yards,' said Josh. 'Ask if anyone knows a Tana who has two tall, athletic daughters.'

KT gave his son a look suggesting that approach would get him into trouble. 'I'll make the calls and then you can check if it's the right Tana.'

Josh beamed. 'Okay.'

'Come back after five,' said KT.

Back on the street, Grace checked the time on her phone. 'That's seven hours away. I could use the time to get some work done, smooth the ruffled feathers of my editor and check in with Sean and my children, who'll claim I've abandoned them. What about you?'

'I'll take Indy for another walk, it's good thinking time. I might do a little sight-seeing too, I've never visited Tāmaki Makaurau before.'

Before Grace could reply, her phone burst into song. Her current ringtone for unknown callers was 'Who are you?'. She looked – *Caller Id Blocked*.

'It could be the police,' said Grace.

'It's definitely The Who,' said Marla.

With a roll of her eyes, Grace accepted the call, answering in a military tone. 'Marks.'

'Marks. Manderson.'

A smile spread over her face, there are moments when the stars align. But before she could keep the *Two Ronnies* sketch running, he said. 'Let's not go there again. What am I going to see?'

'How did you get the files so fast? I thought you operated out of a different station.'

'This may surprise you, Ace,' he said, 'but we don't use courier pigeons. The officer on the desk copied the files onto a shared drive and sent me an image of your message.'

Chastened, Grace explained he would be looking at files from two security cameras that showed a man, not Lauren, parking her car before entering what they believed was her property for four minutes. Manderson listened without asking any questions. When she finished, he asked, 'Is that it?'

Grace wanted to reach through the phone and slap him. 'What do you mean, is that it?'

'Whoa, whoa, whoa,' he said. 'I just mean, when I look at this will I end up at a dead end?'

Gritting her teeth, she said, 'We have, but you lot have more power than we do. You can investigate it as a crime. You can enter her house, see if there's evidence of a crime.'

She heard Manderson exhale. 'I'll have a look when I can. If it's material I'll see if I can get it escalated.'

'I know,' said Grace, 'I won't get my hopes up.' Before he could end the call, she asked, 'Did you check out a man called McMahon? Her colleagues thought he might be involved.'

Over the phone, Grace heard Manderson working his keyboard and mouse. 'Yep, we spoke to him. He said he was out of town last weekend and no, we haven't followed that up.'

Grace waited.

'I'll check out the files. If it looks concerning, I'll get the records pulled to trace her last movements. You know, bank records, mobile phone pings, CCTV. But I have to justify using the resources and it's tough. We've had a spate of firearm incidents – they take precedence.'

'I've seen the reports,' she said. 'Let me know if you need anything more,' and she terminated the call.

'That didn't sound promising,' said Marla.

Grace grunted. 'If they consider the files concerning, the wheels *might* start turning.'

Marla forced a smile.

'What?' asked Grace.

'Even if the police get interested, and that sounds like a big if, they're going to focus on the present – where's Lauren? I think the answer to that question lies in the past, in Lauren's past. Don't get me wrong, having the police investigating will help, it sure can't hurt.'

'What else can we do?' asked Grace. 'Contact McMahon? I doubt he's involved, but it wouldn't hurt to eliminate him. I have his details and I know exactly how to get him talking. Pick me up at 4.45. There's a library a block away, I'll work out of there. It'll be all right staying with Carter again tonight, won't it?'

'I think so, he seemed keen for us to stay. I think he enjoyed the company and we can keep him in the loop. Besides, it keeps me away from hotel security cameras.'

'And me on the right side of RNZ's finance dragons,' said Grace.

CHAPTER 23

Lauren wriggled, moving her muscles to get tolerably comfortable, but it was an impossible task. The most comfortable position she had found was to use the book they had left her as the world's worst pillow. That or wedge herself into the corner of the barren storeroom. With walls on two sides, she found she could doze for short periods.

The room, with its solid timber walls, had one small window, too high for Lauren to see out of. The air that circulated through the window and the small cracks between the equally solid timber floorboards did little to dispel the heat. Even though they let her wash in the morning, by the afternoon, without deodorant, she smelt feral. Featuring a malevolent peephole, the door was locked and bolted. It was the only way in and out. The only other items in the room were a bible and a cheap, blue bucket.

When she had regained consciousness in the familiar room, a wave of panic had flooded her system. Her new life, which she had guarded so preciously, was it over? Her past life, Reverentia, had dragged her back. Yelling, she had struggled to her feet and kicked at the door. No one answered. No one came. They'd never come before either.

The room, she knew, was in a house at the farthest point on the upper level of the farm. It wasn't the first time Lauren had spent time in this room. The elders used it as a punishment for anyone deemed not fervent enough in their work or their dedication to God. The usual 'sentence' was twenty-four hours with no food or drink – just the bible and a bucket to help you find your way back to the path of the righteous.

Fuckers.

Lauren wasn't certain how many days she had been there, at least five. Reverentia adored a regimented approach to life including, it seemed, abduction, imprisonment and interrogation. Each morning, they let her use the bathroom, the windows of which were barred. Two young community members acted as guards under the watchful eye of Melissa Palmer. They gave her breakfast, the food, she recognised, being what they served to all community members.

The morning rituals were conducted in silence. Lauren had tried talking to Melissa, who had looked away, jaw set and glowering. When she had tried talking to one of the community members who she recognised but couldn't remember his name, the wife of the community leader had snapped, 'Do not speak to her, she's evil.'

After breakfast they locked her back in the storeroom to wait for the lowlight of the day – half an hour with the community's leader, Nathaniel Palmer. They tied her hands behind her back and sat her at a table. If she wanted, she could've freed her hands, they never tied them that tightly, but what was the point? With two community members in the room, it would be difficult to overpower them all, though not impossible. If she failed, it would mean they would tie the bonds tighter.

After he had lectured her on God's way, temptation and whatever else he decided to sermonise over, he got to the point.

'What information did you take when you left?' 'How did you manage to fake a copy of Keith's will?' 'What were you planning to do?' There were several variations to these questions as he probed. Interestingly, given that she knew they had gone to the trouble of planting the gin bottle from her house in the car, he never asked about the crash itself.

She kept her answers short and consistent. In answer to her repeated question of, 'When are you going to let me go?', his answer was always, 'when we have come to an arrangement that we both can *live* with'.

Lauren viewed these sessions as a game of chess. When Reverentia's leader had finished his interrogation cum sermon, they gave her dinner, then allowed her to use the bathroom again before locking her away for the night. Left, in Palmer's words, 'to contemplate God's plan for her'.

Each night they left her with nothing but time, the bible and the bucket.

CHAPTER 24

Grace watched Marla's car turn into the small carpark behind the library right on 4.45pm. The carpark was almost full, people using the park and boxing gym replacing the library visitors. Marla pulled up next to where Grace was waiting, Indy giving Grace a hard look when she assisted her out of the passenger seat and into the back.

'What did you get from McMahon?' asked Marla straight away.

'Zip.'

'I thought you were confident you'd get him talking.'

'I was,' said Grace, giving Marla a who-knew shrug. 'It's always worked in the past. I told him who I was and that I was doing a story on his legal challenges to the protection order and that I wanted his side of the story.'

'What did he say?'

'He told me to fuck off and die.'

'He's a charmer, isn't he?'

'It struck me,' said Grace, 'that if you *had* abducted someone, and a journalist rang, how would you react?'

Marla ran a hand over her hair. 'If I put myself in McMahon's narcissistic shoes, and if I was involved in Lauren's disappearance, I'm confident no one suspects me because I'm brilliant, but I'd want to know what you know. Men like him would back themselves to wrap you around their little finger.'

'That's what I thought,' said Grace. 'He didn't hesitate, he didn't take any time to weigh up the consequences.'

'It suggests he's not involved,' said Marla, 'but you couldn't take it to the bank.'

A car wanting to exit the carpark forced Marla to park in a keep-clear zone in front of a building named the *Gerry Preston Pavillion*. They each looked at the sign, then at each other and shook their heads.

Leaving the engine running, Marla said, 'Before we head to KT's, let's review what we have. After Lauren dropped you off at 8.30 last Friday, she went to visit a friend – Tana. We don't know whether she made it, but an unknown man parked her car opposite the church at 2.17, walked to her house where he spent four minutes before leaving, presumably heading for a pre-arranged rendezvous.'

'They knew what they were doing,' said Grace slowly. 'And it means more than one person was involved.'

'It *suggests* that,' corrected Marla.

'Fine, suggests.' Grace tried unsuccessfully to keep the annoyance out of her voice. 'Between 8.30 and 2.17, Lauren disappeared into thin air. She hasn't answered calls or texts and, unless the police decide to take an interest, they won't trace her phone to check her movements.'

'Lauren's been living in fear.' Marla shook her head. 'That's not the right word, she's not fearful, she's … anxious. Anxious that she's able to control her life, possibly her past.'

'That sounds Orwellian,' said Grace.

'It does a bit, but she's gone to extraordinary lengths to keep her life outside of Weeping Angels secret.'

'Except,' said Grace, 'she let Carter in, sort of, though he and her colleagues have been dead ends as far as locating her.'

'That leaves Tana,' said Marla. 'A friend from her past … possibly.'

Grace pursed her lips. 'Tana might be involved – is that where you're heading?'

Nodding, she said, 'It sounds unlikely, given how Carter and Trudi said she talked about him, and that she was happily visiting him. But unlikely isn't zero, which makes him a risk we need to manage. We don't know if KT and Josh will find him but, if they do, we need to approach him with caution.'

'Hope for the best, plan for the worst,' said Grace.

Marla looked at her sideways. 'That saying was, maybe, the only redeeming feature of that character. A gorilla-sized fighting machine with hands the size of saucepans, a toothbrush in his back pocket and an engine-block of a chest who women find irresistible. Put that through an AI image generator and you'd get a Neanderthal with a Donny Osmond smile.

Grace laughed. 'You've read them?'

'Guilty,' said Marla. 'I've had more time on my hands than I expected.'

In less than a minute, the library was literally around the corner, Marla parked her silver Nissan Leaf opposite St James Anglican Church. They looked across the road at KT's house then back at each other.

'Well, well, well,' said Grace.

'KT's made progress,' said Marla.

Parked in KT's driveway was a red and yellow courier van.

After a quick consultation, they decided to go in together and play it however it came at them. As Marla pointed out, if it was a trap, parking the courier van in the driveway was a bit of a giveaway. Added to that, KT and Josh were hardly gangster types. Marla told Grace to keep an eye on her – if she sat down, that was her signal that she considered the situation safe.

An uneasy Josh answered Grace's knock.

'Is everything okay, Josh?' asked Marla coolly.

'Yeah, all good,' he said. 'It's just been an intense day.'

'Is it safe to come in?' said Grace pointing at the courier van.

Smiling, he said, 'Yeah, it's all good – no stress.'

Josh stood back and Grace entered. She heard Marla say, 'After you Josh.' She didn't sound concerned though Marla never sounded concerned. In her game, Marla said that being taken by surprise was a cardinal sin.

'Straight ahead, they're in the lounge,' said Josh.

Grace walked slowly. 'They' were in the lounge. Marla would be even more on guard, if that's possible. Was she armed?

Pausing in the doorway, Grace took in the rectangular, narrow lounge. Assorted bean bags lay in front of an enormous switched off TV at the far end of the room. Sofas lined the walls and a large china cabinet took pride of place in the middle of the internal wall. It was full of family photos taking the place of the more usual plates and spoons.

KT sat in a recliner chair, his leg in the moonboot raised. A second Tongan man, balding with a neatly kept greying beard, sat across from him. He too was solidly built, though not in the manner of an ex-athlete. Wearing a red and yellow courier driver's uniform, he had a stern, unwelcoming face – this had to be Tana.

'Hi, Ace,' said KT, nodding to the sofa next to him, directly across from the courier driver. 'Take a seat.'

As Grace walked towards the sofa, she hesitated. A third man, wiry and much younger, was leaning against the wall in the corner of the room. Māori rather than Tongan, he wore skinny jeans, sunglasses and his white T-shirt showed off one seriously inked arm.

'It's cool, Ace,' said KT. 'He's okay.'

Grace nodded to the man who, surprisingly, smiled back. Josh followed Grace into the room. Back to looking uncomfortable, he sat next to the courier driver.

'Norma.' KT smiled as he greeted her.

Nodding to KT, Marla stopped inside the room and turned to the man in the corner. 'Kia ora,' she said, making it sound more like a question.

'Kia ora,' he said, shifting uneasily, his face serious.

Marla smiled, pushed her sunglasses onto the top of her head and sat next to Grace without hesitation.

The room plunged into silence. KT sat in what was obviously 'his' chair. Opposite, the intense courier driver sat next to a concerned Josh. Grace, next to KT, sat on the edge of the sofa. Marla sat next to her, leaning back, one leg crossed over the other at right angles. The body language of the man in the corner was awkward rather than menacing.

It was the man in the corner who broke the silence. Taking off his sunglasses, his voice warm and friendly, he said, 'I'll put the jug on, eh?'

Without his sunglasses to hide behind, he looked twenty, attractive, with a friendly, mischievous face. This was possibly what Marla saw; after one look she clearly didn't rate him a threat.

The courier driver glared at him as he stole out of the room after asking everyone what they wanted. The fact that nobody else wanted a hot drink hadn't deterred him.

'Okay,' said Grace. 'This is feeling awkward and I don't know why.'

Looking at the stern courier driver, she asked, 'Are you the Tana we've been looking for?'

'Maybe,' he said, his expression unchanged.

'I'm Grace Marks, I'm a journalist with RNZ.' Indicating Marla, she said, 'This is —'

Marla cut in. 'Norma. I help Ace track people and places for her stories.'

Marla had taken no chance that Grace might inadvertently introduce her as Marla. Changing her name at that point would have dented the thin credibility they had built.

Tana's face softened a degree. 'KT told me who you were. I got my daughters to check you out, Ace.'

'Right,' said Grace. 'So … what's going on? Why am I getting an unfriendly vibe?'

'Sorry,' said Tana, his face morphing into what was likely his usual kindly look. 'I'm concerned and confused. That's why I wanted to play it safe.'

The would-be enforcer slunk back into the room, cup in hand.

Tana gave him a hard stare. 'You were supposed to look like a heavy, Wai. Not try to organise a tea party.'

Looking hurt, Wai said, 'You didn't tell me it was two chicks, sorry, ladies … women. I felt like a dick standing there in sunglasses.' Wai sat down between Tana and Josh. 'Budge up e hoa.'

The atmosphere in the room relaxed.

'Let's start over,' said KT. 'As I understand it, Ace and Norma are looking for their missing friend Lauren. She dropped off Ace last Friday telling her she was going to visit her friend Tana. That's the last time anyone's seen her, but our security camera recorded her car outside the church early on Saturday morning.'

Marla took over the story. 'The man driving Lauren's car walked down Tainui Terrace. A house with a security camera in their doorbell showed him going into a house which we think is Lauren's. He didn't stay long enough to get inside.'

Tana sat forwards. 'KT explained why the police aren't interested, but why are you looking for Joy' – he shook his head – 'Lauren?'

'Who's Joy?' asked Marla.

Tana's forehead creased, and he didn't answer immediately. 'That *was* her name. She changed it to Lauren when she moved to Auckland – I forget.'

In answer to Tana's initial question, Grace explained her journalistic role in helping Lauren fight the justice system and their concern when she went missing.

Tana, who had nodded as Grace spoke, said, 'She was always talking about doing that, fighting the justice system.' His face went serious. 'When they told me someone was looking for a courier driver called Tana with two daughters, I headed back to the depot to see what's what. That's why I came up. KT isn't the first person to come looking for Lauren lately. And if she's missing, I want to help find her.'

The room quietened as everyone processed Tana's words.

Breaking the silence, Marla said, 'Who else came looking?'

'I needed to know you were on the level,' said Tana. 'Lauren knew I'd never tell anyone about her, or her life. When two men came to my house a few weeks ago asking if I knew her' – his nostrils flared and his eyes widened – 'I told them if I ever saw them again, I'd take them out the back and barbeque them.' His face softened. 'They took off quick smart.'

'That's why no one will date his daughters,' said Wai. 'He scares them away.'

'Too bloody right,' said Tana. 'I know what I was like when I was in my twenties.'

This time laughter echoed around the room.

Grace took out a business card, handing it to Tana. 'I'm on the level, Tana. I was working with Lauren on stories to fight the justice system. She went missing the day after we met to discuss stories I could run to build pressure on the Government.'

'Ace is a legend,' said Josh. 'She made the wealthy pay tax, helped expose the alt-right and stopped the US from spying on us.'

Grace flashed an eyebrow raise in Josh and Tana's direction.

'And you, Norma, where do you fit in?' asked Tana.

'She won't blow her own trumpet,' said Grace, 'But she's saved my life on at least two occasions when I've chased stories in dangerous places.'

Marla shrugged. 'I'm a little like Lauren, Tana. I need to stay in the shadows too.'

'Okay, I'm going to trust you,' said Tana. He sat back and exhaled. 'Where do you want to start?'

'Let's work backwards,' said Marla. 'Last Friday night Lauren came to visit you. What happened?'

'Just the usual,' he said. 'She texted to say she'd be popping in around 9.30. We caught up – had a lot of laughs. She left around 11.30. I was a bit tired. I start work at five, even on Saturdays.'

'Around 9.30,' said Marla matter-of-factly. 'Where do you live?'

'Hamilton, but I was in Pōkeno, staying with rellies. If I have deliveries for there, I save them until last, stay overnight. I always let Lauren know, if she's free, it's only a forty-five-minute drive. My eldest came with me. She spent most of the time chatting with Lauren. They're sort of sisters.'

'Was it you and your family who helped her move into her house on Tainui Terrace?' asked Grace.

'That's right. Cor, that was a few years ago.'

'Do you visit her much?'

Shaking his head, he said, 'She didn't want to take the chance that anyone followed us. She was scared her previous life was going to catch her. She'd drive down every few weeks, in the weekend usually, and stay the night. I think she just needed time out from the world. She had a tough start in life and she liked to chill.'

Grace asked, 'Did you know what she was doing?'

'Sure. She worked in a lawyer's office for a couple of years before going out on her own, setting up her own business. She told me she was an investigator, helping women get justice. It sounded great and she was loving the work. Loving her new life.'

'Before I forget,' said Marla, who would never forget, 'did you tell her about the men who came looking for her?'

'Sure,' he said. 'She was concerned.'

'Did Lauren know who they were?'

'No, but they weren't from the community. They had on flashy suits, but they weren't cops. My guess was PIs.'

'Whoa,' said Grace shaking her head. 'Community? What community?'

Tana stared at her.

'You can trust us, Tana,' said Marla. 'Besides, finding out where she is and what's happened to her, that's the most important consideration.'

'What I'm about to say can't leave this room,' said Tana. 'Wai, Josh, I'm sorry, but you'll need to leave for a bit. KT, you can stay.'

Looking relieved, Wai jumped up. 'Come on Josh, let's go get a burger – my buy.' A reluctant Josh followed Wai out of the room. They heard the front door open and close, and through the net curtains Grace watched the pair head towards the shops.

Taking out a notepad, Grace listened as Tana took them through Lauren's story as he knew it. Picking her up hitch-hiking on the expressway, how his daughters helped change her look by giving her clothes and how he had dropped her in the middle of Hamilton.

'Where did you pick her up?' asked Marla. 'That first day.'

'It must have been a couple of kilometres outside Taupiri. She was standing on the expressway, thumb out. She didn't know it was illegal and it was too dangerous to leave her. Gosh, eh. It's the little decisions that can change your life. I wasn't meant to be on that route but Ricky was crook with the Covids – I was helping out.'

'Wow,' said Grace. 'If she, or you, had got there minutes earlier or later, your paths would have never have crossed.'

KT shook his and made a low groaning noise.

'It could be all part of God's plan,' said Tana, 'but she was running away from God, so how does that work? Anyway, I didn't expect to see her again, I was just helping a girl trying to escape a backward life in a community of nutjobs. A week later she came to my house in tears. She had no money, nowhere to go, no life, so I said she could stay with us.'

'What do you know about the community she was in?' asked Grace.

Tana's face soured. 'Not much. It's called Reverentia, but she seldom talked about it, or them.'

'Reverentia,' said Grace. 'I've not heard of it. But Lauren lived with you from then?'

Tana smiled as he recalled events. 'Money was a bit tight for a while. We enrolled her at high school for the rest of year thirteen. It was hard for her at first but, as you know, she's bright and soon caught on. My daughters watched out for her too, otherwise the girls might've eaten her.' He made a face. 'Some of them scared *me*.'

'Wouldn't she stand out?' said Grace. 'I mean, if this community was looking for her?'

Tana shrugged. 'She dressed like my daughters and we changed her name to Joy Brown – she fitted in. We told the school she had come over from Australia, a child of my wife's sister. People see what they want to see. They saw a quiet child adopted into a new family – nobody asked questions.'

'Were people looking for her?' asked Marla.

'I don't know if the community were but' – Tana rubbed his hands together as though he was washing them – 'the police were. But they never came knocking.'

Grace and Marla waited. It was clear he knew more but was either reluctant to speak or needed time to find the right words. After a loaded silence, Tana said, 'Her husband crashed his car when he was rat-arsed. He drove off the road on a steep hill and died instantly.'

Leaning towards Grace, Marla asked, 'Is that the same as *rat-ted*?'

Everyone's smile answered Marla's question.

Grace, struggling to keep Tana's story straight, said, 'Hang on, Tana. *Husband?* How old was she when she was married?'

'She told me she was fifteen but they changed the dates to make it look like she was sixteen. Her husband was older, abusive and an alcoholic. He died in the accident. She escaped from the community and she thought the police might be looking for her. That's about all I know about that part of her life.'

Marla, eyebrows raised, said, 'An accident?'

'That's what she told me,' said Tana defensively.

'What next?' said Grace. 'Lauren finishes school ...'

'I landed her a job in the depot. You know, helping in the warehouse, helping with dispatches. She loved it and got on well with everyone, but she was nervous. I told her it was all over now, but she was always looking over her shoulder. So, after a year she packed up and went to Auckland and got a job in a lawyer's office. She earnt enough money to rent a house; she wanted to live alone. I wasn't sure about that but it was her call. We helped her move in and life carried on, as it does. She kept in close touch with us and, as I said, she visited every couple of weeks.'

Grace checked her notes. 'If I have the timing right, Lauren's lived in Auckland for about five years. A few weeks ago, a couple of PIs arrive at your house looking for her. What happened in the previous years?'

Shrugging, Tana said, 'Until now, not much. It was like her past was in the past. I kept my eyes open and ear to the ground – nothing. No police. No PIs. No community members.'

KT, who had followed the back and forth of the story like he was watching a tennis match, asked, 'Do you know what changed? What caused the PIs to arrive?'

'Not really. Lauren kept her secrets close. When I told her about the two men, I remember she said, "bloody social media" and that "they'll be scared of going to court" but …' He ended his sentence with a shrug.

Marla and Grace each asked a few more questions but it was clear that Tana had told them all he knew. They exchanged phone numbers and, just before they left, Tana said, 'If you fullas find out anything, you let me know. I've known Lauren all her *new* life, she's part of my family. And if I can help in any way, you just let me know.'

As everyone was filing out of KT's house, Josh and Wai arrived back.

Back in Marla's car, they sat in a reflective silence. Just as Grace was going to ask Marla for her take on Tana's story, Marla reached over and grabbed her arm.

'What?'

Marla was staring across the road at Tana, who was walking away from KT's house with Wai – in the direction of Tainui Terrace.

'No way,' said Marla, getting out of the car. She called out, 'Tana, where are you going?'

Turning, he called back, 'Just heading to Lauren's house to make sure it's okay. Water the plants, that sort of thing.'

'It's protected with a security system.'

'I know,' he called out. 'I know the code.'

Marla and Grace, now also out of the car, stared at him with open mouths.

Frowning, he called out, 'What?'

Only KT, nursing his injured foot, stayed behind. Marla, Grace, Tana, Wai, an excited Josh and an equally excited Indy walked to Lauren's house.

Grace, walking in front with Marla and Indy, said, 'I cannot believe we nearly missed that.'

'I know,' said Marla. 'I *must* be losing my edge.'

Tana checked Lauren's letterbox, which was empty thanks to the large *No junk mail* sign. As he walked to front door, he said, 'I helped her install the security system.'

'That was five years ago,' said Marla. 'She'll have changed the code.'

'Nah,' he said. 'She would've told me.'

Marla leaned close to Grace. 'If this goes wrong, I'll need to disappear – fast.'

Her eyes on Tana, Grace nodded.

'Don't you fullas look,' he said covering the keypad. 'It's the same code I use for my pin.'

All eyes focused on the word *Armed* on the display. Grace tensed as Tana tapped in the code. The box produced a physical 'chonk' and the word changed to *Disarmed*. The group collectively and noisily exhaled.

'What?' Tana turned around chuckling. 'You thought I'd stuff it up.'

'Well done, Tana. I don't know why I doubted you,' said Marla. 'Let's do this fast, who knows what the neighbours might do. Wai, Josh, you stay at the gate with Indy.' Handing Indy's lead to Josh, she said, 'Keep an eye out for nosy neighbours.'

They grunted in disappointment.

Holding out his keys by a single key, Tana said, 'You first, ladies. You know what you're doing.'

Marla took the keys, opened the door and tossed the keys back to Tana. From her pocket she took a pair of blue rubber gloves. Putting them on she said, 'Keep your hands in your pockets, just in case.'

Doing as she was told, Grace followed Marla into the house. The house was as it looked from the outside, spotless. They walked through an immaculate living area, though an empty coffee mug on a coaster indicated Lauren used the room to watch the moderately-sized TV and relax, if she relaxed.

'It doesn't look like she was a big entertainer,' said Grace.

'Fits with what we know,' said Marla.

A film of dust coated the TV cabinet. Grace went to run her finger through it when Marla, caution in her voice, said, 'Ace.'

She stopped with her finger just above the surface.

'If the police do search,' said Marla, 'it's best your fingerprints aren't on the TV.'

Grace laughed briefly. 'They've always wanted an excuse to lock me up.' She jammed her hands back into her pockets.

In the kitchen, Marla opened the refrigerator. Looking over her shoulder, Grace saw it wasn't full of groceries, but it contained all the usual items you'd expect; milk, butter, cheese and various bottles of sauces and condiments.

'No horse's head,' said Grace.

'No wine either,' said Marla as she glanced around the kitchen. 'That's odd given the empties.'

'Not really,' said Grace.

Marla looked at her.

'It's what I do too,' she said. 'I don't keep alcohol in the house, it removes temptation, but I'm always tempted on the way home.'

'I get it,' said Marla. 'You're trying to limit your consumption, but failing?'

Frowning, Grace said, 'I wouldn't have put it that brutally but … yes.'

'It's a good sense-making observation,' said Marla. 'I wouldn't have seen it in that light.'

In the fridge was an almost full container of milk. Looking closely, Marla read out, 'Best before the nineteenth. When was that?'

'Tomorrow,' said Tana.

Grace walked into the adjacent dining area. 'Looks like she used this room as an office.' On the table sat piles of documents together with the cables and equipment needed to keep the essential devices of the modern world connected and powered. She said, 'There's a docking station but no laptop.'

'That fits too,' said Marla. 'She would've had it with her.'

'So, they took that too,' said Tana. 'And her phone, I guess.'

Next, Marla went into the hall. The two closed doors revealed empty rooms. They might have been the first people to open those doors since Patrick, the previous owner that Glenda had mentioned, had died.

The last door, which was open, led to the master bedroom. They filed in as though they were entering a sacred place, standing around the wall, looking but not touching. Lauren's bedroom, in juxtaposition to the rest of the house, was a relative mess. The bed was unmade. The dresser cluttered with the range of products most women in business needed. There was a pile of clothes on one side of the bed, presumably washed and waiting for Lauren to put away – it's also what Grace did when Sean wasn't staying over.

Grace ventured into the ensuite, Marla's voice following her inside.

'Make sure –'

'My hands are in my pockets,' she called back. The ensuite bathroom was in a similar state to the bedroom, cluttered but with all the products you would expect. Emerging, she said, 'It's tidy enough, like her bedroom.'

'Messy, but not dirty,' said Marla. 'It's like she had one place in her life where she didn't need to care.'

'What's up, Tana?' asked Grace.

Wiping his eyes, he pointed at the framed pictures on the bedside table. One was of a large family group, all dressed in blue and white clothes, presumably Lauren's family in Reverentia. The second was recognisably of a younger Lauren, Tana and presumably Tana's wife and two daughters – everyone was laughing hysterically.

'We'd gone tenpin bowling,' he explained. 'I asked the fulla behind the bar to take a group photo. Lauren wasn't keen but I said it'd be just for us. He took one then … well … I farted.' Grace and Marla stared at him. 'I meant to let out a sly one, but it got away on me bigtime. He caught the carnage on camera.'

They all burst out laughing. Grace had to wipe tears from her eyes, his laugh was infectious. The photo captured a rare moment of pure joy.

When they'd regained their composure, Tana said, 'Those are the only pictures in the house, apart from the art on the walls – I was looking.' He looked at them, the previous humour gone. 'I'm worried.'

'We're worried too,' said Grace. 'That's why we need to find out what's going on.' She turned to Marla. 'What do you think?'

'If there's anything to find, it'll be the room she's using as an office. Every other part of the house feels like a normal home. She might have hiding places, but it looks like she feels safe here. Besides, we don't have time for a deep search.'

Back in the office, Marla used her phone to take photos of the table. 'This is so we can make sure we can recreate the scene exactly. Here' – she handed Grace a pair of blue gloves – 'you better put these on.'

'I'll check on the boys,' said Tana.

After Grace had looked carefully through the piles of documents, the only item that resonated was a thick file labelled *McMahon*. The rest of the items were an eclectic mix of articles and stories detailing family violence cases in the news, legal challenges and government white papers on the legislation.

Almost as an afterthought, Grace opened the newspaper that was at the bottom of a stack of articles. It was the only newspaper and, curiosity growing, she noted it was a two-year-old copy of the *Waikato Times* – a strange item to keep.

The editor had dedicated the front page to rugby, an upcoming All Blacks/Black Ferns international doubleheader. She flipped the newspaper open and a headline on page three drew her attention instantly: *Police to re-open accident investigation.*

The article detailed the death of Keith Leslie, an accountant who had driven his car, an Audi no less, off a steep hill while intoxicated three years earlier. The journalist had relied on interviews with members of the Reverentia community that Leslie belonged to, primarily Nathaniel Palmer who was concerned that, in his words, 'events were not as they seemed'.

First, Palmer didn't believe his friend had drunk as much as the blood-alcohol test from the autopsy revealed. Second, the police had assumed the bottle of gin found in the car accounted for the high blood-alcohol reading but, according to Palmer, Leslie didn't drink gin. A man called Wright, who had previously left the bottle at Leslie's house, confirmed it hadn't been touched. Third, Leslie's clothes were dirty with minor tears. Palmer, who had watched him drive away on the fateful night, had said he didn't leave his house in that state and doubted the police's version that Leslie had fallen over when he had relieved himself. Finally, there was the mysterious disappearance of his wife – Joy Leslie.

Grace re-read the sentence aloud. 'The mysterious disappearance of his wife.' Looking up she saw that Tana, who had come back into the house, was staring at her. 'What was Lauren's last name, before she lived with you?'

'Before she lived with me?' Stroking his beard, he said, 'Leslie. Joy Leslie. Why?'

Grace tapped the story, 'Read this, Tana.'

Marla, having observed their exchange, was already reading.

After Tana had read the story, he stepped back frowning. 'That's my Joy.'

'Did the police interview you?' asked Marla.

He shook his head vigorously. 'I told you, no one knew she stayed with me. I never saw this story, until now. We stopped getting the newspaper ages ago and look at the date, it's over two years old. Those two fullas turned up a fortnight ago.'

'She could've kept it for any number of reasons,' said Grace.

'The story doesn't mention any dispute,' said Marla. 'You said Lauren mentioned going to court when you told her about the PIs.'

'That's right,' said Tana. 'She said they'll be scared of going to court – something like that.'

'Did you –'

'No,' said Tana, cutting Grace's question short. 'If she wanted to tell me she would've told me. That's how we roll.'

Josh burst into the house. Wide-eyed, he said, 'There's an old lady at the gate, she's threatening to call the police. Wai's trying to stall her but she's having none of it.'

'Put everything back in place,' said Marla. 'Take photos of the story, Ace. In case it's not online'

Whipping out her mobile, Grace took images of the story and front page before re-folding the paper. When she had replaced the newspaper under the pile of papers, Marla checked the table against the photos she had taken.

'Perfect,' said Marla. 'Now, let's all take a breath – we've been in every room, what have we forgotten to put back? I hate rushing, it's how monumental cockups occur.'

Grace and Tana each looked around the room, into the kitchen and down the hall. They stared at each other and, in unison, shook their heads.

Nodding seriously, Marla said, 'I'm good too. We lock the door, arm the alarm and go chat with Glenda.'

'Glenda?' said Tana.

'She's the one who had the security camera,' said Grace. 'We'll need to unruffle her feathers, that's all.'

At the gate, Wai, holding on to an excited Indy, was trying his best to keep Glenda in check. 'It's okay, lady. They're just watering the plants. They'll be out soon. Honest.'

'Now look here, young man, if you and your friends don't clear off, I'm calling the police.'

'It's all right, Glenda,' Grace called out as she neared the gate. 'We've just been making sure the house is secure.'

Glenda's face lit up. 'Ahh, it's the two nice lesbians who visited me yesterday. I thought I recognised your little dog.'

Tana, Josh and Wai all turned to Grace and Marla.

In a low singsong voice, Marla said, 'Don't ask.'

The three men collectively nodded.

Unfazed, Grace said, 'You remembered us, how lovely. Anyway, nothing is wrong. We're just –'

'Would you all like to come and have a cup of tea?' cut in Glenda. 'It's really no trouble.'

Taking Glenda by the arm, Grace started leading her back to her house.

Marla took a quick step towards Grace, whispering, 'Give her your phone number. Get her to call if she sees anything.'

Grace flashed an eyebrow raise at Marla. 'That's lovely of you Glenda, but we need to get on. They don't make people like you these days. When we're back this way, we'll pop in for sure.'

It took time for Grace to explain why she was giving her a business card then to detach herself. On the way back to their respective vehicles, they again promised to keep Tana in the loop. Tana got into his courier van but Wai hung from the open passenger door. Giving them a smouldering look, he said, 'Good luck and ahh' – he flashed his eyebrows – 'have fun, ladies.'

He disappeared instantly, dragged into the van by a scolding Tana. 'Don't you get fresh, you cheeky arsehole.'

Marla and Grace were still laughing as they crossed the road with Indy. They could hear Tana lecturing Wai on manners in his unique style as the van sped away.

CHAPTER 26

'What have you found out?' a worried-looking Carter asked as he opened the front door.

With the evening drawing in, and with no concrete plan of attack, they had headed back to Carter's house, buying wine and chocolate to thank him for letting them stay. After insisting they relax with a glass of wine while he cooked, Indy again trotting behind his every move, they related the day's events.

When Grace told him how they almost missed getting into Lauren's house, he laughed. 'Life is fickle. What did you find?'

'Not a lot,' said Marla, nodding to Grace.

'She kept a newspaper,' said Grace. 'It was an old copy of the *Waikato Times* that had a story about a man who died in a car crash.' She paused, watching Carter's reaction as he turned an element down and joined them at the breakfast bar.

'Clearly this is germane,' he said, his manner serious. 'I'm not seeing it.'

Grace took out her phone, finding the image of the story. 'Read it. Tana confirmed that the Joy mentioned is Lauren.'

Using his fingers to expand the story, Carter grimaced as he read. Returning Grace's phone, he said, 'This must be Lauren's past, the one she occasionally mentioned but never spoke about.' After sipping his wine, he said, 'Her husband died in a car crash but they, this Reverentia community, they're suggesting this Joy, Lauren, was involved in something darker. They wanted the police to find Joy Leslie, the missing wife, to ask questions. Do I have that right?'

Marla nodded.

Grace took out a notepad from her bag. 'I need to get my head around the timeline.' Drawing a line in red across the page, at the far end she added a tick mark, writing *Today*. 'This story came out two years ago.' She put a tick mark halfway along the line with the label *Newspaper Story*.

Marla, reading from Grace's phone, said, 'The story says the accident occurred three years earlier. Joy,' – she shrugged briefly – 'Lauren, disappeared after the funeral.'

'Which must have been when Tana picked her up hitching,' said Grace, adding the events to the timeline. 'Then she lived with Tana for around two years before heading to Auckland and getting a job.'

'That's right,' said Carter, keeping an eye on dinner as he talked. 'I met her at karate when she must have worked there maybe nine months. We'd trained together for a while before she picked my business brains for the price of lunch. After that, Weeping Angels started going gangbusters.'

Adding that to the timeline, Grace said, 'That leaves roughly eighteen months between her starting the business and the story coming out. What was going on, Carter?'

Carter talked as he dished up. 'She was still working in the legal firm, being an investigator in the evening when she wasn't at karate. The business was growing, but the business model meant she wasn't getting paid.'

Passing them their plates, Carter explained their services-now-pay-when-you-can model.

Grace, who had heard Lauren's version of the model, said, 'Lauren told me a wealthy patron is funding the debt.'

'That's a recent event,' he said. 'Initially I ran a Kickstarter campaign to give the business some breathing space.'

Marla's eyes narrowed. 'When did you run the campaign?'

'About two years ago, give or take.'

'Around when the story came out?' said Grace, adding it to the timeline.

Forking pasta into his mouth, Carter leaned over. After swallowing, he said, 'Yep.'

They ate in silence until Grace asked Marla, 'Coincidence?'

Marla shrugged. 'Could be, but I'm not fond of coincidences. Did the campaign mention Lauren? Or carry her picture?'

He shook his head. 'Until recently, the entire operation avoided mentioning Lauren. It still runs as a separate company under my name. I did use the name Weeping Angels in the campaign, but that's not linked to Lauren.'

Putting her fork down, Marla rubbed her temples. 'The story comes out after three years. Why? I doubt the community elders woke up three years later with a "hang-on" thought. Whatever they suspected, they must have suspected it from the day of the crash.'

'Before I ran the campaign,' said Carter, 'when we discussed the business's need for cash, she mentioned a legal situation.'

They stared at Carter. Grace and Marla knew this was a time to stay quiet.

Recognising their interest, he hurriedly added, 'She didn't say much more. She didn't seem keen on the idea, but she said if she won, there'd be money. But after we secured money from the Kickstarter campaign, she didn't mention it again.'

'Let's make sure we have the sequence right,' said Marla. 'Lauren's in Reverentia, her husband dies in a car crash and she escapes as soon as she can.'

'Leaves in the clothes she's wearing, according to Tana's story,' said Grace.

Carter chimed in. 'The story says she was married. Does she inherit money or land?'

'I doubt a religious community would allow individuals to accumulate money, or own land,' said Marla. 'But she doesn't stick around to find out. Jump forward a few years, her business needs money. Lauren mentions a legal situation, but you run the Kickstarter campaign around when the story comes out. Does that sound right?'

'I can find out for sure,' he said and disappeared down the hall. In less than a minute he was back, looking at Grace's timeline. 'I started the campaign two weeks after the newspaper ran the story, the campaign ran for three weeks.'

'We don't know what Lauren did,' said Marla, 'but, possibly because of her actions, Reverentia came out swinging. You run the campaign, Carter, ease the money situation so Lauren backs off. Maybe. But, whatever she's done, it's ruffled the community's feathers.'

'The money must have been material,' said Grace. 'Enough to finance the company *and* get the community agitated.'

'Does that make the newspaper story a shot across the bows?' asked Marla. 'If you want to come out of hiding and try to claim what we see as rightfully ours, we'll fight like fury. But everyone stands down – until a few weeks ago.'

'What's happened in the last month or two, Carter?' asked Grace.

Slowly he shook his head. 'Nothing stands out.'

'Tana remembered Lauren saying, "bloody social media", and that "they'll be scared of going to court",' said Marla.

'The image,' said Grace. She fished the picture of Lauren out of her bag. 'Trudi, one of their investigators, gave me this picture of Lauren. She said they published it on social media but Lauren had the post deleted.'

Marla and Carter took turns looking at the picture.

'It's blurry but it's clearly Lauren,' said Carter. 'Do you think someone saw it and put two and two together?'

'It sounds like that's what Lauren thought,' said Marla.

'But why would she be scared of going to court?' asked Carter.

Marla and Grace went to talk simultaneously.

'I'll go,' said Grace. 'Lauren didn't say to Tana that *she* was scared, she said *they'll* be scared of going to court. The inference being that *they* must be the community.'

'That's how I read it,' said Marla. 'Not scared *of* Lauren. Scared of what might happen if everything is in the open.'

'If she thinks she can get money from the community,' said Grace, 'it has to involve the death of her husband, doesn't it?'

Marla nodded slowly. 'She left straight away and never went back. It's hard to imagine a different scenario.' Turning to Carter, she asked, 'And Lauren didn't mention anything out of the ordinary?'

'For the past few months,' he said, 'apart from working cases, her focus was on taking on the justice system. Planning to involve you, Ace,'

'Think carefully,' said Marla. 'You know, when you two were … well, you know.'

Smiling, he said, 'You're back to pillow talk?'

Marla raised her eyebrows. 'In your version of events, you weren't doing much else.'

Sniggering, he said, 'We weren't.' His face changed back to serious. 'No, nothing and if she had, I would've noticed – I love gossip. She's the sort that doesn't say much, but what she says is worth listening to.'

'Could they have been looking for her over the past two years?' asked Grace. 'You know, on the down low.'

'They would've parked it,' said Marla. 'Besides, I can't imagine anyone wanting to pay a PI firm's steep rates if they're bringing in nothing new month after month.'

After taking their plates away, Carter topped up their glasses with the last of the wine.

'You'd make a great husband,' said Grace. 'Or wife, for that matter. Complicated.'

'I know.' His tone suggested he really did know.

They sat in silence. Sipping their wine, thinking.

'What about McMahon?' Grace eventually asked.

Carter grunted. 'Him.'

'You know about him?'

'Sure, he's been a pain in the arse, especially financially, for months. Filing moronic case after case, finding our operations centre.'

'You don't think he's connected, though?' asked Grace.

Frowning, he said, 'He *could* be involved but he's like a little boy who hasn't got his way. A planned abduction doesn't seem to fit. Besides, removing Lauren won't stop us supporting his ex.'

'If we rule him out,' said Grace, 'for now, that leaves this church community, Reverentia. I've read stories in the media of church communities using PIs to spy on former members.'

Grace's phone blasting out 'Who are you?' interrupted their conversation. Grace looked at the screen. The caller wasn't one of her contacts, though she had a hunch who it might be.

'Kia ora, it's Grace.'

'What? Oh yes, of course, kia ora. Such a lovely language. Musical. Why people would prefer to say *gidday* is beyond me.'

Grace raised her eyebrows. 'Glenda, what's up?' Placing a finger to her lips, she put the call on speaker phone, putting her phone on the breakfast bar between them.

'You asked me to call if anything happened across the road. Well, what a kerfuffle. About an hour after you left, sirens started wailing from Patrick's house, they were deafening. I went across the road but there was no one around. I thought you may have come back and forgotten how to turn off the … thingy.'

'What happened?' asked Grace.

'A security company car arrived, eventually. They turned off the alarm and we watched them check the property.'

'We?' asked Grace.

'Most of the neighbours came out to see what was going on, you couldn't hear yourself think with that racket going on.'

'Did you talk to the security guards?'

'Of course,' said Glenda sounding indignant. 'She said they'd found a broken window but whoever had done it had run off. Probably kids, she said. It happens all the time, she said. She was so matter-of-fact, far too serious. In fact, she looked like a lesbian too – maybe you know her?'

Marla put her hand over her mouth, Grace rolled her eyes. Carter looked at each of them.

'The police arrived but they didn't stay long. I tried to talk to them but they were very rude. They said, "Sorry, we're busy". They didn't look busy.'

Grace smiled knowingly when Marla opened her eyes wide.

'Can you do me a favour, Glenda? Can you send me the files from your doorbell camera. Like we did earlier.'

After a short silence, her voice less sure, she said, 'Of course, if I can remember how.'

As Grace patiently talked her through opening the file explorer, Marla wrote down the path where the files were located. In less time than Grace had anticipated, Glenda had selected two files, sending them to Grace's email alias – ace26@proton.me. After congratulating Glenda for being a vigilant neighbour, she ended the call and opened her laptop, setting it up on the breakfast bar.

'God, you two are fun to have stay,' said Carter grinning. His face changed to confused. 'Why does she think you're –'

Marla intercepted Carter's question. 'It's my hair.'

'Right,' said Carter. 'So, who broke in?'

'I initially thought it must be whoever was at Tana's a fortnight ago,' said Marla, 'But –'

'The PIs?' cut in Grace. 'If they're watching Tana, we led them to Lauren's house.'

'It can't have been them,' said Marla. 'How long did it take to drive here?'

'From Church Road?' said Grace. 'About twenty minutes. Why?'

The logic struck Grace and Carter simultaneously, their eyes widening.

'It's what I'd do,' said Marla. 'If I know which house is Lauren's, there's no need to rush. But I'm curious who these two new people are, so I'd follow them. Once I know enough, then I'll go to Lauren's house, see what I can find out.'

'But they set off the alarm,' said Grace. 'They must have had to scarper before the intrepid Glenda caught them single-handedly. Do you think they'll come back here?'

Marla nodded, adding as Carter made to stand, 'Not now. If I was them, and my car's parked in the driveway, which it is, I'd figure this is where they're staying. So, run the licence plate, if they have that sort of access, come back in the morning – early.'

'I assume the plate number won't help them,' said Grace.

'It's registered to a phantom on Waiheke Island.'

'Parts of this aren't adding up,' said Grace shaking her head. 'If it's the same people, and they're responsible for Lauren's disappearance, why are they still following Tana?'

'That's why it can't be them,' said Marla. 'Whoever has Lauren knew where to park her car and they knew where she lived. That means, as strange as it sounds, it's a different crew.'

'I see,' said Carter. Then he shook his head slowly. 'No, I don't see.'

Grace, also trying to put the pieces together, took a moment to collect her thoughts. 'Lauren's former life has reached out to stop her from claiming money from them – that seems possible. The PIs, the ones that approached Tana, they had to have figured out that he knows Lauren – that also seems possible, but I can't see how. What makes no sense is what happened tonight.'

'No,' agreed Marla. 'No trained PI would have missed the alarm system on Lauren's house. That's why the security guards thought it was kids, smash and grab is what kids do.'

'What you're saying …' Carter put a finger to his lips. 'No, I still don't know what you're saying.'

'What I'm *thinking*,' said Marla, 'is that we need to find out who's following us and why. That'll eliminate them and, whatever's left, should hopefully lead us closer to Lauren.'

Grace's laptop ping informed her a new email had arrived. Smiling, she said, 'It's from MangereGlenda10@gmail.com.'

Angling her laptop so they could see, Grace opened the first video file. The street appeared empty, but on the far left of the screen the recording captured the outline of two male figures – one large and bulky, the other short and thin – jumping over the front gate and walking down Lauren's drive. Thirty seconds later the image stopped.

Grace opened the second file. The same street scene appeared, but this time an alarm was wailing. The same two figures leapt over the gate and ran back the way they had come. After a few attempts, she paused the action with the men in the frame. The image was blurry, the men's faces unrecognisable.

She let the action run, the image lurching one way then the other, the camera refocusing on a spry Glenda cutting across her lawn, stopping on the footpath. Neighbours joined her and an animated discussion was audible but not decipherable.

'It's lucky she closed her door,' said Carter.

Marla increased the playback speed to times three, the action reminding Grace of the exit scene of *The Benny Hill Show*. Slowing the action when a branded security car appeared, they saw two security guards head towards Lauren's house. Eventually, the alarm ceased. Back at their car, the security guards conversed with their back to the camera and the crowd. Glenda strode across the road.

'Look out, she's behind you,' said Carter, making them all laugh.

The rest of the video played out as per Glenda's narrative. She remonstrated with the security guards, the police arrived but didn't stay long, then the crowd dispersed. The last person to leave the scene, hopping from foot to foot, was Glenda who eventually retreated inside.

'Well?' asked Carter.

Marla chewed on her thumb nail. 'Those two are amateurs, at best.'

'But what are they doing?' asked Grace. 'If they're looking for Lauren, it doesn't make sense, Marla.'

'*Marla*?' said a confused Carter.

Grace made an I'm-sorry face. 'Oops.'

'It's no big deal,' said Marla. 'I can always shoot you both later … if I need to.'

Carter's look indicated he was unsure how to take this news.

'I'm joking, Carter,' she said.

He blew out a relieved breath.

'And Ace, if I'm honest, not much is making sense,' said Marla. 'Not yet, but the fog is thinning and there's nothing else we can do until morning. We'll chat with the two outside and go from there.'

Marla outlined her plan, which started with them getting up at 5.30am. Grace, who didn't mind early starts, thought Carter might baulk but he was keen to be involved – anything to help find Lauren, he said.

After showering, Grace headed to her room leaving Carter and Marla on the couch drinking a second bottle of wine, Indy between them acting as chaperone. After calling Sean and her children, she checked her emails to make sure she hadn't forgotten any major task. Before drifting off to sleep, the day's events swirling, she heard Carter's bedroom door close quietly, but not Marla's. The last sound she heard was quiet giggling.

CHAPTER 27

A blaring 5am alarm hits you like a physical assault. It took Grace a few moments to realise what it was and where she was. Her chosen alarm was the rocky Green Day song 'Redundant', which she usually snoozed through at least twice before forcing herself out of her warm bed. She didn't have that luxury this morning and, turning it off, she slid out of bed.

Putting on a thin oriental dressing gown she had found in the closet, she headed straight to the kitchen. Switching on the jug, she found a packet of instant coffee in the back of Carter's pantry. She had no experience with coffee machines that needed a pilot's licence to operate.

Carter emerged next, in a blue towelling dressing gown. Trailing him into the kitchen was Marla, dressed in dark activewear. Indy, seemingly grinning, trotted after them.

'Morena *les enfants*,' said Grace.

They both smiled, guiltily to Grace's eye.

'I'll make us *real* coffees,' said Carter.

With his back to them, Marla gave Grace a you're-not-my-mum look. Grace smirked.

Checking her watch, Marla said, 'We go in ten minutes.'

'Can we go through the plan again?' asked Carter.

'You'll leave first, Carter,' said Marla. 'We've got our routes planned and each other's phone numbers stored in case we need to keep in contact. I think you taking Indy works best.'

'Indy?' he said.

'It looks innocent, too innocent. You'll present our amateur PIs with a dilemma. Does one of them follow you or do they both stay watching the house?'

Carter reluctantly nodded.

'I go next,' said Grace. 'The men, or man, in the car has another dilemma.'

'Precisely,' said Marla. 'You walk the other way, circle around the block and you'll be back at the same time as Carter – ten minutes. Depending on the state of play, I'll either leave next or, if they've both gone, have a look inside their car, see if they've left any ID. We'll need to see how it unfolds but I'd like to have a chat with them, one way or another.'

'What say they get tough, or they're armed?' asked Carter.

'If I get any sense that they're armed,' said Marla, 'I'll disarm them immediately. Amateurs and guns are a terrible combination.'

In answer to Carter's look, Grace said, 'She can, she will and it'll be quick. You do karate, she's done the US Marine version.'

'Right,' he said.

'I doubt it'll come to that,' said Marla. 'What I've seen screams two blokes unaware they're miles out of their depth, maybe earning a few bucks on the side.'

'But from who?' asked Grace.

'Who indeed,' said Marla.

Grace was last to finish dressing, once again putting on yesterday's I'm-going-for-a-run clothes. In her last pair of fresh underwear and in a T-shirt borrowed from Carter, she applied liberal deodorant. When she came back into the kitchen, Marla and Carter were staring at a laptop. 'What's up?' she asked.

'Miss superspy here,' said Carter, 'installed a surveillance camera outside last night when she took Indy out for a slash.'

'Placed rather than installed,' said Marla. 'They'd gone home so I figured it wouldn't hurt to get a look at them this morning.'

Grace smiled. Security cameras had come a long way since the early days of black and white grainy images on video tape. The morning was bright and clear and Marla's camera captured the would-be spies in high-definition. The two figures, wearing sunglasses inside their dark coloured sedan, stood out like dog's balls. 'They should have a sign on the top of their car, like a pizza delivery arrow.'

'You head off, Carter,' said Marla. 'I'll text to let you know what they do.'

Taking Indy's lead, he headed for the front door.

'Hang on, you'll need this.' Marla took a green poo bag from her pocket, holding it out to him.

He looked at her open mouthed.

'I'd say it's just in case, but' – Marla shrugged – 'if she has to go, she goes.'

Indy stared up at Carter. Grace could have sworn the little dog gave a short, affirmatory nod.

'Why do I have –'

'Do it for Lauren,' cut in Grace.

Few of Carter's mannerisms were stereotypically gay but the odd look slipped out. His current pout wouldn't have been out of place on *RuPaul's Drag Race*. With a snort, he left.

He turned left, away from the parked dark-coloured sedan, pulled along by a keen Indy. The men in the car talked animatedly before the passenger got out, pulled on a cap and headed after Carter. Short and lean, he resembled one of the men recorded by Glenda's surveillance camera the previous night but not the man who had parked Lauren's car.

Marla shook her head. 'He couldn't look more obvious if he tried.' She sent Carter a text confirming that he had a tail and that the situation was under control.

'How long should I wait?' asked Grace.

Marla's phone pinged. Looking at the message, she laughed, showing it to Grace. It was a picture of Indy looking pleased with herself next to a small pile of poo on a manicured lawn. Carter's message was simply, *OMG* with the Munch scream emoji.

'Give him a couple more minutes,' said Marla. 'He'll take a while tackling the poo without getting his fingers dirty. God know what his tail is going to do.'

When it was time to go, Grace set off towards the car with the lone man sitting in the driver's seat. As she passed, he was staring at his phone as though he was reading a novel. In her peripheral vision she saw his eyes dart her way. She listened for the sound of a car door opening and closing but the hum from the nearby motorway made it difficult to hear.

A few seconds later her phone vibrated but it wasn't a text as planned, Marla was calling.

Not waiting for Grace to speak, Marla said, 'He didn't follow you so we'll pull a switch on him. Take the first side street that isn't a no-exit, get out of sight, text me the street name and wait.'

Grace had barely time to say, 'Okay,' before Marla terminated the call.

The next street met Marla's conditions. After she had texted Marla the information, using Google maps, she studied the surrounding streets to plot a new course back to Carter's house. She had to fight her journalistic curiosity, which wanted her to peek around the corner to see who was coming.

The time it took for Marla to arrive seemed like an age. Over the top of the leggings and dark-grey hoodie she was wearing, Marla had put on a long fawn overcoat, presumably Carter's.

'He's following me,' Marla said, as she took off the coat.

She didn't need to explain her thinking. Putting on the coat, Grace said, 'There's a side street on the left, it's a cul-de-sac but you'll be able to get out of sight.'

Marla sighted the street, briefly looked all around. 'Plot a route that runs into Carter. When you both get back, I'll be at their car.'

Marla sprinted across the road towards the street Grace had indicated. As Grace passed the cul-de-sac, there was no sign of Marla. The remainder of her loop walk was uneventful, boring even. Keeping a measured pace, she walked the quiet suburban streets. Ellerslie was an affluent suburb, each house and garden neat and orderly. No doubt, there would be expensive EVs parked inside security-system controlled double garages as heteronormative couples and their 2.1 children slept peacefully. No one slept in the garage in Ellerslie.

Grace shook her head, now was not the time for moralising about inequality.

The man following her – she had risked a glance when she took the final corner onto the street where Carter lived – was around one hundred metres behind. Dressed in rugby training gear, he looked like neither a PI nor an early-morning Ellerslie resident.

Carter, on his preplanned route, was approaching her position, Indy trotting along in front. The man following Carter was well back in the distance, so she waited. They were around 200 metres away from Carter's house and the car belonging to the two tailing them. Although the distance made it difficult to be certain, Marla looked like she was sitting cross-legged on the bonnet of their car. Their respective tails would soon meet, the position they found themselves in brutally clear.

'Any hiccups?' she asked.

Falling in alongside her, a scowling Carter said, 'Yes.'

'What happened?'

'It was horrific. I won't be able to walk in my own neighbourhood again.'

Grace rolled her eyes. 'Come on Carter, it was only a poo. It's normal.'

His head shot around, eyes accusing. '*One* poo was bad enough. And it was warm.' He made a vomiting noise.

Starting to laugh, Grace said, 'I know I can't use this language, but Jesus, Carter, you are such a poof.' Her eyes suddenly widened. 'Indy had a second poo, didn't she?'

Exasperated, he said. 'How is that even possible. The first lot was immense – a veritable faecal mountain. Then, on number forty-one's immaculate, manicured berm – plop.'

Grace choked back a laugh. 'Roxy, my partner's retriever, has been known to squeeze out three.'

His mouth fell open.

'It's a gift,' she said laughing.

His eyes narrowed. 'You're enjoying this, aren't you?'

They carried on walking in silence. Grace could see that Marla was indeed sitting on the bonnet of their car in the lotus position. She had the passenger's door wide open to send them a message.

Reaching the car, looking behind her to confirm their tails were approaching, she said to Marla, 'All good?'

'All good,' she said. 'Even from here, I can see they're shitting themselves.' Sliding off the bonnet, she took the lead from a stern Carter

Looking at him sideways, Marla asked, 'Are you okay?'

'I'm *fine*,' he said in that tone that unmistakenly meant he was anything but fine.

Grace patted his shoulder. 'How are we going to play this, Marla?'

With a last look at Carter, Marla said, 'Ace, you take the passenger side. You better have Indy. Carter, you take the driver's side. Get your phones out and record the action. I'll do the talking.'

The two men approached slowly, their eyes darting around, faces grim. They knew the confrontation was inevitable but human nature dictated that putting it off, even for a few seconds, was desirable – no one runs to the gallows. The shorter man was Māori and well-dressed, the baseball-style cap he was wearing at odds with his sharp appearance. The man ready for rugby training was fair and built solidly. If he did play rugby, it was in the tight five. They stopped ten or so metres from the car.

The shorter man took off his cap and stepped towards them. He opened his mouth, but Marla, who must have been waiting precisely for this moment, beat him. Her voice low, her American accent strong, she sounded menacing. 'If you threaten me, threaten us, that's going to fuck me off.' She slowly pushed her sunglasses onto the top of her head. 'Now tell me, what are you doing and who are you doing it for?'

Licking his lips, the short man was clearly worried but, to Grace's journalistic eye, calculating too.

'We're trying to locate someone. For a friend.'

Marla stared coldly. Her voice matching her look, she said, 'It's a fair start. Truthful, though light on detail, but we'll get there. I know who you are.' She took two wallets out of her pocket and tossed them over. Landing at their feet, they each bent down to retrieve their wallet, putting them in their pockets without inspection.

'Here's a tip for you – if you take ID on a stakeout, keep it on you. I've taken pictures of your driver's licences – in case you were wondering. Now, who are you looking for?'

'We don't know her name,' said the short man as his larger friend shifted from foot to foot. 'That's what we're trying to find out. We think her first name is Lauren.' The rugby player nodded seriously.

Grace zoomed her phone in on the two men to capture their faces in HD. Marla was right, these two were amateurs. They wanted to get this finished so they could take off as soon as humanly possible.

Taking her time, as though she was considering his answer, Marla asked, 'Wasn't there enough time to find out when you *broke into her house*? Do not tell me you didn't see the alarm.'

Turning, the rugby player hissed, 'I told you it was a dumb idea.'

'Shut up,' snapped the shorter man without turning his head.

The man in the rugby gear was three times the size of his colleague, and could have squashed him like a bug, yet the short man was firmly in charge.

Holding Marla's gaze, he waited until a car had driven past, the driver taking no notice of the streetside theatre playing out. 'How did you know about that?'

'I watched you on video,' said Marla. 'The recording's enough to get you standing in front of judge … answering awkward questions.'

The rugby player shook his head. 'I should've said no.'

Marla patted the air with her hand. 'It's okay, big fella. I have no interest in seeing you two get into trouble. After you tell me what I need to know, you get to drive away. If I see you again, I won't be happy. But, if I don't, it'll be like our paths never crossed. Okay?'

The rugby player nodded keenly. The shorter man licked his lips.

'The offer's not negotiable,' said Marla. She again waited until he was about to speak. 'And it expires soon.'

His shoulders slumped. 'Okay.'

Smiling, Marla said, 'Great. This shouldn't take long. Let's go back to the beginning. How did you know to follow Tana?'

The two men looked at each other. It was unrehearsed.

'Who's Tana?' asked the short man.

A small laugh escaped from Marla. 'Good to know. Who *were* you following then?'

Pointing at Grace, he said, 'Her. Ace Marks. We saw her outside where the woman works, holding up a sign. We followed her and, ahh' – he exhaled – 'we bugged her rental when she went into a church.'

Marla turned to Grace, eyebrows raised.

Shrugging, Grace nodded. 'I made a sign saying *I'm looking for Lauren.* It's how I got their attention through their security cameras. It never occurred to me that *I* might be being followed.'

Turning back to the two men, Marla said, 'Tidy work. Is that why you think her name's Lauren?'

'It was our first break,' he said.

'Then I arrived on the scene,' said Marla.

'You dropped the rental car back, but we knew you were staying here so' – he held up his hands and shrugged – 'we bugged your car too.'

Marla looked at the short man with an incredulous look. 'You bugged *my* car?'

'Sorry,' he said. And he sounded sorry. 'Two nights ago. Last night we went to see what was so interesting about the house.' He lowered his eyes. 'I hoped to grab a few documents, you know, bills and stuff with her name on it. We went around the back. It didn't look like the house had a security system.'

'We saw you strut down the driveaway and sprint away like rabbits,' said Grace, deciding to embellish what they had seen.

'We're getting there,' said Marla. 'Why didn't you follow Ace this morning?'

'We thought you' – he nodded at Marla – 'might be Lauren. We were waiting for you to leave.' He shook his head. 'I thought something was up but I don't do this shit for a living.'

'What do you do for a living?' asked Carter, his voice movie-esque ice-cool gangster.

'I'm a …' He paused as a car drove past them slowly. Everyone waited. 'I'm a manager. This fella's a labourer at our site. If there's any blowback, leave him out of it.'

The rugby player looked a mix of grateful and relieved.

Marla said, 'There'll be no blowback. You don't even have to tell me who you're working for, you just have to nod. McMahon?'

They both nodded.

The short man said, 'He owns the company where we work. To say no would be a career-limiting move. And he pays well.'

'Did he say why?' asked Grace.

'No, but it's always the same. It's usually related to his ex, sometimes a woman he's been seeing. He gets fixated.'

'Have you done this for him before?'

'I haven't,' said the rugby player, shaking his large head.

The short man shrugged., 'It's easy money, or it was; this one was different. He didn't know who she was, wanted me to find out.'

Grace stepped forwards. 'Like where she lives. What colour underwear she prefers.'

'No.' Anger flashed over his face. 'I'm not a pervert.'

'Your boss is though,' said Grace.

An uneasy silence fell over the group.

'I'll tell you what, fellas,' said Marla. 'I can honestly tell you that I'm not Lauren. In fact, *we're* looking for Lauren too though, as you might imagine, for an entirely different reason.' She turned to Grace. 'Do you have a burner email you can give them?'

Grace took out a business card, one with her name but omitted her contact details. She wrote the same email address she had given to Glenda on the back.

Marla took it and walked over to the two would be PIs. The short man took it, though not willingly.

'Here's the deal,' said Marla. 'You get your bug off my car and take off. Keep looking for Lauren. If you find out anything, and I mean *anything*, you email the information through to Ace. If I find out otherwise' – Marla used her finger and thumb as a pretend gun, winking and clicking out the side of her mouth – 'I'll pay you a visit.'

The look the rugby player gave his partner suggested he was keen to get away. The short man didn't move, he asked, 'What do you want us to tell McMahon. I mean, he knows we've been following someone.'

Marla shrugged. 'Tell him you thought you'd found Lauren, but it was a wild goose chase.'

'He won't be happy. He won't pay.'

'Sad,' said Marla. 'How happy will he be if I tell him what really happened?'

'Got it,' he said.

'If I was you two, I would make this my last PI run,' said Marla. 'I've known people who created far less aggravation than you've caused me get cut up and stuffed into garbage cans. I mean, on principle I should shoot you for bugging my car.'

Their eyes widened.

'Just saying,' said Marla. She flashed an eyebrow raise at Grace and Carter, they headed towards Carter's house.

The bigger man dived nimbly, surprising because of his size, under Marla's car to retrieve their bug. Before they were inside Carter's house, the two would-be PIs had performed a fast U-turn, tyres squealing and had driven away. Carter made more coffee, Marla filled Indy's water bowl, then they started their debrief.

'What does McMahon want with Lauren?' asked Carter as he frothed some milk.

'Nothing good,' said Grace. 'He's a serial fuckwit, that's for sure. There must be a law against tracking women's movements.'

'Maybe,' said Marla. 'It'd be hard to prove, though.'

'Which is why Lauren is doing what she's doing,' said Grace. 'The law's stacked in the abuser's favour. And as most abusers are male, the law's stacked for men – what a surprise.'

'Let's put McMahon and the law to one side,' said Marla. 'We can rule him out of Lauren's disappearance. As you said last night, Ace, that leaves us with only Reverentia, the community she fled.'

Frowning, Grace said, 'They put PIs on her who discover the connection with Tana. They stake him out and she arrives late on a Friday. They seize their chance.'

'Would PIs snatch a person?' asked Carter. 'Abduction's a serious crime.'

Marla went to drink her coffee but stopped. 'Good point. PIs would never get involved in an abduction. That would mean jail time – guaranteed.'

'Tana didn't think the men were from the community,' said Grace.

They drank their coffees, each thoughtful. It had been quite a morning. When Marla was around, action tended to happen thick and fast.

'Do we need to join all the dots?' asked Carter.

Marla pouted. 'It's better if you can, but you usually can't. Whatever happened to Lauren, it was planned. You can't snatch her, know where to park her car, know where she lives and not leave a trace. Like you Ace, I can't work out how the PIs, or whoever they were, knew to approach Tana. I can see how they could get to Lauren through Tana, that's understandable.'

'There were two or three weeks in between,' said Grace. 'We have no idea what happened in that time.'

'That's right,' said Carter. 'Were they bugging Tana's phone? His car? Those two idiots managed to bug both your cars.'

'I cannot believe they bugged my car – the fucking cheek of it.' Marla shook away her annoyance. 'The community, probably via the people who approached Tana, they must have joined the dots and worked out who Lauren was and decided they needed to talk to her … on their terms.'

'It's the only scenario that makes sense,' said Grace.

'Carter, you're right,' said Marla. 'If it was the community, we don't need to know how they did it. We do need to pay them a visit.'

CHAPTER 28

Marla, Grace and Carter spent the rest of the morning scoping out the best approach for staking out Reverentia. They needed to get close enough to see if there was any sign of Lauren, ideally without being seen themselves. The size of the community complicated plans.

Taking time out to ring Sean, her children and check her emails, Grace had received a single word email from her editor – *Well?* She followed her reply – *Feeling great, thanks for asking* – with a second email in which she documented her progress. Because she had returned the rental, and wasn't staying in a hotel, she hoped he might lighten up.

Using Google maps to get an aerial view of the community, they saw large buildings clustered around the church on the lower level of what was a single, large farm. Connected by a winding gravel road, the top section contained additional farmland and a few scattered houses. Marla, using Carter's whiteboard, drew what resembled a battlefield plan.

'If they're holding Lauren,' said Grace, 'they'd keep her in one of the main complexes, wouldn't they?'

Marla frowned.

'Wouldn't that mean the other community members would know she's there?' asked Carter. 'Keeping her somewhere remote would mean they could keep her isolated.'

Marla's frown deepened. 'Both options are possible.'

'No one's going to talk, though, are they?' said Grace. 'Those communities are all the same, they brainwash them from birth to believe whatever's spouted at them.'

'We need to look around,' said Marla. 'See the lie of the land.'

'That's not likely,' he said. 'Even if they don't have her, they're hardly likely to let the famous three romp around their farm.'

Grace grinned. 'Am I thinking what you're thinking?'

With a brief eyebrow flash, Marla said, 'You bet.'

'What did I miss?' said Carter, looking at them in turn.

An hour and a half later, having left an unimpressed Indy at Carter's house, Carter pulled his spotless Atlantic-blue Volkswagen Golf into the Kauri Loop Walkway carpark. The walkway ran next to a river that bordered the church's farm before the track headed into the foothills. At the top it briefly ran along the ridgeline, the boundary of the church's farm, before plunging back through the trees. Their initial target was a small picnic area where the loop track diverged.

A five-minute walk from the carpark, the picnic area was clean and tidy with a single combined picnic table and benches in the middle of the clearing. A more recent solid-wood bench was situated on a small knoll that provided a view over the river, across the community's farmland, to the church and buildings nestled near the hills. If someone had wanted to create a base from which to surveil Reverentia, they couldn't have picked a more suitable spot.

'It looks made for us,' said Marla, taking out her DJI First-Person-View drone from its carry bag. She readied it for flight – taking off the lens cover, attaching propellors, slotting in a fully-charged battery and turning on the X-box-lookalike controller.

Carter, wearing a small blue backpack, grunted as he read the sign at the start of the track. 'An hour in total. That'll mean forty minutes uphill and twenty down.'

'You're young and fit,' said Grace. 'Well, youngish.'

Carter smirked. 'That's rich coming from you.'

Grace pressed her lips together to stop from laughing.

'Before you head off, let's make sure we're all on the same page,' said Marla. 'You go, Carter.'

'I head uphill and find a position near the top where I can stay hidden but also see the community's buildings. I text when I'm in position.'

'Twenty minutes after you leave,' said Grace, taking over, 'Marla's going to fly the drone over their farm to get aerial images that we can review later.'

'I'll fly the drone in stealth mode,' she said. 'They'll be able to see it but they won't hear it. Hopefully no one looks up. When I've covered most of the farm, I'm going to buzz the community. That'll give us close-up images we can review plus we'll see what reaction we get.'

Tapping the camera hanging around his neck, he said, 'When you do that, I'm to watch out for' – he used his fingers as quotation marks – 'unusual activity.'

'What do you think they'll do?' asked Grace.

'That's the fun of the fair,' she said. 'I don't know.'

'Are you armed?'

'Always, when I'm in the field,' she said. 'I doubt they'll try strongarm tactics but it doesn't hurt to be prepared.'

After giving Marla's body a careful once over, Carter said, 'Where do you carry it? I can't see an obvious bulge.'

A second later, having retrieved her Glock 19 from a concealed holster, she offered it grip first it to a wide-eyed Carter.

'Jesus, fuck,' he said. 'I am *so* glad you're on our side.'

Holstering it, she said, 'It's a last resort.'

'Like the time I was about to get the shit knocked out of me with a baseball bat,' said Grace. Four alt-right thugs disguised as activists had invaded her house to 'teach her a lesson' for reporting on their activities.

'I recall it vividly,' said Marla. 'Four on one was hardly fair, karate or no karate.'

Carter shook his head in a combination of admiration and disbelief.

'Let's do this,' said Marla. 'Leave your keys with Ace. Just in case it goes tits up.'

Dropping his keys into Grace's outstretched hand, he said, 'Now listen to me you two' – he glared at them in turn – 'do not eat the cake I bought. That's for dessert.' After underlining his sentence with a final hard stare, he headed up the track.

Grace, waiting until he was out of earshot, said, 'I thought he was going to tell us to be careful. He'd be hard work to live with, no wonder he's single, handsome and all.'

Grinning, Marla checked her watch. 'I launch at 2.25. Fancy a piece of cake?'

Grace winced. 'Don't.'

They settled themselves on the wooden bench, taking in the view of the farm, Marla occasionally checking the time. Grace thought about the cake. She was having a *because-I'm-not-allowed-it-I-want-it* moment. Her partner Sean had learnt a long time ago never to say, 'Do you really need another glass of wine?'

Passing her phone over, Marla said, 'You can watch on this,' as she put on the drone's goggles.

'They're not flattering, are they,' said Grace. 'They make you look like a fly.'

'They weren't designed as a fashion accessory,' Marla replied over the angry-bee noise the drone had started making. Climbing slowly at first then rapidly, the drone became a small dot in the sky. Grace became engrossed in the images the drone was capturing.

'Can you zoom in more?'

'That's as good as it gets at this height,' said Marla. 'I'm going to fly a grid pattern. Keep an eye out for buildings that look interesting. When it's time to have a bit of fun, we can check them out.'

Recording the flight, Marla flew the drone in a criss-cross pattern over the farm, documenting the layout of Reverentia. In the centre, its back against the tree-covered foothills, stood a massive church. Five large housing complexes that resembled multi-storey motels radiated out from the church. Further out, smaller farmhouses and buildings dotted the landscape. After capturing the lower level, Marla flew the drone over the upper tier of the farm, which was mainly farmland with a handful of houses. This task completed, the drone landed at her feet like an obedient dog.

As she took off the goggles, Grace said, 'You're handy with that.'

Smiling, she said, 'I've been using it heaps when I'm touring. Did you notice anything unusual?'

Grace shook her head. 'Apart from their huge church, a phallic monument to extravagance, and the accommodation blocks, the rest of the houses and farm buildings look normal.'

'That's what I thought. They could be using any of the buildings to hold Lauren.'

'*If* they're holding Lauren,' said Grace.

'Feeling pessimistic, Ace?'

'Aren't you?'

Before Marla could answer, Grace's phone pinged. Grace read it out, smiling. 'In position. My arse muscles are killing me. I shall need a rub down tonight.'

'Don't look at me,' said Grace as she put her phone in her back pocket. 'I have a partner. Besides, relaxing with a wine versus massaging a gay man's buttocks, it's no contest.'

Marla, making a face, said, 'When you put it like that. He'll have to make do with cake and a sore arse.'

Grace started laughing.

Marla put her hand over her mouth. 'You're bad. Anyway, ready to incite the locals?'

'Damn straight,' said Grace.

Having replaced the battery with a fully charged one, Marla again commanded the drone to soar into the sky. Positioning it directly above the church, she set it to hover. Then, more to herself than to Grace, she said, 'Let's have a bit of fun.'

The church appeared to hurtle towards the screen. Just before a collision seemed certain, the image changed as the drone wheeled to one side, circling the building. With the camera zoomed in, it appeared the drone was only metres from the building. Marla flew the drone around the community, skimming over trees and past houses – it was like watching a video game.

Although the drone couldn't record sound, the propellers drowning out all other noise, Grace could see people shouting and yelling. Flitting above the scene, the drone captured the antics as men and women pointed and ran around in circles. Marla flew the drone slowly around the large accommodation complexes.

'I saw a man with a gun,' said Grace.

'I saw him too,' said Marla. 'Where's there's one, there'll be more. Time to check out the outbuildings.'

Grace's phone pinged. 'Carter says two cars are on the move, heading for the main gate.' Grace could see the cars, dust trailing behind them. When they reached the road, they turned towards their position.

'They're coming our way,' said Grace.

'I thought it might take them longer to work out where we were. Never mind, it'll take them five minutes to get to the carpark and walk here.'

'What are we going to do when they get here?'

'It's a public place,' said Marla. 'I'll be interested to see how they handle the situation.'

'What about the guns?'

Marla, her face unreadable behind the goggles, stayed quiet for a long moment. 'That'll be interesting too. I doubt they'll arrive armed. Too risky.'

Another ping interrupted their discussion.

Grace passed on Carter's message. 'A lone car is heading uphill, fast.' Grace pinpointed the tell-tale dust cloud accompanying the vehicle.

'Oh,' said Grace.

'Oh, what?'

Staring at the dust cloud progressing up the hill, Grace said, 'I've just realised, the road that car's taking ...'

'Is the road that Lauren's husband drove off.' Marla finished Grace's thought. 'Yeah, shit's feeling real.'

The drone climbed skywards, Marla piloting it towards the upper level of the farm.

'Tell Carter to come back,' said Marla. 'Get him to hide his camera in his backpack.'

'Done.'

After sending the message Grace looked at the images the drone was capturing. Marla was hovering the drone where it could take in the whole top section of the farm. The only movement Grace could see, apart from a farmhand on a quadbike moving a herd of cows, was the car heading towards the furthest building.

'How far away are our visitors?' asked Marla.

Standing on the wooden bench, Grace said, 'Almost at the carpark.'

The images from the drone remained steady. The car stopped outside a distant house. Two men got out and, even from a distance, it was clear one was carrying a gun.

'Are you going in closer?' asked Grace.

Marla licked her lips before quietly saying, 'No.'

After the men had gone inside the house, Marla let the drone sink below the ridgeline, flying it towards Carter's position. When she found the loop track, she manoeuvred the drone until it picked out Carter's distinctive blue backpack.

'He's halfway down,' said Marla. 'He'll arrive just after them.'

'Why's he stopped?'

The image of Carter increased as Marla focused the drone's full attention on him.

'Oh, he's having a slash,' said Grace. She sent him a text – *Having a nervous one?*

On the screen, Carter, who was descending, stopped. Taking out his phone, he read her message then scanned the sky until he located the drone. The technology was amazing. On a remote walking track, on the side of hill, she could clearly lip read him – fuck off.

The image on the phone went blank. Marla started packing up as the sound of angry bees grew louder. She almost caught the drone as it landed. Within thirty seconds she had packed the drone away, hiding the bag in the bushes behind the wooden bench.

'Do you think they'll be fooled?' asked Grace.

Marla shook her head. 'But it'll throw them. When people encounter a scene different from what they expect, it creates doubt.'

The cars were now out of sight, presumably in the carpark. Two cars meant two to eight men, there was no chance they would send women on what they would consider 'men's work'. Call it four men, possibly armed. Carter arriving on the scene soon after them.

As they sat waiting on the solid wooden bench, Marla eased closer to Grace until their legs were touching. Turning, Grace said, 'It's a strange time to be trying that?'

Marla laughed. 'I'm just making the scene they're going encounter more awkward.' She held Grace's hand and, staring into her eyes, said, 'Don't worry, I'm not going to kiss you.'

Her spine stiffening, Grace said, 'I should hope not. That'd be … odd.'

Marla looked over Grace's shoulder. 'They're almost here.' Tilting her head, she came to within an inch of Grace's face. 'From this angle,' she whispered, their lips almost brushing, 'when they come into the clearing, that's exactly what it'll look like we're doing.'

'I can see how you honey-trapped that politician now.' To infiltrate New Zealand's newest alt-right funded political party, Marla had attended their conference, allowing one of the candidates – her target – to *pick her up*. Grace, unable to relax with Marla's face so close, said with minimal lip movement, 'How far away are they?'

'Ten seconds,' whispered Marla.

Behind her, Grace heard the noise of the men stomping into the clearing. Marla her eyes closed, squeezed Grace's hand. Grace didn't move.

Marla's eyes flicked open. She leapt up, yelling, 'What the hell?' Grace spun around, eyes wide, holding her breath.

Four men stood in the clearing, forming a line behind the elderly leader of the deputation. Five men in total, no guns on display. Presumably a community elder, he resembled an accountant in an odd shade of blue pants, light blue shirt and black tie. Glaring at them through thick rimmed glasses, his face and grey hair painted him sixty – minimum. The men standing behind him were the closest people Grace had seen to clones. Beatles-era haircuts, the same shade of blue overalls, a light blue office-styled shirt and, incongruently, they were wearing gumboots.

Caught by surprise, as Marla had intended, the elder seemed lost for words, his mouth hanging open. The young men behind stared, wide-eyed. Not only the first time they had likely seen women kissing, they had, perhaps, never considered it possible. In their world, that sort of thing didn't exist.

'First those kids and now you lot,' said Marla. 'What's with this place?'

The elder glared at them, then around the clearing. 'What kids?'

'The kids flying the drone,' she said. 'They were here when we finished walking the loop track.'

Grace maintained an annoyed, concerned look. The utter confusion on the faces of the four young farmhands was priceless. They clearly didn't know where to look or what to think. Grace decided to add to their discomfort by standing right behind Marla, an intimate hand on her shoulder.

'I didn't see any kids,' the elder said.

'They left on a motorbike when we arrived,' said Marla.

'I think we scared them away,' said Grace. 'You know, young boys can feel threatened by two women.' She raised her eyebrows to the four fidgeting farmhands. 'Can't they?'

'You were on the loop track?' the elder asked. He had an edge to his voice that said he knew they had staged the scene.

Marla nodded slowly. 'Our friend's still coming down.'

'Why isn't she with you?'

'*He* stopped for a slash,' said Marla. 'And what's it to you? What are you and the barber shop quartet doing here?'

Grace gritted her teeth to keep from smirking.

His gaze grew hard. 'Someone was flying a drone over our farm. I think it was you two.'

'Why should I give a damn what you think?' said Marla. 'Besides, it was only kids having fun, why the posse?'

'Because' – he pursed his lips – 'it was dangerous.'

'Boys will be boys,' said Grace, 'as people like to say to excuse all manner of misogynistic behaviour.'

Looking confused, the man was about to speak when Carter arrived. The section of the track that led into the clearing was steep, and he literally ran into the clearing. 'Made it,' he said panting, doubled over, his hands on his knees. Straightening, he said, 'Oh, we've got company. Interesting company but a bit weird. There's too much blue going on.' His hand outstretched, he strode confidently towards the community elder. 'Carter.'

The elder, once again thrown off kilter, shook his hand. 'Christian,' he said.

Carter shook his head seriously. 'No, I'm gay. I mean, there didn't seem much point if I was going to hell anyway – why not enjoy myself?'

The man snatched his hand back.

'You can't catch it, you know,' said Carter. 'Despite what you're telling these young men. What is the church's stance on masturbation these days?'

Two of young farmhands went bright red, but remained silent.

'Sorry lads,' said Carter. 'Didn't mean to give you away. You won't go blind, either. I'm living proof.'

'Let's go,' said the elder after giving them each a steely glare. 'If any *kids* fly a drone over our community again, we'll shoot' – he left a long pause – 'it down. And we'll be calling the police.'

'*We'll call* the police,' said Carter.

'What?' The man's face contorted.

'You're setting a bad grammatical example for your disciples,' said Carter. '*We'll call* the police. Not, *we'll be* calling the police.' He turned to Marla and Grace. 'And what's he talking about?'

They both made you-tell-me faces.

Clearly having had enough, the leader trudged back towards the carpark, the four farmhands falling in behind like ducklings.

Grace let go of Marla, reclaiming her personal space.

They watched them go.

Carter slumped onto the bench with a tried groan. 'That was fun,' he said.

Marla, her hand on his shoulder, said, 'You were brilliant, and hilarious. "What's the church's stance on masturbation?" Classic.'

'What do you think?' asked Grace. 'Is Lauren there?'

'It's hard to be sure,' said Marla. 'I get why they wouldn't want a drone flying over their community, buzzing the flock. Their response is over the top but they're a weird religious community worried about the outside world.'

'What about the car heading to the upper farm?' asked Carter. 'That looked strange?'

'That was the oddest part,' said Marla. 'And they were armed.'

'If it's connected,' said Grace. 'Why didn't you get a closer look at the house?'

'If that's where they're holding Lauren, and I buzzed the drone in, it would've tipped our hand.'

'Ahh,' said Carter. 'They'd move her.'

'Something like that,' said Marla. 'It looks as good a place to start as any and we need to act now, before it crosses their mind.'

Marla went to retrieve her drone. 'Make sure both cars head back,' she called out.

As they watched, the two-car convoy drove sedately through the community gates.

'Let's get out of here,' said a recovered Carter, setting off at a jog. He called over his shoulder, 'Last one back doesn't get any of *my* cake.'

They shared an eyeroll as they walked after him.

CHAPTER 29

Lauren massaged her wrists.

The large old man sitting opposite her said, 'I hope they didn't tie them too tight.'

Lauren breathed in deeply through her nose. They had broken their routine – something had happened. She'd already suffered through her daily half-hour sermon cum interrogation with Nathaniel Palmer, Reverentia's leader, but he was back. And while he was trying to look in control, he was perspiring heavily.

'What's happened?' she asked. 'I heard a commotion before.'

'It was nothing,' snapped Palmer. He forced a beaming smile, adding more calmly, 'Just kids being a nuisance.'

Reverentia kids are never a nuisance.

'Have you thought about what I suggested?' His voice was gravely, as if he needed to cough. 'Coming back to the community?'

Licking her dry lips, she forced herself to concentrate. 'I thought even you had given up on that. I told you, I want nothing to do with *your* community.'

'Your parents have been praying that you'll come back.'

'You've told me that.'

He sat back in his chair, his watery eyes staring at her through his thick glasses. 'Tell me again how you created a *fake* will for Keith.'

Lauren paused for a beat before answering. 'It wasn't fake. The one you produced for your lawyer, that was fake. You know that.'

'If that's true, where did it suddenly spring from after, how long was it, four years?'

Lauren paused, idly brushing non-existent dust off the sleeve of the long blue dress they had made her wear. They hadn't forced her, not physically, but Palmer had made it clear that unless she wore what the community demanded, she wouldn't be fed. She resisted at first but it didn't seem a battle she needed to win.

'It was in among the papers I took with me,' she said. 'I've told you that too.' This was a battle she needed to win. Palmer wanted to know how much she knew, to know he was safe. And if he discovered that she had taken a copy of Reverentia's accounts with her when she escaped … that would make her situation precarious.

Palmer's voice rose. 'Are you telling me that Keith kept papers that I didn't know about. That Keith was untrustworthy?'

'I took papers relating to me. I have no idea what papers he did and didn't keep.' She kept her voice even, adding, 'As you preach, it's not a *woman's* business. Can I have a glass of water, please?'

Sucking his teeth for a moment, he turned his head, speaking to one of the two young community members who had brought her out of the storeroom. 'Get her a glass of water.'

The glass was organised in silence. Palmer stared at Lauren, who held his gaze. When the water arrived, she drank it slowly.

When she had finished, he asked, 'Why didn't you contest the will, then? If you believe your will was authentic, why just slink away … again?'

'Because you were trying to frame me. You had that bottle of gin planted in the car.'

Sitting back, smiling with his eyes mockingly wide. 'Planted? That's a serious accusation. Why would anyone here want to do that?'

She shrugged away the question. *You know why.*

Drumming his fingers on the table, he eventually said, 'We'll continue this conversation later. I have the Lord's work to do.' Looking over at the young man, he said, 'Lock her up.'

As she was being led away, he said, 'We need to come to an understanding, Joy.'

She stopped and turned. 'It's Lauren.'

'If you prefer, *Lauren*. And we need to come to it tonight.'

'What sort of understanding and why tonight? Tell me why I won't go straight to the police when I get out of here. And I will get out of here.'

Palmer laughed, his jowls wobbling. 'The police? They're keen to see you too. You can explain why you disappeared' – his voice dropped octaves – 'after you killed your husband, Joy Leslie.'

Lauren went to speak, but Palmer carried on talking.

'You can tell them how you forged papers to create this Lauren Brown person you think you are. I, and the all the community, will tell them how you arrived here disorientated.' His voice changed to that of a concerned parent. 'We suspected you were on drugs, but we looked after you.' He leaned forwards, elbows on the table, his voice again low. 'No one outside the community knows you're here. No one knows how you arrived. It'll be your word against ours. A person on the run from the police versus an entire god-fearing community.'

Lauren glared at him.

'Are you going to save us time by giving us the password for your laptop?' he asked.

Lauren shook her head.

'We'll get into it,' he said, staring hard. 'We have contacts who are excellent with technology.'

You have no chance.

'I know you will,' said Lauren. 'It's not that hard.'

'Lock her in,' he said to the community member.

One of the young men led her gently back into the storeroom, bolting and locking the door.

Palmer called out, 'Have a good think, *Joy*. I'll be back later tonight. The sooner we can come to an understanding, the sooner we can all get on with our lives.'

Lauren heard the door shut, an engine start and a car drive away, the faint sound of tyres crunching over gravel.

Kicking the bible into a corner, she sat awkwardly on the floor. *What's changed?*

CHAPTER 30

'I think one of us should come with you,' said Grace.

Back at Carter's house, they reviewed the footage from the drone. The farm looked ordinary, at least for a religious community. It was the house at the far end of the farm's upper level, where the armed men had headed, that seemed the logical place to check first. After a rapid-fire planning session, they had decided that the sooner they found out if Reverentia was involved in Lauren's disappearance the better.

It was 7pm, still light and warm, when they again parked in the Kauri Loop Walkway carpark. Tramping uphill, they were soon at the place where Carter had positioned himself hours earlier. The evening was cooling as the sun dipped behind the hills. Soon it would be dark enough for Marla to go.

'We went through this,' said Marla. 'No offence, but I prefer to operate on my own. Besides, you'll see what I see, give or take.'

Marla was wearing a helmet with a high-definition video camera mounted at eye level, the images streamed to Carter's phone. Marla had dressed from head to foot in black, the pants she had borrowed from Carter. As he was a full head and shoulders taller than her, she had hemmed them using black electrical tape like bicycle clips, to Carter's dismay.

'We won't see anything,' said Carter. 'You said the camera doesn't have night vision. All we'll see is a mass of swirling blots like a Rorschach test.'

Holding up a powerful torch, Marla said, 'If it's worth seeing, you'll see it.'

'Is there sound?' asked Grace.

Walking a few paces away, she said, 'Testing, testing, one, two.'

They heard her voice clearly from Carter's phone.

'You can keep up a running commentary,' said Grace. 'We'll know when you're getting close.'

'Just don't expect me to be verbose. The wind carries voices for miles. That's another reason for you staying behind, Carter.'

'I don't have a foghorn for a voice.'

'It's loud enough,' she said. 'Aromas travel too. That deodorant you use, it's … strong. Any dog will smell you a mile away.'

'You are too much at times, Marla …' He paused. 'I don't know your last name, do I?'

'No.'

'Don't feel bad, Carter,' said Grace. 'I only found out through the SIS.'

They waited until the evening had drawn in sufficiently, the sky still with a faint red-orange tinge. Marla surveyed the hillside. 'Remember, any light will stand out like dogs' balls.'

Grace grinned. 'Talking like a Kiwi at last.'

'If you use your phones, make sure you're low to the ground, that's all.' They exchanged awkward fist bumps. Marla said a quiet 'Oorah', before she headed towards the ridgeline.

Grace and Carter made themselves comfortable on the blanket they had brought, putting Carter's phone between them. The image was pitch black, the odd flash of light on the screen as Marla presumably looked around. It was a clear night, and once their eyes acclimatised the moon and stars provided enough light for them to make out their surroundings.

'Just climbed the boundary fence.' Marla's voice was icy through the phone. 'Skirting towards the road as planned.'

They had plotted a path she could follow that would take her to the house in question without going near other houses or farm buildings. They couldn't tell much from the live stream except that Marla was moving, the odd incomprehensible light darting across the screen.

'What do you think?' asked Carter.

'I've been trying not to think,' she said. 'But, if Lauren's not here …'

'Do you think she's dead?'

'No.' Grace almost barked the word out. Clearing her throat, she said, 'I think she's here but, and you know Lauren better than anyone, what's the chance of her coming here willingly?'

'Zero. In fact, less than zero. She was obviously paranoid about them finding her.'

'As Marla said, the chances of this being random are also zero,' said Grace. 'She has to be here, it's the only logical conclusion. And we'll find her.'

They resumed their silent vigil. The wind rustling the bushes made a sinister background noise.

'On the gravel road.' Marla's voice cut the stillness.

'She's halfway,' said Carter.

After a small pause, Grace asked, 'What do you think of Marla?'

He stared upwards. 'She's a great friend to have. I mean, she doesn't know Lauren from a bar of soap, but it sounded like she dropped everything to help. Now she's running around in the dark, putting herself on the line.'

Grace stayed quiet.

'Did you mean as more than a friend?' he asked.

'Maybe.'

'Are you asking for me or for yourself?'

He was grinning like the Cheshire Cat and she slapped his arm. 'Twat. I didn't *sleep* with her last night.'

'Neither did I,' he said. 'Well, technically, we did sleep together, but we didn't get *jiggy*. It's comforting to sleep with someone without the complication of sex or a relationship.'

'Pyjamas?'

He sniggered. 'I haven't worn pyjamas since I left home.'

'That's the bit I don't get,' said Grace. 'When you jump into bed with someone, *naked*, I can't see how sex isn't top of mind.'

'There's always the chance of sex, I agree. But if you're not attracted to women, like me, sleeping with a woman who knows it's platonic, that makes it relaxed, companionable. We chatted, spooned and fell asleep.'

'What did Marla —'

It was Marla who cut Grace's question off. 'Approaching target, approximately one hundred metres away.' After a pause, she added, 'You journalists are fucking nosey.'

Grace wasn't sure what to say.

Marla continued. 'I should've mentioned, we're on a two-way circuit. As entertaining as your conversation has been, let's keep the chat operational.'

'Sorry,' said Grace. 'I'm all business now.'

They stayed silent, staring at the screen as the image of a house became more distinct. It was a well-lit single-storey house, most of its windows illuminated behind curtains. The image bounced as Marla must have jumped a fence, landing in what Grace presumed was the house's backyard. As Marla edged around the house, towards the back door, Carter blurted out, 'There's a car coming.'

They had been watching the phone so intently that they hadn't heard or seen the car driving up the gravel road. The image on the screen panned from side to side.

'How far away in minutes?' Marla asked quietly.

The car's headlights were roughly a third of the way up the hill, it wasn't travelling fast but it didn't have far to travel. Grace, recalling the drone image of the farm, said, 'Three minutes to the top. Another two, maybe three, it'll be at the house – if that's where it's heading.'

The image blurred. It was impossible to work out what Marla was doing. She appeared to jump two fences as she ran. As they watched, the car breasted the hill, it's light disappearing from their view. The image on the screen steadied on the front of the house.

'It's reached the top,' said Grace.

The image pivoted towards a car's headlights, still distant, but dazzling. From the angle, Marla was lying on the ground behind a post and rail fence.

'It's coming this way,' said Marla. 'I'm in cover, the headlights will only splash over me if they do a U-turn.'

'What's the plan?' asked Carter.

'No plan,' she said. 'We're winging it.'

'Do you want us to move closer?' asked Grace.

Marla was quiet for a long moment. Through Carter's phone, they heard the car approaching Marla's position, its tyres crunching over the gravel. 'I was thinking the opposite,' said Marla. 'Move back to the picnic area, nearer the car in case you need to get away.'

'And leave you?' said Grace.

'Only temporarily. I'll need a lift home. I think you two staying put makes sense until we know what we're dealing with.'

The crunching noise grew louder. Marla said, 'I'm going radio silent. You can talk, only I'll hear.'

The car drove past Marla's position. Slowing, it stopped outside the house. From her vantage point Marla could see the car and front door of the house. She had picked a great position – if they didn't see her.

The driver turned off the engine and the headlights of the car blinked off. The image took a few seconds to adjust, the lit house now the major focus of the camera. The passenger got out, his clothes identifying him as a man from the community. He went into the house.

'Was that the man from this afternoon?' Grace asked Carter.

'He looked the same, but, Jesus, they all look the same.'

The image remained static. Marla not moving, the driver sitting behind the wheel. Whatever was happening, he wasn't anticipating it taking long. Time crawled, minute by long minute. The night wasn't cold, but it wasn't warm either. Marla hadn't dressed for a lengthy stakeout.

Having kept an eye on the time, Grace knew that the front door opened again twelve minutes after the man had first entered the house. Two figures emerged this time – a woman in a long dress and headscarf followed by the man who arrived in the car, or his clone. Two community members stood at the front door, watching.

'Fuck, that's Lauren,' hissed Carter.

Before Grace could look closely, the man had put the woman into the back seat, like a police officer putting a criminal into a patrol car. He leaned into the car as if he was talking to her, then he got in the front seat.

'Are you sure?' asked Grace.

'Not a hundred percent,' he said. 'But ninety-nine. And she would never dress like that voluntarily, not the Lauren I know.'

The car's engine roared into life, its headlights flicking on. As it started a slow U-turn, the image went black as Marla ducked her head to limit the chances of being seen or light reflecting off the camera. An instant later the screen showed the car's red glowing tail lights as it drove away at pace. The image swept back to the house. The front door was closed, the two men had gone back inside. The image remained locked on the front door, Marla making sure no one was going to emerge – the house was still. Then the image started dancing. Marla grunted as she jumped the fence and started after the car.

'I can't see the car's headlights yet,' said Grace. 'Let us know what we should do when it's safe to talk.'

The glow of the car's headlights was getting brighter. They could hear Marla's breathing over the audio. She was moving fast, but she wasn't running.

Between breaths, she asked, 'Carter, are you sure that was Lauren?'

'As sure as I can be.'

The image on the screen danced around. In the distance, the car's headlights briefly lit up the ridgeline before they plunged downwards as the car started its descent.

'Watch where it goes,' said Marla, breathing harder now. 'I'm not sure what else we can do, at least tonight. I'll be at your position in five.'

Grace and Carter watched mesmerised as the car's lights wound down the hill. Seconds later, before their eyes, the scene silently imploded.

CHAPTER 31

The moon and stars bathed the hillside in a faint, silver light. Grace and Carter stood watching the headlights of the car as it ducked in and out of visibility, weaving its way down the steep gravel road. They watched its progress in silence as Marla hurriedly made her way to their position. It was impossible to gauge how far away the car was, maybe two kilometres, the sound of its engine oscillating as it competed with the wind gusting in the trees.

The dark, patchy image on the phone gave them no clue as to Marla's progress. It appeared to Grace that she was covering the ground in a fast walk – her breathing hard, but not laboured.

'What do you –' Carter cut his sentence dead.

The car's headlights had blazed for a split second before they dropped straight down and out of sight. They heard a vague crunch, a noise like someone biting into a crisp apple, the wind snatching the sound away. The car's headlights had vanished.

Jumping in the hope of seeing the headlights, Carter said, 'Fuck. Fuck.'

Grace stared hard where she had last seen the lights, though it was impossible now to pinpoint the exact place. All she could see was blackness, a dark sea of rolling trees. Without the car's headlights, it was featureless.

'Talk to me.' Marla's voice, distant now they were standing, shook them into action. They both started talking, Marla cutting them off. 'Stop, take a breath. Ace, what's happening?'

Blowing out the breath she indeed needed, she picked up the phone. 'The car, it drove off the side of the hill.'

Staring at the phone, they heard Marla take her own advice. Then she asked, 'Are you positive?'

Looking at Carter, who nodded emphatically, she said, 'We both saw it. The lights plummeted straight down. We heard a sound, it was faint, then the lights were gone.'

Marla had stopped. She was looking down on the community,

checking the church and surrounding buildings. They too looked for a response but the scene was static. No lights had snapped on. No cars were racing towards the scene.

'There's no response from up here,' said Marla. 'And I can't see a reaction from below.'

'Do they even have mobile phones?' asked Carter. 'Lauren wouldn't have hers.'

'The man in charge must be carrying one,' said Grace. 'The young muscle from earlier today, they were carrying phones. I saw rectangular shapes in their back pockets when they left.'

'Solid work,' said Marla. After a few seconds silence, she said, 'Here's the plan. If we're the only ones who know, we're the only ones who can help Lauren and whoever else was in the car. Follow the track I took to my current position. It'll take you about three minutes. We're going to double back and head down the road. If we see a response from the community, we'll make for Carter's car.'

They didn't need telling twice. Turning off the phone, cutting the comms link, Carter led the way, pushing through the scrubby seldom-used path towards the farm's upper level. Billions of stars provided centuries-old light that let them make out the path. When they found the farm's boundary fence, they leapt over, following it towards where Marla was waiting.

Creeping along as fast as the light allowed, Carter turned his head and hissed, 'We should've found her by now.'

It was Marla who answered. 'Keep moving, I'm behind you.'

'Jesus,' whispered Grace through clenched teeth. She pushed Carter onwards as he abruptly stopped when he had heard Marla's unexpected voice.

'We're nearly at the top of the road,' said Marla. 'Pick up the pace a little, Carter.'

His karate training stood Carter in good stead as he responded to Marla's request, although the going was tricky, the ground uneven, pock marked by hooves and tractor tyres. Thankfully it was firm, it didn't look as if it had rained for weeks. Keeping up a strong, steady pace, they soon stood at the top of the gravel road.

Marla performed a 360° survey of their position as Grace took the opportunity to take in oxygen. Although she didn't like to admit it, she wished she was their age, or even the age she pretended she was. Carter, buzzing with nervous energy, was staring around.

Signalling for them to huddle up, Marla said, 'We're going to head towards the crash site. If this goes pear-shaped, we'll need to pick our way back, without being seen, then head to Carter's car. If the police arrive, I'll have to disappear. Don't worry about me, I'll reappear when I can.'

Grace asked, 'What are we going do when we get there?'

'If they've crashed, and it's bad, we'll have to ring 911. We'll do what we can in the meantime.'

'What's our story?' asked Grace.

'We don't have time to nail one,' said Marla, 'but let's stick as close to the truth as we can. Ace, you're trying to find Lauren for a story. Carter and I are helping. Let's keep it that simple.'

'Got it,' said Carter.

Marla led the way, followed by Carter with Grace taking the tail-end Charlie position. Descending the gravel road at a fast-walking pace, they had to stop themselves from running on the steep sections. Starlight lit parts of the road, allowing Grace to pick where to step, but the sections in inky shadow were treacherous, each step felt like a lottery. Grace was hoping she didn't go over on her weak ankle, an old karate injury.

At times on their descent they could see for miles, the landscape laid out before them like a huge relief map. The busy expressway in the distance, the foreboding hills all around and, seemingly at their feet, Reverentia's buildings, the church nestled close to the trees, lit like a giant wedding cake.

Without looking, Marla called back, 'Any idea where they went off the road?'

'It was about a third of the way down,' said Carter. 'It must be soon.'

They came to a relatively long, straight part of the road, the incline reducing giving it the appearance of a makeshift runway for small planes. At the end of the straight, the road bent sharply to the left and upwards.

It was the missing fence straight ahead that told them they had found where the car had left the road.

Without talking they slowed, fanning out as they cautiously approached the now unprotected edge. The light from the night sky illuminated a sheer drop before a scrubby section of hill sloped acutely into blackness. The broken fence hung like an uninviting rope ladder. The car would have plummeted straight down and, as they couldn't see it, into the dark, densely treed area.

Listening hard, Grace couldn't hear anything other than the wind gusting in the trees.

'I need to use the torch,' said Marla. 'If anyone's looking, and they might be by now, they'll see the light so keep an eye out for movement.'

Putting her hand over the torch, Marla turned it on, her hand glowing red. Aiming towards the trees where the car must be, she took away her hand. The powerful light picked out the rear of a car – its reflective tail lights shining brilliantly. Marla danced the light over the car, which looked neatly parked between two large pine trees.

'Ace, call 911,' said Marla. 'I don't see movement.'

Taking out her phone, Grace stepped away from the edge and placed the New Zealand equivalent, a 111 call, where she reported the nature of the crash and that it would involve serious injuries – or worse. She gave her phone number in case they needed directions when they arrived.

'I saw movement,' said Carter. 'In the car.'

Marla aimed the torch at the car's intact rear window. A hand was waving weakly. 'I see it,' she said. 'Lauren's alive. She was the only one in the back.'

'Can we get down there?' he asked.

Using the torch, Marla investigated the hill and its surrounds.

Glancing down at the community, the picture had changed. It reminded Grace of when she was driving home, alone without a care in the world, when 'nek minute' her rear-view mirror was full of the brilliant headlights of a car driven by two US agents. Near the church, two cars had turned on their headlights but they remained stationary. She could see people moving around the compound, some ran towards the vehicles.

'We're going to get company,' said Grace.

'I've found a way down,' said Marla. 'How long before they get here, Ace?'

'They're not coming yet, but no more than five minutes.'

'What about the police and ambulance?' asked Marla

'They'll be coming from Hamilton, so' – Grace trilled her lips – 'in twenty.'

'I'm not sure what I'll be able to do,' said Marla, 'but time matters. You two work out how to handle the hillbillies. Keep them at arm's length until the police arrive.'

With that, Marla climbed for a few steps before she started carefully picking her way down the hillside. As they watched her progress on what was possibly an old sheep or goat track, Carter asked, 'How are we going to handle the Clampetts? They're on their way.'

Her laughter came out hard and Grace shook herself to relax. Two cars were moving towards the gravel road. She said, 'I'm not sure.'

'If they know the police are coming,' he said, 'they'll have to behave themselves, won't they?'

'Good thinking,' she said. 'We can make sure they know the cavalry is coming. Besides, two of their … flock are in the car. Marla will help them too, if she can.'

Grace and Carter watched in silence as though they were at the tennis. First Marla's progress, then the car headlights climbing the hill. Repeat.

Marla reached the stricken car with the cars charging towards their position around two minutes away. Her torch darting around gave the scene an inappropriate strobe-light effect. She tried to open the driver's side back door, but it wouldn't budge. She went to the front door but didn't try opening it, shining the torch through the window.

'How long?' she yelled.

'They're almost here,' Grace shouted. 'What's it look like?'

'The car's wedged solid. Lauren's alive, I'm going to see what I can do. The two in the front look bad.'

'Can you get to her?' Carter called out.

'The other side looks less damaged,' she called back.

The torchlight moved to the other side as Marla carefully picked her way around the car. As she did this, the noise of engines and the crunch of tyres on gravel grew louder. Marla opened the door easily this time, sliding in next to Lauren.

The night changed to brilliant daylight. Carter and Grace moved away from the edge, having to shield their eyes. The headlights on full beam were bright enough, but the twin spotlights mounted on the roof of the ute lit the scene as if they were actors on stage. The ute graunched to a stop twenty metres in front of them, the lights of a second vehicle stopping behind the first. Four men got out, forming a line in front of the ute. That was all Grace could determine as the dazzling lights behind gave them the form of movie-esque humanoid aliens.

Two of the men stepped closer. Dressed identically, they were slightly younger versions of the elder they had encountered earlier in the day. Concerningly, they both carried rifles. As Grace readied herself to answer whatever came, Carter strode towards them, his hand acting as a vizor.

'Put those guns away, for fuck's sake.' He barked his words out like an army drill instructor. 'We saw a car drive off the edge of the hill, we're trying to save people's lives.'

The indistinguishable man left of Carter, said, 'What car? And what are you doing –'

'We can deal with that later,' Carter interrupted. 'Move your vehicles up the road, the police and an ambulance are on their way.'

'What? The police?' the man stammered.

'Yes, the police,' said Carter. 'Who do you think attends car crashes? God?'

'They're nearly here,' said Grace, pointing towards Reverentia's main gate where a single set of blue and red flashing lights had turned into the driveway. They must have been in the vicinity to have arrived that fast.

The armed men were struggling to comprehend what was happening, what had happened, who was coming and what they should do. Taking her lead from Carter, Grace took charge. 'Park your vehicles over there,' she said pointing to the straight stretch of road. 'The police will need to access the crash site.'

The men looked at each other.

'Now,' yelled Carter. 'My friend's down there and I'm losing my fucking patience.'

As the community members started to move, Grace called out, 'If I was you, I'd hide the guns. I'm not sure the police will take kindly to finding armed citizens at the scene of an accident.'

As Carter helped with traffic management, Grace kept an eye on the crash site. The light was steady inside the car, Marla must have found a place to wedge her torch. Grace could see Marla's silhouette attending to Lauren, but that was all.

Grace's mobile rang. Knowing who it would be, she accepted the *Caller ID blocked* call. 'Grace Marks.'

'It's the police,' said a female voice. 'We're on the property, approaching a set of buildings. Can you give us directions to the accident?'

'I can see you,' said Grace. 'Keep going straight, you'll hit a gravel road leading uphill. We're two-thirds of the way up, you can't miss us.'

'Can the road take a fire truck?'

Grace yelled the question to Carter.

In a few seconds, Carter called back, 'No problem. Stock trucks use the road, they turn around at the top.'

Grace relayed the information.

The flashing lights of the police car drove steadily past the buildings before accelerating up the gravel road. The parked ute, although facing the wrong way, they had turned its spotlights around so the area where the car left the road was brilliantly lit. Carter and the four identically dressed men joined Grace near the edge. Having stowed their guns, they had armed themselves with torches. They took turns shuffling close to the edge, peering over before stepping well away.

'Did someone go down there?' The question likely came from the man who had spoken previously, presumably the senior member of the small delegation. His tone had changed, more respectful, more worried.

Pointing to the track Marla had used, Grace said, 'Our friend found a path.'

The men played their torches on the side of the hill, searching for the track.

'There's no point now,' said Grace. 'You'll just get in the way of the police.'

The torches clicked off in unison.

With a mix of suspicion and accusation in his voice, their spokesperson asked, 'So … what happened?'

'We were watching on the *public* loop track,' said Grace. 'We saw a car drive off the hill, we scrambled to help.'

'Why were you watching?'

'Why did you abduct my friend?' countered Carter.

'What?' said the man.

The situation made it hard to tell, but his laconic answer seemed filled with genuine confusion.

A short, silent standoff ensued which Grace broke. 'There'll be plenty of time to sort this out, especially with the police involved. Right now, we need to help the police once they get here.'

All they could do was wait. The men again took turns peering at the car, its interior lit as if by a single glowworm. Marla would be doing all she could. The police were seconds away, a fire truck with rescue equipment possibly minutes away.

When the police car arrived, Carter directed it to park behind the two utes, leaving space for the fire truck when it arrived. A single uniformed police officer came over, putting on a high-viz jacket as she walked unhurriedly. When she arrived near the edge, she looked at Grace and asked, 'Was it you on the phone?'

Grace nodded.

'What are we dealing with?'

This wasn't the first accident Grace had witnessed and she kept her reply short and factual. 'A car went over the edge about twenty minutes ago. My friend found a track down, she's doing what she can but she has no first-aid equipment.'

'Was another car involved?'

Grace shook her head.

'I need to talk to the person at the scene. What's her name?'

Normally a simple question, Grace paused for a beat. 'Norma.'

They all moved to the edge. Grace, Carter and the community members fanned out to watch but the officer intervened. 'I'm going need space, please step back.' Carter reluctantly edged away – it was his friend who was in the car. For the members of Reverentia, this was new territory – a woman telling them what to do.

'Now please, gentlemen,' she growled. Reality dawning on them, they stepped back, forming a small huddle well away from Carter.

As Grace, fighting her journalist's desire to remain, stepped away, the officer said, 'Not you. I might need you.' Licking her lips, Grace joined the police officer at the edge of the hill.

Flashing her torch over the car, the officer called out, 'Norma, can you hear me?'

'Loud and clear,' called Marla who was standing next to the car.

'What's the situation?'

'The car's wedged tight, it's not moving anytime soon. There are three in the vehicle, one's dead and the other two need medical assistance asap. There could be neck damage, I haven't moved them.'

The police officer mumbled, 'She's had training.' Clearing her throat, she called down, 'Backup is on the way. What can you use until they get here?'

After a short pause, she called out, 'Not much. Until the paramedics get here, the situation's stable.'

'Okay, hold tight.' Clicking off her torch, the officer stepped away from the edge.

A second police car, which Grace hadn't seen arrive, added to the impromptu parking lot. The fire engine took an age to climb the hill, Carter guiding it opposite where the car had run off the road. A FENZ crew member, who must have been baking in full fire-fighting garb, moved to the edge of the hill, flashing his torch onto the crash scene. The remaining crew members disembarked; there was no panic as they efficiently checked the surroundings, checked the site and unloaded equipment.

The two police officers, the female officer joined by a male colleague, conferred before joining the FENZ team. The female officer said, 'It's all yours. How do you want to handle it?'

'First, we need to get down there,' he said. 'Check out the scene. Then we need to get them out of the car and up here, an ambulance is on the way. Who's down there?'

The police officer ran through the situation, the firefighter listening intently. After she had finished, he went to the edge and called, 'Norma. I'm from Fire and Emergency. How's it going?'

'Slowly,' she called. 'I'm glad you're here.'

'We're going to throw some ropes down. Can you secure them to the trees?'

'Sure.'

The emergency responders acted in harmony, everyone knew their role. 'Let's give them room,' said the male officer stepping away, taking a reluctant Grace with him.

First, two firefighters abseiled to the crash scene with a stretcher. The first person hoisted to the top was Lauren, a neck brace in place, her arm bandaged and her face looking like she had gone a few rounds in the boxing ring and lost badly.

Carter rushed to her side. 'Lauren?'

The ambulance team, who had arrived minutes before Lauren had reached the top, worked on Lauren – again without panic. Lauren's eyes flicked open but she couldn't move her head, her eyes darting around until they locked on Carter's face.

'Carter?' her voice was faint. 'What the fuck. Where am I? Did Allen smash me?'

Smiling, tears in his eyes, he said, 'No, and you're going to be okay.'

Her eyes darted around, then at her body. 'What am I wear –' Whatever drug they had given her, it worked fast. Her eyes rolled backwards and she was out cold. As they placed her in the ambulance, the unconscious driver was hauled up from the crash site.

Finally, and this time in a body bag, the community member who they had seen take Lauren out of the house was stretchered to the surface.

Marla arrived seconds later, brushing herself down, joining Grace and Carter who were standing well away from the serious-looking community members. They were talking quietly, but animatedly, among themselves.

Carter hugged Marla. 'Thank you.'

'I'm a little surprised to see you back here,' said Grace.

Scrunching her face, Marla said, 'I considered it, but the going looked tough. Plus, disappearing would've made the police jumpy. Let's roll with it, see what happens.'

The ambulance was the first to leave, having to do a thirteen-point turn, the male police officer assisting. As the firefighters packed away their equipment, the police finished taking everyone's details and statements. Grace talked the police through what they had been doing – that they believed Lauren had been abducted and they had been staking out Reverentia to see if they could identify where they might be holding her. Normally at an accident scene everyone is either part of the accident or an innocent bystander. When Grace used the word 'abducted', the officer's eyes widened.

'You're going to have to come to the station,' she said.

'Oh God?' said Grace. 'Tonight?'

The officer shook her head. 'Tomorrow. We need to sort out this first.'

A relieved Grace exhaled. By the time they drove back to Carter's house, it would be late enough without a few hours at the police's incredibly slow pleasure. Other people's time was not a consideration as they meticulously plodded along, dotting i's and crossing t's.

When the police had interviewed the community members they had pointed over several times in response to the police's questions. No matter how hard they tried to push the blame away, it was going be tough for them to answer why Lauren was in Reverentia, presumably against her will. Their only hope was if Lauren's injuries had impaired her memory, but her recognising Carter instantly was a positive sign.

Marla was the last person the police interviewed. Grace, her journalistic curiosity piqued, listened to Marla's answers as the male officer questioned her. In her strongest American accent, she sounded friendly and open. 'Norma Smith'. 'Ellesmere Street, Christchurch'. 'I'm on holiday'. 'Ace needed help tracking a missing person'. 'That's about all I know'. The officer asked several more questions, but Marla's answers were variations of 'I'm on holiday' or 'I have no idea'.

After the police had affixed hazard tape where the fence was missing and put out orange cones, the female officer came over. 'Tomorrow at two o'clock at Hamilton Central, that work for you three?'

They exchanged glances, Marla speaking for them. 'Sure.'

Grace was confident Marla wouldn't be with them, but there was no point having that discussion now. What Grace needed when they met with the police tomorrow was an answer as to why.

'What about the hillbillies,' asked Carter. 'Will they be there too?'

Shaking her head, the officer said, 'We'll come back tomorrow with the Serious Crash Unit. We'll talk to them then.'

Nodding, he asked, 'Can you give us a lift to my car? It's in the loop track carpark.'

Giving him a steely gaze, and possibly grinding her teeth, the officer said icily, 'Sure.'

The utes left first, driving up the hill followed by the fire truck. After they'd gone, the second police car to arrive performed a fast three-point-turn and headed away in a shower of stones. The police car they were in was last to leave the scene, the officer driving carefully.

As they neared the bottom of the hill, Grace broke the uncomfortable silence. 'Will the serious crash people be able to work out what happened? I mean, with all the traffic and people stomping over the scene?'

Rocking her head from side to side, the officer said, 'They're smart. They can usually piece events together. Why?'

'Just curious,' said Grace, deciding to park her curiosity. In her experience it was best to say little to the police.

The excitement of the strange vehicles with their flashing lights had seemingly brought out the entire community from their motel-like accommodation. A sea of blues and whites, they stood around staring, their faces a mix of curiosity, hostility and wonder. It reminded Grace of the aftermath of a sporting event in which everyone was wearing the home team's colours, but it was obvious from their faces that they had lost.

Had the word gone around? Did they know a car had crashed, that at least one member of Reverentia had died? Did they know about Lauren? Were her parents among the staring mass? Or had the community eradicated Lauren's name and existence, as though she had never lived among them?

After dropping them off in the carpark, the police car didn't leave immediately, its engine idling.

As they walked to Carter's car, Marla said, 'She's checking your car.'

'She won't find anything,' he said. 'Not even a parking ticket.'

'No, she's making sure you're who you said you were.'

'Oh,' he said. 'Luckily, I am.'

The police car didn't linger.

They sat in the car for a few moments, not knowing what to do or say.

'Shit, it's past eleven,' said Carter. 'By the time we get home and unwind, it'll be one in the morning.'

Putting her hand on his shoulder, Marla said, 'Let's get going. We can unwind on the way back. I just hope Indy is busting when we get there.'

It took a second for Carter to follow Marla's logic. He let out a combined sigh and groan as he shook his head.

'I'll call Tana,' said Grace. 'He'll be over the moon we found Lauren. What did you make of her condition, Marla?'

'I think she'll recover fully, though it depends on how bad the whiplash was and how much of a whack she took to the head. Only her arm needed bandaging, the other cuts looked superficial.'

'Do you have any contacts at Weeping Angels you can tell?' asked Carter.

'I do,' said Grace. 'Trudi, one of the investigators. I'll text her, tell her the good news.'

Carter drove a tick over the speed limit on the quiet night-time roads back to Auckland. Grace sent the text to Trudi then called Tana, waking him. His delight at hearing they had found Lauren changed to concern when she took him through the accident. He was keen to head straight to the hospital. Grace advised him, as Lauren would be receiving treatment, he wouldn't be able to see her. Reluctantly, he said he'd go in the morning.

The traffic became denser as they neared Auckland.

'It doesn't matter what time of day or night it is, the roads into Auckland are stagnant,' he said.

In a faux-surprised tone, Grace said, 'Wasn't your new crusty mayor going to fix Auckland?'

'Yeah right,' said Carter. 'Local government puts me off democracy.' Glancing at Marla, he said, 'You're not coming to the police station tomorrow, are you?'

'I can't,' she said. 'When they put "Norma Smith" through their computer, I'm confident that will result in zero hits related to me, which will get them thinking.'

Taking an exit off the motorway, Carter said, 'We'll need a story.'

'The same play we used before will work,' said Marla. 'Stick to the truth, it's easiest to remember.'

'That'll work for me,' said Carter. 'I mean, I hardly know either of you. What about you, Ace?'

'I've been mulling over that question. I think I can claim I'm protecting a source, which is true, sort of.'

'Will they buy it?' asked Marla.

'I'm hoping it won't matter, but I'll do a little research before we go. Even if they forced me to give you up, what could I give them that the SIS doesn't already have? You have a dog and live in the South Island – turn left or right at Blenheim.'

They arrived at Carter's house, the automatic garage door opening as though it had been waiting patiently for their return. After parking in his immaculately ordered garage, he looked at them both. 'What are the chances of me spending time in jail for being in cahoots with you two?'

Marla looked at Grace. 'Fifty-fifty, I'd say. Ace?'

'At best,' she said. 'The police will need a patsy.'

'Arseholes,' he said.

It was 12.38am when they went inside, laughing.

Grace put down her phone, she had been doing the Wordle, when Lauren opened her eyes. Lauren blinked, her eyes darting around the sterile hospital room, a look of confusion on her face.

'Hey, Lauren,' said Carter in his quietest voice.

Focusing on him as he moved closer to her bed, she appeared to go cross-eyed. 'Whoa, Carter. Where did you spring from?'

He took her hand. 'We just came in for a visit, to see how you were. Grace is here too.'

Stepping next to Carter, Grace said in her normal voice, 'Hey, Lauren. You look surprisingly good for what you've been through.' And she did. Given the crash claimed at least one life, Lauren's two seriously black eyes, swollen face and one arm bandaged from wrist to shoulder appeared minor.

'Ace,' she said hoarsely as though she was pleased to be able to recall her name.

How do you feel?' he asked.

'Trippy.'

'That's understandable,' said Grace. 'They're bound to have given you a decent dose of drugs. Are you in much pain?'

Closing her eyes, Lauren wriggled gently. 'I'm sore all over but the pain's dull. And even with the drugs, my head is pounding.'

'That's how I felt too,' said Grace. 'After I was in a crash.'

Carter glanced at her.

'It's a long story,' she said.

'We popped into the operations centre,' he said. 'The team is over the moon that you're okay.'

'They don't know who you are,' said Lauren.

'They do now,' he said. 'They recognised Grace, let us in and you had obviously told them about how great I was.'

Lauren smiled weakly. 'How's the operation running? I haven't been there for …' She closed her eyes, the effort at remembering obviously taxing.

'It's been just over a week,' said Carter. 'And everything is running smoothly. Trudi wanted to let you know –'

Grace cut in. 'I'll give you two time to catch up. I'll go grab a coffee and be back in fifteen. Carter and I are heading to the police station.'

'Why?'

'Carter can tell you, it's nothing to worry about. When I get back, I'd like to ask you a couple of questions, if you're up to it.'

The route to the hospital café was like navigating an intelligence test for mice. Eventually finding it, Grace found a table with a dispiriting view of an over-crowded carpark. She checked her emails as she drank what she considered an average at best coffee. Looking at the people in the café, she gave herself a mental upper-cut for being a twat – most people at the hospital were having far worse days than her.

Having lost her way on the return journey to the ward, there was little time left to ask Lauren her questions. As it turned out, it didn't matter.

'She was tired,' said Carter, meeting Grace at the door.

On tiptoes, looking over his shoulder, Grace saw that Lauren had gone back to sleep.

'No matter,' said Grace. 'There'll be time later. How was she?'

'Great, considering,' he said. 'She said the police had visited earlier, asked her lots of questions. She said the past few days were fuzzy, like an image that kept moving in and out of focus.'

'How was she when you talked to her?'

'Not bad,' he said. 'She was lucid enough.'

'That's a good sign,' she said. 'Come on, we need to get a move on. I'll follow you. I have no idea how to get out of this rabbit warren and there's a slim chance the police will be on time.'

Having hustled across town, arriving punctually at 2pm as requested, it was clear that the police were not ready for them. Suspecting as much, Grace had come prepared.

'Snap!' Grace's hand crashed onto the pile of cards. 'You're pretty average at this, Carter. I should've played you for money.'

'I've never played *Snap* before,' he said. 'You're like an evil machine. *Snap. Snap.* I'll have nightmares.'

Laughing, Grace dragged the pile of cards towards her. 'My children still do. Taught them —'

'That their mother was related to Ming the Merciless?' cut in Carter.

Supressing a giggle, she organised the cards in her hand. He tossed her his last two remaining cards.

'Do you want to play a different game?' she asked.

'No. I want the' — he leant close to her — '*fucking police* to interview us. No wonder you brought cards.'

'It's the way they roll,' she said.

When the police finally arrived to interview them, at 3.10pm, they were each trying to build a card house.

The female officer from last night was first into the room, dressed in her police uniform minus the cap. Following her was an older male wearing a suit and with a salt and pepper beard — undoubtedly a detective. Detectives didn't usually get involved in motor vehicle deaths. The stakes had increased.

'Sorry to interrupt your fun,' said the female officer.

Most people feel a pang of fear when confronted with the police, even when they are innocent. After her numerous run-ins with the police and the SIS in her career as a journalist, Grace had lost that. Without looking at them, she said, 'They teach you so much at Police College except how to tell the time. I'm surprised you cope in the real world.'

Carter's eyes widened. Grace gave him a short shrug as she toppled her card house, dragging the cards towards her.

Unsmiling, the two law enforcement officers sat. In a monotone voice, the female officer said, 'I'm sorry to have kept you waiting, but we're very busy.'

Grace stood slowly. 'We'll come back later. When you've more time.' They weren't under arrest; they were there making a voluntary statement and that meant they could leave anytime they liked.

Carter's eyes remained wide. The female officer's eyes narrowed. It was the detective who calmed the waters.

'Please, sit down, Ace,' he said. 'Can I call you Ace?'

Staying standing, she said, 'Sure.'

'We're sorry, you can blame me for the delay,' he said. 'I needed time to go back through the files and come up to speed with what happened last night.'

Sitting slowly, Grace said. 'Why didn't you say that when you came in. Why be arseholes?'

The detective smiled. 'It's a fair point. In our defence, most people we deal with aren't like you two. Let's start again. I'm Detective Jeffries, this is Sergeant Collins.'

Collins asked, 'Where's Norma Smith?'

'That's a little tricky,' said Grace. 'She's a journalistic source of mine that I need to protect, as set out in the Evidence Act of 2006. Section 68 if you need to bone up on it.' In answer to their continued stare, she added, 'She had to head away.'

'Did she supply a false name?' asked the detective.

Well used to playing this game, Grace said, 'Why are you asking me that?' As the detective's jaw clenched, she said, 'What I can tell you is that what she told you was true. She was on holiday and joined me to help find Lauren, who you had listed as a missing person. *I* can tell you what *we* did.'

'You'll have to divulge her name if this goes to court,' said the detective.

'Only if it goes to the High Court,' said Grace. 'And even then, judges are reluctant to open that can of worms. Besides, this won't reach the High Court.'

The detective's face indicated he was having trouble controlling his annoyance. The police liked to dominate situations. Having their bluff called, or being out-manoeuvred, tended to piss them off.

'Okay,' said the sergeant taking over. 'Let's park that. Take us through the events that led to you *three* being at the accident site.'

'Can we record this?' asked the detective taking out his phone.

'No,' said Grace, stretching her arms over her head and flexing her neck, ignoring the dual look she received. The detective exhaled noisily as he took out a notepad and pen. She took them through a sanitised version of the events, leaving Tana out of the story. Marla was right, it was easiest to tell the truth, and she was just omitting unnecessary details.

She walked them through meeting Lauren to discuss stories focused on family violence and the justice system, ending with their arrival at the scene of the accident. After Grace had finished, the police sergeant stated, 'So you were nowhere near the accident when it occurred. You arrived at the scene to help.'

'That's right,' said Carter, who must have felt the need to contribute.

'If you've nothing to add to your statements from last night,' said the sergeant, 'I'm good.' Looking at the detective, she said, 'I'll leave them with you.'

As she went to stand, Grace asked, 'What did the serious crash people find?' The look Grace received wasn't warm. 'I mean, if you wanted a free and frank chat about events.'

After the briefest glance at her colleague, her face pinched, she said, 'Not much. The tyre marks were compromised, but all the evidence points to the car going too fast and skidding straight over the edge. Strange though, the driver must have known the road well. The passenger wasn't wearing a seatbelt, the driver and the woman in the back were, which saved their lives. It's the second fatal crash at that spot which, given its remoteness, is … unusual.'

Grace nodded, keeping her face neutral. The second fatal crash? Lauren's husband had to have gone off at the same spot.

After the sergeant had left, the detective looked at them in turn. 'How much do you know about Joy Leslie?'

Grace looked at Carter. They had spoken at length in the morning about the best approach and, as per Marla's advice, sticking to the truth was the smart move.

'Not much about Joy Leslie,' he said. 'I've always known her as Lauren Brown. I didn't know her last name had ever been Leslie.'

'What's your relationship with her?'

'I'm her business advisor and she's my closest friend.'

'Are you two in a relationship?'

'I'm gay, detective.'

Seemingly thrown for a moment, the detective briefly shrugged then regained his thread. 'When did you meet her?'

Carter took the detective through their early history, karate, his helping her with her business and that she stayed over at his house.

'She never spoke about her past?' asked the detective.

'Lauren was protective of her past, I didn't push it,' he said. 'Friends know where to draw the line.'

'I find that hard to believe, Mr Donaldson.'

Carter, eyes wide, said, 'She spoke in riddles, when she was down, but nothing specific. I only found out her first name used to be Joy through helping Ace.'

'What are you hoping for, Jeffries?' asked Grace. 'A late-night drunken confession? And to what?'

The detective turned to Grace.

'Carter's not protecting her,' she said. 'Lauren played her cards close to her chest.'

Scratching at his beard, he said, 'What about you, Ace?'

'What do I know? I had no idea she had a past until I heard she was missing. I figured I was possibly the last person to see her, and I knew what she did could attract unwanted attention.'

Tapping his pen on the table, the detective made a low humming sound. 'The troubling aspect, as the sergeant observed, is that it's uncommon for two fatal crashes to occur at the same remote place and involve the same person.'

Grace kept her face blank while her mind raced. Jeffries had confirmed her suspicion but added a massive complication. If Lauren was in the car that killed her husband, no wonder the community was suspicious. And how could she be hitch-hiking a week later, uninjured? It didn't add up.

'Lauren was *in* both crashes?' asked Grace.

The detective pressed his lips together. They were playing information chess, each wary. 'No.' He spoke slowly. 'I said she was *involved* in both crashes.'

'I'm not sure where you're heading with this,' said Grace. 'As far as I know, and I've told the police this, the god-fearing members of Reverentia abducted Lauren and were holding her against her will when last night's crash occurred. I don't see what her husband's crash, which she wasn't *in*, has to do with this except, as you say, it being uncommon. I know detectives don't like coincidences, I don't like coincidences, but the word exists for a reason.'

Jeffries inhaled through his nose and turned back to Carter. 'In all your time with Lauren, did she ever mention her husband's accident?'

He shook his head, which Grace knew was the truth. 'She made it clear that part of her life was a no-go zone. I respected that.'

Grace, sensing an opportunity, asked, 'What is it about her husband's accident that's concerning?'

The detective tapped his pen. 'For one, why she disappeared afterwards.'

Grace's eyes narrowed. 'Are you suggesting she was involved with the accident?'

After a long moment, he said, 'Let's just say a couple of aspects of the case are puzzling. We want to clear them up.'

'She was entitled to leave,' said Grace.

'I'm well aware of that,' he said. 'But innocent people don't tend to abandon their lives. There's also the matter of her using a false name.'

'She was escaping,' said Carter. 'Rather than abandoning her life, she was reclaiming it.'

'Escaping what though?' said Jeffries. 'That's what we want to clear up. The case remains open. Members of the community were adamant that she was involved.'

'Or do they want her involved?' said Grace. 'That way she's out of the way and there are no awkward legal challenges. As for changing her name, you can't seriously want to chase that angle.'

'I don't, as it happens.' The detective snapped his notepad closed. 'Thanks for coming in,' he said standing. 'I'm assuming you two aren't going to disappear, we may need to ask you more questions.'

'I assume it was you who spoke to Lauren this morning,' said Grace. 'What did she tell you?'

The detective looked at the door but turned back to them. 'She was vague, struggling to recall what happened last night, let alone five years ago. She did say she ran away because she thought the community was trying to frame her.' He gave them a final shrug before he left the interview room, leaving the door open.

They sat in silence for a moment.

Grace sat back in her chair and exhaled a grunt. 'What you reckon, Carter?'

'I don't know what to think.' Then his eyes lit up. 'But you, the way you handled the police, you were magnificent.'

CHAPTER 33

'What do we do now?' asked Carter.

He was in his kitchen, cooking dinner for three. Indy was following him dutifully, hoping he would drop a few morsels. Grace and Marla leaned on the breakfast bar watching Carter, each resting their head on a hand, drinking white wine.

'I need to head home,' Grace said. 'Check on my children, write some stories and see if I still have a partner.'

'I know,' he said, 'but we're in the middle of … well, something. Aren't we?'

'I think we're at the end of something,' said Marla. 'Once the police are crawling over events, they crowd out everyone else.'

'It doesn't feel like the end,' he said whisking eggs. 'There's loads of, what do they call them on TV, loose ends.'

'There are a few,' said Marla, 'but it's the police's job to tie them up.'

'And they will,' added Grace. 'They love to close cases. They like neat, tidy endings, which is why Detective Jeffries was digging away so he can stamp *Closed* on the accident that killed Lauren's husband.'

'It will take them a while,' said Marla. 'Weeks or months, not days. It isn't the only case they'll be working.'

'I suppose you're right,' he said. 'But it was so exciting. I can't go back to listening to academics, who fantasise that they're corporate hard-hitters, prattling on about finance – it's too depressing.'

'It has been a rush,' said Grace. 'But when Marla's on the scene I'm usually in mortal danger. A little quiet time might not be bad.'

Marla, her mouth open in semi-outrage, said, 'You make it sound like I'm the cause of the trouble. It wasn't me who ran you off the road – or abducted Lauren, for that matter.'

Grace laughed. 'I know.'

'So, what's going to happen now?' asked Carter.

Briefly drumming her fingers on the table, Marla said, 'The police need Lauren to fill in the gaps between when she dropped Grace off to when she was in the backseat of that car, halfway down the hill. Assuming the community sticks together, only she can tell the other side of the story.'

'The detective said she was vague about details,' said Carter. 'Maybe she won't be able to remember what happened.'

Grace and Marla exchanged a glance.

'What?' he said.

'Was she vague when she talked to you at the hospital yesterday?' asked Grace.

'No, she seemed ...' Carter smiled. 'Oh, I see. You think she's being deliberately vague.'

'Lauren has lived her entire life playing her cards close to her chest,' said Grace. 'At the very least, she's buying herself time to work out what parts of her story she *wants* to tell.'

'Why wouldn't she just tell the truth?' asked Carter. 'I mean, the community abducted her. Why wouldn't she throw them under the bus?'

'That's the right question,' said Marla. 'She's had the chance, why didn't she?'

For a minute the only sound was the oven humming and Carter's wine glass singing as he ran his finger around its edge.

'Only Lauren knows what happened and why she's doing what she's doing,' said Marla. 'Put yourself in Reverentia's shoes, Carter. What would you do if you were them?'

His face creased, he said, 'Blame everything on their leader. The one who died in the crash.'

'It would be the smart play,' said Marla. 'I can't imagine many knew what he was doing and those that did won't be keen to admit it. If they all sing from the same hymn sheet ...' She finished her sentence with a resigned shrug.

'Which they will,' he said.

'Unless Lauren implicates other community members,' said Grace.

'It's all conjecture,' said Marla. 'It'll play out over the next days and weeks. You'll be the closest to finding out what happened, Carter. Once she's recovered, I assume Lauren will be keen to resume her life – Weeping Angels, karate and hanging out with you. Ace will write several insightful stories that will embarrass the Government, hopefully enough to make them act, and Indy and I will resume our holiday.'

'Christ,' said Carter. 'It sounds like a and-everybody-lived-happily-ever-after ending.'

Over Carter's delicious, healthy dinner, they continued to pick away at events, laughed and drank too much wine. After a shower, Grace headed to her room, once again leaving Carter and Marla sprawled on the couch, wine in hand, with Indy acting as chaperone.

Grace called her children, who were having a great time leveraging her credit card and guilt, then Sean, who she always missed when her world quietened. Her emails contained the usual mix of spam, bills and work problems. Her always-keen editor wanted to know when she would be filing her promised stories. It was a tomorrow problem, but when she shut down her devices and turned out the light, her brain seemed determined to kick it around.

For all the excitement of the past few days, did she even have a story? The family violence stories, Weeping Angels and the failing justice system, they needed to wait until Lauren was better – that could be weeks. The rest of the story – the twin car crashes, Lauren's escape, the abduction, the strange Reverentia community – that was closer to a thriller than a story for the media.

A deep sigh escaped her. For all her success, and she'd had more than her share over the past few years, her life remained at five-minutes-to-midnight – more likely a pumpkin arriving than a coach. Her world would have turned more smoothly if she had remained a business consultant, dredging wodges of money out of the system to lavish on herself and her whānau. She was in no doubt, they were living through an age of greed and selfishness – maybe fatally. If you weren't born into money, or played the game hard, you were collateral damage. Inequality? Human rights? Democracy? Surveillance? Climate change? Poverty? Who cared about them? The answer – she did, and with a passion. She would never drink the *Flavor Aid* the wealthy were pushing on society.

In the quiet, as she eased towards sleep, she heard Marla letting Indy out for a final call of nature. The lights in the lounge clicked off and stealthy feet moved along the hallway. Carter's bedroom door closed as though he was frightened of making a sound. The last sound she heard before sleep claimed her was quiet giggling.

CHAPTER 34

'That's more like it,' said Grace, getting out of Lauren's car.

In the six weeks since she had last visited Weeping Angels, it had changed dramatically. It was as though the company had stepped out of the shadows, no longer content to work behind the scenes, it was now in your face. The freshly painted building, sign-written with the company's name, also featured the classic image of a weeping angel from the British TV programme *Dr Who*. In shades of grey, with powerful wings on either side, the angel's hands covered her face, ostensibly hiding her tears – in reality they hid a face radiating vengeance.

'I thought you'd approve,' said Lauren.

'It looked great in the last story, but it's more impressive live. And we need to get updated photos of you as well.'

As they walked towards the front door, Lauren said, 'But I had photos taken a few weeks ago.'

'Don't take this the wrong way,' said Grace, 'but you still looked' – she waved her hands around – 'grey.'

'Grey?'

'Yeah. A shadow. I mean, look at you now. Long hair, a sharp suit, a crimson shirt that matches your lipstick and shiny black heels – you make quite a statement.'

Smiling, Lauren opened the security door. 'Carter insisted I get fashion advice. Is it really such a big change? I don't feel any different, maybe a little more confident.'

As they walked through the 1970s tribute doors, Grace asked, 'How old are you, Lauren?'

'Twenty-four.'

Grace shook her head. 'Twenty-four. The CEO of an organisation that wants to change the world, and you look fantastic.'

Lauren's face reddened.

'If we were at a party, lining up the same bloke, I would be forced to casually spill my red wine on you.'

Lauren laughed.

Grace's visit was mostly business, part pleasure. The pleasure part was that Lauren had invited her, Tana, Carter and Marla to a dinner party with Weeping Angels picking up the expenses. It included travel, which meant Grace didn't have to lock horns with her parsimonious organisation. It was, Lauren had said cryptically, a chance to bury the past before she and Weeping Angels could advance into the future.

In Lauren's office, getting down to the business part, Grace said, 'I think it's time to go for the jugular.'

'Whose jugular?'

'The Minister of Justice and, by association, the Government.'

'They're the ones that can change the law,' said Lauren.

Nodding, Grace said, 'We've been laying a solid media foundation. Highlighting cases, getting one of your clients into *Woman's Weekly* – that was a score. I didn't think they'd touch family violence with a barge pole.'

'They did make the story, what do you call it – puffy?'

Grace laughed. 'A puff piece; they sure did. I'm surprised they didn't want a bikini shot, but great impact. Weeping Angels – allowing women to live their best lives.'

'It's not your style, is it, Ace?'

'Certainly not. My style is what comes next – kicking the Government in the throat. I mean, they've been playing along, happy to take the kudos that "justice is being delivered", even though they're doing four-fifths of fuck all. It's time to squeeze the minister's testicles.'

'I do love your language, Ace, it leaves nothing to the imagination. How should we play it?'

'Funny you should ask that,' she said. 'I think we should employ a classic karate attack – a *uraken* followed by a *mae-geri*.'

'Stun them, then kick them in the balls,' said Lauren. 'I prefer that metaphor to squeezing testicles. Have you seen the Minister of Justice?'

Grace laughed. 'Good point. The initial stories, the *uraken*, we increase the focus on the appalling position that the law puts women in.'

'And that we can't help everybody,' said Lauren. 'Even if they did fund us, which they've said they can't, we're helping maybe one percent of women.'

'The call to action will be for the minister to launch an inquiry into "access to the justice system".'

Lauren grinned. 'Sounds great.'

'It might even work,' said Grace. 'But I doubt it.'

'What's the *mae-geri*?' asked Lauren.

'We demand the minister's resignation,' she said. 'We march, start petitions and maybe we camp in the parliamentary grounds.'

'They wouldn't let us, would they?'

'No,' said Grace. 'But what great coverage if they drag you off, looking gorgeous, and throw you into a paddy wagon.'

Eyes wide, Lauren said, 'I'm in.'

Grace and Lauren spent the rest of the afternoon sharpening the concept, looking for other angles and working out how they could generally create a public outcry. Carter joined them at 4pm, giving Grace the most intimate hug she had experienced outside a sexual encounter. He helped them develop, in his words, 'a strategy so simple a child could understand it'. The tagline they developed, which Grace knew would play brilliantly in the media, was 'Make the system dispense justice, not sell it'. As Lauren had observed, Grace and Carter had appeared to climax when they arrived at that phrase.

Grace tried to steer the conversation to events surrounding the car crash, but Lauren, looking a mix of serious and coy, had twice said, 'Wait until tonight'.

'She hasn't told me yet,' Carter said, ' and you know how close we get.'

An intrigued but frustrated Grace carried on plotting the demise of the justice system's status quo.

After they had finished, they indulged in a celebratory glass of champagne. Carter explained that they had changed the company ownership officially to Lauren and there were three directors now: Lauren, himself and Julianna Leftbridge, a name Grace recognised from the media pages that covered the lifestyles of the rich and famous. In response to Grace's questioning stare, a smiling Carter had added,

'It's okay, Ace. She's not one of the deluded wealthy – she didn't take any equity.'

'Really?' said Grace. 'No equity? That'll get her kicked out of the EP One Club.'

'What's that?' asked Lauren.

'Elite Priority One,' said Grace. 'It's Air New Zealand's invitation-only club. Think of it like a fawning Koru Club for pretentious snobs.'

When they'd finished the champagne, Grace said, 'Lauren, I'm curious about tonight –'

'There's a surprise,' said Carter, cutting her off. 'You'll have to wait, like me.' Taking her hand, he helped her out of her chair. 'Come on, Ace, you're coming with me.'

CHAPTER 35

'Six people?' said Grace.

Lauren had headed home to change, while Grace had gone with Carter to his house, which he had set up to host a dinner for six. Opening a bottle of wine, Carter said, 'You, me, Lauren, Marla, Tana and Wai. Wai's driving so Tana can have a few drinks.'

Grace smiled. If anyone deserved a few celebratory drinks, it was Tana. After showering, she put on what passed for semi-casual clothes – tight jeans, a T-shirt with a picture of George Orwell saying, "I fucking warned you", that she couldn't wear on many occasions, and a black and white checked jacket which she had bought for the occasion.

'Wow, you look great. I love the T-shirt,' said Carter when she emerged. Pointing to the wine with his elbow as he mixed ingredients that smelled of garlic, he said, 'Help yourself.'

Pouring herself a glass, she said, 'So, Carter, tell me. What do you think's going to happen tonight?'

He carried on making dinner while he talked. 'I don't know, I really don't. I thought we already knew what happened. Maybe Lauren just wants to rule a line under that part of her life.'

'Maybe,' said Grace swirling her wine around in her glass.

'What do you think?' he asked.

'There are a couple of areas that don't add up,' she said. 'They're not major but, well, they're indicative.'

'What are –'

'I let myself in,' Lauren called out, interrupting Carter's question. Her face was radiant as she came into the open-plan lounge, and her casual clothes too had lost their grey hue. Previously she had dressed to make sure no one gave her a second glance. Now, still understated in three-quarter length jeans, a tight-white top and double-breasted navy jacket worn open, she was blossoming.

Carter gave her a big hug, pointed to the wine and she joined Grace at the breakfast bar. A knock on the door interrupted them before they could start talking,

'I'll go,' said Grace. 'My bet is Tana and Wai. Marla doesn't often use the front door.'

It was Tana, holding a liquor store carry bag. He looked different out of his uniform, smarter.

'Hey, Ace. Jeez you look great.'

'So do you Tana.' She hugged him before asking, 'Is Wai coming?'

'He is. I'm just making sure nobody's following us. This is the first time I've visited Lauren in years. I wanted to make sure, so he's keeping watch until everyone's here. Then I'll text him.'

Putting his bag on the breakfast bar, he said, 'I brought some wine, I know you fellas like it. I also brought beer, in case you forgot.' Tana took out a six-pack of Waikato Draught.

Carter, opening the fridge, pointed to a six-pack of the same beer. 'Lauren told me "Chateau Kato" was your preferred drink.'

Tana chuckled in his usual style. 'I didn't know they'd heard of it in the big smoke.'

Carter suggested everyone should head outside while it was still sunny. Picking up a platter of snacks, he opened the sliding door, stepped outside and was accosted by a small, excited barking dog. Grace, Lauren and Tana peered around Carter and saw Indy, her front paws on Carter's leg, and Marla, sitting on Carter's passionate-blue wicker outdoor settee.

'I was invited,' said Marla.

When Marla had a drink in hand, a curious Tana asked, 'How did you get past Wai? He's outside watching the house.'

'I'm not sure Wai is your best choice for surveillance,' said Marla. 'I waited in my car until a woman in tight leggings jogged past. I followed her and while Wai just about put his neck out perving, I slipped around the back.'

Tana puffed out his cheeks as he took out his phone. He walked into the house, his voice drifting outside. 'Jeez, Wai, you're bloody useless. You may as well come in and have a feed.'

Carter had made a sumptuous dinner – he would definitely make a great husband or wife. Grace kept an eye on Lauren throughout dinner. She was bubbly and having fun, but when she was out of the limelight, she looked concerned, maybe even calculating. Grace caught Marla looking as well, Marla giving her the slightest of nods.

After dinner, they retired to the lounge where Tana, who had kept an eye on Wai to make sure he hadn't snuck a drink, took out his wallet. 'I didn't tell you about this part of the evening, Wai. I kept it as a surprise, but you need to take off for a couple of hours.'

'What? Why?'

'It's none of your business why. Here's two hundy, I want you to go to Sky City and win us some cash.'

Wai's face beamed. 'True?'

'Just keep an eye on the time,' said Tana. 'I want you back here by eleven.'

Wai took the money. 'Sweet. I've always fancied myself as a high roller.'

When Wai had gone, Tana explained, 'He's always wanted to go so I figured it's time he learned casinos are a mug's game.'

No one had told Grace about 'this part of the evening'. The room went ominously silent. All eyes turned to Lauren, who gave a forced smile. She sipped her wine and then breathed in deeply, letting her breath out in a slow stream. 'I guess it's time.'

The room stayed silent.

'Get comfortable,' said Lauren. 'There's a bit to tell. It started with his – that's my deceased ex-husband – with his last will and testament in which he left everything to the community. At least, they claimed he did. When he went off the road, for reasons which I didn't know at the time, the community leader tried to make out that I was involved. He had a bottle of gin put in his car which raised questions about the sequence of events of his crash.'

'When did you find that out?' asked Marla.

'It's so long ago,' she said. 'After I left the community, the police came to the backpackers where I was staying, they told me about the bottle. That's why I went to Tana's house and changed my identity. I became

Joy Brown, then Lauren Brown. That's why I kept that part of my life a secret – only Tana and his family knew anything about my past. As you can imagine, the members of Reverentia would faithfully repeat whatever they were told to faithfully repeat. At the time I was sure they would've framed me, the court convicted me and I'd have been thrown in jail. I was seventeen. Running, hiding, stopped all that.'

Lauren looked around the room – she had everyone's attention. After drinking more wine, she took off her watch, putting it on the coffee table. As much as Grace wanted to, now was not the time to hurry her along.

'For a few years it went quiet, like it was dead and buried. With the will settled, Reverentia carried on as before. The police didn't know where I was and I can't imagine they were that desperate to talk to me, it was an accident after all. Then, as Weeping Angels took off, thanks to Carter, I needed money to keep the business afloat until enough women were paying. I stumbled over some information. It was a cold, rainy day and I was at home in a mood that often caught me – sad, frightened but angry too. I was going through the papers I took from Reverentia and I found the flash drive that I had used to copy the files – in case I lost the documents I had taken with me. I wasn't that computer savvy then –'

'You still aren't,' interrupted Carter.

Everyone except Lauren frowned at him.

'Sorry,' he said.

Lauren patted his leg. 'Anyway, before I escaped, I copied my husband's computer files including, as it turned out, the Reverentia accounts – he was the community's accountant. The only folder I had looked in when I first escaped was one called *Personal files* – it contained a copy of his insurance policy. He was insured for $100,000 but, because of his will, it all went to them.'

The tension in the room was building as Lauren, Poirot like, continued to slowly pull back the curtain.

'This time I looked through the documents carefully,' she said. 'I found a copy of his will in a subfolder which, according to the date of the file, he had made just after our wedding – he left half of his estate to me. I thought it must be an old will but, when I checked, the date on both wills was the same. They altered his will to cut me out.'

'That's a dirty trick,' said Tana.

'It sure was,' said Lauren, 'but if I hadn't copied the files I would have never known. In my mind, they owed me $50,000 – half his life insurance. I needed the cash, at least I did until Carter weaved his magic.' She smiled at him warmly and he looked down, blushing. 'I couldn't use a lawyer, I didn't exist. So I contacted the community directly using an anonymous email address, sending them a copy of the will. They didn't reply straight away. They must have pulled a few strings and made the police reinvestigate the accident, which got the story into the newspaper. They emailed back, equally anonymously with a link to the newspaper article and a biblical reference – Deuteronomy 32:35.'

'Go on,' said Marla. 'I'm sure you looked it up.'

'Oh, I didn't need to look it up,' said Lauren. 'It was one of Nathaniel Palmer's favourites. "It is mine to avenge; I will repay. In due time their foot will slip; their day of disaster is near and their doom rushes upon them".' She rolled her eyes. 'He used to trot it out every other Sunday.'

'Charming,' said Grace. 'Christian charity at its finest.'

Nodding, Lauren continued. 'I wasn't sure what to do when I read the story, but Carter came to the rescue. I stepped back, but I guess Palmer was worried. He knew I was around and that I must have copied information from *his* computer … before Palmer had taken it away.'

She paused.

'What else was on the flash drive?' asked Grace.

'I was wondering that too,' said Marla.

Lauren grinned. 'You're both quicker than I was. I thought it was all about the insurance money, but it dawned on me later that, while $50,000 was a huge sum for me, it wasn't that much for them among all the farms and buildings. Long story short, he and Palmer were siphoning money out of the community into private assets – property, shares and, of all things, racehorses. When they were away on community business, they lived the high life, trotting about New Zealand and Australia. They told everyone in the community that we were just scraping by – keep up the hard work.'

Wide-eyed, Carter said, 'Really? What fuckers.'

'I think he must have kept evidence implicating Palmer in case Palmer tried to throw him under the bus. There were photos and document in a folder called *GST return copies – do not delete*.'

'What sort of photos?' asked Grace.

'Drinking beer at the races – that sort of thing. The community probably thought they were at a Christian leadership retreat.'

'Surely his wife suspected?' said Grace.

'Melissa?' Lauren grunted. 'Maybe.'

Realising she was almost leaning on the table, Grace eased back. 'They were leading double lives.'

Lauren nodded. 'Maybe that's why *he* was the way he was – conflicted, trapped, battling demons.'

'That doesn't excuse anything,' said Tana.

'No, it doesn't,' she said.

'So, when you approached them with the real will,' said Grace, 'Palmer, the leader of the community, he suspects you know everything.'

'Like a cornered cat, he comes out scratching,' said Lauren. 'He knows if I want to press the issue, I'll have to come out of the shadows – I'll have to take them to court.'

'And if you come out of the shadows, with the community's help, the police might be waiting,' said Grace.

'A stalemate,' said Lauren. 'And then, with the money issue dealt with, it became a risk I didn't need to take.'

Grace glanced at Marla who was pulling at her bottom lip.

Lauren slowly put her glass on the table. 'Three months ago, Carter thought we needed a presence on social media. A first step towards coming out of the shadows.'

'And that goes to prove I'm not always on my game,' he said. 'And not because of what happened next, because on social media you're the product, not the consumer. They pimp you and your data to the highest bidder.'

Grace smirked – he was right.

'We hired a young, keen uni student majoring in communications

– part time,' said Lauren. 'We wanted to start focusing on highlighting injustice and our results. But, and it's totally my fault, I didn't impress upon her enough to keep staff images off the sites we joined. She found a photo on our secure intranet of a team-building event we ran with family – Tana was in the photo.'

'Ahh,' said Marla.

Nodding, Lauren continued. 'It looked harmless so she posted it online. When I saw it, I couldn't breathe. I had to pull myself together so I could call her, get her to delete it, but it had been up for over a day – people had commented and shared it. I'm not sure how they did it, and it might not have even been that, but they found Tana. Then me.'

'Who's they?' asked Grace.

'I don't know,' said Lauren. 'I presume they were PIs, like Tana thought they were, but that part puzzles me.'

'How long had Weeping Angels been on social media when the photo was posted?' asked Marla.

'Maybe two months.'

'Did the post carry your name?'

Shaking her head, Lauren said, 'But it did identify me as GM.'

'This is speculation,' said Marla, 'but if other PI firms have been monitoring you, keeping an eye on the new competition, then your image appears. Who is this person?'

Grace added, 'And after a search they're still wondering who you are. But they're PIs and there are clues in the photo. Cogs whirr. Dots join.'

'That makes sense,' said Lauren. 'More sense than anything I've come up with. It must have taken them a couple of weeks to track me down, maybe bug my car. I guess it doesn't really matter how they found me.'

After helping herself to more wine, Marla asked, 'What can you remember about the night they snatched you?'

'After I dropped you off, Ace, I drove down to see Tana.'

'I was staying in Pōkeno,' he said.

She smiled. 'It was a fun night. I remember leaving the house and heading to my car. My next recollection was waking up in the community – locked in an empty storeroom.'

Tana and Carter scowled.

'It didn't take me long to realise where I was,' said Lauren. 'I'd spent time in that storeroom before. They used it as a punishment for the least infractions. I bashed on the door, yelled, but either no one was there or they had decided to ignore me. It was dark when they let me out to use the bathroom and, if I put on the prescribed Reverentia dress, feed me. I was starving.'

'What did they want?' asked Carter.

'Initially, Palmer wanted to find out what I knew. I had to keep alert, to make sure I didn't let on that I knew what he did, what he must have been still doing. I think he was starting to believe me, that I only knew about the will, but he was suspicious. He said we needed to come to an "understanding we could both live with".'

'Meaning?' asked Carter.

Lauren licked her lips. 'It was like a standoff – if you don't go to the police, we won't.'

Marla opened her mouth but must have thought better of it, staying quiet.

'Anyway,' said Lauren. 'Carter told me about how you launched a drone – that must have spooked him. I knew something had changed because when Palmer came back that evening, he said we needed to come to our understanding now. I'm not sure how it would've played out, but I didn't get the feeling they had my best interests in mind. They tied my hands behind my back and put me in the back seat of a car. They were in a hurry. We were going too fast. Then Palmer's yelling and we're plummeting down the hill. I thought I was dead for sure. I came to when Marla shined a torch in my face.'

The squishing noise from a can of beer momentarily broke the tension. 'Sorry, sorry,' said Tana.

'You know the rest of the story,' said Lauren, 'or you've guessed. Palmer wasn't wearing a seat belt, that killed him. The new leader of the community visited me in hospital. I knew who he was, but that was about all. He said he knew nothing about the abduction, laid all the blame at the feet of Palmer.'

'We figured that was the smart play for them,' said Grace.

'It was,' said Lauren. 'With the community parroting that line, that's all the police will have too. I asked him if he was involved in siphoning money out of the community. The look on his face told me he had no idea what I was talking about. Palmer must have taken over running the accounts after *he* died in the car crash. I told him that I'd send him copies of the photos and documents.'

Grace spoke slowly. 'So, you get your name cleared. Reverentia will sort out their dodgy affairs behind closed doors. And what, that's that?'

'And *hopefully* that's that,' said Lauren.

Carter raised his glass. 'Here's to Lauren and Weeping Angels. And, with Ace's help, we're going to kick the justice system into shape.'

Raising their glasses, everyone echoed the toast.

A reflective silence fell over the group. Lauren looked first at Grace, then at Marla, who was still pulling on her bottom lip.

'That's quite a story,' said Marla. 'But I'm a little confused about a couple of aspects.'

Lauren slowly topped up her glass.

Carter and Tana shifted uneasily while Grace drank some of her wine – Marla was right. Although it seemed a tidy explanation, aspects didn't sit right. Lauren was taking an age to fill her glass, was she calculating what to say?

'Really?' said Lauren, an overly-wide smile on her face. 'That's interesting. Which aspects?'

'I don't want to put you on the spot,' said Marla. 'This is your dinner party, not mine. It was lovely you invited me.'

Closing her eyes for a long moment, Lauren rolled her head around as though she had a stiff neck. When she opened her eyes, she said, 'When I considered doing this, having this dinner party with everyone here, I was in two minds. I've haven't felt safe enough to tell my two best friends my secrets, let alone a journalist. And I didn't really know who you were, Marla.' She laughed briefly. 'I asked my best investigator to do some digging – she found nothing.'

'Good to know,' said Marla cooly.

'Carter told me all about you, though,' said Lauren. Carter gave Marla a what-could-I-do look. 'He was highly impressed and he doesn't impress easily. And what you and Grace did to help me – without you two, the story would have ended very differently. You both needed to be here but … I wasn't sure so please, Marla, which aspects are confusing?'

'Okay,' said Marla evenly. 'I watched you get into the back seat of the car that night, your hands tied behind your back. The driver in the car kept his seatbelt on while he waited. And the passenger, the community leader as it turned out, after he buckled you in, he put on his seatbelt.'

Lauren looked at a frowning Carter biting a fingernail.

'But when I reached the crash site,' said Marla, 'your hands were free and it was clear that Palmer hadn't been wearing his seatbelt. When parts of a story don't fit, it makes me wonder about the whole story, about what really happened.'

Smiling, but this time sadly, Lauren said, 'I've kept secrets ever since I can remember. It's time to bury some of them, that's why I invited you all here, I just wasn't sure I could do it. But if I'm going to front the charge on the justice system, I need to get things out of my head. You're the four people in the world I know I can trust with my life because each of you, in your own way, have saved my life. I intend to take as much misery out of society as I can as my way of repaying you … and the past. Maybe you'll look at me differently after I've unburdened myself.' She shrugged. 'I'm going to take that chance.'

Grace sat back. Marla remained impassive. Carter and Tana both looked between confused and intrigued – clearly neither knew what Lauren was about to say.

'I need to take you back in time,' said Lauren. 'Back to when I was seventeen …'

CHAPTER 36

The night of the first accident.

Joy Leslie stood looking out the large lounge window watching glimpses of a car's headlights as it drove up the steep, winding, gravel road. It was her husband behind the wheel of his Audi, no one else would be on the road. He would be drunk, or well on the way. She inhaled deeply, her breath coming out unevenly. Shivering though it wasn't cold. She wanted to cry, to scream, but what was the point? Tears were futile in the community, a sign of weakness. A sign, they said, that you needed to commit yourself more fervently to God.

From where she stood, the headlights were visible only on a few parts of the road that coiled its way up the hillside. She prayed he would drive off the road. That the lights would disappear – along with her husband. But they never had. They never would.

Leaving the window, she set about reheating dinner. There was a chance that he wasn't in a black mood though it was unlikely on a Friday. His temper would darken if he kept drinking … and he usually kept drinking. His rage became almost visible, bubbling beneath the surface.

From the kitchen window she saw headlights sweep around the section. A few seconds later, his car skidded to a stop in front of the garage, his arm dangling out of the open driver's window. He stared straight ahead as he emptied the last vestiges from a bottle of spirits.

Shit.

Closing her eyes, she placed her hands on the bench. Tonight, of all nights, she had to keep it together.

As she busied herself in the kitchen, the car's headlights went out. Slowly he got out of the car, his keys in one hand, an empty bottle in the other. She focused on dinner as he yanked the back door open. Turning as though she hadn't been watching, she said, 'Hi. Dinner's almost ready. Did you have a fun night?'

Grunting in the affirmative, he went looking for more alcohol. Bottles clinked in the lounge as he searched. Having hidden his bottle of bourbon, she hoped he would settle for what was in easy reach. When he drank bourbon, he became particularly violent – unpredictable. Tonight she needed predictability.

'Where've you put the bourbon?' His voice hissed into her ear.

Her body stiffened. 'What?' The word came out as a squeak. He was inches behind her. The pungent smell of hard liquor on day-old breath. Putting on a smile, she turned around and said, 'What bourbon?'

The severity of the blow, although not unexpected, caught her by surprise. She slammed into the fridge. A blinding flash of pure white light before blackness and stars. She slid slowly to the floor – the coolness of the fridge door on her cheek.

He seemed far away as he yelled and swore. Blinking, trying to stay still, making herself small, she put a hand on her jaw, moving it back and forth – it was sore but it didn't feel broken. He had used a closed fist. He seldom did that though it was becoming more common. He was always careful not to leave marks, let alone bruises.

'Where's the bourbon?' he yelled.

'It's … it's in the shed.'

She could sense him standing over her, swaying, waiting for her to say something, anything. She lay still, her eyes closed, hardly breathing. Eventually he stalked from the kitchen, slamming the back door.

Using the kitchen table for support, she dragged herself back to her feet. Holding her jaw again, she moved it from side to side – not broken. *Thank Jesus.* She staggered over to the bench. Were they all like him? All the community elders, when they were alone? Did Palmer beat and rape Melissa too? Did they all abuse alcohol while preaching piousness?

This Friday would be no different, the pattern the same. Violence, followed the next morning with regret, mumbled apologies and promises to reform. But the violence was escalating, the punches harder, the sex more brutal. Later tonight he would threaten to leave her, to ruin her – to get her thrown out of the community. But he would never leave her, she knew that. She might be trapped in Reverentia, but so was he. Here he was a big shot accountant with a fancy car. An important man. It was an empty threat. It was an empty promise.

She knew that his anger, at least part of it, stemmed from his not having had children. It was important to him, important to his status. He was desperate, but not because he especially wanted children; it was because the community expected him to have children. As the congregation liked to say, 'God had not yet blessed them'.

When she had confided to her friends, they had told her she needed to be a better wife. 'You're exaggerating.' 'Your husband is a pillar of the community.' 'You're bringing this on yourself.' And the worst comment of them all, 'You don't know how lucky you are.'

'*You* don't know how lucky you are,' she whispered.

Their advice made no sense, but she had tried to do better – it made no difference. The pattern of her life was on repeat, slowly spiralling to what she saw as its obvious conclusion – her death.

The door slammed. Stalking in with the bottle of bourbon, he pointedly ignored her as he took a bag of ice from the freezer, slamming it on the table. Thankfully he was in no state to grasp that she had watered down the bourbon to lessen its impact. Bizarrely, he could be the warmest of husbands, if he was sober or others were watching. Without the judgmental gaze of another human being, he became cold, withdrawn and, when he drank, a violent bastard.

She glanced at him briefly as he was fixing his drink. There was no remorse in his eyes. That wouldn't appear now, not until morning, maybe not ever. It took all her willpower not to stiffen as he put a hand on her shoulder as she heated a large, heavy, black frying pan for the steak she had taken out of the fridge.

'Let me see your chin,' he said as amiably as he could manage.

She obeyed, turning her head, tilting it upwards so he could see where his blow had landed.

He took her jaw in his smooth accountant's hand, looking at it with detachment, as if it was a financial report of little interest. 'It's not bad. You can say you fell off the porch.'

Forcing a smile, she said, 'Sit down. The steak won't be long.'

Although he was in reasonable shape, lately he had put on weight and he grunted as he sat heavily at the kitchen table.

The steak sizzled as she dropped it into the heavy, unoiled frying pan. Glancing over her shoulder, she made sure he was sitting where he usually sat – his back to her. He had one fist clenched, the other wrapped around his drink, the bourbon within reach. Whatever had happened to make him the way he was, it was too late for him to change – he was irredeemable. This was her life and its end was rushing ever closer. No one would save her. She had to save herself.

Closing her eyes, she drew in a calming breath through her nose. She lifted the heavy but familiar frying pan in two hands, hovering it above the flame. Then, as she had practiced many times in the shed, she turned first one way before spinning back in a confident, controlled turn, swinging the frying pan hard but in a controlled arc, keeping it steady, keeping it level. She had one chance.

'I'm –'

He might have been going to say 'I'm starving'. It was unlikely to be 'I'm sorry'. But his time had run out.

'I'm –'

Cutting his sentence dead, the heavy frying pan crunched into his neck, just behind his ear. The sound was a dull thud, like the sound of wood when struck with a rubber mallet. The steak stuck fast in the unoiled pan. Recovering her balance, drawing the frying pan back, ready to strike again, she held her breath and stared. The slowing sizzle of the steak the only sound in the room.

The scene froze.

Hardly breathing, she waited. Her husband had swayed in his seat before collapsing, his face hitting the kitchen table.

She stared at his motionless body.

Joy had stumbled across a particularly sad and tragic story on the internet. A cricketer had suffered a blow to the back of his neck that had led to a vertebral artery dissection that led in turn to a subarachnoid haemorrhage. The vertebral artery supplies oxygen-rich blood to the brain and a blow to the back of the neck can create life-threatening complications. In the cricketer's case, he never regained consciousness.

Her husband remained face down on the kitchen table, motionless.

CHAPTER 37

Joy held the cooling frying pan like a baseball bat, ready. She didn't want to have to hit him again, that would jeopardise her plan, but if he stirred, she would – repeatedly if necessary. Wide-eyed, she watched for the slightest movement. But apart from taking shallow, jerky breaths, he remained still.

She stood over her husband's inert body until her arms ached. Without taking her eyes off him, she put the pan back on the stove, turning off the element. If her blow had done the damage that befell the unfortunate cricketer, her husband would never regain consciousness, he was beyond medical attention. If not, how long he would stay unconscious was anyone's guess. When she had searched online, she had found the unhelpful advice of 'it depends'. It could be a few seconds; it could be much longer.

Even though she had long ago lost her faith in prayer, when she turned back to the table she muttered, 'Our Father, who art in heaven …' – she stopped, grimacing, before finally adding – 'deliver me from evil'.

She slowly pulled out a chair and eased herself down opposite him, not wanting to disturb the image in front of her. Without looking, she picked up the bottle of bourbon, taking a deep drink. Even watered down, it burned.

He didn't move.

She shook her head and stood. *Focus.*

He wasn't a big man, she was as tall as him, but he was solid, heavy. Using her shoulder, she pushed him off his chair. He slumped to the floor much like she imagined a dead body would. She paused, looking for signs of movement, before grabbing him under his armpits and dragging him out the back door, onto the porch.

The night was clear but windy, the moon nearly full. She stared at the stars, mouth open and breathing hard. Having never driven his car – her experience limited mainly to studying how her husband drove – it took her many slow attempts to manoeuvre the Audi until it was parallel with the porch. As she opened the driver's door, it brushed past the porch – perfect. With the car parked a metre away, the height of the porch lined up with the height of the car's back seats.

She created a bridge from the porch to the back seat of the car from a solid wooden door she had found in the shed and cut down to the right size. Then she dragged him over, laying him with his feet on the makeshift bridge. Getting in the opposite rear door, she crawled across the back seats and onto the door. Then, with a lot of small, incremental tugs, she pulled him inside the car so that he was lying, seemingly peacefully, across the back seat. Buckling his knees, she dumped the bridge on the porch and closed both rear doors.

Briefly stretching her arms and legs, she got behind the wheel and performed a slow U-turn. Then she drove carefully towards the gate, her foot covering the brake pedal. At the gate, she braked too hard, the car's tyres biting into the gravel. Headlights off, breathing in deeply through her nose, listening to her heart thud and the blood in her ears, Joy waited for her eyes to adjust. There would be no traffic to contend with – she could drive as slowly as she needed.

When objects took a more solid form, she eased her foot off the brake pedal, the car gently easing forwards. At this limited speed it was a slow, tense trip. She could have gone faster but for the urge to turn her head every few seconds to make sure he remained still. She had visions of seeing him struggle upright in the rear-view mirror.

When her husband needed to turn around, swearing when he forgot something, it took him seconds at a point where the road was wider. Sweating, clutching the steering wheel tightly, it took her many small, jerky movements to point the Audi back uphill.

Driving slowly, she parked just before a section of the road that sloped downwards before it curled in a tight hairpin into a straight, gentle uphill climb – the longest straight section of the road. Leaving the car idling and in park, she engaged the handbrake and carefully got out, leaving the driver's door open.

As she opened the rear door on the driver's side, her husband's head turned and he stared up at her.

Screaming, she fell backwards, her heels kicking at the gravel as she scrabbled to get away. Taking short, panicked breaths, she stared in disbelief but he didn't move – he was seemingly gazing up at the stars. Her breathing slowed as she realised his head must have been leaning against the door. When she opened the door, it had lolled towards her.

Getting up slowly, she said, 'You can do this.' *You have to do this!*

After dusting herself down, she put her hands under his armpits, the smell of his oily hair in her nostrils as she bent close and dragged him out of the car, laying him on the gravel. In unchartered territory, she had mentally rehearsed getting him into the driver's seat. Now it looked impossible. She looked into the night sky. There would be no help from that quarter but, given what she was doing, maybe that was right.

She dragged him around, his heels making twin tracks in the gravel, so his head was close to the driver's seat, his body at a right angle to the car. Standing astride him, she bent down and put her arms around his chest lifting his torso, dragging him and propping his back against the car. With his chin resting on his chest, he looked as though he was taking a nap. She stepped back, panting hard.

There wasn't time to recover fully. She stepped back over him, bending down, putting her arms around his chest. Even given the situation, it wasn't lost on her that this was the closest they'd had to an embrace for months. She tried to stand, to lift his body, but he was too heavy. Letting him go, she stepped back, eyes wide. *Fuck*. If she couldn't do this, everything would be lost. She would be lost.

Trying again, this time rather than bending she crouched, imagining he was a sack of grain. Drawing him as close as she could, she used her legs to lift him. This time it worked; she put his backside on the edge of the car's floor, balancing him there. Adjusting her feet, she hugged him again and repeated the effort, this time getting him onto the edge of driver's seat. With a final effort she shoved him backwards until enough of him was on the seat so he couldn't fall out.

Not letting him go, she twisted his upper body, pushing him into the seat. Then she unwrapped her arms, putting a hand against his chest to keep him in position. Her eyes closed, she took in long breaths, wiping the sweat off her face with her sleeve.

She stood there, waiting for her body to recover. After a single deep breath, she put a hand behind his head to keep him in position while she used her other arm to lift his legs into the car – like the way she used to put her little brother into bed. Finished, she stepped back. Her husband sat slumped behind the wheel, not wearing his seat belt. It was exactly as she had envisioned, except his clothes were dirty from the gravel road. She shook her head, there was no way she could clean his clothes, though he had occasionally come home with ripped pants, presumably from tumbling over drunk.

Technically he was alive but he was beyond feeling. She was thankful that in what was about to happen he wouldn't suffer. Despite the torment he had inflicted, she didn't want revenge – that never featured in her thinking. It was a simple equation: at some point he would kill her and *they* would cover it up. It was either him or her – he had to die. It was the only solution, at least it was the only solution she could see.

From her dress pocket she took out a list. Although it was hard to read in the weak light, she knew the list by heart. She shook her head when she read the first item – *Undo zip*. Why hadn't she done that before now? With difficulty she performed the grim task that provided a rationale for why he wasn't wearing a seatbelt.

Make sure driver's window is down. It was. He always drove with the window down no matter what the weather. She checked off several more items before, at the bottom of the list written in capitals was, *TURN ON HEADLIGHTS.*

This was it, not that she could turn back. From the moment she had hit him, there was no back.

Taking a moment, she looked around. It was a beautiful place to live, if it wasn't for the community. The wind blew plants out of the ground and in the winter the cold made life hard, but the view was spectacular. At night, far from the city lights, the stars painted a wonderous picture. When he was away on business, she liked to stay up late staring at the vastness of the universe. On those occasions, it was hard to imagine that there might not be a God.

Shaking her head vigorously, she refocused – time was running out. Putting away the list, she took a triangular-shaped rock from the passenger side footwell. Using it like an aircraft chock, she wedged it under the Audi's right, rear tyre.

As she circled the car, she made a final inspection to ensure all was ready. Leaning in the open passenger door, with great care she put the car into drive. It strained forwards, the handbrake and rock keeping it in place. Then, having to use both hands, she disengaged the handbrake holding the tension, easing it off until it was fully disengaged. The triangular-shaped rock was all that held the car in position. She shut the door as gently as she could, then rushed around to the driver's side, where her husband remained alive and dead at the wheel.

Mentally, she rehearsed the last act. Turning on the headlights, kicking the rock away. The car, freed from restraint, would lumber towards the drop. She reached in the open driver's window and turned on car's headlights. They snapped on like twin laser beams. Impossibly bright, they seemed to light up the entire hillside.

She rushed to the back of the car and kicked the rock – it didn't budge.

Eyes wide, she kicked twice more, pain shooting up from her toes.

'Fuck!'

The headlights blazed and the engine hummed.

Looking around, she saw there were fist-sized rocks on the side of the road. Grabbing one, she skidded on her knees to the rear wheel, blood from her knee instantly forming a black patch on her dress. She bashed at the stubborn chock but her blows were as ineffective as her kicks. Sweating, her eyes bulging, she stopped, sitting back on her bleeding knees, breathing hard.

Calm down. Calm down.

Staring at the rock and the wheel pressing down on it, she saw her mistake. She had kicked and hit the rock in the centre of its mass – it was futile. She needed to strike the furthest edge of the rock with blows away from the wheel. Concentrating hard, and using a backhand action, she swung the rock in her hand lightly, focused on the edge of the rock – her blow turned it a few degrees. She struck again, a few more degrees, then a few more – it needed a final well-aimed blow.

The rock squirted out from under the tyre.

Expecting violent movement, she flung herself backwards, but the car moved away sedately, with no fuss or screaming tyres. Accelerating smoothly down the slope, it headed towards the wire fence, the only obstacle between it and nothingness. Again, with a minimum of fuss, it brushed through the wire before disappearing, the back of the car seeming to hang in mid-air for longer than possible.

The tyres had crunched over the gravel. The fence wire had screeched briefly against the front of the car before it gave way. There had been no ear-splitting boom or spectacular explosion. The car had simply disappeared, replaced by silence before a metallic crunch – like a giant taking a bite out of a stick of metal celery.

Joy stared in disbelief.

The wind moaned.

Staring at where the fence had been, her mouth open and dry, she stumbled towards the edge. Taking small steps, she peered down. It wasn't difficult to see, light reflected off the back of the car. It was upside down on a lower section of the gravel road, its lights, as she had prayed, off – smashed in the impact. The only sound was the wind.

She stared at the car for a long moment. She had done it. She was free. Now she had to make sure she stayed that way.

Returning to where she had parked the Audi, she used her foot to erase the marks left in the gravel. Then after retrieving the triangular-shaped rock, she ran up the gravel road.

CHAPTER 38

Grace, Marla, Carter and Tana had listened to Lauren's story transfixed. As she took them through the night's events years before, at times her eyes were distant, as though she was seventeen again. When she had finished, she looked at each of them in turn, her eyes back with their intense focus.

Marla broke the deafening silence. 'That's how you knew the community were trying to frame you,' she said. 'You *knew* there was no gin bottle in the car when it went over the edge.'

Lauren nodded. 'I never figured on them doing that, but I didn't know what was at stake. Nathaniel Palmer didn't know that I was completely ignorant … at the time. Maybe he wanted an insurance policy, just in case – to keep me in line. He certainly wouldn't have thought I'd escape.'

'He must have shat himself when you scarpered,' said Tana.

'He must have,' said Lauren smiling at the thought. 'But when the will went through, and I hadn't made any waves, he must have thought that he was safe.'

'His safest play was always to take you *right* out of the game,' said Marla. 'If he couldn't do it, he knew the police could.'

'And even though I'd planned well,' said Lauren, 'I had no idea what would happen – I was seventeen. The gin bottle, his dirty clothes and the detective's suspicion about the injuries he had suffered. I was scared – I knew what I had done.'

'When you found out they were siphoning money out of the community,' said Grace, 'why you didn't go to the police then?'

Briefly closing her eyes, Lauren said, 'I couldn't risk it. I killed him.'

'Now the community have admitted that Palmer organised for the bottle to be planted in the car,' said Carter, 'it's a freak accident.'

'The lead detective, Jeffries, told me they were closing the case,' said Lauren. 'That he was sorry for what I'd been through. I couldn't read him. I wasn't sure if he was genuinely sorry or still suspicious.'

'How did the latest crash happen?' asked Grace. 'Marla said your hands were free when she arrived.'

Carter nodded. 'I was wondering that.'

Running her fingers through her hair, Lauren sighed. 'I thought I had to act. I didn't know what they had planned, but I couldn't see how they could let me go. I told him often enough during our sessions that he was going to jail. Maybe they were considering a deal, an understanding. Maybe. As you now know, I knew that section of the road intimately. I decided to strike and let the chips fall where they may.'

They gave Lauren space to tell the final part of her story.

'The car had inertia seatbelts. I let mine out to its full length and I moved forwards until I was on the edge of the seat.'

Grace interrupted. 'I thought they put you in the car with your hands tied behind your back.'

'They did,' said Lauren, 'but they never tied the knots that tight. When I talked to Palmer, I could have freed my hands then, but there were always three people in the room. As soon as I was in the back of the car, I started working to free my hands.'

Marla's eyes narrowed as though she was testing if this was possible.

'Once I'd freed my hands, I inched forwards slowly, slackening the seatbelt. The driver was going fast, confident because he knew the road. Halfway along the short straight, I reached through and unclicked Palmer's seatbelt. As it retracted noisily, I lunged past the driver and held the steering wheel straight. If he'd braked immediately, we *might* have stopped in time. But Palmer was yelling and grabbing at his seatbelt, it distracted him. Just before we went over the edge, I pushed back hard into my seat, hoping the seatbelt had enough time to retract. I was lucky – it did.'

They sat quietly, each imaging the scene.

Marla asked, 'Were you hoping to be fit enough to escape on foot?'

'That, or grab one of their phones and call for help,' she said. Looking down, she shook her head. 'I didn't mean to injure the driver. They tell me he'll recover fully, but it'll take time.'

Grace interrupted another prolonged period of silence. 'How do you feel about it, Lauren? I mean … everything?'

Lauren took a moment before answering. 'I've come to terms with what happened – with what I did when I was seventeen. I've stopped agonising over whether I should've taken a different path. In the eyes of the law, I'm guilty of premeditated murder. But the same law expected me to take whatever he threw at me until I died. Then the law *might* punish my killer, sitting back and saying "Justice has been done".' She shook her head angrily. 'I did what made sense to an alone, unhappy, scared seventeen-year-old who didn't want to die.' She looked down. 'I thought about killing myself, too. Escaping that way.' Looking back up, she wiped away a single tear from her cheek. 'But I wanted to live. As for Palmer, I don't know how I feel about that – it's too soon. I feel bad about the driver, he shouldn't have been there.'

Tana cleared his throat the way people do when they're about to take centre stage. 'I didn't know about any of this, Lauren. I always wondered what happened all those years ago, but, as I've always said, it's your life.' He paused but nobody interrupted. 'I can't put myself in your shoes. I can't say what I would or wouldn't have done. But if I found out that one of my daughters was being beaten and' – he gulped – 'raped, could I kill the person? Sure. In a blind rage, easy. So, nothing's changed for me, girl. I'll carry your secrets to my grave.'

Lauren went over to him and they embraced. When they finally separated, there were tears in both their eyes.

When Lauren sat back down, Carter put a hand on her leg. 'Nothing's changed for me either. The Lauren I know is self-sacrificing and generous to a fault. And Tana's right, I have no idea what I'd have done in your shoes. My situation was a picnic compared to yours, and I thought my world was ending.' They embraced too.

'I grew up in a small US town,' said Marla, sitting comfortably, smiling. 'Small people with small minds. It wasn't a community like Reverentia, but everyone was a god-fearing pillar of society. It was a town where being different, or even curious about being different, was a sin, according to those in charge. One night, two men … straightened me out. Their unforgettable words, not mine.'

'Christ, Marla,' said Grace. 'What did you do?'

'At the time, nothing. There was no point reporting them, one was a police officer. Not that anyone would've believed me. Like Lauren I escaped too. I joined the army when I turned seventeen.'

They waited in silence, everyone sensing Marla had more to tell.

'I was much older when I went back. I could've worn my uniform, medals pinned to my chest, but I arrived looking like a vagrant, on a Greyhound bus. I walked the town – it was like I'd never left. I walked past the house where I had lived. I didn't see my parents but I saw people who I recognised – they had aged along with the town. I left two days later in a car one of the rapists didn't need anymore – Uncle Sam had trained me well. I totally get it, Lauren.'

The end of Marla's story ushered in a heavy silence. Grace, unsure, put a hand on Marla's shoulder. She then nodded to Carter. 'Any secrets you want to spill?'

'No,' he said sitting upright. 'I mooned the principal once.'

Giggling as he spoke, Tana asked, 'Did he recognise you?'

Everyone laughed, then the tears came.

Lauren went over and hugged Tana again, wiping her eyes on his sleeve. Carter hugged Marla then Grace. Indy leapt onto anyone who wasn't in an embrace, keen to get in on the action. When everyone had wiped away their tears, they refilled their glasses, Tana opening another 'Chateau Kato'.

Lauren exhaled loudly. 'Thanks. I mean, I can hardly get counselling. I know you might think differently about me now, I think differently about me now. I wish none of it happened, but it did and it happened to me. I can't change the past but I can influence the future. Maybe I can help someone in a similar situation escape without having to …' Her sentence didn't need finishing.

'This is where that part of your life remains,' said Grace. 'In this room, with us.'

'No one else knows,' said Carter. 'The police have closed the case and the Reverentia elders know their late leader tried to frame you.'

Marla laughed briefly. 'It's almost the perfect crime.'

A loud knock on the door – like a judge's gavel bringing proceedings to a close – made everybody jump.

'Crikey, it's after eleven,' said Tana jumping up, slopping his beer. He rubbed it into the carpet with his foot, causing Carter to wince. 'Sorry, Carter. That'll be Wai.'

They heard Tana greet Wai in his fatherly style.

'Kia ora, kia ora,' said Wai, coming into the room sporting an over-confident grin. 'Can I have a beer, Tana? One won't hurt to drive, eh'

'Go for it. Any chance you've some of my money left?'

Standing next to the breakfast bar, Wai opened a beer, smiled and dug a wad of notes out of his pocket, tossing them to Tana.

As he caught the money, Tana's eyes opened wider than Grace thought possible.

'Jeez, Wai. I didn't tell you to rob the place.'

Sitting next to Marla, Wai said, 'I lost half your money on the stupid poker machines. I wandered around for a bit, watching people chucking their cash around like it was monopoly money. I sat down at a $10 roulette table, that was the cheapest they had. I watched for a bit then put a chip on my jersey number, seven. It didn't come in so I waited a few spins and tried again – boom. The lady spinning the wheel gave me only five chips, I thought she'd ripped me off, but three of them were hundies. I counted the chips – 360 bucks.'

Grace tutted. 'Kenny Rogers wouldn't approve of that behaviour.'

'What's that?' said a confused-looking Wai.

'Keep going, Wai,' said Marla, smiling at Grace.

'I was rapt. I was thinking about a celebratory beer, but I didn't,' he added quickly. 'Then the lady pushed over another five chips. I told her I hadn't bet but they don't give you back your winning chip. It was still on the table and seven came in again. And it came in three more times in the next half hour.'

Shaking his head, Tana asked, 'How much is here?'

'Just over one and half K. Fifty-fifty, eh?' He asked this with a slight pleading note in his voice.

Giving him his well-practised parental glare, Tana took four $50 notes out of the wad. 'I didn't expect to see it again – your honesty is pretty impressive.' Keeping the four notes, he tossed the wad of cash back to Wai. 'You keep it. Spend it wisely, like buying new footy boots. And something for your mum.'

A grinning Wai pocketed the money. Leaning back, he stretched his arms out, one going behind Marla like they were teenagers at the pictures. With his warm, beaming smile he looked around the room. 'What did I miss?'

When the evening was over, after long hugs, Tana and Wai were first to leave. Walking to Tana's van, they could hear him dishing out advice, Tana style. 'Don't you blow that money, Wai. If I hear you've gone back to the casino, your life won't be worth living.'

Their voices drifted away into the night.

Carter started cleaning, but after he had put away the leftover food in the fridge, he threw his tea-towel on the bench. 'It can wait until morning.'

'Where's everyone sleeping?' asked Grace.

'Lauren's in with me, you two are in the rooms you had last time.'

'Am I?' said Lauren.

'I'm not having the couch,' he said. 'Not after I cooked –'

Lauren interrupted him by throwing her arms over his shoulders and pressing her face close to his. 'But will I be safe?'

'Are you tipsy?' he asked.

Lauren ran her tongue over her teeth.

'That's enough of that you two,' said Grace. 'I'm off to bed.'

Grace had warned Sean and her children that she would be late and that she would call in the morning. In the dark, snuggled into the soft bed, her mind shuffled conflicting thoughts. Lauren's was an act of cold-blooded murder. Sure, the extenuating circumstances were massive, but did that make her actions right? What was *right*? If her husband had killed Lauren, the Crown would have probably charged him with manslaughter – how was that right? Lauren was absolutely the victim. Full stop.

Then there was Tana's point. What if Sophie's partner, or Kane's for that matter, were beating and raping them – was she capable of killing? She doubted it but she wasn't sure – it was far from a categorical no. And she was fifty something with a partner, family, friends, colleagues and decades of life skills. Not seventeen, isolated, self-educated and living in a backward community.

As for Palmer's death, she shrugged under the covers. There was the fact that he'd had her abducted and was holding her as a prisoner – and it was doubtful the police would have pressed charges, even if they had known that Lauren had caused the crash. Palmer had lived and died by the sword.

Grace let out a soft laugh. You can never *unknow* so would it have been better to not know? Would knowing Lauren's past change anything? She shook her head. Who was she to judge Lauren when she couldn't rule out taking a similar course of action. One thing was for sure, her brain would keep chewing over events for weeks, if not months.

As sleep was finally claiming her, she heard Marla calling Indy inside. A tipsy Lauren, trying to whisper but failing, asked, 'What's the worst that could happen?' Carter's door closed with a light click.

Grace shook her head, pleased her life and sleeping habits were comparatively simple. If her hearing was right, sharing a bed were Carter – a handsome but gay man attracted to neither woman. Lauren – a heterosexual with a dark past seemingly attracted to Carter. And Marla – possibly bi-sexual with an even darker past maybe attracted to them both. That was a level of complexity that would require professional help to untangle.

The last sound she heard before she fell asleep was not-so quiet giggling.

EPILOGUE

Three months later

Grace stood drinking a coffee near the floor-to-ceiling windows of Wellington's domestic airport terminal. The day outside was miserable. Wellington had turned on the sort of day it was unfairly famous for – windy and wet. It hadn't, thankfully, disrupted flights.

Just after 10.15am, Grace spotted Lauren among the current of passengers making their way into the terminal. Over the past months, Weeping Angels had featured prominently in the media, as had Lauren – her days of hiding were over. With the increased media attention, Lauren's fashion sense had sharpened. The black suit, white shirt and sunglasses look she was sporting reminded Grace of her SIS contact, agent Jenna Parata.

Finishing her coffee, Grace waved. Smiling, Lauren headed towards her.

'Ace, it's great to see you.'

They exchanged a warm hug. Although they had been working together on the stories over the past months, Grace hadn't seen her in person since the night of the dinner party.

'You too, Lauren. You look great and ... taller?'

Showing off her shoes, she said, 'It's the heels. Carter suggested I wear them because people in business have a *thing* for height.'

'I've always wondered why I wasn't a millionaire,' said Grace. 'Do you have luggage?'

Shaking her head, Lauren patted the backpack-come-laptop bag over her shoulder.

'We can share my umbrella,' said Grace. 'I parked close to the building but it's bad out.'

As they left the shelter of the undercover carpark, Grace opened the umbrella and gave it to Lauren. 'If I hold it, it'll poke your eye out.'

After they had scrambled into Grace's car, they set off across Wellington, heading for the Beehive.

'So, how's the business going?' asked Grace.

'Nuts. The stories and publicity have brought a flood of inquiries, loads from areas where we don't operate. Carter's fulltime now, helping me manage the operations.'

'What about financially?'

'If we stopped growing, we'd be in a great position – that's what our accountant tells me. But having Julianna as our patron has not only solved our money problems, she's out there needling people to get involved financially. That's a big part of Carter's role now – chief schmoozer.'

'He would so love that,' said Grace.

'He does,' said Lauren softly.

Grace, sensing Lauren had more to say, stayed silent as she navigated through the slow inner-city traffic.

'He's met someone,' said Lauren, trying to sound perky and disinterested.

'Good for him,' said Grace. 'Are you okay with that?'

'Of course,' she said too quickly.

'But?'

Sighing, Lauren said, 'You journalists. I miss how Carter and I used to be, that's all. I know that's incredibly selfish. I mean, if I was dating, they aren't going to want a handsome man hanging around, even a non-threatening gay one.'

'Have you told Carter how you feel?'

Lauren shook her head vigorously. 'No.'

'You need to tell him. He won't want to lose you as a friend – a very special friend. You've shared a lot.'

Silence descended, the windscreen wipers tapping out a metronomic rhythm.

'How's Tana,' asked Grace, deciding to change the subject and mood.

Lauren looked across smiling. 'He's wonderful. Now I'm earning a living, I tried to repay him for looking after me.'

'I bet he didn't take it.'

'No, he didn't. He said' – Lauren did her best to imitate Tana's voice – "'What do I need with all that money? I'd buy a motorcycle and break my stupid neck." We agreed to donate the money to a local charity that helps children who have come from dysfunctional homes. I didn't know, but he had volunteered to be a father figure for Wai when Wai was thirteen.'

'Wow,' said Grace. 'Look how cool Wai's turned out.'

'Anyway, that's enough about me,' said Lauren. 'How's your world spinning?'

'Great,' said Grace. 'Children are doing well. Sean's still lovely, busy but attentive, and, with the stories I've been writing, even my editor has forgiven me for what he called "running amok with the RNZ gold card".'

Lauren laughed. 'Any major stories on the radar?'

'Yeah, there are. I've been poking my nose deep into the union movement. Successive governments have royally shafted them. Now they're making a comeback, but the current Government seems hellbent on crushing them. We need unions, now more than ever, so I'm digging into why the Government is so anti-union – who's really pulling their strings?'

As they closed in on the Beehive, Grace asked, 'Are you ready for today?'

'No, but yes,' said Lauren. 'I've done all the prep I can, and I know the subject inside out, so why do I feel so fucking nervous?'

Grace shrugged. 'It's your mind's way of telling you that it's important, that you care about what happens. You'll be great. Besides, the chair of the select committee invited you to speak first. And for half an hour. Most people get five minutes. They want to hear what you have to say.'

Drawing in a deep breath, Lauren said, 'You're right.'

Grace said, 'I have a saying when I have to present and I feel like you do – what's the worst that can happen?'

'I stammer my words and forget my own name?'

'There is that,' laughed Grace.

Lauren paused before saying, 'Actually, the worst that could happen is they don't change the system.' She huffed. 'I'll be fine.'

The trip across Wellington would normally take twenty minutes, but in places the rain was slowing traffic to a crawl. It took them closer to forty minutes.

'Where are you going to park?' asked Lauren looking out the window at the dismal day.

'In my wildest dreams,' said Grace, 'I never thought I'd get a pass to park *under* the Beehive.'

'Really?'

'I know. I'm going to take a selfie and send it to my contact in the SIS – she wouldn't believe it otherwise.'

Grace stopped in front of a set of bollards blocking the Molesworth Street entrance to the parliamentary grounds. Looking around, she could see that a malevolent fish-eye camera was watching them from a metal cabinet well away from where she had stopped.

'I'm going to get saturated,' said Grace. 'I bet they put that box way over there on purpose.'

Just as Grace was about to open her door, the lights on the bollards started blinking green and the bollards descended into the asphalt. 'I had to register my number plate,' she said as she drove towards the entrance of an underground carpark, 'but that's still spooky.'

As they descended into the carpark, Lauren said, 'I would've thought they'd have searched your car.'

Parking, Grace pointed out another ominous, all-seeing orb. 'They'll be watching us closely. If I opened the boot and took out a cello case, they'd arrive from all corners.'

'Tempted?' asked Lauren.

'You bet, but we're on a different mission today.'

Taking the lift, they arrived as instructed on floor two where they passed through a security check. Grace showed them her pass and they had to surrender all their possessions – the pass allowed Lauren to keep her laptop.

'So far, so good,' said Grace 'Fifteen minutes until they start. Let's find room three and wait outside.'

They walked down the corridor with its plush red carpet and high ceilings – it smelt old and reassuring. It was a short walk, the electronic screen over the door confirmed they were in the right place – *Select Committee Inquiry into Accessing the Justice System.*

'Stand underneath it,' said Grace taking out her phone. 'You're the reason this inquiry is being held.'

'You were meant to leave your phone with security,' hissed Lauren.

'Oops,' said Grace. 'My bad.'

Lauren held back a laugh as she stood next to the door. Grace snapped away on her phone as if it was a photo shoot. Directing her, Grace said, 'Look stern. Now look confident. Lean on the door. No, don't lean on the door.'

Lauren started giggling as Grace kept taking photos.

'These will look great on your website,' said Grace. 'I'll definitely use one for the story I'm writing about the inquiry.'

They sat on budget office chairs that looked out of place in the opulent, windowless corridor. A security guard wandered past, giving them a friendly smile.

'They can't have been watching,' said Lauren.

'The point of security cameras is to make you believe they're watching, then you self-police,' said Grace. 'Anyway, have you thought about what'll you do if you get the law changed?'

'With Weeping Angels? I doubt the machinery of government will move quickly, if at all. But if by some miracle they *fix* the justice system, I guess I'll refocus our operation on another part of society that needs fixing.'

'There are plenty of those,' said Grace. 'Housing, fucking banking, water quality, youth justice, brain-injured babies –'

'Brain-injured babies?'

'ACC,' said Grace. 'You wouldn't believe, but now's not the time.'

The door opening startled Lauren. Grace saw a phalanx of well-dressed politicians seated around a large U-shaped table – some she recognised, most she didn't.

'Ms Brown?' asked a tall, well-dressed young man. 'I'm the clerk for this committee.'

Lauren stood.

'They're ready for you,' he said with a friendly, charming smile.

Standing almost at attention, Lauren took in a final deep breath before striding confidently into the room. The door closed behind her.

ABOUT THE AUTHOR

Riley Chance, whose first novel – *Surveillance* – was short listed for the Ngaio Marsh awards, is passionate about giving readers fast-paced, engaging novels that also provide a window into societal issues.

Since being made redundant in 2001, Riley has juggled raising a family, work and life. A seasoned, but unenthusiastic, member of the precarious workforce, Riley has had a myriad of jobs – computer programmer, IT manager, consultant, project manager, mentor, lecturer and, of course, writer.

When headspace allows, Riley loves to read as well as follow politics, often visiting parliament to watch question time. It is within the political sphere where society can be changed for the better (or worse) and fiction can be a catalyst for change.

Visit Riley's website at www.rileychance.com.

If you can afford to, please donate to Women's Refuge
– they are there when it matters.

https://womensrefuge.org.nz/make-a-donation/

If you or someone is in immediate danger call 111
– if it's unsafe to speak, push 55.

Women's Refuge – 24/7 crisis line 0800 733 843

Are You OK – 24/7 support for unsafe relationships. 0800 456 450

Shine National Helpline – 24/7 helpline and live webchat . . 0508 744 633

Shakti – 24/7 multilingual crisis line for migrant women 0800 742 584

If you are concerned about your own behaviour.

White Ribbon – www.whiteribbon.org.nz

www.ingramcontent.com/pod-product-compliance
Lightning Source LLC
Chambersburg PA
CBHW010314100726
47906CB00005B/983